Dear Readers,

What would you do if you could travel [back in time?]

In scientist Chuck Della Croce's case, as the man who developed the theories and created the means for time travel, the answer was clear—go back just a few years in time, and convince his earlier self *not* to develop time travel!

After a rogue organization uses time travel as a weapon to change the past and control the government, and after Maggie Stanton, a former girlfriend of Chuck's, is killed in the cover-up, Chuck attempts to do just that.

But he slightly overshoots his target date, and ends up knocking on Maggie's door *before* they originally first met. He knows this woman extremely well, but to Maggie, he's a complete stranger.

First impressions are everything, and Maggie can't deny that the man at her door is extremely good-looking and charismatic. But he's also buck naked and spouting nonsense about time travel. According to him, she's in serious danger. . . .

Time Enough for Love was a fun story to write. It allowed me (a card-carrying Trekkie!) to blend romance with science fiction, and show how love can transcend the boundaries of space and time.

It was also tremendously fun to write a book with a love triangle between Maggie and two different versions of Chuck—one from the present day and one from the future!

I'm delighted that Bantam has reissued this special 2-in-1 edition of *Time Enough for Love,* combining it with *Stand-in Groom,* a marriage-of-convenience romp, which features another favorite hero of mine, a chef from my hometown of Boston named Johnny Anziano.

Happy reading!

Love,
Suz

OTHER TITLES BY SUZANNE BROCKMANN

SUZANNE BROCKMANN

Stand-in Groom

Time Enough for Love

Suzanne Brockmann (signature)

BANTAM BOOKS

STAND-IN GROOM / TIME ENOUGH FOR LOVE
A Bantam Book / August 2007

Published by Bantam Dell
A Division of Random House, Inc.
New York, New York

Bantam Books and the rooster colophon are registered trademarks of Random
House, Inc.

ISBN 978-0-553-38523-6

These titles were originally published individually by Bantam Books.

Printed in the United States of America
Published simultaneously in Canada

www.bantamdell.com

10 9 8 7 6 5 4 3 2 1
OPM

Stand-in Groom

For Melanie and Jason

---

one

CHELSEA WAS BEING FOLLOWED.

It was crazy.

True, this wasn't the best neighborhood in Boston, but it was seven o'clock in the morning. It was broad daylight.

She glanced behind her. There were three of them—lean, dangerous-looking young men dressed in gang colors. She slipped the strap of her purse securely around her neck as she moved more quickly down the sidewalk. She could be wrong. Maybe they were heading toward the H&R Block that was three doors down from her office. Maybe they were looking to have their taxes done.

They were right behind her now, and she moved aside, toward the street, praying that they would walk on past.

They didn't.

"Hey, blondie." The taller of the three leered at her—if it was possible for a sixteen-year-old to leer.

They were only kids. Kids with fuzz on their upper lips and chins that was supposed to pass as facial hair. Kids pretending to be grown men. Kids who were taller and wider than she was. Kids who probably carried knives and could hurt her badly before she could even shout for help.

"You part of the beautification program in this part of the city?" the shortest of the three asked, laughing at his own joke. He wore an enormous ring in his nose—obviously to make up for his lack of height. He couldn't have been more than fourteen years old.

The third boy made animal noises—part dog, part barnyard pig—as he invaded her personal space.

Chelsea stepped out between two parked cars, into the street. "Excuse me. I need to get to work, and you should probably get to school—"

She had to stop short to keep from bumping into the tall one.

"Excuse me," he mimicked her. "Excuse me. We don't go to no friggin' school."

"Maybe you should reconsider. You could use a little help with your grammar." She stepped around him, but the dog-boy blocked her path. He grinned, and she pulled back. His teeth were all filed to sharp little points. He snorted and woofed at her obvious alarm.

That's all they wanted. They wanted to scare her. Well, okay. She was scared. They could let her go now.

"You got some money we can borrow?" the nose-ring wearer asked. "We'll pay you back—we promise."

She felt a flash of anger, wondering how often that had worked—how often the people they intimidated simply handed over their money.

As the other boys laughed Chelsea pushed past them onto the sidewalk, aware of the cars moving down the street, aware that not a single one of them had even slowed to see if she needed help. "Go away," she said sharply, "before I call your mothers."

It was the wrong thing to say.

The dog-boy pushed her, hard, and she went down onto her knees. The tall one grabbed the strap of her purse and it lifted her back up as it caught around her throat.

He was running now, all three of them were, and she was dragged and bounced along the cracked, uneven sidewalk. She heard herself screaming and she felt her shoe come off, felt her toes scrape along the concrete. Her head snapped back and her arm twisted behind her as the boy yanked her bag free.

God! All the work she did at home last night—those disks were in her purse! Chelsea pushed herself up off the sidewalk, kicked off her other shoe, and ran after them.

They were nearly a block ahead of her, but she could think of nothing but all those hours of work, and she ran faster.

And then it happened.

With a squeal of tires, a white delivery truck bounced over the curb, right onto the sidewalk in front of the three kids. The driver swung himself out the open door of the cab, landing directly on top of the tallest boy. The kid was no match for a full-grown man, and the truck driver was *extremely* full grown. All it took was an almost nonchalant backhanded blow, and the big kid went down, her shoulderbag pulled free from his hands.

But the dog-boy and the kid with the nose-ring were both behind the man. Chelsea saw a glint of sunlight reflect off the blade of a knife.

"Look out!" she shouted, and the man turned. The way he moved was graceful, like a choreographed dance, as he disarmed the kid with a well-placed sweep of his foot. He moved threateningly toward the dog-boy, who turned tail and ran after his friends.

Chelsea slowed to a stop, aware that her heart was pounding, that her panty hose were torn, her clothes askew, her hair loosened from her usual French braid and dangling around her shoulders, aware that the soles of her feet burned and stung from her shoeless run down the rough city sidewalk. She had to bend over to catch her breath, hands braced above her bruised knees.

She tilted her head to look up at the man who'd rescued her

handbag. He looked even taller from this position, his shoulders impossibly broad. He was dressed in well-faded blue jeans and worn white leather athletic shoes. He wore a Boston Red Sox cap backward over a dark head of unruly curls and a T-shirt that proclaimed in large red letters I'M TOO SEXY FOR MY SHIRT. Given a leather jacket and a studded dog collar, he could have been those kids' older and far more dangerous brother.

"You all right?" he asked her, moving closer, his dark eyes even darker with concern. "You need me to call the paramedics?"

Chelsea shook her head no, taking quick stock of her bruises and scrapes. Both knees were bleeding slightly, as were both elbows and the heel of one hand. The top of her right foot and most of those toes were sore. Her neck felt raw where the strap of her purse had given her a burn.

"I'm okay." She straightened up, trying to tuck her blouse back into her skirt, trying to ignore the fact that her hands were shaking so hard, she couldn't get the job done.

The man didn't ignore it. "Maybe you should sit down."

Chelsea nodded. Sit down. That would be good.

She let him lead her across the sidewalk to a building that had a stone stairway going up to the front entrance. He helped her sit on the third step up, then sat next to her, setting her handbag between them and pulling off his baseball cap.

She glanced at him, aware that he was gazing at her.

He wasn't what she'd call classically handsome. His nose was big and crooked, as if it had been broken one too many times. His cheekbones were rugged and angular, showcasing a pair of liquid-brown, heavily lidded eyes. His mouth was generously wide, with full, sensuous lips that seemed on the verge of a smile. His hair was dark and curly and long, and as he steadily returned her curious gaze he pulled it back into a ponytail at the nape of his neck.

"I've seen you around the neighborhood for a couple of weeks," he told her. His voice was deep and husky, with more than a hint of urban Boston coloring it. "You opened up that computer consulting business around the corner, right?"

She nodded. She hadn't seen *him* around. She would've remembered. "I'm Chelsea Spencer." She held out her hand.

"I know," he said, finally letting his smile loose as he gently clasped her fingers.

It was a smile that was set on heavy stun. Chelsea was not normally affected by such things, but this man's smile was off the scale. It was a smile that seemed to echo the words on his T-shirt. She glanced at those words again. He followed her gaze and actually blushed, a delicate shade of pink tingeing his rugged cheekbones.

"A friend got me this shirt," he explained sheepishly. "I'm visiting him today, and I wore it, you know, kind of like a joke?" He was still holding her hand. "I'm Giovanni Anziano. My friends call me Johnny."

"Thank you for saving my bag."

His smile faded as his gaze swept her scraped knees and dirt-streaked clothes. "I wish I got there sooner. They didn't do more than knock you over, did they?"

He was watching her closely. His eyes may have been lazily hooded, but Chelsea got the sense that this man missed nothing. She shook her head. "No."

He ran one hand down his face. "Jeez, will you listen to me? 'They didn't do more than knock you over'—as if that wasn't enough. I saw you bounce when you hit the ground. You sure you don't want some professional help getting cleaned up? There's a hospital not too far from here and it won't take too long."

"Oh, no!" Chelsea pulled her hand free and closed her eyes. "Oh, God, I've got a meeting with a client in an hour." She laughed, but it sounded faintly hysterical, so she stopped. "I look like I've been hit by a train."

"You look like you've been mugged."

Chelsea stood, searching the street for a taxi. "If I hurry, I can take a cab home and get cleaned up and only be a few minutes late." She turned to face him. "Thank you again. If you hadn't come to my rescue..."

Johnny stood up, too, and again she was startled by how very tall he was. "Lookit, I'm running a little early. Hop in the truck, and I'll give you a ride home and back."

She gazed at him in surprise. He laughed, as if he could read the trepidation in her eyes.

"I'm not dangerous," he told her. "I promise. Come on, I work for Meals on Wheels, delivering food to helpless little old ladies who unlock their apartment doors for me without batting an eye. Hell, I've got a key ring the size of New Hampshire for all the people who can't get up to answer their own door."

Meals on Wheels. The words were painted on the side of the truck that was still parked in the middle of the sidewalk. Meals on Wheels was a charity organization that delivered precooked meals to shut-ins. Some of them were ill, some elderly, all of them unable either to get to a grocery store or cook their own meals for whatever reason. Whoever this Giovanni Anziano was, the Meals on Wheels organization trusted him enough to allow him to make deliveries.

He smiled again, and Chelsea felt her stomach flip-flop. She could imagine him smiling at her that way as he leaned over to kiss her, as he pulled her against that rock-solid body, encircling her with those powerful arms. She could imagine him smiling at her as he helped her out of her clothes and ...

Where on earth had *that* thought come from? She wasn't prone to having on-the-spot fantasies about strange men—no matter what they looked like. No matter if they were, indeed, too sexy for their shirts.

"Hop in," Johnny said again. "I'll go get your shoes."

Chelsea Spencer.

She was sitting in the Meals on Wheels truck. She was sitting next to him, holding tightly to her bag as he took the right turn onto Beacon Street, heading out toward Brookline, where she lived.

Johnny glanced at her again, smiling as he met her eyes. Man, she was the definition of incredible.

It was weird, because she wasn't especially pretty—at least not in the conventional sense. Her nose was a touch too pointy, her chin too sharp. But taken with the rest of her face, she was strikingly attractive. Her eyes were a shade of blue Johnny hadn't even known existed before he first caught sight of her. Her hair was silky and golden blonde. And her mouth . . . Her lips were gracefully shaped and gorgeously full. It was the kind of mouth he fantasized about. And God knows he'd been doing a hell of a lot of fantasizing lately. . . .

"I'd been meaning to stop in your office and introduce myself for a couple of weeks now," he said, pulling up to a red light and turning to look at her.

She glanced at him again, and he could see an answering flash of attraction in her eyes.

He felt his pulse accelerate and forced himself to slow down. He had a shot here. If he asked her out, there was actually a chance that she would accept. But he had to chill out, take it slow, be cool. Be very, very cool.

The light turned green, and he stepped on the gas.

He couldn't believe it when he'd seen the three punks knocking Chelsea down to the ground. And he *really* couldn't believe it when she started chasing after *them*. The lady had guts. When most people were mugged, they got up and ran in the opposite direction. "Are you going to press charges?" he asked.

She snorted. "Of course."

Johnny nodded. "Of course." He tried to hide his smile. "Silly question."

"Will you do me a favor?"

Oh yeah. Especially if it involved full body contact . . . He nodded again, aware that she was watching him. He forced himself to sound cool. Nonchalant. "Sure."

She smiled. "Don't you want to know what it is first?"

"Nope."

"Hmmm. In that case, maybe I better think about whether there are any other big favors I need done . . ."

She was flirting. Chelsea Spencer was flirting with him.

"How about we discuss the terms of this favor over dinner tonight?" he countered. There. Damn! He did it. He asked her out.

But she just laughed. "There're no terms. I just need you to file a statement with the police. You probably got as good a look at those guys as I did."

"All right, but . . ." He shook his head. "Just don't expect the police to be able to do too much with what we tell them."

Her smile faded. "I know there's only a small chance the police will be able to find those boys, but . . ." She suddenly sat forward in her seat, pointing. "Take the next left. My building's the second on the right."

He followed her instructions and double-parked in front of her building. This block was all high-priced condominiums. The buildings were perfectly maintained, their grounds well kept. It was Nice, with a capital *N*, and a silent but very present dollar sign in front of that capital *N*.

Chelsea Spencer had money. A lot more money than he'd imagined. Johnny gazed up at the ritzy building. It was possible this lady was out of his league. Not that *he* necessarily thought so, but if *she* thought so, the game was over.

Chelsea opened the truck door and turned to look back at him. "I'll be quick."

"Don't be so quick that you forget to wash out those scrapes with soap."

She smiled. "You sound like my mother."

"No, I sound like *my* mother. She was a doctor."

"No kidding."

"Nope."

She was just sitting there, one hand on the opened door, gazing across the truck into his eyes. Johnny gazed back, hardly daring to breathe.

"I'll, um, go change," she said breathlessly.

"I'll be right here."

It took her thirteen and a half minutes.

For thirteen and a half minutes Johnny sat behind the wheel of the truck and planned. He'd take her out to dinner tonight to his restaurant. He rolled his eyes in self-disgust. *His* restaurant? Try, the restaurant in which he worked. *His* restaurant was the one that was still in fantasy form. *His* restaurant was pre-embryonic—an idea, a gleam in his eye, the beginnings of a small fortune in his savings account. But it was only a matter of time before he had enough money to make that dream come true.

But until then, he had to settle for the distinguished title of Head Chef at Lumière's, among the best of Boston's four-star restaurants.

He wasn't on shift tonight, but he could easily go in during the late afternoon and prepare a dinner for two. Veal. Chelsea Spencer would go for veal, in his special sauce and...

Tomorrow he'd meet her for lunch. He'd bring a picnic basket and they'd walk over to the Common, spread out a blanket and a few of his garlic-dijon chicken-salad sandwiches and...

He had to work both Friday and Saturday night, but Sunday he had the entire day off.

Sunday. Sunday, he'd pull out all the stops. Sunday, he'd seduce her. He'd show up here at her condo early enough in the morning so that she'd still be in her nightgown. He'd bring warm butter croissants and he'd kiss the crumbs from her lips and...

Chelsea quickly descended the front steps of her building, brushing out her long blond hair. She wore flowing, loose-fitting pants and a long-sleeved blouse. A wide belt accentuated her slim waist. No one would've believed she'd been mugged not quite an hour ago.

She smiled as she climbed in the truck. "Police didn't hassle you for double parking?"

He smiled back at her as he started the engine. "Meals on Wheels trucks don't get hassled."

She fastened her seat belt and began braiding her hair. "I don't know how I can thank you for doing this."

It was the perfect segue. "Well," he said. "Actually, I wasn't kidding about that dinner. If you're not busy tonight, I'd love to—"

"I'm sorry, I can't." Chelsea Spencer shook her head, not meeting his eyes. That was a bad sign.

He was silent then, just driving. She didn't want to go out with him. He didn't need a rejection stamped onto his forehead. But then she glanced at him. Eye contact. It was all the encouragement he needed.

"Look, I've got all of Sunday off," he said, turning to gaze at her as he pulled up to a red light. "And if you're busy then, let me give you my phone number, and that way, if you're ever not busy, you can give *me* a call and—"

"I'm busy Sunday." She met his eyes, firmly, squarely.

Johnny was the one who had to look away as the traffic moved forward. He was about a block and a half from Chelsea's office, and he pulled into the right lane, keeping his signal on so that the cars behind him knew he was going to stop.

"I'm sorry," she said softly, and as he put the truck into park he looked over at her.

She was still watching him and she *did* look sorry. Was it the money thing? Or maybe it was the class thing. She probably came from a family who could trace their roots back before the time of the *Mayflower*. Johnny's father, however, was a first-generation American, paternity unknown.

Or maybe it was just an unspoken rule. Girls from Brookline didn't date guys from his part of town. But maybe someday she'd decide to break the rules.

He reached alongside the seat for his clipboard and the pen that was attached. "Let me give you my number—"

Chelsea was shaking her head. "I don't think so. Because on Sunday—"

"Take it anyway," he said, writing his home number on a scrap of paper. "'Cause you never know, you know?"

" . . . I'm getting married."

Johnny looked up. She was still looking at him, her blue eyes apologetic. "Married," he repeated.

She nodded. "On Sunday."

"*This* Sunday?"

Another nod.

He looked out the window. "Oh." He put down the clipboard, glancing over at her. "I'm sorry. I didn't mean to make you uncomfortable . . ."

"And I didn't mean to make *you* uncomfortable." She slipped out of the truck. "Don't forget to make that police report."

"I won't."

"Thanks again." She gave him one last smile and shut the door.

"Hey, Chelsea."

She pulled herself up on the running board and looked in the open window.

"This guy you're marrying on Sunday . . ."

"Emilio Santangelo," she said.

Emilio Santangelo. It was as Italian-American a name as Giovanni Anziano. It could have been him. He, Johnny Anziano, could have been standing at that altar come Sunday morning.

Not that he wanted to marry Chelsea Spencer. He just wanted a date or two. Or twelve. Or thirty...And hell, if she was going to marry some guy named Santangelo, she would've had no problem going on a date with an Anziano. It was his tough luck, though. He was too damn late.

"Tell Emilio congratulations for me," Johnny told her. "Tell him he's one hell of a lucky guy."

Chelsea smiled at him. "Thanks, John. For everything."

---

two

"HI, CHELS. IT'S ME, 'MILIO. IT'S REALLY important that you call me back. It doesn't matter what time it is here in Rome, just *call me*."

Beep.

"Chelsea, it's Emilio again. There's something wrong with your phone at home and I can't get through. As soon as you get this message, call me. Day or night."

Beep.

"Chelsea. Where are you? If you're in the office, pick up the phone."

Beep.

"Chelsea, It's three in the morning here, and I can't put this off any longer. I didn't want to leave this on your answering machine, but . . . I can't marry you. I can't do it—I'm sorry. I've canceled my plane ticket. I'm not coming on Saturday. I met a woman, Chels. I swear to God, I didn't mean for this to happen, but . . . I fell in love. I know you're probably never going to talk to me again, but call me, all right? Just . . . call me."

Chelsea sat at her desk, pressing the replay button on her answering machine and playing the series of messages from Emilio again and again.

Love. Her fiancé had gone and fallen in love.

With her digital answering-machine system, his smooth, faintly Italian-accented voice sounded as if he were standing right there, with her in her office.

He wasn't coming on Saturday. He wasn't going to marry her.

Moira O'Brien stood in the doorway, silently listening as Chelsea played Emilio's last message for a third time.

"Breach of promise," Chelsea said as her best friend and business partner came in to sit down across from her desk. "This was more than a marriage—this was a business proposition. He's reneging. I can't believe it."

"So sue the son-of-a-bitch."

"Moira, he's my friend. I can't sue him."

"You wanna bet?" Moira reached for the telephone. "My brother's a lawyer. Let me give him a call—"

"I'm not going to sue Emilio." Chelsea pulled the telephone out of reach. "But the next time I see him, you better believe I'm going to make him crawl to beg forgiveness." She put her head down on the desk with a thump. "Oh, Moira, what are we going to do?"

"About the bank loan?"

Chelsea lifted her head to meet her friend's worried eyes. "No, about the five hundred and fifty-seven shrimp cocktails that will go to waste—*Yes*, about the bank loan. The first payment is due three weeks from Monday. If I don't get married on Sunday, I don't get my hands on the money from my trust fund."

"You've looked at the terms of your grandfather's will?" Moira asked. "There're no loopholes?"

Chelsea opened the file drawer of her desk and pulled out a folder. She took the photocopied page that was clipped to the inside cover and passed it across the desk to her friend.

"Chelsea Jasmine Spencer to receive the first payment of funds from a trust to the amount of two hundred and fifty thousand dollars, plus all interest accrued, upon the first business day following the return from a honeymoon, preceded by her wedding." Chelsea recited the words she knew by heart. "Additional terms regarding release of funds to be revealed at that time."

Moira chewed on her lower lip. "Additional terms?"

"Knowing sweet, rich, manipulative, *controlling* old Grandpa, it could be anything," Chelsea told her. "I might have to wear a clown suit to work for the next five weeks." She took the paper back from Moira and returned the file to its place. "Of course, now I'll never know."

"Your mother's going to have a heart attack when you tell her the wedding's off. She's going to die."

"Or worse yet," Chelsea said wickedly, "she'll live, and spend the rest of her life reminding me how *I* embarrassed *her* by being jilted three days before my wedding day."

"Jilted. That implies a certain emotional attachment, doesn't it? You don't love Emilio and he doesn't love you. Maybe this is for the best."

"Moira, if I don't get my hands on that money... Let me see. How can I put this delicately? How about: We're *screwed*!" She gestured at the room around them. "If we don't come up with that loan payment, this whole business gets flushed."

"You could borrow the money from your dad. Or one of your brothers."

"I could also sell my soul to Satan," Chelsea retorted, pushing her chair back from her desk and starting to pace.

Moira ran her fingers through her mass of red curls, making them even wilder than ever. "I know getting your family involved in Spencer/O'Brien Software is the last thing you want to do..."

"If I let them lend me money, they'll be breathing down my neck," Chelsea said. "Every single little tiny minute obscure move I make will be criticized. 'Are you sure you want to do that, sweetie?' 'Why not try it *this* way instead, Chelsea-bean? That's the way *I* did it, kitten, and it worked for me.'"

". . . but it's better than bankruptcy, isn't it?"

"No."

"Yes, it is."

"No, it's not. Believe me, you've never been called 'Chelsea-bean.' In front of a client." Chelsea turned to look at Moira, her eyes narrowing. "Your brother Edward's not married, is he?"

Moira knew exactly where this was leading. "No, but he's living with someone."

"Your older brother—Ron? He's the lawyer, right?"

"Chelsea, as your maid of honor, I have to advise you to cancel the wedding. This isn't like some daytime soap opera where one of the actors calls in sick." Moira assumed a television announcer's ultrasmooth voice. "'Today, playing the part of Chelsea's groom will be Moira's brother Ron.'"

Chelsea stopped pacing. "Do you think he'd do it?"

"Not a chance. He's married. I was just using him as an example of your insanity—"

"What about your younger brother?"

"Jimmy? He's thirteen."

But Chelsea had already dismissed him. "He's also a redhead. I need to find someone who looks Italian. My parents haven't met Emilio, and if I can find someone who looks—" She broke off, staring out the plate-glass window onto the street below. A white truck was driving past, bouncing and clattering as its wheels hit a pothole. "Giovanni Anziano," she whispered.

"Who?"

Chelsea turned to face Moira. "If you were a truck driver, probably earning just a little over minimum wage, and someone offered you, say, seventy-five thousand dollars to get married, take a free trip to the Virgin Islands, and then get the marriage annulled, would you do it?"

"Depends who I'd have to marry. Orlando Bloom, yes. Homer Simpson, no way. Who's Giovanni What's-his-name?"

"Anziano. He's the man who got my purse away from those kids." Chelsea picked up the phone and dialed information. "He's the man who's going to save my butt again— Hello? Boston, please. I'd like the number for Meals on Wheels."

"See you tomorrow, Mr. Gruber! Remember, medium high for five minutes in the microwave."

"All right, Martin," came the elderly man's quavering reply. "Don't let the cat out when you open the door."

"I won't." He wouldn't let the cat out because the cat—as well as Albert Gruber's son Martin—had been gone for nearly forty years. "And it's Johnny, remember? Johnny Anziano from Meals on Wheels. Catch you later, Mr. G, all right?"

Johnny locked the door behind him. He rolled his shoulders and neck as he took the stairs down from Mr. Gruber's fourth-floor apartment. The old man was slipping further into the past. It used to be his moments of confusion were few and far between, but lately, Mr. Gruber had been calling him "Martin" more often.

Johnny stepped out onto the sidewalk. Today had been a particularly bad day for Mr. Gruber. There was no way the old guy was going to remember to heat up that plate of food in the microwave come dinnertime. Johnny was going to have to call him from the restaurant's office and remind him and—

Chelsea Spencer was leaning up against his truck.

Johnny stopped short, doing a quick double take. Yes, that was definitely his truck. There were no other Meals on Wheels trucks parked on this street. And yes, that was definitely Chelsea Spencer. Her blond hair was pulled back into a French braid and she was wearing some kind of dark business suit with wide-legged pants and a jacket that managed to be both mannishly cut and thoroughly feminine. Or maybe it was the fact that Chelsea was wearing it that made it seem so feminine.

She straightened up as she caught sight of him, obviously waiting for him.

"Hi, John. Remember me?" She looked slightly self-conscious, slightly nervous. "Chelsea Spencer."

Johnny had to laugh. Did he remember her? It was a ludicrous question. "What are you doing here?"

He looked around at the crumbling brownstone apartment buildings, at the littered sidewalks, at the bent and fading street sign. Yes, this was definitely one of the crummiest streets in one of the crummiest parts of town. He looked again and Chelsea Spencer was still standing next to his truck, impossibly out of place.

"Are you all right?" he asked.

She nodded, another flash of something faintly shy and sweet in her blue eyes. "You're . . . taller than I remembered."

Her eyes lingered on the front of his T-shirt, and he glanced down, suddenly panicked that he was wearing another embarrassing slogan across his chest. But no. Today he was a walking billboard for athletic shoes. JUST DO IT, the white letters on his shirt proclaimed.

Chelsea tried to hide a smile, meeting his eyes only briefly, and he knew without a doubt that she was remembering the words he had been wearing the last time they met. *I'm too sexy for my shirt*. She was going to remember *that* until the end of time. No doubt he'd made one hell of a first impression.

"I wanted to talk to you about something, and the Meals on Wheels office wouldn't give out your phone number. It's kind of urgent, so instead of leaving you a message, I talked them into telling me your route. I was starting to worry this wasn't really your truck," she added. "You were gone an awfully long time."

Johnny nodded. "Mr. Gruber's my last delivery of the

morning. Sometimes he needs a little extra attention. Today I played a couple of games of cards with him and helped him re-pot a plant. But if I'd known you were waiting..."

"I didn't mind waiting." She shifted her weight and cleared her throat and jammed her hands into the pockets of her jacket. She was definitely nervous and Johnny was intrigued. "If you're done for the day... Do you have to get the truck right back? Or can you take some time to talk?"

His curiosity kicked into overdrive. "What, did they find the kids who snatched your purse? You need me to testify or something?"

She shook her head no. "I noticed there's a coffee shop just around the corner. Would you mind if we sat down and talked?"

"Sure," he said. "That'd be great."

Johnny forced himself to be cool. She'd asked him to have a cup of coffee. So what? It wasn't like it was a date or anything—after all, the lady was getting married in just a few short days.

"Have you ever been married?" she asked, glancing up at him as they walked down the cracked and uneven sidewalk.

"No. Have you?"

She shook her head again. "No. So you're not separated, or waiting for a divorce to come through or something like that?"

She was watching him closely, as if his answer were very important.

"Nope."

"No steady girlfriend? No significant other?"

Johnny stopped walking, suddenly realizing where this line of questioning was leading. "You're going to set me up, aren't you?" he guessed. "You have some friend who needs a date for your wedding, right?"

Chelsea hesitated, chewing slightly on her lower lip. "Well, sort of... You see..."

She was gazing up at him, her blue eyes so wide that she

looked about twelve years old. He could drown in those eyes, Johnny realized. He could just fall right in and never come back out.

She took a deep breath and gave him a somewhat tentative smile. "You see, *I* need a date for my wedding."

He stared at her, convinced he'd misunderstood. "You need a *what*?"

"Groom," she said. "I need a groom. My fiancé canceled on me and—"

"He *canceled* on you?" Johnny's voice went up a full octave in shock. "You mean, he *ditched* you? *You*?"

She smiled very slightly. "I appreciate your disbelief, but yeah, he ditched me. Three days before the wedding."

"What kind of fool is he, anyway?"

"The kind of fool who's in love with someone else," she said.

"Whoa. That must've hurt."

"No, it's not that bad, really. The marriage was just a business arrangement, anyway. I needed a husband, and Emilio wanted a green card, and . . ." She shrugged. "It hurt, but not in the way you mean because, well, I wasn't in love with him."

Johnny couldn't believe what he was hearing. "You needed a husband badly enough to marry someone you didn't love?"

"I still need a husband," she told him quietly.

He gazed back at her. He heard her words. He understood them. He just couldn't believe them. "What are you telling me, Chelsea?" He knew. He just had to have it spelled out. He wanted to hear it from her own lips.

"I'm not telling, I'm asking," she said. She took a deep breath and squared her shoulders. "John, I'm asking you to marry me on Sunday."

three

"*THIS* SUNDAY?" JOHNNY ASKED, AS IF THAT were the incomprehensibly insane part of her crazy request.

Chelsea nodded, gazing up at him. She'd shocked him. Utterly. She could see his surprise clearly in his eyes—for once they were open wide. He was floored, and she couldn't blame him. If a virtual stranger had approached her and asked her in all seriousness to marry him, she'd long ago have been running as fast as she could in the opposite direction.

So far Giovanni Anziano wasn't running.

She glanced over her shoulder at the door to the coffee shop. "Can we go inside? I'd like to explain."

He was noticeably silent as he followed her into the tiny restaurant, but at least he was following her.

There was a booth free by the window, and Chelsea slid onto one of the vinyl banquettes. Johnny sat down across from her. Some of the shock in his eyes had changed to wariness. He was willing to hear her out, but she knew he was far from giving her a yes.

"Why do you need a husband?" he asked. "Are you in trouble? Are you going to have a baby?"

It was funny, but Chelsea had the feeling that if she said yes, he'd seriously consider helping her out and marrying her so that her baby would have a name. Or maybe it wasn't funny. After all, Giovanni Anziano was the kind of man who voluntarily spent several mornings each week delivering food for Meals on Wheels. He wasn't paid for driving that white truck—she had learned that after talking to the receptionist at the charity organization. And he was the kind of man who took the time from his busy schedule to play a game or two of cards with one of the lonely old men on his route.

"I'm not pregnant," she said. "I'm in a different kind of trouble. I'm in kind of a financial bind."

He had been watching her intently, but now he glanced up. A waitress had come to their table.

"I'll have a coffee," he said. "Cream and sugar." He looked at Chelsea. "You too?"

"Herbal tea, please."

The waitress shook her head. "Don't have it. Only regular tea or coffee."

"Then just a pot of hot water with lemon, please." Chelsea glanced at Johnny as the waitress left. "I don't do caffeine."

"Too bad. I make a mean espresso."

Chelsea had to look away. There was something highly volatile that seemed to spark and burst into flames every time she so much as glanced into this man's eyes. That wasn't good. She wasn't looking for a sexual playmate—she was looking for a business partner.

But this guy was so damned attractive, it was hard to keep her mind on business.

Still, now that Emilio had backed out, too attractive or not, John Anziano was the only man around. He was her only hope.

"My college roommate and I started our own business last year," she explained. "Computer software. Moira—she's my friend—is a programmer, too, and we figured why work for someone else when we could work for ourselves. But we under-estimated our start-up expenses and reached a point a few months ago where we either had to call it quits and lose every-thing or get creative in our financing."

The waitress returned with their order, and Chelsea poured steaming-hot water from a tiny, silver-colored teapot into her mug. John added cream and sugar to his coffee as she continued.

"We streamlined, moving into that office in a lower-rent part of town. We also got creative with our assets. You see, when my grandfather died a few years ago, he left money in trust for all of his grandchildren. But according to his will, we can't get our hands on that money until we're legally wed."

She glanced across the table and into Johnny's chocolate-brown eyes. Chocolate was one of the few things that she truly missed since she'd cut sugar out of her diet several years ago.

"So you're getting married in order to get your hands on your inheritance," he said.

She shielded her slice of lemon with one hand as she squeezed the juice into her mug of hot water. "It's a little more complicated than that," she admitted. "After Emilio agreed to marry me, I went to a bank and got a loan—kind of an advance on the money I'd be receiving from the trust fund. I have to start making those loan payments in a few weeks, and the business isn't up to bringing in that kind of money yet, so . . ."

"Why not just borrow the money to repay the loan?"

She took a sip of her hot water and lemon. "Do you know someone who'll lend me over two hundred and fifty thousand dollars, interest-free?" she asked.

He nearly dropped his coffee mug. "*That's* how much you need to pay back the loan?"

"No, but that's how much I'll get from my inheritance. I was intending to sink that money into the business." She gazed at him. "I *need* to get married. And not just for the money. This whole thing has gotten bigger than I imagined. The ceremony, the reception—I have relatives already arriving from out of town. I can't cancel now."

"Chelsea, you know, it happens sometimes. It's really not that big a deal. People call weddings off."

"Yeah, well, Spencers aren't 'people.' Spencers are above making such nasty little messes with their lives. Or so I'm told."

"Emilio's the one to blame. He's the one who walked. You had no control over his actions."

"I should have—at least that's what my parents will say. I should have made certain that a prize catch like Emilio Santangelo didn't get away. After all, he's in a power position at one of the biggest financial institutions in Rome—not to mention the fact that he's descended from royalty. That went over really well with Mother and Daddy."

"He is?"

"See, even *you're* impressed. You can bet I'll be lectured for years on how it was *my* mistake that I let him get away. The same way I've been lectured for the past seven years on what a mistake it was not to get married right out of college. My parents believe a woman isn't complete without a husband. Forget your degrees and all those years of studying—you can become the CEO of General Motors, and you still won't be whole until you find a man and get married. After that you can fool around with your little career all you want—as long as it doesn't get in the way of your devotion to your beloved lord and master."

Johnny was laughing at her vehemence.

Chelsea sat back in her seat, giving him a rueful smile. "Sorry. I'm a little irate about the whole thing. They've been pressuring me to get married for close to an eternity now. It gets old after a while. If it was up to me, I'd never get married. I'm quite complete on my own, thank you very much."

"So you didn't tell your parents that you and Emilio were only tying the knot to get the money," Johnny said.

"No, I didn't. I just told them I was finally getting married and let them take it from there. And they took it and ran. The reception is going to be huge. My parents have a guest list of nearly six hundred people."

Johnny whistled. "Holy God, who's catering that?"

"I don't know. I don't *care*." She gazed down at her mug and sighed. "I just wanted it to be over." She glanced up at him. "Here's my offer: I'll give you seventy-five thousand dollars and a trip to the Virgin Islands if you show up at the church on Sunday and pretend to be Emilio. After the reception, you'll fly out to Vegas with me and we'll get married for real. We'll go from there to St. Thomas, spend a few days at the beach, then show up at the lawyer's office with our marriage certificate in hand. We'll get the money, and in a few days—a week or two at the most—we'll quietly get the marriage annulled."

He took a long sip of his coffee, watching her over the rim of his mug. When he put the mug down, he laughed in disbelief. "This is definitely one of the more bizarre days of my life."

"I know it sounds crazy, but, John, I really need your help."

"You don't know me. What if I'm some kind of weirdo?"

"You work for Meals on Wheels. Little old ladies open their doors for you, remember?"

"Explain to me the part about Vegas again," he said. "I'm not sure I follow that. We get married *twice*?"

Chelsea felt a burst of hope. Was he actually considering doing this? She tried to keep her voice even and matter-of-fact. "Vegas is to make it legal. I've already checked into it—there's no way we can get a Massachusetts marriage license by this coming Sunday."

He nodded slowly. "Seventy-five K, huh?"

"Yes." She held her breath. She could almost see the wheels turning in Johnny's head. God, what she would have given to know what he was thinking.

"And a honeymoon in St. Thomas too? How many days?"

"Four days, three nights." She crossed her fingers under the table, making a wish. Please, please, *please*, say yes.

"I've got some time off coming to me," he said, thinking aloud. "Rudy, my boss, isn't going to like me springing it on him with hardly any notice, but . . ."

"Does this mean . . . ?" she whispered, hardly daring to hope.

He smiled. "If we're going to do this, we oughta do it right, don't you think?" He reached across the table and took her hand, lacing their fingers together. "Chelsea Spencer, will you marry me—for a week or two?"

Chelsea felt a rush of tears fill her eyes. His hands were big and warm and they seemed to engulf hers completely. It was an odd sensation. "Yes," she said. She smiled at him across the table, blinking back her tears. "Thank you, John, so very much."

This was one crazy idea.

Of course, Johnny had had some experience with crazy ideas in the past. He'd pulled some particularly insane stunts before— like hopping aboard the red-eye to Paris with a friend from the Culinary Institute simply to settle an argument over whether it was lovage or cilantro that master chef Donatien Solange of the Hotel Cartier used in his world-famous lemon-lime chicken.

It was lovage.

Johnny had been right. He'd won the argument, but the round-trip ticket had cost him all of his second-semester spending money.

He squeezed his VW Bug into a half of a parking spot on Boylston Street, wondering what this latest crazy idea was going to cost him.

He was marrying Chelsea Spencer on Sunday. The thought still made him laugh out loud. It was one hell of a first date, and one amazingly crazy idea.

Supposedly it was going to cost him nothing. Supposedly he was going to get seventy-five bills gigundo for the pleasure of giving the lovely Ms. Spencer his name—albeit only temporarily. But if there was one thing he'd learned so far in life along with how to make a near-perfect crêpe, it was that crazy ideas *always* had hefty price tags.

But how could he turn down seventy-five grand? The money would put him a year and a half closer to owning his own restaurant. And how could he not notice those tears of gratitude that had flooded Chelsea's crystal-blue eyes when he'd told her he'd help her out? And how could he not think about the fact that he'd be flying to some Caribbean paradise to share the honeymoon suite for three hot, tropical nights with a lady who made his blood pressure rise?

The possibilities were endless and extremely tantalizing.

He got out of his car, glancing again at the address Chelsea had scrawled on the back of one of her business cards. Her attorney's office. It was a Newbury Street address—just a few blocks away.

He picked up his pace as the first fat drops of rain began to fall.

Newbury Street was made up of graceful old brownstones, some elegantly restored, but some renovated with gleaming metal and shining glass. It was a jangling mixture of old and new, a vibrant neighborhood filled with trendy restaurants, upscale fashion boutiques, and avant-garde record and CD stores. Offices and condos were nestled in among the shops, and on the other side of the heavy wooden front doors, those offices tended to be either crumbling and slightly seedy or gorgeously preserved.

Johnny took the stairs up to the attorney's building, betting he was going to see an office that was gorgeously preserved.

He wasn't disappointed.

The reception area was something out of an old movie. The wood trim around the windows and doors gleamed. The ceilings were high, and polished brass gas fixtures were still in place.

An elegant-looking receptionist was sitting behind an enormous oak desk, gazing at him over the top of a pair of half glasses. "Are you here to pick up the delivery?"

Johnny had to laugh. Figures he'd be mistaken for the hired help. "No. Actually, I'm here to see Tim von Reuter."

"Really?" She gave him a very pointed once-over, lingering disapprovingly on his shoulder-length hair, his faded jeans, and his rain-spotted T-shirt.

He returned her gaze just as steadily, feeling his temper start to rise. "Yes, really."

"I'm sorry, you don't seem to be in *Mister* von Reuter's book. You'll have to call for an appointment. Good day." She turned away from him.

Johnny knocked on her desk to get her attention. "Hate to disappoint you, lady, but I do have an appointment. One o'clock. You can tell Mr. von Reuter that *Mister* Anziano is here to see him."

"John. Good, you made it."

He turned to see Chelsea coming into the outer office, closing the door behind her.

His fiancée.

Nobody would mistake her for a delivery person.

She was still wearing the same dark suit she'd had on this morning, and she still looked like about a million very elegant bucks. He forgot all about the snob lady behind the desk as Chelsea set her umbrella in a brass stand and smiled at him. It was a sweet smile, almost shy. She met his eyes only briefly as she set her enormous purse on a chair and shrugged out of her raincoat. "I was half-afraid you wouldn't come."

"I said I'd be here."

"John, it's okay if you want to change your mind—"

"Do *you* want to change your mind?"

"*No!*" She looked up at him then, her blue eyes wide. She glanced at the receptionist and lowered her voice. "I just ... I know you must be having second thoughts and doubts, so ..."

"I definitely have some questions to ask the lawyer before I sign anything," Johnny said evenly.

She took a deep breath and gave him a somewhat wobbly smile. "Then let's do it. Let's talk to Tim." She turned to the receptionist. "Mrs. Mert, will you please tell Mr. von Reuter that we're here."

"We?" the lady asked icily, with another grim look at Johnny.

"My fiancé and I," Chelsea said, with a hint of that same chill in her voice. "We're here to sign a prenuptial agreement."

Mrs. Mert stood up and moved silently down a corridor with one last disapproving look back at Johnny.

"Is that a class you can take in private school?" Johnny asked. "You know, Chilly Disapproval 101? She's definitely a master, but you're not so bad at it yourself."

"Oh, God, please don't compare me to Mrs. Mert. She wasn't exactly hired for her tolerance."

"No kidding. I think she likes me about as much as she likes getting a piece of bubble gum stuck on the bottom of her shoe."

She smiled at him. "The gum she can take care of with some ice and a putty knife. You look a little bit more difficult to get rid of."

"Why, because I'm not wearing a business suit and a noose—I mean, tie—around my neck?"

"That's part of it." Chelsea gazed at him. "But I think it's mostly your hair," she said.

"My *hair*?"

"Wait a sec." She sat down and dug to the bottom of her purse, coming up with a ponytail holder. "Try this."

He sat down next to her. "It's more than my hair. It's the 'us versus them' theory. Mrs. Mert thinks she's 'us,' and I'm definitely 'them.' You're 'us,' too, although your status is shaky now that you've been seen with me."

Chelsea studied him almost pensively as he raked his hair back with his fingers, gathering it into a ponytail. "You're probably right," she said. "People like Mrs. Mert feel threatened by people like you."

"People like me." Did she mean people in his tax bracket, or people who were born in a crummy part of town with a less-than-pure pedigree?

"People like you," Chelsea repeated, "who are too sexy for their shirts." She was doing her best not to smile, but she couldn't hide the sparkling amusement in her eyes.

"Damn," he said with a laugh. "You're never going to let me live that down."

"You know what they say about first impressions."

"Let's see, if I remember correctly, I wrestled your handbag away from muggers, staring down a pretty nasty-looking switchblade knife in the process, *and* okay, yes, I *was* wearing a dumb T-shirt. But somehow you only seem to remember the shirt part."

"Some things just stand out above the rest." She grinned at him. "I heard that song on the radio just about an hour ago, and it occurred to me that we should use it for our first dance at the reception."

"Your parents would *love* that." Dance. They were going to have to dance at the reception. He would have to hold her in his arms and—

"I would ask the band to play an instrumental version—my parents would never know."

"Whoa, you're not kidding, are you?"

She just smiled at him. "We need to get you fitted for a tuxedo," she said. "And do you happen to know your ring size?"

"Ring size? Not a chance. But I already have a tux."

"Black shoes?"

"Got 'em. Italian leather—Emilio would approve."

She pointed to his ponytail. "That's definitely the way an Italian investment banker would wear his hair. It's very high finance."

"Are you sure I don't need a scrunchee with dollar signs on it or something?"

"No scrunchees. Unless they're Italian leather." She paused. "John, it's occurred to me that you may not know much about banking and the stock market and all that. I mean, I don't even know where you work—besides Meals on Wheels."

"I work at Lumière's—it's a restaurant downtown." He could see from her eyes that she didn't recognize the name. He could also see that she was not impressed. Most people weren't—until they tasted his cooking. "And you're right," he said. "The most that I know about banking is that my savings account doesn't make nearly enough interest anymore. And as far as investments go, right now my sole investment is a two-dollar quick-pick lottery ticket I've got for next Wednesday's drawing."

"I'm going to have Emilio give you a call," Chelsea decided. "He can give you a crash course in international banking."

"It's not necessary."

"Oh, yes, it is. What are you going to do when my father starts asking you questions about the Italian economy?"

"I'll do this." Johnny leaned forward slightly, bringing his finger up to his lips in a gesture of silence. He spoke with a faintly foreign-sounding accent. "Shhh. Today is a day of pleasure and celebration, not business. We will talk of such things another time."

Her graceful lips quirked upward in a smile and she snorted, trying not to laugh. "I hate to break it to you, but you sound like Mr. Roarke from *Fantasy Island*."

He gave her a mock scowl. "No, I don't. I sound like Emilio."

"Hmmm. Do you speak any Italian?"

Johnny rubbed his chin. "Only a few phrases. And *definitely* nothing I can toss out at your wedding reception, believe me."

She began searching for something in her purse, glancing at him out of the corner of her eye. "I guess Mr. Roarke will have to do."

Johnny stretched his legs out in front of him and crossed his ankles. "So which of my tuxes do you want me to wear on Sunday? The light blue polyester or the maroon velvet?"

The look on her face was priceless. She actually believed he was serious.

"I've got this pink ruffled shirt that goes great with either of 'em. . . ." he continued, unable to keep from smiling at her look of total horror. "Chelsea, I'm kidding. Black. My tuxedo is black. I was just getting back at you for saying I sounded like a character from a bad TV show."

"But I loved that show. I adored Mr. Roarke. . . . Until he turned into Khan and killed Mr. Spock in *Star Trek II*." She paused. "You did say your tuxedo is black, right?"

"Black and only a year old. Right in fashion. Designer label. Fits like a glove. Women faint when I wear it in public."

"I'll bet." She found whatever she was looking for in her purse, pulled it free, and handed it to him. "Here, Don Giovanni, try this on for size."

It was a jeweler's box, covered with soft black velvet. It was a ring box. Johnny popped it open, and there, inside, was a gleaming golden band. He looked up at Chelsea, suddenly subdued. She, too, had fallen silent.

This was a wedding ring. An age-old symbol of commitment and love. But Chelsea was joining him in holy matrimony on Sunday, and neither of them was expecting either.

"I tried to guess your size," she said softly.

The ring was gorgeous in its simplicity. Johnny ran one finger lightly over it, but when he pulled it from the box he fumbled and dropped it on the plush carpeting.

Chelsea bent over and picked it up. "Here," she said, reaching for his hand.

She slid the ring onto his finger.

It seemed far too intimate an act. Far too personal for two people who barely knew each other. Chelsea looked up into his eyes, and for Johnny, time seemed to stand still.

"It fits," she whispered, still holding his hand.

It did fit. Snugly. Perfectly. About as perfectly as her hand fit in his.

"Good guess," he said. His voice sounded odd too. Breathless.

"Mr. von Reuter will see you now," Mrs. Mert announced, appearing suddenly, like a specter from the mist.

Chelsea jumped and dropped Johnny's hand as if he'd burned her.

Johnny looked down at the ring he was wearing on his left hand.

Married.

On Sunday, he was going to get married. He should be searching his soul, questioning the moral implications of so casually entering into one of the holy sacraments. He was, after all, at least half-Catholic.

But instead, all he could think was how much he couldn't wait to kiss the bride.

four

CHELSEA LIKED HIM. SHE HONESTLY LIKED
Johnny Anziano.

He was charming and smart, and he had a good sense of humor, thank God. And he certainly wasn't difficult to look at, that
much was for sure. As if he felt her watching him, he glanced in
her direction and she quickly looked away.

She found Johnny much too attractive. This was a huge mistake. How on earth was she going to live with this man for a
week or two without getting in too deep?

Control. Willpower. She took a deep breath. She could do
it. She was going to *have* to do it.

Tim von Reuter droned on, explaining the terms of the prenuptial agreement as Johnny read over the documents.

"I have a question," he said in his smoky voice when Von
Reuter stopped for a breath. God, even his voice had the power
to send shivers up and down her spine.

This had to stop. Johnny Anziano was just a man. She'd had
working relationships with men before, with absolutely no shivers up or down any part of her anatomy.

Johnny glanced at Chelsea again. "About the annulment . . .
You mention annulment as a means of ending the marriage,

but . . . Clue me in here, Tim. If annulment is so much easier and faster, why does anyone bother with divorce?"

Von Reuter cleared his throat. "We have connections to a judge who will grant unopposed annulments provided the marriage has not been consummated. Most marriages are consummated."

Chelsea looked up and met Johnny's gaze. Instant fire. He didn't smile this time—was it possible, he, too, couldn't manage to move any of his muscles at all?

Somehow she managed to pull her gaze away and she heard him shift in his chair as if he, too, had suddenly been freed.

Her lawyer leaned toward Johnny. "This marriage is going to be a business partnership. You do understand that you're going to be married in name only?"

Johnny nodded. "I understand that. But . . ." He paused, as if searching for the right words. "What if . . . ?" He cleared his throat. "I'm not saying that it's going to happen, but if something does happen, I mean . . ." He was embarrassed, but this was clearly important enough for him to plow on through. "If something happens of, um, an intimate nature between Chelsea and me, then we'll have to go through the whole divorce procedure, is that what you're saying?"

"Nothing's going to happen." Chelsea wished she felt as confident as she sounded.

Von Reuter put in his two cents. "Such *an* . . . *event* would be difficult to prove, if you know what I'm saying."

"In other words, if we slipped and 'accidentally' had sex—if such a thing is possible—we could lie about it under oath when it comes time to end the marriage?" Chelsea snorted and shook her head. "That's unacceptable. I won't do that." She turned to Johnny. "If a sexual relationship is an important part of what you're hoping to get out of this deal, you may as well walk out the door right now."

God, were they actually sitting here in her lawyer's office discussing *sex*? Chelsea could hardly breathe.

Johnny was sitting back in his seat, obviously going nowhere as he gave her one of his extremely potent smiles. "It's no
big deal. I was just wondering how many cold showers I'd have
to take over the next few weeks."

"As many as you need," she told him. But how many would
she need? As many as it took, she decided grimly. There was no
way she was putting this deal in jeopardy.

She made a mental note to take a vast amount of work with
her to St. Thomas. And she'd call the hotel again this afternoon
to be absolutely certain that the connecting rooms she'd reserved
had a door with a working lock between them. Control was always easier when temptation was reduced.

Johnny sat forward, reaching for a pen, and glancing once
more in her direction, he signed the agreement.

Chelsea felt giddy as the document was passed to her. "I
don't have your card," she said to Johnny, thinking aloud as she
initialed the pages and added her signature to the bottom.

"I don't have a card," Johnny told her as they both shook
Von Reuter's hand and rose to leave the room.

"Do you have a phone number?" she asked, opening her appointment book to the back as Tim walked them out to the reception area. She jotted down the numbers Johnny gave her for
both home and work. "The wedding's at noon on Sunday at the
First Congregational Church. Do you have a fax at work? I can
send you directions...."

"I'll see you both on Sunday," Von Reuter said, disappearing
toward his office.

Johnny held the door to the street open for her. "I know
where the church is."

It was raining in earnest now, and Chelsea slipped on her
raincoat and opened her umbrella. It seemed so odd. She and
this stranger had just signed a marriage agreement. She and this
stranger were going to be married in a matter of days....

And the marriage would be annulled in a matter of days after that, she reminded herself.

"There's a rehearsal and a dinner scheduled for Saturday evening." Chelsea held the umbrella up high enough so he could stand underneath it too. What a mistake. Now he was standing *much* too close. Whatever the faint cologne was he was wearing, it should have been illegal. It was impossibly enticing. "But I know that you have to work."

"There's no way I can get that time," he apologized. She could feel his body heat even though they weren't quite touching. "My boss nearly had a heart attack when I told him I needed a few days off after the wedding."

"It's probably better this way," she said, her mouth remarkably dry. She gazed out at the street, afraid to look up into his eyes. He was so tall and so . . . close. She tried to sound casual, matter-of-fact. "I'll cancel the rehearsal and the dinner and we'll just . . . wing it on Sunday. Just be ready for the minister to call you Emilio, all right? We'll use your real name in Vegas. Oh, do you have a copy of your birth certificate?"

Johnny nodded. "Yeah. I'll bring it. Look, can I give you a lift somewhere? My car's right around the corner."

"No. Thank you. I'm heading all the way out to Brookline. It's out of your way—I'll just catch a cab."

"It's not that big a deal."

"No, I don't want to make you late for work." What she really didn't want was to spend a fifteen-minute ride through heavy traffic sitting next to Johnny in his car. With the rain drumming on the roof and the windows steaming up, it would be far too close quarters.

"How about we get together for lunch tomorrow?" he asked.

"Tomorrow . . ." She let him take hold of the umbrella as she flipped open her book, already knowing what was written there. "No, I'm sorry. I'm doing lunch with my parents."

"Saturday?"

Chelsea shook her head, grateful that she had another excuse. "My mother's made me promise her the entire day," she told him. God knows she'd be spending enough time with him immediately after the wedding. Why start testing her willpower any sooner?

"I guess I'll see you Sunday, then."

"Call me if you're going to be late, or . . . something."

"I won't be late."

She looked up into his eyes and found him smiling at her.

"Really," he said again. "I won't be late."

His gaze flickered down to her mouth, but when he leaned forward, he kissed her gently on the cheek.

Chelsea's heart was drumming in her chest. This was insane. This was totally crazy. How was it possible that one little chaste kiss on the cheek could make her feel as if she were going to explode?

Johnny stepped out from underneath the umbrella, pressing the handle into her hands. She almost dropped it.

Control. Willpower.

Chelsea forced her mouth up into a friendly smile, forced herself to turn and walk toward the street, forced herself to lift a hand to beckon to one of the cabs that were racing by.

She could feel him watching her as a cab jolted to a stop beside her. He was still standing there as she got in and the cab pulled away. She let herself sag back against the seat.

Control. Willpower. Something told her this was going to be her mantra over the next week.

"I remembered what it was that I didn't tell you."

Johnny gazed blearily at the red numbers of the digital clock on his bedside table: 3:40 A.M. "Chelsea?" he said into the phone.

"Yeah, it's me. I know I probably woke you, but all I could think about was what if I waited until the morning to call, and then you weren't home and..." He heard her draw in a deep breath. "I'm sorry, John. God, I'm really losing it. Please, will you do me a favor and call me first thing in the morning? It's really important."

He reached over and turned on the light, squinting in the sudden brightness. "No, it's all right," he said, running his hand over his eyes and the roughness of his cheeks and chin. "I haven't been asleep for that long. I only get home from work at twelve-thirty on a Friday, and then I'm usually too wired to go right to bed. And tonight I was bouncing off the walls. Too much coffee, probably." Tonight he'd stared at the ceiling for a solid hour after he'd gotten into bed, thinking about the fact that he was getting *married* day after tomorrow. "What's up?"

"Can you really talk now? I mean, you're not busy, I mean, you don't have company?"

Johnny had to laugh. "Maybe after we get to Vegas there'll be time for us to talk—get to know each other a little bit better. And then I can tell you things about myself like, I don't do one-night stands, and that I certainly wouldn't start an affair two days before I was planning to marry someone else."

Chelsea was silent for a moment. "I'm sorry. I didn't mean to offend you."

"Hey, no offense taken—it takes more than that to offend *me*. But of course you wouldn't know that either, would you?"

"We don't know each other at all," she said quietly.

Johnny leaned back against his pillows, tucking the phone under his chin. "So let's make a date for Vegas. Whaddaya say?"

Another pause. "Maybe it's better if we just...don't get to know each other."

"Aren't you curious about me?"

"Well, yes, but..."

He could hear rustling on her end, as if she, too, were

settling back in her bed. The thought brought all sorts of incredible pictures to mind and his throat suddenly felt tight. His voice was husky when he spoke. "But what?" he asked.

"It's not like we're really getting married," she pointed out. "It's a business deal. I've done business with people I've known absolutely nothing about."

He cleared his throat. "Yeah, well, you haven't had to go on a honeymoon with *them*, have you?"

She laughed. "No, thank God."

"I'm way curious about you," he said. "I don't even know your favorite color."

"You also don't know anything about my family—and that's why I called."

"You called at three-forty in the morning in a near panic to tell me about your family? That's . . . interesting."

She laughed again. She had an incredibly musical laugh. Johnny closed his eyes, letting it wash over him. He wondered what she was wearing, wondered if she slept naked, the way he did. Forget about her favorite color—there was a whole hell of a lot of other things he was dying to know about this woman.

"It occurred to me that you would be arriving at the church on Sunday morning," Chelsea said, "and my entire family would be there—except for me. You won't see me until I'm walking down the aisle. I won't be there to introduce you to anyone."

Johnny forced himself to concentrate on her words. She would be walking down the aisle, coming to meet him at the altar. . . . "Are you going to be doing it up, you know, wearing a fancy wedding dress?"

"It's a gown," she said. "And yes. It's extravagant. I don't even want to tell you how much it cost."

"I bet you're going to look beautiful."

"I bet you say that to all of your fiancées. John, about Sunday morning . . ."

"I'll be there, tuxedo clean and pressed, shoes shined, hair back in an extremely conservative ponytail."

"But I'm not supposed to see you until after the wedding, so who's going to introduce you to my parents?"

"I think maybe since I'm the groom, your father would probably take it upon himself to approach me and shake my hand."

"Yes, but he would expect my fiancé to already know my brothers' and sister's names. But I forgot to tell you, and that's why I called and woke you up."

Aha. Now it all made sense. "How many brothers?"

"Two. Michael and Troy. Michael's going to be your best man. He's the one with glasses."

"Michael. Glasses. Best man." Johnny grabbed a pen from his bedside table. There was no paper around, so he jotted the words on the side of a tissue box. "And Troy. Got it."

"Maybe you should write it down."

"I'm already a step ahead of you, pen in motion," he said. "Sisters?"

"One. Her name's Sierra."

"Like the mountains?"

"Well, that's one memory aid. She's eight months pregnant, and kind of reminiscent of a mountain range."

"I'll be sure to tell her you said that."

"Don't you dare!"

"Husband?"

"Absolutely. We don't do unwed pregnancies in our family. Sierra got married the day after she turned twenty-two. Her husband's name is Edgar Pope and you'll recognize *him* right away too. He looks just like his name."

"Big pointy hat, long robe, funny way of waving his hand?"

Chelsea laughed and he could hear her relaxing. She had obviously envisioned an incredible screwup on Sunday in which he was exposed as a fake after failing to know her family's names.

"No," she said. "Little wire glasses, receding hairline, two-thousand-dollar hand-tailored suits—although he'll probably be wearing his tuxedo. He looks kind of like a 1930s stereotype of a millionaire—without the yacht."

"Is he a millionaire?"

She snorted. "If he's not, he should be. He's the international vice-president of some Fortune 500 company, and he works about twenty-two hours a day. These days he's always flying off on business trips to Japan and Australia and Outer Mongolia. He's never home—it's a wonder Sierra managed to get pregnant at all this time. My theory is that they met for a quickie in the airport ladies' room between his flights."

Johnny nearly choked.

"This is their third demon offspring," Chelsea told him. "They come already equipped with two junior-model Popes. An Ashley and a Skippy."

"Skippy, huh?"

"His birth certificate says Edgar Pope, Junior, but his real name is Monster. Have you heard of the terrible twos?"

"Yeah."

"Monster's going for his fourth consecutive year of the terrible twos."

"I guess you don't like kids, huh?"

"I don't like what my sister has let Edgar do to her life. She's some kind of a *trophy* wife, and she won't even acknowledge it! She does *nothing* besides take care of Edgar and the kids."

"Maybe she's happy doing that."

"Maybe she's had a lobotomy and everyone forgot to tell *me*," Chelsea huffed. "Do you know that five years ago, she and Edgar were living in San Francisco? It was just after the Monster was born, and Sierra auditioned for a really fabulous semiprofessional community chorus. She was so excited about it—it was an interracial, intercultural, inter-everything group that did all kinds of music and it was a really big deal that she got in. She told me it was a chance to unite the diversity of the community through music, without homogenizing the cultural differences. She was *so* into it—she majored in both music and anthropology in college. After about three years she was elected to sit on the board of directors, which was one heck of an honor. But then two weeks later Edgar was transferred back to the Boston office. Just like that, she had to give it up."

"But that's part of being married," Johnny said. "You know—compromise."

"Exactly," Chelsea countered hotly. "Women and men get married, and the women are the ones who have to compromise. We lose our individuality and our importance along with our identity—even our names are taken away. I'm *never* getting married."

"Correct me if I'm wrong here, but aren't you getting married in less than forty-eight hours?"

"Don't remind me."

There was real trepidation in her voice. Johnny pushed himself up, resting his weight on one elbow as he held the phone closer to his ear. "You're scared about Sunday, aren't you?"

"Hell, yes. Aren't you?"

"I guess I'm a little nervous," he told her honestly. "But I'm excited too. It's funny—it's kind of like I'm taking you to a Halloween party for our first date. You're dressing up as a bride, and I'm going as a groom."

"This isn't a date—it's business deal," she said.

She could call it a deal—he was going to call it a date.

"Have you still got your pen handy?" she asked. "Because my parents' names are Howard and Julia."

Dutifully he wrote the names down. "Got it."

"Whatever happens on Sunday," she said, and he got the feeling she was saying this as much to herself as to him, "just grit your teeth and *smile*."

five

"BREATHE," MOIRA SAID AS SHE ADJUSTED Chelsea's wedding veil. "Come on, Chels, in and out. Focus only on that. Oxygen into the lungs, then exhale. Atta girl."

"What if he doesn't show?" Chelsea asked. "Oh, *God*! What if he *does*?"

"He's here," Sierra announced, coming into the little room in the back of the church. "Chelsea, you never told me Emilio Santangelo was a hunk."

"I gotta get a peek at this guy." Moira went to the door and opened it a crack. "Whoa!" She turned to Chelsea in disbelief. "*This* is your truck—"

Truck driver. She'd almost said, "This is your truck driver," right in front of Chelsea's sister, who still believed that Johnny was Emilio, the investment banker from Italy.

"Sierra, will you please go and check on the flowers?" Chelsea could hear the desperation in her voice, but there was nothing she could do about it. "And run interference with Mom? She's the last thing I need right now—criticizing my makeup and hair. You know how she gets when she's tense."

"You only have about three minutes before you have to get out there," her sister warned as she closed the door behind her.

Three minutes. "All right," Chelsea said weakly. Three minutes. And then she'd have to walk down that aisle on her father's arm. It was the kind of symbolism she really despised—being "given" by one man, her father, to another, her soon-to-be husband, as if she were some sort of booty or prize.

It wasn't going to be real, she tried to tell herself. It wouldn't be legal. Johnny Anziano *wasn't* Emilio, and this ceremony wouldn't bind them in the eyes of the law or God or *anyone*. They were going to do the legally binding ceremony later this afternoon, in Las Vegas. And in Vegas no one was going to *give* her to anyone. She was going to meet Johnny Anziano as an equal, as a business partner, and together they would stand before a justice of the peace and set in motion a business deal.

"*This* is the guy you manage to *scrounge* up only three days before your wedding?" Moira asked, opening the door again and peering out at Johnny again. "I think I'm going to steal your wedding gown, lock you in the closet, and marry him myself."

"He's doing it for the money," Chelsea told her, unable to resist taking a peek. But Moira shut the door before she could see him. "Is his tuxedo black?"

"Black and very nicely tailored. So tell me again where you found this guy? At an evening out at Chippendale's?"

"I'm scared to death and you're making jokes. What if he contests the annulment? Or challenges the prenuptial agreement?"

"What if he doesn't and everything works out hunky-dory?" Moira pointed out. "You get your money, he gets whatever percentage you've offered him, your parents get to throw their party. Everyone's happy. And, hey, you can give your ex my phone number after it's all over."

After it's all over. This part of it, the wedding and the reception, would be over in just a few hours. By three o'clock, she and Johnny would be on their way to Logan Airport. By four, they'd be in the air, heading for Las Vegas.

Chelsea closed her eyes, willing herself not to think beyond three o'clock, trying not to think about getting married for real. First things first, and first she had to get past this hurdle. Standing up in front of nearly six hundred people made her knees feel weak, and standing up in front of them to pledge eternal devotion to a man she had no intention of spending a month let alone an eternity with made her mouth dry.

And then there was the possibility that something could go wrong. Out of the six hundred wedding guests, what if one of them knew and recognized Johnny Anziano?

She took a deep breath, telling herself that she couldn't think that way. Everything was out of her hands now. All she had to do was hold on to the roller-coaster car and wait for this crazy ride to end at three o'clock. Three o'clock was only a few hours away. She could endure damn near anything for a few hours.

Her father opened the door and Moira slipped out, giving Chelsea a smile and a thumbs-up.

Howard Spencer looked impeccable, as usual. His salt-and-pepper hair was combed straight back from his face, each strand securely in place. He smiled at her, with a definite misty quality to his eyes. "Chelsea-bean, are you ready for this?"

She nodded, feeling a pang of remorse at her deception. Her father thought she was marrying for good, until death do us part. Not until annulment do us part. Still, when he found out, he'd probably congratulate her on her shrewd ability to get her hands on the money she so desperately needed.

Her father pulled her into his arms in a clumsy embrace. They weren't a touchy-feely family, the Spencers. They were the types who kissed the air next to someone's cheek or briskly shook hands.

For a fraction of a second Chelsea let herself imagine what it would have been like to grow up with a father who was more like the dad on *The Cosby Show* than a walking financial predictions computer.

But that kind of thinking was a waste of time. Her father was who he was. And her childhood was long since over.

"They're waiting for us," he told her. "Your mother's been seated and Moira and Sierra have just gone down the aisle." He opened the door and held out his arm for her.

The organ stopped playing as she moved toward the back of the church, toward the edge of the red carpet that had been rolled down the ordinary wood floor of the aisle. As she stood at her father's side in the back of the church, the organist began the traditional wedding march.

Here comes the bride. All dressed in white. For some reason, Chelsea could hear Bugs Bunny's voice in her head, singing the childish words that had been put to the tune. It would have been funny if she hadn't been so damn scared.

Everyone stood, turned to face the back of the church, smiling at her. Didn't they know she could barely breathe?

She searched for and found Moira's familiar face. Her friend and maid of honor was standing with Sierra at the altar. Her red hair had defied her attempts to tame it, and tendrils and curls escaped her French braid. On anyone else it would have looked messy, but on Moira it looked romantic and windswept.

Moira smiled at her, then turned slightly to glance across the aisle.

That was when Chelsea saw him.

Johnny Anziano.

The butterflies in her stomach exploded, flying everywhere, several of them lodging securely in her throat.

He had been right—his tuxedo was black, and it fit like a glove.

He looked impossibly good. He looked like one of those models in magazine ads where you knew the photo had been touched up because no one could possibly look so good in real life. The black of the tuxedo accentuated his trim waist and narrow hips, yet at the same time seemed to show off the broadness of his chest and shoulders. His legs looked fantastically long, and as she watched he shifted his weight slightly and the powerful muscles in his thighs moved against the soft fabric of his pants.

In today's performance of Chelsea Spencer's wedding, the part of the groom will be played by Giovanni Anziano. This was totally insane.

He was watching her, his handsome face serious, his dark eyes intense. Their gazes locked and the butterflies that were left in her stomach accelerated the steps to their frantic dance.

She was actually going to marry this man.

She searched his eyes, wondering what he was thinking, wondering—inanely—whether or not he liked her dress. And then she was there. At the end of the aisle.

Her father lifted her veil, kissed her gently on the cheek, then handed her over to the man he thought was Emilio. But it wasn't Emilio, it was Johnny.

Johnny's hands were warm while hers were blocks of ice. He gave her a thoroughly relaxed smile. "Hey." How could he look so calm and cool?

Her own lips and face felt brittle, but she tried to position them into something approximating a smile too. "Hey."

Underneath his heavy lids, his gaze was as sharp as ever. "You okay?"

Chelsea nodded, the sound of his husky voice somehow soothing her. She'd wanted to call him again last night as she had lain awake, tossing and turning. She'd liked talking to him on the phone the night before. She'd liked lying in the darkness of her bedroom, snuggling under her blankets, the phone and his voice nestled close to her ear. She'd liked it too much—and that was why she *hadn't* called him again.

"You sure?" he asked, his voice low. "You look a little pale. You know, it's okay if we call a time-out here."

Her smile felt more genuine this time. "We're not in the middle of a basketball game," she whispered back to him.

"Yeah, well, it's your wedding, right? You want a time-out, you can have a time-out."

"I'm fine, really." She took a deep breath, willing herself to be fine. Head up, shoulders back, nose slightly in the air. She'd learned it as a child. Stand as if you're in control, hold your body as if nothing that happens will perturb you in the least, maintain a slight disinterest, a distance from the events happening around you. It worked, as it nearly always did. She glanced at Johnny, raising one eyebrow very slightly. "I'm fine," she said again, and she was.

"Good." He was still watching her, as if he weren't quite sure whether or not to believe her.

The ceremony passed in a blur. She refused to think about the words she was saying as she promised to love and honor this man through richer and poorer, sickness and health. Till death do us part. She tried to repeat the words as nonsense syllables.

Johnny, too, spoke the wedding vows softly, as if he didn't want God overhearing his untruths.

She tried not to look at him as he slipped the wedding ring onto her finger, and as she did the same for him.

And then the minister declared them husband and wife. "You may kiss the bride."

This was the part she'd been dreading. She didn't want to kiss Johnny Anziano. She didn't want to—because she'd dreamed about kissing him when she finally fell asleep last night. And she'd dreamed it the night before too. And even the night before *that*.

Chelsea had dreamed about kissing this man the night after he'd saved her purse from those kids. Shoot, she'd *daydreamed* it moments after meeting him. And she was afraid that when his lips touched hers, he somehow would know.

She had a plan. She would wait until the last split second,

and when his mouth was just a fraction of an inch away from hers, she would turn her head away and he would kiss her cheek.

In theory, it was a fine plan. In practice, it was thoroughly flawed.

Because he took his sweet time. He reached up and gently touched her face, pulling her chin and her mouth up to his, holding her firmly in place. That, combined with the warmth she could see as she looked into his eyes, was something her plan hadn't made provisions for.

And in a shot, all of her carefully maintained calm disintegrated, leaving her defenseless.

She couldn't pull away. The truth was, she didn't want to.

His lips brushed against hers in the gentlest, most chaste of kisses, and she felt a flash of disappointment. That was hardly a kiss.

But he wasn't done.

He kissed her again, still gently, but leaving no doubt in her mind as to what he wanted. He wanted a real kiss, a deep kiss, a curl-your-toes and melt-your-bones kind of kiss.

And she wanted it, too, God help her.

With a soft moan of disbelief, she parted her lips, meeting his tongue with her own. He tasted like sugar-sweetened coffee and peppermint, a combination that hardly seemed compatible.

It was sinfully delicious.

His mouth was warm and soft, his dizzying kiss so far beyond her fantasies, Chelsea almost laughed out loud.

But then she remembered. She was standing in a church filled with her parents' closest business associates and friends. She pulled back, and he released her. He was as shocked as she was—she could see it in his eyes.

The wedding guests were standing, applauding for them. Little did any of the six hundred realize, but they were cheering for Chelsea and John's first kiss. It was downright bizarre.

Except as far as first kisses went, this one was *way* off the scale and thoroughly deserving of a round of applause.

Chelsea could feel Johnny slip his hand around her waist as he drew her down the altar steps toward the aisle that led out of the church. His touch was possessive, proprietary, and far too confident. He would take off her clothes that same way, she realized. Without hesitation, and as if taking possession of what naturally belonged to him.

He'd probably gotten far with a large number of women by simply taking control like that. Before they knew it, they were thoroughly seduced. And if that kiss at the altar was any indication, Chelsea had a sneaking suspicion that those women probably hadn't minded.

But she minded.

"The minister said you could kiss the bride—not inhale the bride," she whispered sharply as they plunged down the aisle.

There was amusement in Johnny's eyes. "Hey, it takes two, and I wasn't alone back there. You know that as well as I do."

He was right. She had kissed him as passionately as he'd kissed her. "I'm sorry," she said, at the exact moment he, too, apologized.

They were outside of the church, the heavy wooden doors separating them from the thundering organ music. They were alone—if only temporarily.

"No, *I'm* sorry," he said again. "You're right—I went too far. I knew you were off balance, and I took advantage of that. It's just...I've been dying to kiss you like that for a while now. I couldn't resist."

She made the mistake of gazing up into his eyes. Just a glimpse of the fire smoldering there was enough to make her heart pound.

"I still can't resist," he whispered, leaning forward to brush her lips with his.

He would have deepened the kiss again and she would have stood stupidly still and let him, were it not for the wedding photographer, who was striding toward them.

"*Perfect* picture," he enthused. "The absolutely *sweetest*, most genuine kiss I've ever taken. You're going to want that shot for your memory album, I can guarantee it. How about we get a few in front of the forsythia now?"

The look in Johnny's eyes was unmistakable. Underneath the rueful, good-natured humor was a clear message. He wanted more. And soon.

Dear God, Chelsea was in *big* trouble here.

Because she did too.

---

six

"ABSOLUTELY NO TALK OF BUSINESS TODAY," Johnny said for the twenty-seventh time. He spoke in what he considered his best "godfather" accent, but what Chelsea insisted sounded like Ricardo Montalban. What was wrong with these people, anyway? They seemed so surprised that he refused to talk business on his wedding day. If he were a doctor, would they be approaching him for free medical advice?

He could see Chelsea's blond head all the way across the elegant country-club ballroom and he excused himself and worked his way toward her. She was talking with a group of elderly ladies. They were her great-aunts—at least that's the way he seemed to remember her introducing them on the receiving line. Some receiving line—everyone was so solemn and reserved.

In his neighborhood, people at a wedding smiled and laughed and kissed one another on the face or the mouth, and men embraced with resounding slaps on one another's backs. And the bride and groom started the dancing as soon as they arrived at the party. It was expected that they wouldn't stay long. They would barely even touch their dinners, instead escaping out the back door to celebrate their wedding in a far more private, intimate way.

He skirted the dance floor as he headed toward Chelsea. She'd been avoiding him rather skillfully since he'd kissed her outside of the church. That was going to stop. Right now.

He touched her arm and she glanced up at him, giving him a smile that didn't quite reach her eyes. She looked around for the quickest route to escape, but there was none. So she did the next best thing. She transformed into the Ice Princess.

This time he was ready. This time he was watching for it to happen, and sure enough, right before his very eyes, she turned into the Queen of Cool.

He bowed slightly to the older ladies. "You'll allow me the pleasure of dancing with my bride," he said to them.

Chelsea was the only one who protested as he gently pulled her onto the dance floor. "John, it's not time yet. We're not supposed to dance until—"

"Ladies and gentlemen," the bandleader said into his microphone. "May I present Emilio Giovanni and Chelsea Santangelo-Anziano-Spencer."

"What did he just say?" Even the Ice Princess couldn't keep from laughing, and when she did, Johnny caught a glimpse of the real Chelsea underneath.

"I told him we were hyphenating our names, and while I was at it, I thought I might as well throw in mine too. Santangelo-Anziano-Spencer. It has a nice ring to it, doesn't it?" He smiled. "Of course, our children will have to spend years in therapy to recover from having a name that doesn't fit on an address label."

She bristled. "There aren't going to be any children."

"Relax. I was making a joke." He pulled her into his arms as the band began to play.

But she pulled back slightly to gaze up at him. "This isn't the song I asked them to play."

"No, it's the song *I* asked them to play. The bandleader agreed it was more dignified than 'I'm Too Sexy for My Shirt.'"

"I recognize the melody, but I don't know the name," Chelsea said, frowning slightly.

Across the room, someone started tapping their water glass with their spoon—a request for the bride and groom to kiss.

"It's called 'Misty,'" he told her as a dozen more spoons joined in. "It's a jazz standard. You're probably not into jazz, right?"

She shook her head. "I listen to Top 40—when I have time to listen to the radio."

The ringing sound was unmistakable. He gazed into her eyes and caught a glimpse of trepidation—she knew what it meant. "They're not going to stop until I kiss you," he said softly.

She moistened her lips. "I know."

He lowered his head, but she stopped him, her voice low and serious.

"John, it's acting—you know that, right?"

"Acting."

"When we kiss each other," she explained. "When I kiss you . . . it's not real."

For a minute he just stared at her. She looked incredible. Her wedding dress was out of this world, with a snugly fitting top and a heart-stoppingly low-cut neckline. It was a dress that had been made to be worn with a Wonderbra, and Johnny was willing to bet that Chelsea had one on. His view, as he looked down at her, was something to behold. God bless the designer who had introduced that fashion phenomenon.

But despite his enticing view, it was Chelsea's eyes that kept drawing his gaze. She was looking at him calmly, steadily. Despite that one flash of nervousness he'd seen back at the church, she now seemed utterly cool and almost distant.

Johnny had always considered himself to be a good judge of women, in tune with their desires, aware of their needs. But Chelsea Spencer was a bundle of contradictions—one minute warm and friendly, filled with good humor and laughter, and the next cool and aloof, impossibly calculating and businesslike.

Which was the act?

Johnny had thought the Ice Princess was the disguise, but now he honestly didn't know.

It's not real.

The sound of the clinking was nearly deafening now, so he lowered his mouth to hers, kissing her harder and deeper than he probably should have. But hey, it wasn't real, right? And the wedding guests deserved to get their money's worth.

He pulled her closer, molding her slender body tightly against his as he took possession of her mouth. It wasn't real as she trembled, as she drove her fingers into his hair, as she kissed him back with a passion that took his breath away.

There was no way, plastered against him the way that she was, she could have failed to notice his instant hard-on. That was all too real.

She pulled back, a faint blush tingeing her cheeks, her eyes wide as she gazed up at him.

It was then, in that fraction of a second before Chelsea conjured up her Ice Princess persona, that he saw it. Molten desire burning in her eyes.

She was lying. The way she responded to him was real. And if that were true, he had to believe the Ice Princess was the act. It had to be.

"You're one hell of an actor," he murmured into her ear.

She didn't say a word.

"I'm glad Chelsea's finally found someone."

Johnny turned to see one of Chelsea's brothers standing next to him. No eyeglasses. It was Troy.

He looked more like Chelsea than the other brother did.

He was blond and slender with a more masculine but no less elegant face.

"So has my little sister told you all the nasty family gossip?" he asked. "All of our dark secrets?"

Johnny shrugged. "We haven't had time to talk about much of anything besides the wedding plans."

"Oh, good, that means I can fill you in."

"I'm not sure I want to be filled in—"

"Yes, you do. You're part of the family now. You deserve to get a look at the skeletons in the closets. See the guy over there, about fifty years old, dark suit, bald spot, heading toward the bar?"

There were a dozen men who fit that description, but Johnny nodded anyway.

"He's my father's second cousin, Philip Spencer. Former CEO of a company called Tristock. He spent eight years in jail for vehicular manslaughter. DUI. Got offered another job with the company on the day he got out. After all, he'd only killed a young woman—he hadn't done something truly awful like embezzle corporate funds. Oh, and look. See the couple sitting all alone at the table in the corner of the room?"

Johnny followed Troy's gaze.

"That's my cousin George and his wife. We don't remember what her name is, because she grew up in the projects in the South End. We call her George's Wife, or That Gold Digger from the Projects Who Married George. After all, it's obvious that she married Georgie for his money—never mind the fact that he chose to teach school instead of work for my uncle, and never mind the fact that he spent most of his share of my grandfather's trust on a tiny little house in the suburbs. The rest of it he's spending lavishly on renovations on that house so that the Wife can bake bread or something ridiculously low-class. See, she never went to college, which, as we all know, is either a sign of total stupidity, sheer slothfulness, or pure evil."

Troy clearly didn't buy in to any of what he was saying, but Johnny couldn't keep from commenting. "Your family really believes that?" God, what would they think of him?

Troy rolled his eyes. "You should hear my uncle Ron—George's father—go on and on and *on* about the Wife. Sometimes even right in front of her, the tactless bastard. She could be a prizewinning rocket scientist, and my family would still call her That Girl from the Projects." He smiled at Johnny. "Don't worry about it—Chelsea told me you come from royalty."

"That shouldn't matter."

"Yeah, but in *this* family, it does."

"Excuse me," Johnny said. "I should go find Chelsea—"

But Troy caught his arm. "She's right there—dancing with Benton Scott—he's an old Harvard friend of mine."

Sure enough. Chelsea was on the dance floor, in the crush of dancers. She was laughing at something her partner said.

"When Chelsea was in high school, she had the biggest crush on Bent. He went out with her a few times, but it wasn't serious—she was seven years younger than he was. Then Bent knocked up his law-firm partner's daughter, and like a good little law clerk on the fast track toward making partner himself someday, he married the girl. Chelsea cried for about six months."

Johnny looked more closely at the man Chelsea was dancing with. He looked like money. Everything about him, from his perfectly coiffed dark blond hair to his quietly expensive tailored suit and his Hollywood movie-star face, screamed dollar signs. His fingernails looked manicured. His shoes were freshly shined, presumably by one of the servants. His straight white teeth gleamed as he laughed with Chelsea.

It was hard to imagine Chelsea crying for six months over anyone—except possibly this man. Who was married, and had gotten married not for love, but for money.

Just as Chelsea was in the process of doing.

Johnny headed for the bar, in search of a drink. He was

willing to bet that he wasn't just a stand-in for Emilio, but that he was a stand-in for this Bent guy as well.

The revelation made him feel all kinds of things he didn't want to feel. Disgust. Envy. Frustration. Jealousy.

He wanted to go onto the dance floor and cut in. But that was stupid. Chelsea might have pretended to marry him in a church just a few hours ago. She was intending to marry him for real at a wedding chapel in Las Vegas before the day ended.

But he had no right to feel jealous. He wouldn't—and would probably never be—anything more to her than a business partner.

There was a line at the wedding chapel.

Johnny was still wearing his tuxedo. When he found out that they'd be going to the wedding chapel straight from the airport, he'd refused to change into jeans and a T-shirt for the flight. But he'd been comfortable enough on the plane to put his head back and go straight to sleep during the flight to Nevada, even without changing his clothes.

Chelsea had changed, though. She'd put on a pair of wide-legged white pants with a white silk blouse. It was what she would have chosen to get married in—if she'd had a choice. In fact, this Las Vegas setup was entirely the way she would have planned. The ceremony was going to be short and sweet, and she and Johnny were going to walk toward the justice of the peace together, as equals. And—if she had her way—they would seal the deal with a handshake.

She'd had enough of Johnny Anziano's soul-shattering kisses earlier today.

She glanced at her watch, trying her best not to be nervous. Why should she be? She'd done this once today already. The second time should be a piece of cake.

"What time does our flight to St. Thomas leave?" he asked.

Of course, this time when they said "I do," it would be for real. She had to clear her throat before she could speak. "In two hours."

"We have plenty of time."

"Yeah."

Johnny was watching her, his dark eyes unreadable. "So what *is* your favorite color?"

"Red." She glanced at him. "Yours?"

"Blue."

Chelsea looked down at the forms they'd had to fill out to get a marriage license. "I didn't even know how old you were until I read this."

"I'm twenty-six."

"Yeah, I can do the math. I minored in math in college."

"Now, you see, I didn't know that. What was your major?"

"I did a double major—computer science and physics. And then I went on to get my business degree."

Johnny whistled through his teeth. "Well, *I'm* impressed. I had no idea I was marrying a scholar."

"How about you? What was your major?"

He shook his head, smiling slightly. "I didn't go to college. At least not exactly."

Chelsea was embarrassed. She shouldn't have assumed. Quickly she changed the subject. "Your birthday's in October."

"Yep. I'm a Libra." He looked over her shoulder at the forms she held in her hand. "You were born late in January—an Aquarian, huh?"

She lifted an eyebrow. "Are we compatible?"

"Librans are pretty much compatible with everybody," he said with a smile.

"What a relief."

"What's your favorite holiday?"

Chelsea had to think. "I don't know. Christmas, I guess."

"Mine's New Year's Eve. It's such a high-energy night—

everyone's all jazzed up for the coming year, with high expectations. And hope. The hope on that night is off the scale." He paused as the woman who was acting as a sort of hostess came out into the waiting room and took the couple who had arrived directly in front of them into the chapel.

They were next.

Johnny looked back at Chelsea. "Who's your favorite dead president?"

She blinked. "What?"

"For most people it's a toss-up between Washington and Lincoln, with Kennedy running a close third, but I'm an FDR fan, myself."

"I don't think I have a favorite president—dead or alive."

"You must've had one when you were a kid."

"When I was a kid, it was Washington," she said. "Definitely. That whole story about the cherry tree. 'Father, I cannot tell a lie, I chopped down the cherry tree.' I always thought he was a lot like Mr. Spock on *Star Trek*. Vulcans can't tell a lie, either. It's supposedly physiologically impossible."

"Except Spock *could* lie because he was half-human," Johnny pointed out.

"Which says a lot for humanity, doesn't it?" Chelsea sighed, her smile fading.

"You feel bad, don't you," he guessed perceptively, "for fooling all those people at the church today."

"My dad was so . . ." Chelsea shook her head, smiling ruefully. "God, for the first time during the twenty-eight years I've been alive, I actually saw him with tears in his eyes. All I could think of was the way I was lying to him." She miserably blew out a short explosion of air. "And not only was *I* lying to everyone, but I've gone and dragged you into it too."

"At least now when you go to hell, I'll be there with you, so you'll have someone to talk to."

"That makes me feel *so* much better."

"It's not too late to back out," he said. "We can just walk out of here, spend the next twenty-four hours playing the five-dollar blackjack table at Circus Circus and drinking beer with whiskey chasers on the house."

Chelsea had to laugh. "Sounds tempting."

"Then when we've had too much to drink to keep our balance at the blackjack table, we can get a room upstairs and sleep it off for another twenty-four hours straight."

Sleep. As in share a bed. Yeah, right, they would sleep.

Johnny smiled, as if he were following her thoughts.

"I don't think so," she said.

"After a couple of days you could run home to your parents, claiming that Emilio was heavily into bondage and discipline, and that you left him, because that's not quite your style."

"How do you know that B and D isn't my style?" she couldn't resist asking.

He laughed in surprise, but recovered quickly. "Even if it is, I'm betting that you wouldn't share that fact with your mom and dad."

"Oh, that's a bet you'd win."

"Spencer and Anziano."

Chelsea looked up to see the wedding-chapel hostess beckoning to them. "Oh, God," she said. "It's time." She turned to Johnny. "It's not too late for you to back out."

"For seventy-five K," he told her, "I'm not going anywhere. Unless we can add to that Circus Circus scenario and say that after we get a room upstairs, we get to take turns tying each other up."

He hadn't realized that the wedding hostess was standing right behind him. He turned to see her there, and realized she'd overheard him. She was trying her best not to look shocked.

Johnny gave her one of his best smiles. "It's a wedding-night tradition in Chelsea's family," he said conspiratorially.

"He's kidding," Chelsea said, but the woman didn't look convinced.

As she followed the woman into the chapel she turned to give Johnny a chilling look.

"Oh, good, the Ice Princess is back," he said with a grin. "I was hoping I'd get to marry both of you—it'll make married life *really* interesting."

Ice Princess? Marry both . . . ? "What are you talking about?" she asked, but he just smiled. With his light banter and silly questions, he'd managed to make her feel thoroughly relaxed. She liked having him around, she realized. And then she remembered those kisses. She liked having him around too much.

Chelsea's pulse started to accelerate at the thought that within the next few minutes she was going to marry this man, and she tried not to think, not to feel, not to anticipate.

The hostess took the forms they'd filled out and the copies of their birth certificates from Chelsea. "One moment, please."

"No kissing this time," she told him under her breath. "We shake hands, do you understand?"

"No way. The man says you may kiss the bride, not you may high-five the bride."

"This is a business deal. We should shake—"

"Where I come from, people embrace and kiss when a deal is made."

She stopped short. "Where *do* you come from?"

"I was born in the North End, but while I was growing up, I lived about a block away from the Projects."

"The . . . Projects?" It was an impossibly tough part of town, filled with gang violence, drug abuse, struggling welfare mothers, and drive-by shootings. And Johnny had grown up there.

"Yeah. I won't tell your daddy if you don't."

"Oh, God, someone told you about George's wife, Cathy."

"So she does have a name. Troy filled me in. Her status as a

Projects kid hasn't exactly won her any popularity awards with the Spencer clan. Or should that be Klan, spelled with a *K*?"

Chelsea briefly closed her eyes. "I'm so sorry. You have every right to be offended."

"You can make it up to me—by letting me kiss the bride."

"John . . ."

He took her hand, squeezing her fingers gently. "Chelsea, this may be the only time I ever get married. Yeah, I'm doing it for the money, and yeah, it's weird, but please, let me at least do it right. And doing it right means when the guy says kiss the bridge, I kiss the bride."

She gazed up at him. "It matters to you that much?"

"Yeah. It does. Absolutely."

"One kiss, and then you'll retire your lips—permanently?"

"Are you sure you want me to?" He lowered his voice. "I can do an awful lot with my lips—without running the risk of consummating this marriage."

Chelsea felt her cheeks heat. "I can't believe you just said that to me."

To her surprise, he actually looked embarrassed too. "I can't believe I did either." He took a deep breath. "Although, one thing my mother always taught me was, you can't have what you don't ask for."

"Please don't ask for more than I can give you," she said softly. "John, we talked about this when we signed the prenupts. No sex. Of any kind. Just this one last kiss and that's it, all right?"

Johnny nodded. "If that's the way you want it . . ."

It wasn't the way she wanted it. It was the way she *needed* it to be.

"Giovanni Anziano and Chelsea Spencer?" The justice of the peace was a little, wizened old man wearing a western-cut jacket and an enormous cowboy hat. "Please approach."

"I don't know about you," Johnny whispered almost silently to her as they moved forward, "but the hat works for me."

"Chelsea Jasmine Spencer, do you take Giovanni Vincente Anziano as your lawfully wedded husband?"

Chelsea took a deep breath. "I do."

"And do you, Giovanni Vincente Anziano take Chelsea Jasmine Spencer—"

"I do."

The justice of the peace gazed at Johnny from the narrow band between the tops of his half glasses and the wide brim of his hat. "In a hurry there, are you, son?"

"Yes, sir."

He smacked the counter with a gavel. "By the power vested in me by the state of Nevada, I pronounce you man and wife."

Johnny looked at Chelsea in surprise. "That's it?"

"I asked for the short version. I hope you don't mind."

He looked at the judge. "We're married?"

"You truly are. Go ahead, son," the old man said. "Kiss your bride."

Chelsea braced herself, but Johnny didn't move. He just gazed at her.

"This time's for real," he told her.

Chelsea nodded. Yes. This time it was real. This time they were really married.

He moved closer then, drawing her into his arms before he lowered his mouth and then . . .

He kissed her.

This time, it was real. This time, he wrapped her in his arms as if he intended never to let her go. This time, his lips were impossibly gentle, his mouth impossibly sweet.

And this time, when her heart pounded crazily, she had no excuses handy.

Still, she let herself kiss him, losing herself in the sweetness of their embrace. Because he was right. Because this could very well be the only time she ever got married too. Because he was quite possibly the most desirable man she'd ever met. Because despite that, from this moment forth, their relationship was going to be pure business.

She was going to make damn sure of that.

seven

"YOU BOUGHT ME A *PRESENT*?"

Johnny smiled at Chelsea's look of total amazement as she turned to gaze at the neatly wrapped and beribboned package he had put into her hands.

They were sitting in the first-class section of a jet heading directly to the Caribbean. He was on his way to paradise with the most beautiful, most appealingly complex, and attractive woman he'd ever had the pleasure to meet. But just a short time ago she'd given him his final warning. This wasn't a honeymoon. It was a four-day-three-night-long business meeting.

In other words, hands off.

He'd never seduced a woman with his hands tied behind his back before. But there was a first time for everything.

Oh, not that he'd go and mess up her chances for getting an easy annulment. No, he could wait. But by the day that the annulment was declared, he was determined that Chelsea Spencer would be more than ready to fall into bed with him. And then they would consummate and celebrate their *not* being married to their hearts' content.

"What are *you* smiling at?" she asked, but he just shook his head, watching as she unwrapped the gift he'd bought for her. He opened the little cardboard box. "It's a . . . What *is* it?"

"It's a miniature music box." He fingered the unfamiliar weight and bulk of the thick gold wedding ring on his left hand. "If you wind the little key on the bottom, it'll play a very square version of 'Harlem Nocturne.'"

Intrigued, she wound the key and laughed as the melody came tinkling out. "I know this song."

"It's supposed to swing a whole lot more, but there's not much you can do with an old-fashioned cylinder-style music box that's this small. I'm amazed they managed to fit eight bars of the tune onto something that tiny."

"It's such a pretty melody." She looked up at him almost shyly. "This is so sweet."

"I'm glad you like it." Damn, it would be so easy to just lose himself in her blue eyes. . . .

"I feel like a jerk—I didn't get you anything."

"In that case, I'll let you pick up the tab on the champagne."

"Champagne?"

Chelsea watched as Johnny gestured for the flight attendant. The young woman came over almost immediately, ready with a big smile and a flutter of her eyelashes. "Yes, sir?"

Johnny reached for Chelsea's hand, turning it over to look at her wristwatch. "In about three minutes we'll be celebrating our two-and-a-half-hour wedding anniversary. Do you think you can get a bottle of champagne opened in time?"

"Only two and half hours since you were married? Oh, aren't you so sweet!" She rushed toward the food-preparation area.

"Two and a half hours," Chelsea echoed. Johnny was still holding her hand, and she gently pulled it free. "Are you sure you don't want to skip the fractions and go for the solid hours—wait for three to celebrate?"

"I'm not real good at waiting." He fished in his jacket pocket, trying to pull something free. "Besides, we need to have something to drink right now—to wash down our wedding cake."

He tossed a double package of Twinkies onto the tray table.

Chelsea looked from Johnny to the Twinkies and back. *"That's* your idea of wedding cake?" She couldn't keep from laughing.

"I could have done a whole lot better if I'd had a couple hours and a bakery kitchen," he admitted. "Instead, all I had to work with was an airport vending machine. It was this or Yodels. And I figured wedding cakes are supposed to be vanilla, so . . ."

Chelsea picked up the Twinkie package. "There's no way in hell you're going to get me to eat one of these."

"You don't have to eat an entire Twinkie," he told her, somehow managing to keep a perfectly straight face. "You just need to take a little, tiny bite."

"I eat only healthy food," she told him, still laughing. "Twinkies are the total antithesis of both healthy *and* food. No way is this getting anywhere near *my* mouth."

"But isn't eating the wedding cake supposed to bring good luck?" Johnny asked, tearing the package open. "Don't we risk the wrath of the wedding-cake god if we don't partake? Isn't that, like, bad juju or something?"

"Believe me, it would be *very* bad juju for me to take even the tiniest bite of one of these."

He took a bite and waved the half-eaten Twinkie in front of her nose. "Sure I can't tempt you with its flavorful aroma?"

She laughed, pushing his hand away. "Oh, God, it smells like my elementary-school cafeteria. Tiffany Stewart *always* brought three packs of Twinkies in her lunch—she told her housekeeper that there was a special table where privileged students could leave food donations for the scholarship kids, and since her father had more money than God, her housekeeper always let her take two extra packs. Of course, there was no such table. Tiffany threw away her sandwich and existed on a pure Twinkie diet for about three years."

"You went to a private school, huh?" he asked.

"The Wellford Academy. Pre-K through twelfth grade."

The flight attendant brought two plastic glasses of champagne. "Congratulations." She turned to Chelsea, nearly beaming with happiness. "You're so lucky—he's good-looking *and* romantic."

"So why is it you're not married?" Chelsea asked, taking a sip of her champagne after the attendant had walked away.

He gazed at the cabin lights through the plastic glass and the bubbling wine. "Just unlucky, I guess."

She shifted in her seat to face him. "I sense a story here."

He took a sip of his champagne. "I thought you didn't want to get to know me that well."

He was right. She shouldn't be asking him questions. She shouldn't try to find out who he was, where he'd been, what he thought, how he felt. She should keep her distance. She turned away, forcing herself to feel nothing but detached. It was only a matter of time before she received her inheritance and this whole ridiculous game ended. All she had to do was endure. She could do that. She *would* do that. "You're right. I don't. Consider the question withdrawn."

She signaled for the flight attendant, who appeared almost instantly. "I'd like a pillow and blanket, please."

Johnny cursed softly. The sudden chilly drop in the cabin's temperature was his fault. He'd gone and conjured up the Ice Princess—because of the one subject he didn't want to discuss.

"Thank you," Chelsea said politely to the attendant, who had handed her a pillow and blanket. "You can take the champagne, too, please. I'm done."

"She was from Paris." Johnny waited for the attendant to leave before he spoke. "Her name was Raquel, and I was with her for three years—"

Chelsea reclined her seat. "I really don't want to hear this."

"We were pretty hot and heavy right from the start, and the last two years we actually lived together. This was down in Washington, D.C.—we were both students at the International Culinary Institute. Can you imagine someone coming to America from Paris to learn how to cook? I would have sold my soul for a chance to study in Paris."

He'd gotten her attention. "You know how to cook?"

"Some people think so. Anyway, Raquel's dad had a heart attack, and she had to fly home. She was supposed to be gone for a month, but she never came back. She wrote me a letter telling me to toss her stuff. She said she didn't need it. And oh, by the way, by the time I got the letter, she would already be married to some old family friend. Two *years* we lived together, and she types me a note."

"I'm sorry," she said quietly.

"Yeah, I was too. But before that I was angry, and then I was hurt. I thought you know, first you live together and then you get married. It seemed the natural order of events—not first you live together and then you marry someone else. I had no clue she didn't feel the same way I did. I mean, right up until she left—the night before her flight home we . . ." He shook his head, smiling ruefully. "No, you definitely don't want to hear about that. Sorry."

They sat for a moment in silence.

"I guess I got you on the rebound, so to speak," Chelsea finally said.

"It's been five years. I think I'm past the rebound stage."

"But you still haven't found somebody new."

"Nope. But then again, I haven't exactly been looking. I work kind of crazy hours. Don't get me wrong—I haven't exactly been a monk these past five years. I've had girlfriends—I just haven't let anything get too serious."

Chelsea was watching him. The Ice Princess had vanished. There was nothing but compassion and warmth in her eyes.

"Do you still love her?" she asked quietly.

"No," he said. But he could tell from the way she was watching him that she didn't believe him.

"How about you?" he asked. "Do you still love what's-his-name? Bent?"

Her eyes widened. "Who told you about Bent?"

"Troy."

"Troy *knows*?"

"Knows what? Troy told me you had some kind of teenage crush on his friend—that you guys dated a few times and then he married some girl he got pregnant."

Chelsea was curled up in her seat, her cheek pressed against the reclined back, watching him, as if deciding how much to tell him. She hitched her blanket up higher underneath her chin. "Troy didn't know, but Bent and I did more than date," she finally said. "It was really just dumb luck that he didn't manage to get me pregnant too."

"How old were you?"

She paused before answering, her eyes assessing him, trying to gauge his reaction. "Sixteen."

In his neighborhood, girls lost their virginity at age sixteen all the time. But in hers? He did his best to hide his shock. "And he was how many years older?"

"He was twenty-three."

"Christ, what the hell was he thinking?" So much for hiding his shock.

Chelsea smiled. "I don't think Bent particularly paid attention to the parts of his anatomy that did the thinking. And as for me, I was impetuous and independent, and trying much too hard to be all grown up." She laughed, rolling her eyes. "I was so naive. When he told me that Nicole was pregnant—that was her name, Nicole—I honestly didn't understand. I thought he was somehow being coerced into marrying some dumb girl who'd gotten herself into trouble. It took me two days before I made the connection that he'd been sleeping with Nicole on the nights he wasn't with me. It was a crash course in reality."

"You were just a kid—it must've been hell to have to deal with that."

"I didn't deal with it very gracefully," she admitted. "It took me years to get over the bastard. You know, the really stupid thing was, if he had been faithful, if he had really honestly loved me, I would have married him right out of college. I would've become everything that I hated most about my mother and my sister, and all those other good little wives who live and breathe only for their husbands. I would have been driven slowly insane. Nicole saved me years of expensive therapy, attempting to discover the underlying causes of my deep unhappiness."

"How do you know you would have been unhappy?"

"Oh, *please*."

"No, I'm serious." Johnny reclined his own seat, so that they were nearly nose to nose. "I met your sister, Sierra. She seems really happy. And her husband, Ed Pope—he seems like an okay guy. True, he's not *your* type, *you* wouldn't be happy with him, but maybe your sister is. Not everybody wants to be president of their own company, you know." He gazed at her, well aware that she hadn't answered his question. She hadn't told him whether or not she was still in love with her former—and probably her first—lover.

"But *I* want to be president of my own incredibly successful business," she told him. "How could I do that with a husband like Edgar Pope or Benton Scott, who at any moment could come home and tell me he's being transferred to the Philadelphia office?"

"Obviously the trick is to marry someone like me. A townie. Even if Lumière's burned down, I'd find another job in Boston. It's my home—I'm not going anywhere, except on vacation."

"Except—suppose that we were really married, suppose we really were trying to make it work," she said. "And what if I had the opportunity to sell my business for a million dollars to a buyer in Texas—with the contingency that I move to Dallas and continue on in my salaried position as president for the next five years?"

"Five *years?*"

"You wouldn't want to do it."

Johnny shook his head. "There's no way I can know what I would or wouldn't do. I mean, everything would be different. If we loved each other..." He shrugged. "If I loved you and you were in Dallas...Hell, I guess I'd go to Dallas. If I knew I could go back to Boston in five years—"

"What if you didn't know that?" she asked. "What if you didn't know where you'd end up, whether you'd stay in Dallas *another* five years, or then go somewhere totally different? And what if the only job you could get was at a Texas barbecue restaurant, waiting tables? And what if you knew that the ten most talented chefs from Paris were coming to Boston to spend a year teaching a small group of students—and you'd been chosen to participate?"

Johnny had to laugh. "Well, that would make the choice a little tougher. I'd see if we could compromise—you'd put off selling the business for a year and after that I'd go to Dallas."

"What if the deal wouldn't wait a year? What if it had to happen immediately?"

She was damned good at thinking up worst-case scenarios. "God, Chelsea, I don't know."

"Or here's a good one: What if I didn't tell you about the deal until after it had been done? What if you didn't have a choice? What if I just came home and said, 'Guess what, honey? We're moving to Dallas!'"

Johnny was silent.

"Both my mother and Sierra have lived that scenario more than once," she told him. "But I refuse to put myself into that situation. Because if it were *you* who had to go to Dallas, and I was the one who had to give up my job and my home and my friends . . . I wouldn't go." She gazed at him unblinkingly. "And *that's* why I'll never get married."

"Hey. Hey, Chelsea. Seat-belt sign's on. We're coming in for a landing. . . ."

Chelsea stirred. She was so comfortable and *so* soundly asleep, but now someone was touching her shoulder, trying to wake her up.

"Time to sit up," the voice said again. It was a familiar voice, husky and deep and sexy. She'd recognize that voice anywhere. It was . . . It was . . . ?

"If you sit up, you can see the sunrise. It's incredible—you've got to get a look at this."

The voice was very persuasive—and very familiar. Why couldn't she remember who it belonged to?

"Please let this just be a dream," Chelsea mumbled, snuggling into her pillow. "I'm too tired to wake up."

"Come on, sleepyhead, open your eyes."

"They're open," she murmured.

He laughed, and she remembered who he was. He was her husband.

Her *husband* . . . ?

Chelsea opened her eyes and found herself staring directly at the fly on Johnny Anziano's pants. She sprang up, bumping her back on the tray table in front of her seat and hitting her head on the overnight compartment.

She had been sleeping with her head in his lap.

"Whoa," he said, reaching out to steady her and help her down into her seat.

"I'm sorry." She was out of breath, her heart pounding. "I didn't know I'd taken over your seat as well as mine."

"I didn't mind."

Chelsea found herself gazing into Johnny's chocolate-brown eyes. He was smiling very slightly and she knew he was telling the truth. He hadn't minded. In fact, on the contrary . . .

Her hair was falling down, and she used the excuse to look away from him as she pulled the remaining pins free. Searching her handbag, she found her brush and ran it through her hair.

"Check out the sunrise," he said, gesturing out the window.

It was amazing. The tops of the clouds were pink and orange and glowing. It didn't look real, yet there they were.

There they were, indeed.

He shifted uncomfortably in his seat.

"Did you sleep at all?" Chelsea had to ask.

Johnny didn't say yes or no. He just smiled. "I'm fine."

In fact, he was better than fine. True, he hadn't slept, but he hadn't wanted to sleep. Chelsea had fallen fast asleep, leaning against the side of the plane. But then she'd shifted, trying to get comfortable, resting her head against his shoulder. He'd pulled up the armrests that were between their two seats in an effort to make her even more comfortable, and his movement had pushed her down so that her head was on his lap.

That had fueled a few hundred thousand fantasies or so.

He'd allowed himself the luxury of touching her silky-smooth hair. It was baby fine and so soft underneath his fingers, glistening in the dim cabin light like the most precious gold.

He'd spent the night watching her gentle breathing, letting her hair slide between his fingers, thinking about all that she'd told him.

If Chelsea loved him, *really* loved him, there was no place he wouldn't go to be with her. Dallas, Boston, Timbuktu. If she were there, he'd be there, guaranteed. *If* she loved him.

But she'd made it more than clear that love wasn't on her agenda.

He'd spent some time thinking about Benton Scott. Chelsea had been in love with the man—maybe she was still in love with him. If there were ever a guy more different from Johnny than night was from day, it was Benton Scott.

Could the man's name sound any more Anglo-Saxon? He was one of Troy's *Harvard* chums. He was the crown prince of the "us" club, while Johnny was the heir apparent of "them," born into his place—or lack of place—in the social registry, the same way Bent Scott had been born into his.

Money. Education. Bent Scott had it over Johnny in every way imaginable. Looks. A woman who went for fair-haired, blue-eyes, slender men like Bent wouldn't give Johnny a second glance.

Night and day.

He'd had to stop and untangle a lock of Chelsea's hair from where it had gotten caught around his wedding band, and he'd realized something he'd been trying his best to ignore.

It wouldn't take much for this woman to entangle herself around his heart. If he wasn't careful, he could very easily fall head over heels in love . . . with his wife.

eight

"YOU SURE I CAN'T TALK YOU INTO COMING into the water?" Johnny asked. "It's *great*. You should see the fish, just swimming around out there—all colors, like something you'd see in someone's tank, only *huge*. They'll swim right up to you."

Chelsea looked up from her powerbook to see Johnny smiling at her, water dripping off of his hard-muscled body, his wet hair plastered against his head, water beading on his eyelashes.

His bathing suit was the loose-fitting, knee-length kind, but on him, it looked transcendently sexy.

Standing there on the white sand, with the turquoise Caribbean ocean and the crystal-blue Caribbean sky behind him, her husband looked like a walking, breathing advertisement for hedonistic temptations.

Husband in name only, she reminded herself.

He held out his hand. "Come on, Chelsea. You can do whatever you're doing later, can't you?"

She steeled herself before looking into his eyes. "I really can't," she lied. "I have to fax these reports to Moira first thing in the morning."

He sat down on the edge of the lounge chair next to hers.

"Okay," he said reasonably. "You take a couple of hours, finish up those reports, and then we'll have dinner together. I was reading one of the guidebooks about this place called the Mafali—it's an open-air restaurant up on the side of the mountain, overlooking the harbor. The food's not fancy—mostly grilled steaks, but the view's supposed to be—"

"I can't."

"—fabulous. Why not?"

He knew damn well why not. Sure, she could give him more excuses. She had more reports to write, more work to do. She'd brought enough with her to keep her occupied every waking moment of this trip. But she didn't want to play games.

"I don't want to have dinner with you," she told him bluntly. "I don't want to pretend that we're newlyweds, I don't even want to be friends with you. I think it would be best if we just went our separate ways over the next three days."

Johnny laughed. "This is perfect," he said, shaking his head in disbelief. "Here I've gone and *married* you, and you *still* won't go out on a date with me. How pathetic is that?"

It was pathetic. But she couldn't help it. She couldn't dare let herself get any closer to him. Instead of waking up with her head in his lap, God knows where she'd find herself waking up next.

"I can't talk you into changing your mind?"

Chelsea shook her head. She refused to acknowledge the disappointment she could see in his eyes. She focused all of her attention on her powerbook screen as she tried to distance herself from him, to pull back, to not care. After all, disappointment was a part of life.

From the corner of her eye, she could see him, still sitting next to her, just watching her work for several long minutes after she had, in a sense, dismissed him.

Finally, he stood up and walked away.

Chelsea looked up then, unable to resist watching him head

for the resort bar, unable truly to keep her distance, despite what she would have him believe.

Because she cared. Somehow Giovanni Anziano had gotten under her skin, and try as she might, she couldn't help but care.

"Do the names Edward and Susan Farber ring any bells?" Johnny said into the telephone as soon as Chelsea picked up.

"Um," she said, "yeah. The Farbers. Friends of my parents—from the country club, I think?" He could picture her doing a mental double take, realizing what he had asked her. Her voice went up an octave. "Oh my God, are they *here*?"

"They're sitting in the resort dining room right this very minute," he told her.

Chelsea swore sharply. "Have they seen you?"

"Of *course* they've seen me." Johnny let his frustration ring in his voice. This trip wasn't turning out the way he'd hoped— not by a long shot. The last time he'd even gotten within range of Chelsea had been two days earlier, in the afternoon, on the beach. She'd been plugged into her computer and had barely even looked up to tell him to forget about dinner, forget about talking, forget about *any*thing. She wasn't interested. Since then, she'd done her best to avoid him. "You don't honestly expect that I'd recognized *them* after meeting them for fifteen seconds in a receiving line—two out of the five hundred and something people I met for the first time a few days ago?"

"You sound annoyed." There was real surprise in her voice.

"I *am* annoyed. You better get your butt down here, unless you want Eddie and Sue getting the word back to Mumsy and Dadsy that they saw Chelsea's bridegroom eating dinner all by himself three days after the wedding."

"Can't you come up—pretend we're ordering in tonight?"

"No," Johnny told her flatly. "I was already sitting in the

restaurant when they saw me. I told them you were running late—that you'd be down in a minute."

There was silence on the other end of the phone. "You're mad at me, aren't you?" she finally asked.

He had to answer her truthfully. "No," he said. "Not mad. Disappointed. I thought we were starting to become friends."

He heard her sigh, heard the rustling of papers on the other end of the telephone. "Have you ordered your dinner yet?"

"Yes, I did. I thought I'd give the so-called chef a chance to ruin some swordfish steaks tonight."

She laughed nervously. "Wow, this is a side of you I've never seen before."

"Yeah, well, I guess the honeymoon's over, huh?"

"Could you order me a large salad?" she asked. "No cheese, no bacon, vinaigrette dressing on the side? Then give me three minutes, and I'll be right down."

Johnny hung up the phone and briefly closed his eyes. God bless the Farbers. Chelsea was going to have dinner with him.

It took Chelsea a little bit longer than three minutes, but not much. When Johnny spotted her coming into the lobby, she was wearing a loose-fitting, long flowing blue island print sundress, and her hair was up on top of her head.

She looked beautiful, and Johnny let himself stare while she was still all the way across the room, while she stopped at the Farbers' table and said a brief hello. He knew that once she sat down across from him, he wouldn't be able to look at her this way. She wouldn't want him to.

How the hell had he ever gotten himself into this situation?

"Hi," she said almost shyly, and he rose to his feet to greet her.

"How's work?" he asked, sitting down across from her.

There was a candle in the middle of the table, and its flickering flame threw light and shadows across Chelsea's face as she gazed at him. "I've gotten quite a bit done." She looked out across the patio, toward the beach and the moonlit water. "It's a beautiful evening, isn't it?"

Johnny felt a flash of frustration. Small talk. They could go on like this all night. But he didn't want to talk about the weather. He had bigger fish to fry. He leaned forward. "I don't understand what the problem is, Chelsea," he told her. "I signed the agreements you wanted me to sign, and I promised to keep sex out of the picture. I gave you my word, but you won't trust me. And I'm finding that hard to deal with."

He more than expected her to slip into Ice Princess mode and regard him with haughty disdain. But she didn't. Instead, she sighed, and gazed out at the moonlight, unable to meet his eyes. Up close like this, she looked a little anxious and a little tired, as if she weren't sleeping well at all. "I guess you don't want to talk about the weather."

"The weather here is perfect. There's nothing to say about it."

Chelsea took a sip from her water glass, trying to pretend that her hand wasn't shaking as she glanced up at him. "So what *do* you want to talk about? My deeply rooted problem with trust? It probably goes back to my childhood—we could be here for quite some time."

"I've got time."

Chelsea let herself really look at the man sitting across the table from her. He was quite possibly the man they had in mind when they coined the phrase *tall, dark, and handsome*. He usually seemed to be on the verge of smiling—except for now. Right now he was uncharacteristically solemn, his dark eyes sober yet no less intense as he watched her.

"Maybe we could start by talking about something easier," Chelsea said.

"You're afraid of me, because I'm legally your husband," he guessed with unerring perception.

She drew in a deep breath. "Or we could start with something even harder."

"Or maybe you're afraid that you're going to like being married to me too much."

Chelsea forced a laugh. "Don't be ridiculous—"

"Why don't you tell me what the problem is, then?" He spoke softly, urgently. He really wanted to know. "We were doing fine on the flight from Vegas, then all of a sudden, we're at the hotel and you're telling me that you don't even want to be my *friend*? What the hell is that about? What did I do? Did I offend you in some way? Chelsea, did I say or do something that makes you think you can't trust me?"

She briefly closed her eyes, then told him the truth. It was the least she could do. "I do trust you," she said, gazing at him in the candlelight. "It's my own self I don't have any faith in."

Johnny struggled to understand. He couldn't believe what he had just heard. "You don't trust *yourself*...?"

"To stay away from you," she finished softly, glancing up at him almost shyly, her eyes filled with chagrin.

He was stunned. Of all the things he'd expected her to say, that was last on the list.

"Every time I'm near you, I want...things I shouldn't want," she admitted quietly. "I can't stop thinking about the way you kissed me...."

She looked away from him, as if embarrassed, and Johnny reached for her hand, moving out of his own chair and into the seat next to hers, wanting to reassure her she was not alone. "Is that really so awful?" he asked.

"Yes." She spoke vehemently, her blue eyes sparking as she looked up at him, but still, she didn't pull her hand away.

He tried to make a joke. "Last time I checked, no one went to hell for kissing."

"It's not the kissing—it's where those kisses would lead that has me worried."

Where those kisses would lead...They wouldn't lead anywhere—at least not if he kissed her here, in the resort's restaurant. And not if he kissed her anyplace else, either. Not unless both of them absolutely wanted it to.

Johnny leaned even closer to her, catching her chin with his other hand. Her skin was as soft and as smooth as he remembered, and he felt a wave of giddiness. He was going to kiss her. Right now. The way he'd been dying to kiss her since Vegas. "Let's try it and see exactly where it will lead."

"John—" She tried to pull away and he let her go.

But his soft words kept her from standing up and running away. "The Farbers are watching."

Johnny saw her glance across the room, saw all of her uncertainty and trepidation in her eyes. But he saw longing too. And he knew without a doubt that she wanted him to kiss her—as much, if not more, than she *didn't* want him to kiss her.

He leaned forward, closing the gap between them, capturing her mouth with his, drinking her in. Whether she parted her lips willingly or in surprise, he didn't know—and he didn't care. For every inch she gave him, he was determined to take a mile. He pulled her closer, touching the softness of her arms and the delicate fabric of the dress that covered her back. He kissed her harder, deeper, feeling her hands against the back of his neck, first tentatively, then possessively, as she kissed him with equal abandon.

And he knew in that instant that he was dead wrong. This kiss wasn't just a kiss. It didn't lead nowhere. In fact, it did quite the opposite. It led directly to temptation. It burned an unswerving path out of the restaurant, into the lobby, and up the stairs to the second floor, where they had adjoining suites. It pushed open the door to Chelsea's bedroom and flung them both down upon her bed, arms and legs intertwined, clothing quickly removed until they were pressed together, skin to skin, soft flesh against hard muscle, straining to become one.

The images that flashed into his mind were sharp and clear.

Chelsea, naked, on her bed. Pale skin, perfect and smooth. Blond hair like spun gold fanned out against the stark white of the sheets. Her smile of welcome as she reached for him. Her soft hands gliding across his body. Her drawn-in breath and the expression of sheer pleasure on her face as he filled her . . .

With herculean effort, Johnny pulled back, away from Chelsea's lips. He watched her eyes flutter open, watched her pulse pounding in her delicate throat.

His own breathing was ragged, and as she met his eyes he knew he'd only succeeded in thoroughly proving himself wrong.

"Okay," he said, reaching for alternatives. "So we *don't* kiss. We can spend tomorrow together and just . . . not kiss."

She put her head in her hands. "How did I ever get myself into this?"

"Tomorrow's our last day here. I just want to be with you, Chelsea. I want to *talk* to you—"

She didn't even lift her head. "I don't think I'm strong enough."

"I can be strong enough for both of us."

"But if you can't?"

"I can," he insisted. "This is about more than just sex. I want to go to the beach with you tomorrow. I want to show you this great place to snorkel—I want to spend the day with you."

She rested her chin in her hand, looking at him for several long seconds before she spoke, searching his eyes, as if trying to read his mind. "And what about tonight?"

Johnny took a deep breath. "I can say good night to you at the door to your room and then walk away. I can do that."

Her eyes lingered on his lips and she didn't try to hide her attraction for him as she looked back up into his eyes. "And what if I tell you I want you to kiss me again? What if I ask you to come into my room and spend the night with me? Would you be strong enough to turn me down?"

"I don't know—" He cut himself off as he held her gaze, as he, too, let her see how badly he wanted her. "No," he said honestly. "No, I wouldn't be."

Time seemed to stretch way out as they looked into each other's eyes, the truth laid out on the table before them.

Chelsea was the first to look away. She took a sip of her water, knowing that it wouldn't help at all to cool her down. "Tomorrow, if you see the Farbers at the beach," she said, amazed that her voice could sound so normal, "tell them I've had too much sun—that's why I'm not with you."

Johnny nodded. "Yeah, all right."

The waiter appeared, carrying Chelsea's salad and his swordfish steak.

Johnny looked up at him. "Sorry for the inconvenience," he said, "but can you have room service bring this up to our rooms?"

"No problem at all, sir." The food disappeared back toward the kitchen.

Johnny got to his feet, holding out his hand for Chelsea. "Come on," he said. "Let's make it look good for the Farbers."

Chelsea stood and he pulled her close, looping his arm around her shoulders. She caught a glimpse of Susan Farber's knowing smile as they left the restaurant.

If Susan Farber only knew . . .

Chelsea was stepping into the warm water of a bath when the phone rang. Thinking it could only be Moira, she sat down among the bubbles and reached for the telephone's bathroom extension.

"It's about time that you called," she said as a greeting as she nestled the phone against her ear.

There was a pause, then a voice that was decidedly *not*

Moira's spoke. "I don't know who exactly you expect this to be, but it's not. It's me."

It was Johnny Anziano. Chelsea nearly dropped the receiver into the bubbly water. She was undressed and in the bathtub, which seemed an utterly inappropriate place to have a conversation with him.

"I thought you were Moira," she admitted.

"Well, I'm not," he said.

She stood up, water sheeting off of her as she reached for her towel. But she stopped mid-grab, catching sight of her reflection in the big mirror over the double set of sinks. She was naked, her body glistening in the dim light of the candle she'd brought into the bathroom. But so what if she was naked? Johnny couldn't see her. And if she got out of the tub to talk to him, the water would be cold by the time she got back in.

Besides, it would be fun to talk to him, knowing that he'd damn near have a heart attack if he knew where she was and what she was doing. She could just imagine the look on his face. . . .

She sat down among the bubbles, smiling at the thought. "What's up?"

"You know, it just suddenly occurred to me that we could talk on the phone." His voice was smoky and resonant—and capable of sending shivers down her spine and heat coursing through her entire body. "You're over there and I'm over here, and the door's locked between us, so the whole temptation thing is pretty much taken care of."

He was right. They could talk on the phone without running the risk of winding up in each other's arms. And she wanted to talk to him. She *liked* talking to him. She leaned her head back and closed her eyes. "What do you want to talk about?"

He didn't hesitate. "You."

She opened her eyes. "That's not fair. How come we can't talk about *you*?"

"We can take turns," he suggested. "I'll ask you a question, and then you can ask me one."

"How come you get to go first?"

Johnny laughed. "All right. *You* go first."

"Okay." Chelsea gazed up at the moisture dripping down the steamy tile walls. It seemed to gleam in the candlelight. She sank down into the water until the bubbles covered all but the tops of her breasts. "Let's see. . . . What kind of car are you going to buy with the seventy-five grand?"

He laughed again. He had a really fabulous laugh. "Who says I'm going to buy a car?"

"The woman at Meals on Wheels told me you drive an ancient VW Bug," Chelsea told him, sinking farther into the water, so that the back of her head was wet, careful not to drop the receiver in. "Allegedly, the car's already died, but both you and it refuse to acknowledge that."

"That car's a classic," Johnny told her. "I might spend a few hundred dollars getting a tune-up, but no way am I buying a new car."

She sat up, squeezing the water out of her hair with her free hand, then reached for the soap. "What kind of man would prefer a museum artifact to a zippy new sports car . . . ?"

"The kind of man who's saving all of his money so he can open his own restaurant," Johnny told her.

"Is *that* what you're going to do with the money?"

"That's right."

She lathered up her washcloth. "What kind of restaurant?"

"The best," he said. "The kind where people drop huge bills for dinner, and leave feeling they got the better end of the deal because the food was so good."

"I had no idea," Chelsea murmured, tucking the phone under her chin as she ran the washcloth up her arm.

"Are you . . . splashing?"

"Splashing?" Chelsea asked.

"Yeah," he said. "It sounds like you're splashing. Like, with water?"

The slightly rough texture of his voice seemed to slide exquisitely against her skin, like the sensation of the soapy washcloth against her breasts and stomach. "Really?"

"There it is again," Johnny said. "Holy God, you're in the tub, aren't you?" His voice sounded odd—choked and tight, as if he were suddenly having trouble breathing.

She smiled, lifting one leg to run her washcloth from her ankle to her thigh. "I take baths at night to relax."

She heard him draw in a deep breath, and when he spoke again, his voice was intimate and low. "So how's it going? Are you relaxed?"

"I'm working on it."

"Anything I can do to help?"

nine

CHELSEA FOUND HER RAZOR ON THE EDGE of the tub, and resting her leg along the edge, she began to shave. "Isn't it your turn to ask me a question? A *real* question?"

She didn't need to see him to know he was smiling. "Yeah. I guess I can cross 'What are you wearing?' off the list."

"I guess so."

"Maybe you should run more hot water into the tub," he told her. "I wouldn't want you to get cold."

She'd turned off the air-conditioning and opened the windows before she'd run her bathwater. It had to be close to eighty-five degrees in there. A bead of sweat ran down her neck and she used her washcloth to cool herself off. "Believe me, I'm in no danger of getting cold. It's steamy in here."

He drew in another deep breath. "I bet. Yow."

"I'm still waiting for your question."

"My brain is immobilized by the pictures my vivid imagination is creating."

"*I* have a question, then," she said. "I want to know where you learned to kiss."

Johnny laughed. "Would you believe through years of dedicated practice?"

"Yes."

"Actually, when I was seven, my mother and I lived next door to a kid named Howie Bernstein. Howie had a sixteen-year-old sister, and—I can't remember her name, but she used to lecture us on how to kiss a girl. Apparently, she went out with a couple of boys who had no finesse—they did little more than grab and suck, if you know what I mean."

"Oh, I know exactly what you mean." Chelsea closed her eyes, using her hands to rinse the soap from her skin, letting his voice wash over her as well.

"So Howie's sister was determined that Howie not grow up to be an insensitive jerk, so she regularly cornered him—and me with him—and told us that when we kissed a girl, we had to re-member to take it *really* slow—even twice as slow as we thought. She said we had to pay attention to little details and take our time. I was only seven, but I can still remember her telling us that. So I guess I owe it all to Howie Bernstein."

"God bless Howie Bernstein's sister, whatever her name is."

"Howie used to call her Butthead, but I know that's not her real name."

"Probably not."

"She was beautiful and funny and smart. I remember wish-ing I had a sister like her. It got kind of lonely sometimes with just my mother and me."

"What happened to your father?" Chelsea asked.

"He died in Vietnam when I was around three. I never really knew him."

Chelsea closed her eyes. "God, I'm sorry."

"Yeah, me too," Johnny told her. "More now than I was as a kid. I mean, I grew up in a pretty tough neighborhood, and a lot of kids had dads that beat the crap out of them—so I didn't mind not having a father back then. But when I got older, I could've used having a guy around the house—you know, like a role model. But all I had were the stories my mother used to tell.

About how my father wanted to go to college and become a schoolteacher, but his parents died when he was a kid, and he had no money. So he enlisted in the army, thinking he could sign up and serve for a few years and then go to school courtesy of Uncle Sam. He didn't factor dying into the equation."

"How did he die?"

"His transport plane was shot down. According to the stories, he was one of about seventy-five men who survived the crash, but he died trying to pull the pilot out of the plane. It was burning, and they could hear the pilot screaming, and my father was the only one who went in after him. The whole thing went up in a fireball, and they were both killed."

Johnny paused, but Chelsea didn't speak. She sat, watching water drip down the tile walls, trying to imagine *her* father going into a burning plane to try to save the pilot's life. She couldn't picture it—because he'd never do it. Oh, he'd have gone in without batting an eye if his money had been in danger of going up in flames, but not for some stranger.

"But then, after my mother died," Johnny continued, "I was going through some of her papers, sorting things out, you know, and I found my father's army records, along with some letters he wrote to her. It didn't take me long to realize that that story she told me about him wanting money to go to college— that was something of a rather huge white lie. The truth was, he was busted for knocking over a liquor store, and since he was only eighteen and it was his first known offense, he was given a choice: jail or the army. That was right around the time he'd gotten my mother pregnant and married her. He had a wife and kid to think about, so he took his chances in 'Nam. He actually made it through his first tour without even being injured.

"The way I figure it, he came back and kicked around for about a year before he started to get into trouble again—or at least until he started to get caught. This time he served about six months in prison, and when he got out, he reenlisted. I read a letter he wrote to my mother from Walpole right before his release, telling her he didn't know what else he could do besides go back to Vietnam. He couldn't handle the grind of nine to five, and he was a lousy criminal too. The only thing he'd ever been good at was patrolling the jungles of Southeast Asia. So he went back, and he died trying to save some stranger's life. He was the only one who went into the burning plane to help that pilot. The *only* one." He was silent for a moment. "I could never figure out why my mother didn't just tell me the truth."

"Maybe she wanted you to remember him as a hero," Chelsea said softly.

"But that's just it," Johnny said. "Didn't she realize that the truth was better than the story she told? I mean, here's this two-bit criminal, this total screwup of a guy who can't hold a job, who's done hard time in Walpole, and he's the only man—one out of nearly a hundred soldiers—who can't just stand there and listen to another man burn to death. My father didn't go into that plane because he wanted to die. He wasn't trying to be a hero. He probably went in there cursing that pilot to hell and back. But he did go in. He couldn't keep himself from trying to save that guy. Everyone thought he was some good-for-nothing lowlife, but inside, he was a better man than all of them. To me, it makes him even more of a hero, since he wasn't a hero to start with."

"You're right, but I can see it from your mother's point of view too," Chelsea told him. "I could see how she wouldn't want her son growing up knowing his father had done time in prison. Didn't you tell me that she was a doctor?"

"Yeah. She went back to school to get her degree about four years after my dad died. It took her that long to deal with it. My old man may not have been able to hold a job, but he was one of those guys that charmed the socks off of everyone he met. Everybody loved him." Johnny laughed. "My mother had this note written to him by the warden up at Walpole, wishing him the best of luck upon his parole, can you believe it? It was in with his letters and stuff.

"Anyway, she never really got over his death, but she finally reached a point where she had to move forward with her own life. I remember when she sat me down and told me she was going back to college—that she was going for a medical degree. I was eight that year, and she gave me my own key to the apartment, because I was going to have to let myself in after school, while she was in class. That was when I first learned to cook." He laughed. "I had to, or I would've starved to death. My mother almost never got home before eight-thirty for about six years. I started cooking *her* dinner."

"You must've been scared—eight years old and alone for all that time every day."

"I was used to it. It was no big deal."

"When I was twelve, I spent three days totally by myself— and it was a *very* big deal," Chelsea said. "And necessity *wasn't* the mother of invention in my case. I *didn't* learn to cook—I just ate junk food the entire time. You know—and this is something you should know about me, seeing as how I *am* your wife—but I *still* can't cook. I'm the kind of person who can burn water."

"Maybe I could give you a few lessons."

Chelsea closed her eyes, not wanting to think about the kind of lessons she wanted Johnny Anziano to give her. "I don't think so. If I learned how, then I'd have to cook all the time. As it stands, I've got a great reason for ordering takeout."

"I love to cook. I loved it when I was eight too. I'd much rather cook my own dinner than eat out. I'm too critical of other people's cooking."

"Do you really know how to cook?" she asked. "*Really* cook?"

"Isn't it my turn to ask a question?"

"No, I think it's still my turn," she told him, knowing full well that she was wrong.

"No way! You just asked me about fourteen questions in a row," he told her. "It's definitely my turn. And I want to know why you spent three days by yourself when you were twelve."

Chelsea stretched her foot toward the faucet, and with her toe she lifted the toggle that opened the drain, letting some of the cooling water out of the tub. "I was in some really intense negotiations with my parents about trying out for the middle-school field-hockey team. I didn't want to do it because Sierra had played and won Field Hockey Goddess of the East Coast, or some major award like that. The way I saw it, Sierra was Miss Perfect, and this was just going to be another way that I would fail to live up to her glorious standards."

She closed the drain with her toe, but then scooted forward to add more hot water to the tub. She raised her voice to be heard over the rush of the water. "So after they told me that I *would* play on the team—I didn't have a choice in the matter—I counternegotiated by packing up my things and moving out."

Johnny laughed in surprise. "Are you saying that you ran away from home?"

"Yep. And you want to know the really stupid thing?"

"Oh, yeah," Johnny said. "I get the feeling this is going to be good."

"After I left, nobody missed me."

"You're kidding."

Chelsea shut off the hot water. "Nope. I happened to run away on the weekend of the big Harvard/Yale game. My entire family spent all of Saturday preparing for the game, all of Sunday tailgating in Cambridge, and all of Monday recovering. Everyone just assumed I was home, pouting."

"Where did you go?"

"I drove out to our beach house in Truro—on the Cape."

"You *drove*?"

"Yep. Took Daddy's Jaguar and headed for Cape Cod."

"I'm assuming that wasn't the first time you'd been behind

the wheel of a car." Johnny paused. "Of course, I realize that with you, I probably shouldn't assume anything."

"No, you were right the first time. Troy taught me to drive when I was ten. I was kind of like his pet monkey—it amused him to teach me to do all sorts of grownup things. That same year he tried to get me to drink beer and smoke, too, but I was a smart kid. I hated the taste of beer, and I knew smoking would give me cancer." She swirled the water around in the tub, trying to mix the cool with the hot. "But I *loved* to drive. I had to sit on about three pillows and pull the seat all the way up so I could reach the gas pedal. Troy used to take me out a couple times a week. Sometimes he'd even wake me up in the middle of the night so I could get a chance to drive on the highway without anyone around to see me and call the cops. By the time I was twelve, I was an excellent driver. I'd probably already clocked a few thousand miles."

"Driving, smoking, drinking... I guess what Troy couldn't teach you, his good friend Bent did, huh?" Johnny asked.

"Is that your next question?"

"No, I was just marveling at the irony. So back to this story: You took Daddy's Jag, and you actually made it all the way out to Truro without getting stopped?"

Chelsea put her head back and watched the flickering candlelight reflecting off the moisture-laden walls. "It was off-season. No one gave me a second glance. At least not until I'd been at the beach house for three days. That was when I was nabbed—by a patrol cop who knew there wasn't supposed to be anyone staying at the Spencer cottage that week. He brought me down to the police station and called my parents—who still didn't even know I was gone." She laughed, but there wasn't much humor in it. "What a joke."

"So did you have to play on the field-hockey team?"

"You bet. I was grounded for everything *except* field-hockey practice for three months. It was not a happy year—that was only the first of a long string of power struggles I didn't stand a chance of winning."

"Maybe that's really why you don't want to get married," Johnny suggested. "Because your parents want you to."

"Thank you so much, Dr. Freud. I think *maybe* I'm a little bit more in control of my own life now that I'm twenty-eight years old."

"Ready for my next question?" Johnny was smoothly changing the subject. He was a very smart man.

"Isn't it my turn yet?"

"Nope. If there was one single thing in your life that you could do differently, what would it be?"

Chelsea didn't have to think about that for long. "I wouldn't have had that affair with Benton Scott. Definitely not."

"That wasn't your fault—you were too young," Johnny said. "*He* was the one who should have known better."

"I wasn't too young," Chelsea countered.

"You think sixteen's not too young?"

She hadn't been sixteen, not the second time. Chelsea was silent for a moment, wondering how much to tell him. The truth? Why not? He was her husband, after all. Why not share her darkest, most dreadful secret with him?

She moistened her suddenly dry lips, wondering what he was going to say. "I wasn't talking about the first time I had an affair with Bent," she said. "I was talking about the second. After he was married."

Johnny was noticeably quiet.

"It was about five years ago," she went on, "and I was working for my master's degree. I hadn't seen Bent in years, and I ran into him downtown. He looked almost exactly the same. It was weird, as if he'd time-warped through the past seven years. He told me he and his family had just moved to a house out in one

of the W suburbs—Weston or Wayland or Wellesley, I don't remember which. But because they weren't living in town anymore, he'd gotten a small apartment near the courthouse for the
times when he had trials and he wanted to stay overnight . . . and
you know exactly where this is leading, right?"

"Yeah."

"Disappointed in me?"

"Yeah."

Chelsea squeezed her eyes shut. "Do you hate me now?"

"Of course not. Hell, everyone makes mistakes."

"It wasn't as tawdry as I've made it sound," she told him. "I
didn't go to his apartment with him right away—not for a few
weeks, anyway. But he started calling me regularly, and we had
lunch, and then dinner, and then . . ." She closed her eyes again,
wondering what Johnny was really thinking. Sure, everyone
made mistakes, but she'd knowingly slept with a married man. It
had not been her finest moment.

"It *was* tawdry," she admitted. "Unbearably tawdry. I only
went there once, but once is enough, isn't it? I guess I did it
mostly to get back at Nicole—Bent's wife. But she probably
never knew, and *I* was the one who felt like crap afterward. Of
course, it didn't help matters that I was still in love with the bastard." She took a deep breath. "So there it is. The one thing I'd
do *much* differently if I could only do it over."

"Maybe your mistake was in letting yourself fall in love with
a man like Bent in the first place," Johnny said quietly.

Chelsea snorted. "Yeah, like we can control who we fall in
love with?" She sat up, letting the water out of the tub. "I'm
turning into a prune. I've got to get out of here." She stood up
and stepped out of the tub.

"Are you still in love with him?"

His words stopped her. "I don't know," she admitted. "I . . .
haven't been with that many men, if you want to know the
truth. And I haven't been with anybody who made me feel even

close to the way Bent did." Except Johnny. Those kisses Johnny had given her had been totally off the scale.

"That sounds like a challenge to me." His voice was as soft as the towel she reached for to dry herself with.

"Well, it's not. I don't want to be someone's challenge, or someone's prize or someone's bonus or—"

"How about someone's partner?"

"There's no such thing as a true partnership," she told him as she dried herself off. "Someone always has more power. In everything from a business deal to a love affair. There's always someone who wants more. And if you want something—or someone—too badly, you're definitely in the weaker position." Chelsea hung her towel up and reached for the moisturizing lotion on the counter next to the sinks. "That's what happened with me and Bent—the first time around, I mean. I wanted to go out with this exciting, handsome, grown-up man—enough to get myself involved in a sexual relationship that I probably wasn't ready for. And I ended up losing more than I bargained for—my trust and innocence as well as my virginity. I've been careful ever since then never to want anyone that much."

She tucked the phone between her shoulder and her chin as she squeezed some of the fragrant lotion into her hand. "Of course, that's not so hard—I just compare anyone I meet to Bent. He was a remarkably talented lover. And I don't necessarily mean in the physical sense, although he was no slouch in that department either. But I'm talking about presentation."

"Presentation?"

"Yeah, he was romantic. He would take me places, treat me like an adult, order me champagne or wine with dinner. He took me to fancy hotels, treated me as if I were special. And for someone who was so damned selfish, he spent a huge amount of time *giving* pleasure. Sometimes I wish . . ."

"What?" Johnny's word was as soft as a breath.

She hesitated.

"Tell me what you wish."

"Sometimes I wish I could have a physical relationship of that intensity now. At the time I didn't fully appreciate it."

"You can, you know." His voice was just a whisper, just a caress. "*We* can."

What was she doing, discussing the intimacies of her past sexual experiences with Johnny. Talk about playing with fire. "I should go. It's getting late—we should both be in bed."

Johnny didn't say anything right away, and Chelsea felt her words seem to echo across the line: *we should be in bed*.

When he finally spoke, his voice was hoarse. "We should definitely be in bed. Together. I think you probably know that I've been sitting here, listening to you take your bath, listening to you talk about your first lover, imagining the way you must look lying back in that tub—" He broke off, swearing softly. "I wasn't going to say anything like this, but as long as I've started, I've got to tell you that I've been sitting here, wishing to God that I could walk in there, climb into that tub with you, and make you forget Benton Scott's name. I want you so bad, Chelsea, I may not live through the night."

His words sent a wave of desire pulsating through her, heat pooling sharply in her belly and between her legs. She gazed at herself in the mirror, at all that bare skin reflecting the flickering candlelight. Her hair was slicked back, her face clean of makeup, making her look like a stranger. A naked stranger. A stranger who didn't need to be careful about wanting someone too much.

"I wish I could show you," Johnny murmured. "I wish I could walk into your room and show you just how much I want you."

Chelsea gazed at the stranger in the mirror, who was gazing back at her. Her breasts were peaked with desire, her nipples tautly erect, enticingly sensitized, so that even the slight breeze blowing in through the open window was enough to make her shiver.

She could remember how it felt—the excitement, the need, of wanting something she knew she shouldn't have. She remembered the total release of letting that wanting consume her completely.

"I want you, too, John," she whispered, watching the woman in the mirror rub lotion down her arms and across her breasts.

Johnny drew in a ragged breath at her words. "Damn, I want to touch you."

"I want you to touch me too." In the mirror, the stranger's chest was rising and falling rapidly with every breath she took. And then she was sixteen again. Sixteen, and recklessly carefree. Now was all that mattered. Feeling good right *now*. She could barely believe the words that came out of her mouth. "John. We could unlock the door." The door that adjoined their two rooms. They each could unbolt it from their own side, and...

His voice vibrated with his intensity. "Are you sure you want to do that?"

She didn't hesitate. She only wanted. "Yes."

He laughed, a short burst of amazement and disbelief. "Wow. You sound...convinced."

"I am. Right now. But don't make me think too hard about it."

He took a deep breath. "I do want you to think hard about it. You made me promise—"

Chelsea didn't want to think about legal complications. The naked stranger in the mirror wouldn't give such things a second thought. Nor would her sixteen-year-old self. "I don't care. I want you more than I've ever wanted anybody."

He was silent for a moment. "Are you serious?" When he spoke, his voice was thick with his own desire.

"Meet me at the door, okay?"

"More than Bent?" he asked, then quickly added, "Forget I asked that. I shouldn't have asked you that."

"Yes." She answered him anyway. "More than Bent. Meet me at the door, John. Please?"

"Oh, God," he breathed, then took a deep breath. "Chelsea, I *promised* you we wouldn't do this." He took another deep breath. "Okay," he said.

"Okay?"

"No! Not okay, I'll meet you at the door. I meant, okay, I've figured out what we can . . . Look, just listen to me, all right?"

"I'm listening."

"Put down the phone and go into the bedroom, and pick up the extension that's next to the bed, okay? Then go and hang up the bathroom line. I'll meet you back in your bed."

"Don't I have to unlock the—"

"No," he said. "You don't. Just do what I said, all right?"

Johnny took a fortifying swallow out of one of the bottles of beer he'd ordered more than an hour ago from room service as he waited for Chelsea to come back to the phone.

He stood up and paced, carrying the phone with him, and he found himself standing in the bedroom doorway, staring out into the darkened living room, at the private door that connected their two suites.

Chelsea wanted him. She wanted him to walk through that connecting door and make love to her. She was his wife, he was her husband. They were legally wed.

So what the hell was he doing, standing over here?

He wanted her so badly, he was in serious pain.

If she wanted him even half as much, she would be dying for his touch—just as he was dying for hers. He wished he had the strength to go through those doors and make love to her only with his hands and his mouth, but he knew if he got near her he wouldn't be able to resist loving her completely. Those words he'd spoken in the restaurant were the truth. He wouldn't be strong enough to stop himself from making love to her.

And if he did that, he would be breaking the promise he'd made to her. And tomorrow, when she woke up, the impact of what they'd done would fracture the growing friendship between them, possibly destroying it beyond repair.

And he wouldn't do that. He couldn't.

The truth was, he liked her. A lot. Enough to want more than just one night of incredible sex.

Enough maybe even to want a lifetime.

The thought caught him off guard, and he shook his head, pushing it away. He refused to think that way. Not about a woman who so clearly didn't want *anyone* around forever.

"John?" Chelsea was back on the phone, her voice slightly breathless.

"I'm here," he told her, turning his back on that door, walking back toward his bed.

"I know," she said, her slightly husky voice thickened with desire. "But I want you over *here*."

"Lie down and close your eyes," he told her. He could hear her pulling back the bedcovers, hear the rustling of the sheets. "Are your eyes closed?"

"Yes."

"You know I can't really be with you tonight, Chelsea," he said quietly. "Not if I want to keep the promise I made to you. But you know I'd knock down this wall to get to you if I could."

"John—"

"Shh. Just listen. Because the day that annulment comes through, well, I'm probably going to have to work that night, but after work, I'm going to come over to your place. I'll have a key to let myself in, because by the time I get there, it's going to be pretty late. You'll be in bed already, just like you are right now. Maybe you'll even be asleep."

"No, I won't." Chelsea spoke with such certainty. "I'll be waiting for you."

"You're naked under the sheets," Johnny told her, letting himself lie back on his bed, his feet still on the floor. If he closed his eyes, he could picture her all too clearly. "And I still have all my clothes on. I just stand there for a minute, looking down at you, you looking up at me, both of us knowing exactly what's going to happen next."

"And then I pull back the sheet," Chelsea said.

Johnny smiled. He hadn't been sure at first if she would be willing to play along, or if she'd simply want to listen to him talk. But it didn't surprise him that she'd want to take an active part in this game. He felt a rush of heat and desire at the thought of her lying in her bed, willing to let him guide her so intimately.

"I'm still standing there, looking at you in the moonlight. God! You're so beautiful. I can't believe you're going to share yourself with me."

"I sit up and reach for you. . . ."

Johnny groaned at the powerful visual images in his head. "I can't keep from touching you any longer. So I sit down next to you, and I kiss you. Your skin is so soft and smooth—I'm touching you everywhere—I can't get enough. Your back, your arms, your throat, your breasts—they fit in my hands so perfectly. Do you feel me touching you? You have to help me a little bit here, Chelsea. Can you do that?"

"Yes."

She was breathing harder, and he was too. Because now he had the fantasy *and* the reality to think about, and both were overwhelmingly erotic. He'd never done anything even remotely like this before. He'd never been one to spend time on words and talking when it came to making love. But right now all he could give Chelsea were his words and his voice. He was determined to give her as much pleasure as he could, and the words seemed to flow.

"I want to taste you, and you want it, too, so I do. I touch the very tip of your breast with my tongue, very lightly—just a little. And then I look at you to see if you like the way that feels."

"Oh, yes," she breathed. "I like that."

"So I do it again, and this time you want more, so you push yourself up, up into my mouth, and I *really* love that. And now I've got you in my mouth, sucking and pulling, tugging at you, and you taste so good, I think I'm gonna die...."

"I want to take your clothes off," Chelsea said, surprising him again by taking the lead. "Your clothes are getting in the way. I unfasten your jeans, pull down the zipper—it's not easy to pull it down because you're... you're so hard."

The sound of her voice, whispering those words in his ear was mind-blowing. "I am," Johnny said, and it was true. "Chelsea, I am *so* hot for you...."

He wanted her—in every way imaginable. He wanted to walk into a crowded room and know he'd find her waiting for him, smiling as he came closer, her smile telling of secrets shared and promises made. *Do you take this woman...?* Yes. Yes, he wanted to take her—and keep her. He wanted to make love to her, and to love her.

To love her... God help him, he was falling in love with his wife.

"You help me push down your jeans," she murmured into his ear, "and God, you're not wearing any shorts. There's just your jeans... and you. I touch you, my fingers against your skin—do you feel me touching you?"

"Chelsea—"

"And then you reach for me, too, touching me...."

She moaned, and Johnny could barely speak.

"Chelsea," was all he managed to say.

"Yes...?"

Somehow, he had to get back into control. Somehow, he took a deep breath and brought the focus back to her. "I'm touching you," he rasped. "You're so soft . . . and hot. So smooth, like silk. I touch you lightly at first, then harder. Deeper."

"Yeah . . ."

"It feels so good—you touching me that way"—his voice sounded harsh in his own ears, rough from his desire—"and me touching you. You push your hips up, against me—you want more."

"Yeah . . ."

"And I want to get inside of you—"

"You are," she said. "You're on top of me, and you're inside me, and it feels *so good*, and we're moving together and oh, John—"

He heard her cry out, and it pushed him over the edge. He heard her drop the phone, heard it bounce along the floor, heard it rocking slightly before coming to a rest.

And then there was silence. One minute stretched into two, two into three.

"Chelsea?" Johnny said when he could finally speak. "Are you all right?"

He heard a rustling sound, and then a scraping as the phone was probably pulled along the tile floor by its cord.

Then: "Hello?" She sounded out of breath.

"Hi," Johnny said. "Are you okay?"

She laughed. "Yeah. I'm . . . extremely okay."

He had to know. "Did you just . . . ?"

"Yeah," she said. "Did you?"

"Yeah," he admitted. "I wasn't exactly planning to, but . . ."

"Oh, my God," she said. "We just had phone sex."

"It beats a cold shower," he said. "No pun intended."

Chelsea laughed. But when she spoke her voice was softer. "What do you say to someone after you've had phone sex with them?"

"I don't know," Johnny admitted. "This is a first for me too."

"You're kidding. You must be a natural."

"Oh, man, if anyone's a natural, it's you. You could make a fortune on one of those 900 lines."

"No, thanks. I prefer the real thing."

"Be patient. That'll come in just a few more days."

He could hear her smile. "No pun intended?"

Johnny smiled too. "No pun intended."

He heard her sigh, heard the rustle of her sheets. "I really like you, John Anziano," she said. "I can't wait to jump your bones for real."

He had to laugh. "I'm looking forward to that too—especially when you put it so romantically."

"Good night, John."

"Good night." Johnny heard the click as the connection was cut. "I think I'm in love in you, Chelsea," he added, knowing that he'd never dare say the words aloud if she were listening.

---

ten

CHELSEA SAT IN THE EARLY-MORNING RUSH hour, waiting for the light to turn green, knowing that she had allowed herself more than enough time to battle the traffic and find a parking spot before her eight-thirty appointment with her lawyer. Shoot, she had enough time to leave her car right here and *walk* the last few miles to Tim von Reuter's office, if need be.

No, the butterflies in her stomach weren't from fear of being late. They weren't even in anticipation of finally receiving the money from her grandfather's trust.

They were from the thought of seeing Johnny again.

Johnny . . .

The driver behind her hit his horn, startling her out of her reverie and she put her car into gear and lurched forward through the green light.

It was hard to believe that just yesterday she and Johnny had been in St. Thomas. And the night before last . . .

God, she couldn't let her mind stray in that direction. The thought of what she'd done—what *they'd* done—still made her cheeks heat with a blush. God, who would've ever thought she could feel the things that she'd felt?

Johnny had called her late the next morning, and she'd felt

tongue-tied, almost shy. But he said nothing about the night before as if he'd known she'd be too embarrassed to speak of it. He'd simply been himself—friendly, funny, and impossibly attractive.

They had only one more short day on the island—their flight was scheduled to leave just before sunset. He'd asked her to spend the afternoon with him, and she'd hesitated until he suggested they go into town and explore the port of Charlotte Amalie. He told her he thought it would be smart if they were careful only to go where they were sure there would be crowds.

In other words, no deserted beaches, no out-of-the-way scenic lookouts, and definitely no meeting *anywhere* remotely near their hotel rooms.

Chelsea put away her laptop and briefcase and had gone with him, and it had been very strange indeed. She'd met him in the lobby—his idea—and when she stepped out of the elevator and met his eyes from all the way across the room, her heart had very nearly stopped beating.

She could see his desire, his wanting, his *need* for her in his dark brown eyes. She felt nearly scalded just from looking at him, and she wondered if everything she wanted, everything she felt, was as transparent.

They'd taken a shuttle into town and wandered through narrow streets and alleyways filled with brightly colored shops and markets. St. Thomas was a duty-free port, famous for its bargains and exotic merchandise, but Chelsea couldn't remember much of what she saw. She'd been aware only of Johnny, of him watching her, wanting her, always careful never to get too close.

He'd made a point not to touch her, not even to brush his hand against hers. He didn't speak of it, but she knew he was as aware as she was that even holding hands would have been too much. Their desire was far too volatile.

Later, on the plane back to Boston, Chelsea had pretended to read, aware of Johnny watching her for the entire flight. Even his five-thousand watt smile wasn't enough to mask the heat in his eyes.

In Boston, they'd taken separate taxis to their separate homes. But Johnny had called her later, to make sure she'd gotten home safely, and to say good night. Again, they'd stayed up for several hours, talking—about books, movies, music. Talking about everything and anything that popped into their heads. Their tastes didn't always agree and they'd argued good-naturedly more than once.

It was odd, when they'd spent the day together, Chelsea had to search for things to say. But on the phone she felt safe. Relaxed. Well, almost relaxed. There was always an undercurrent of danger as she constantly wondered if and when they were going to talk about what they'd done the night before.

Johnny had told her things about himself that she hadn't known. He played jazz clarinet, and on his nights off, he often sat in with the house band at a club near his apartment downtown. He also had a black belt in karate. She'd seen evidence of that the first day they'd met, when he'd made short work of the gang of kids who'd snatched her purse.

Chelsea, in turn, had found herself telling him things she'd never told anyone—about how much it hurt to be labeled the family's black sheep, about how, no matter what she did, she couldn't seem to win her father's respect. About how she wasn't even sure she *wanted* the respect of a man like her father—with his preference for money and business above all else, with his prejudices and narrow-minded way of thinking.

Johnny had listened, letting her talk, as if he were somehow aware that this was not something she shared with just anyone.

They'd said good night at close to four in the morning, without having mentioned their encounter from the night before even once. Which was a good thing, because Chelsea wasn't quite sure what to say.

Except to break down and confess to him that she wanted him so badly that she couldn't eat or sleep or even think straight.

Chelsea tried to count the number of days before she could start the legal proceedings necessary for the annulment. She didn't know precisely how long the process took. She promised herself to make a point of talking to Tim von Reuter about it this morning. She'd also ask him about the logistics of a divorce. It was her understanding that a divorce—even an amicable one—was both time-consuming and costly.

She turned down Newbury Street and pulled into the entrance of the parking lot on the corner of Clarendon. She took the receipt the attendant handed her, and leaving her keys in the ignition, she grabbed her briefcase and her jacket and got out of the car.

And ran directly into Johnny.

"Whoa!" he said, then, "Hey, hi!" in recognition. He'd put his arms around her to steady her, but he didn't take them away.

She'd forgotten how tall he was, how broad his shoulders were, how hard his muscles were. Her breasts were pressed tightly against his chest, her hips locked against his. And still he didn't let her go.

"Good morning," she whispered, aware that she was gazing up at him like a complete fool. She would have been absolutely unable to move even if he had released her.

He was wearing a gray suit today, in honor of the meeting at the lawyer's, no doubt. His shirt was a lighter shade of gray, his tie slightly darker. It was a style of fashion that she hadn't particularly liked before, but on Johnny, it looked wonderful.

He was gazing back at her with that now-familiar molten heat in his eyes getting stronger by the second. She could feel his arousal, instant and unmistakable against the softness of her stomach, and she felt her insides flip-flop as if she were experiencing zero gravity.

"Oh, damn," Johnny whispered, his gaze locked onto her mouth as if he were hypnotized. And then he kissed her.

It was a kiss of pure desire, of near-delirious need. Chelsea dropped her briefcase as she kissed him back with the same fierce hunger. They were standing on the sidewalk, with pedestrians heading for work streaming past them, and they were kissing passionately, as if no one and nothing else existed in the world.

She felt his hands sweep down her back to cup her rear end, pulling her even more possessively against him, even as his tongue claimed her mouth.

Chelsea experienced instant nuclear meltdown. Her bones turned to jelly and her blood turned to fire.

And she knew in that moment that if there were ever a man she'd want to be possessed by in every awful, nonfeminist, un-liberated sense of the word, it was this man. She was ready to do anything to keep this kiss from ending. She was ready to give up her plans for a simple annulment. She was ready to sign on to be his slave or to sell her soul simply to keep him near her.

He made a tortured sound deep in the back of his throat that made her wonder if maybe he wasn't ready to do the same.

It was insane. She'd sworn to herself she'd never let a man control her in any way, shape, or form. Yet here she was, ready to ruin all of her careful plans. Here she was, kissing this man as if there were no tomorrow, right on the sidewalk on Newbury Street.

He pulled back as if it had taken everything he had and then some to stop kissing her. "Chelsea..." He was breathing hard, his eyes faintly wild as he held her stiffly at arm's length.

"John, will you get a cup of coffee and a bagel with me after we meet with Tim?" she asked him.

It was not the question he'd expected, and she could see from his expression that it threw him slightly, coming off of that kiss. But she hadn't known what else to say. She couldn't ask him simply to rush home with her to consummate their marriage immediately after the meeting with the lawyer, could she? If they were going to take actions that would require a more complicated and involved legal proceeding to end their mock marriage, they'd need to talk about it first, wouldn't they?

And maybe, between now and then, this insanity that possessed her would subside and she'd awaken to find herself back in control of her life, instead of being tossed about like a mindless piece of cork in a stormy sea of sexual desires and fantasies.

"Um, yeah," he said. "Coffee." He let go of her arms, raking his hair back with a hand that was shaking slightly before turning to pick her briefcase up from the sidewalk. "Bagel. Sure. We better . . . We better get to that meeting, though . . . now . . . don't you think?"

Chelsea looked at her watch. They had a little time, but it definitely wasn't enough for them to dash down to Arlington Street and get a room at the fancy Ritz-Carlton Hotel. And that was a *good* thing, she tried to convince herself. "We're a few minutes early. We don't have to rush."

He carried her briefcase as they started down Newbury Street. He was doing his best to pretend that kiss hadn't totally turned him upside down, but Chelsea knew better. It had turned *her* upside down, so much so that she couldn't think about much else besides kissing him again.

And why shouldn't she kiss him again? After all, they had *some* time, but not enough to do anything too outrageous. . . .

She slipped her hand into the crook of his arm, and she could feel the sudden tension in his muscles. He looked at her and shook his head.

"Chelsea, if you want me to try to keep my hands off of you, that's not the way to—"

"We have eleven minutes before we're scheduled to meet with Tim," she told him. "We could either spend it in the waiting room with Mrs. Mert, or we could . . . do something else with our time. And our hands."

Johnny turned and met her eyes and she could see his surprise as he hesitated.

"Now it's ten minutes and fifteen seconds," she told him, glancing again at her watch. "Are you going to kiss me again, or what?"

He laughed aloud, but he didn't pull her into his arms. Instead, he took a quick look around at the stores and buildings that lined the street. Then he moved swiftly, taking her by the hand and pulling her with him into the entrance of one of the brownstone buildings. The door was locked, but it was recessed from the sidewalk, offering some privacy from the people passing by. He pulled her with him into the corner, near a row of apartment mailboxes, dropped her briefcase on the tile floor, and smiled into her eyes.

"Okay, now ask me that again."

She was lost in his eyes, her fingers sunk into the darkness of the hair that curled around his neck. "Will you kiss me?" Her voice was barely a whisper.

"Absolutely," he said. Then slowly, so slowly, he leaned forward, searching her eyes, his smile fading as he got closer.

Each heartbeat seemed an eternity, but finally his lips brushed hers impossibly gently.

He closed his eyes then, his lashes long and dark against his cheeks as he kissed her again.

Chelsea closed her eyes, too, and allowed herself to luxuriate in the sheer sweetness of Johnny's lips.

He pulled her to him, her body fitting against his as if they had both been made with each other in mind. His hands swept down her back as he kissed her harder, deeper, the sweetness now laced with searing flame.

He lifted his head then, showering kisses on her cheeks, her nose, her eyes, her neck, in between the words he spoke. "I guess you figured ten minutes wasn't enough time to get a room at the Ritz."

Chelsea had to laugh. That was exactly what she had been thinking.

"You told me last night that Tim has to leave for court by nine forty-five," Johnny murmured. "You said we can't be late for this meeting. That's why I got down here so early."

"I'm so glad you were early."

He pulled back to look into her eyes, and he didn't try to hide the flurry of emotions that crossed his face. "You really are, aren't you?"

This time she kissed him, her arms sliding up underneath his suit jacket, the crisp cotton of his shirt a poor substitute for the sensation she truly wanted—the feel of his skin beneath her hands. Still, she loved touching the powerful muscles of his back and she kissed him harder, wishing he could climb inside her mind and experience the pleasure he gave her with just a kiss.

She explored lower and she felt the leather of his belt and then the perfect curve of his derriere beneath the light wool of his pants. She knew this was neither the time nor the place for what she wanted, but she pulled him even closer to her anyway.

He seemed to explode at her touch, and he pressed her against the mailboxes, the solidness of his thigh firmly between her legs. He took control of the kiss, his tongue claiming her mouth as his. His hand swept between them, along the soft silk of her shirt, across her breasts, caressing her, possessing her. His touch was as proprietary as his kisses. He didn't doubt the fact that she belonged to him—every last inch of her.

She did belong to him.

The thought alarmed her, and Chelsea pulled back, suddenly frightened at the intensity of the way this man made her feel.

Johnny felt her hesitation and made himself back away from

her. Leaning on the other side of the entryway with his back to her, bracing himself with both hands against the wall, he tried to steady his ragged breathing.

"I can't go for coffee with you after this meeting," he told her. "Because I want a whole hell of a lot more than a bagel."

Chelsea rested her forehead against the cold metal of the mailboxes. "I do too," she whispered, forcing herself to acknowledge the truth. "I want more too."

He turned and looked at her. "Your problem is that there's a difference between what you think you want ... and what you want." He laughed painfully, running his hands down his face. "Or maybe that's *my* problem, huh?"

"I do know what I want," she said quietly.

He pushed himself forward, off the wall. "I know. You want the money from your grandfather's trust. It's time—let's go get it."

Johnny straightened his clothes, then grabbed her briefcase.

Chelsea gazed at him, unable to speak. He was wrong. She knew what she wanted. She wanted Johnny. She wanted him to go home with her after the meeting. She wanted him to be her lover. She wanted him to belong to her as surely as she was his. But she couldn't say the words aloud.

Instead she fixed her hair and followed Johnny back into the harsh glare of the morning sunlight.

As Johnny watched, the Ice Princess made an appearance for the first time in days.

"I beg your pardon?" Chelsea said to Tim von Reuter. "The first payment is only one hundred dollars, and I won't receive the second payment until I've been married for *how* long?"

"One year." The lawyer sat behind his desk, clearly unhappy with the news he'd given her. "There was nothing in the description of this trust fund that led me to believe it wasn't set up identically to the funds your grandfather left for your brother and sister and your cousins, which allowed them to receive the money directly following their wedding."

"Yet now you're telling me that it's different. *My* trust was set up entirely differently. How could you not have known?"

Von Reuter was definitely starting to get a bad case of frostbite from Chelsea's chilly gaze. "You saw me break the seal on the envelope," he told her. "This is as much of a surprise to me as it is to you."

"Can we contest this? Challenge it in some way?"

The lawyer shook his head, gesturing with the document that had been in the sealed envelope. "The terms of the trust fund are in writing. It's been signed and witnessed. This is the way your grandfather wanted it, this is what you're going to have to do if you want this money."

"May I?" Johnny asked, reaching for the papers in question. He skimmed them quickly, trying to get past all the wheretofores and thereupons. Von Reuter was right. Amid all the legal mumbo jumbo, Chelsea's grandfather's wishes regarding the money were as clear as day. Chelsea was to receive only a paltry hundred dollars from the trust until her first anniversary.

He looked up to find her gazing out the window, distant and untouchable. She glanced in his direction. "He knew," she said, more to herself than to him. "He knew I'd never willingly get married. He knew I'd try to cheat the rules."

To his surprise, despite the fact that she'd tried to hide behind her Ice Princess facade, her eyes filled with tears.

And when she spoke, her words surprised him. "God, I miss that nasty old man. He always swore he'd get back at me for all those times I beat him at chess." She laughed, one fat tear escaping down her cheek. "I guess this is his idea of a good joke."

"The good news is that he left you nearly eight times the amount he left your brothers and sisters," Von Reuter told her.

Eight times? Johnny flipped to the back of the document

and there was the amount of money that had been placed in trust for Chelsea. That money, combined with the interest it would have made all these years, was the equivalent of winning the lottery. Chelsea would be set for life.

"Screw the money. I don't want the money. If I can't get to it now, it doesn't do me any good." Chelsea stood up, wiping her face. "How long will it take to get this marriage annulled?"

It was obviously not a question Tim von Reuter had been expecting. "Why don't we finish talking about the ramifications of this trust before we—"

"I want to talk about the annulment now. How long will it take?"

Von Reuter shifted uncomfortably in his seat. "Well, that depends on a lot of different variables. . . ."

Chelsea swore, leaning over his desk almost threateningly. "If you don't know, will you *please* just say you don't know?"

The lawyer nearly choked on the words. "I don't know."

There was a note of desperation in her voice. "Give it your best guess, Tim. Please?"

"Best-case scenario? I know we'll need to schedule a court date. . . . Maybe a month?"

Chelsea seemed to crumble, holding on to the edge of the desk. "Oh, my God. *That* long?"

Johnny stood up. "Lookit, Chelsea, I know you're disappointed, and I know that you don't want to be married to me for even one second longer than you have to, but a month's really not that much time in the grand scheme of things."

"Oh, John, no—you don't understand." She turned to face him, her blue eyes enormous in her face. "This doesn't have to do with me not wanting to be married. This is about not wanting to wait a whole month to"—she glanced almost furtively at Von Reuter and lowered her voice—"to be with you."

Johnny nearly staggered from the impact of her words. She was upset, *incredibly* upset, because she didn't want to have to wait an entire month to make love to him. His heart was in his throat. "So we'll have to get a divorce. Big deal."

She shook her head. "Without that money, I probably couldn't afford a divorce. *Everything* I've got is tied up in my business. I haven't even made the mortgage payments on my condo for the past three months." She looked as if she were about to burst into tears.

Johnny turned to Von Reuter. "Tim, is there somewhere Chelsea and I can talk privately?"

The lawyer stood up. "Use my office. Please. If you'll excuse me?"

Johnny waited until the door closed behind Von Reuter. Then he turned to Chelsea. "Here's what we're going to do, okay? We're going to stay married for a year. After that you'll be able to afford all the divorces you want."

She stared at him in total disbelief. "You'd do that? For an *entire* year?"

"Let's see, an entire year, married to the most beautiful, incredible woman I've ever met?" he asked, pretending to consider it. "Somehow I'll suffer through."

He couldn't tell if she was going to laugh or cry.

She took a deep breath and did neither. "So what's your cut?"

Johnny shook his head, not understanding. "My cut?"

"Yeah. What percentage do you want?"

"Percentage?"

"Of the money."

Johnny didn't want a percentage. The money was the last thing he'd been thinking about. But letting her think he was in this for the money was better than telling her the truth and scaring her to death. He shrugged. "I don't know. Ten percent?"

"That's *all*?"

"Ten percent of the money waiting for you in that trust fund is nothing to sneeze at."

"I'll give you twenty-five percent."

He had to laugh. "If this is the way you negotiate, no wonder your business is short of funds."

"We're talking about a solid year of your life—I still can't believe you would do this for me."

"In case you haven't noticed, I kind of like you," he told her. "I asked you out first, remember?"

"You asked me to go to dinner," she reminded him. "Not to marry you for a year."

"If my choice was between zero or three hundred and sixty-five dinners, I'd take the three sixty-five."

Chelsea's eyes were filled with tears again.

"I get more than the money for doing this, you know," he continued softly. "If we're going to be married for a year, we're going to be *married* for a year. Starting tonight, you'll be my wife. For real."

She took a tissue from a box near Von Reuter's desk and wiped her eyes and nose. "Only starting tonight?"

Johnny checked his watch, dizzy from the possibilities. But it was nearly nine-thirty. They still had to talk to Tim, tell him what they planned to do, make sure there were no loopholes they'd overlooked. Even if that took only five minutes—and it would surely take longer—that still left them only an hour. And an hour wasn't long enough to do what he wanted to do. He swore softly.

"I promised my boss I'd be at work by ten-thirty," he told her.

"I thought you worked in the evenings."

"I do. Mostly. But there's a private party that starts at four, and he's counting on me to be in early to help prepare."

She was looking at him as if he were one of his gourmet dinners. "I don't want to wait," she said suddenly.

He didn't want to, either. The thought suddenly occurred to him that they could lock Von Reuter's office door and get it on right there on the lawyer's desk. But as appealing a thought as that was, he knew he didn't want to make love to Chelsea that way for the first time. He didn't want to rush. He wanted to take his sweet time.

"Since the party starts early, it'll end early," he promised her. "I'll be home by ten."

Home. "Where do you live?" she asked. "God, I don't even know where you live."

"I have a condo near the harbor, but . . . why don't I just plan to come out to your place." He smiled. "As a matter of fact, why don't you give me a key?"

eleven

"SO YOU THINK WITH TODAY'S MARKET, WE can list it at five hundred K?" Chelsea asked, making a note on her pad as she spoke on the phone.

"I would even try five twenty-five," the real-estate agent told her. "In that building, in that part of town, with two bathrooms and all those renovations you've done . . . For the type of upscale condominium that you have, it's definitely a seller's market."

"But I need to sell it fast," Chelsea said. "Immediately. As in, the day before yesterday."

She did the math on her notepad for both numbers, figuring in the agent's commission, the closing costs, the amount of equity she had, minus the last few mortgage payments she'd missed and the ensuing penalties. If she sold the place for five hundred thousand, she'd walk away with just under forty thousand, of which she'd have to pay about half in taxes. But if she wanted to *sell* for five hundred, she'd have to list it higher. . . .

"Let's go with five hundred twenty-five," she told the agent. "How soon can you get it listed?"

"I'll messenger the paperwork to your office for you to sign. And I'll put the listing in the MLS computer this afternoon," he said. "We'll have to set up a time for the agents in my office to see the unit."

"The sooner the better," Chelsea told him. "You set it up—I'll adjust my schedule to fit yours."

As she hung up the phone she looked up to see Moira standing in her doorway.

"I can't believe you're really going to do it," her friend said. "You're selling your condo and moving in with a guy named Giovanni Anziano."

"I'm selling my condo to make the first payment of the loan," Chelsea reminded her.

Moira sat down across from her, resting her elbows on the edge of Chelsea's desk and her chin in her hands. "Do your parents know?"

"That I'm selling my condo? No. I just made that decision."

"I'm not talking about the condo," Moira said. "I'm talking about the truck driver. Do your parents know that the guy you married isn't descended from Italian royalty?"

"John's not a truck driver," Chelsea said. "He works in a restaurant . . . or something."

"He's a waiter? That'll go over almost as well."

"He's not a waiter," Chelsea said. "At least I don't think so. I think he's some kind of assistant cook . . . or something." She didn't know. In all of the conversations she'd had with Johnny, she hadn't asked him what, specifically, he did at the restaurant downtown. God, she couldn't even remember the restaurant's name. Had he even told her?

"Your parents are going to have a cow." Moira was grinning. "Can I be there when you tell them?"

"Even if he *is* a waiter, there's nothing wrong with that," Chelsea said, defending Johnny. "He's not going to be a waiter forever—he wants to open his own restaurant."

"With your money, I bet."

"No, with his *share* of the trust fund."

"Relax, I'm just teasing."

Chelsea forced a smile, but truth was, her friend's teasing hit too close to home. Johnny *was* getting paid for the favor he was doing for her. But really, did she honestly expect that he'd agree to stay married to her for an entire year and *not* get paid?

"On an entirely different note," Moira told her, "there was a nifty little stash of crack vials and needles in the doorway when I came in this morning. I talked to Sylvia—you know, the woman who works over at H&R Block—and she gave me some special trash containers marked 'Biohazardous Waste,' that her office gets from the board of health."

"You need to be *really* careful when you pick up those needles," Chelsea said.

"No kidding. But as I was out there, being really careful, it occurred to me that we may want to find a location for our office that doesn't double as a nightly hangout for addicts."

"Moira, God, you know we can't afford to move. Right now we can't even pay the rent on *this* place!"

Moira pushed herself out of her chair. "I know." She shook her head. "Do you think Sears sells needle-proof gloves?"

"Tomorrow, I'll pick up the trash," Chelsea told her.

"You mean, the biohazardous waste." Moira turned back to look through the doorway. "You know, the sad part of what you just said is that we both know there most likely will be vials and needles there again tomorrow."

Chelsea pressed her forehead against her palms. Damn, she needed cash, and she needed it fast.

But what she really needed was Johnny.

She longed to hear his voice and she nearly picked up the phone and called him at work. But wanting to hear his voice didn't seem like a good enough excuse to call him—and certainly one she'd have trouble admitting.

She glanced at her watch. It was only two o'clock. Would

this day never end? The phone rang, and she scooped it up, hoping that it was Johnny.

It wasn't. It was the real-estate agent again. "I just spoke to some of the people in my office about setting up a realtors' open house at your condo," he told her, "and I found out if we don't do it first thing tomorrow, it won't happen until next Wednesday at the earliest."

"First thing as in what time?" Chelsea asked. She had plans for the morning. They involved sleeping late, breakfast in bed . . . and Johnny.

"Seven-thirty."

She cringed. "Can't you do it later? Say, noon?"

"Not tomorrow. If you want, we could set it up for next Wednesday at noon."

"Wait. No," Chelsea said. "Go back to tomorrow at seven-thirty. Do I have to be there?"

"Absolutely not."

"In that case, it's fine. I'll send over a key with the paperwork."

Chelsea hung up the phone and glanced at her watch: 2:07. Time had never dragged like this before.

But . . . Now she had a good reason to give Johnny a call.

She flipped to the back of her date book and quickly dialed the number he'd given her. The phone rang six times before it was picked up.

The man who answered had a heavy French accent, and Chelsea didn't catch the restaurant's name. It might have been Lou's or Louie's, but she wasn't sure.

"Is John Anziano there, please?" she asked.

"Who this is?"

"Chelsea Spencer."

"Who?"

She tried to speak slowly and clearly. "Chelsea."

"You say you call from Chelsea?" Chelsea was also the name of one of the towns north of Boston.

"No, Chelsea's my *name*," she tried to explain.

"*Oui*, is what I asking you. For your name?"

"Please," Chelsea said, giving up. "Just tell Johnny his wife is on the phone."

"Aha! Hold now."

It was nearly a full minute before the line was picked up, and Johnny said, "My *wife*'s on the phone." He laughed. "Sorry it took me so long, but I'm not used to having a wife, and I was sure Jean-Paul had made a mistake, and that the phone was for Jim or Philippe, who *do* have wives. Jean-Paul's English is a little basic."

"So of course he's the one who answers the phone," Chelsea said, happy beyond belief to hear his familiar, husky voice.

"He's the dessert chef. He just happened to be the only one of us not up to his elbows in lobster bisque. So what's up?"

I'm drowning in an ocean of debt and despair and I wanted to hear your voice. "Actually, I'm calling because I was hoping it would be okay if we changed tonight's plans a little bit."

He was silent for a moment, and when he spoke she could tell he'd stopped smiling. "Change them, huh? You mean, cancel them?"

No! she nearly shouted into the phone before she caught herself. "God, no. I was just wondering if you'd mind if I came to your place instead."

"No, but . . . Are you sure that's what you want to do?" He lowered his voice. "I was looking forward to using that key you gave me."

Chelsea swallowed. "I was too. But I put the condo on the market this afternoon, and there's going to be about two dozen realtors walking through the place at seven-thirty tomorrow morning."

"You're selling your condo?"

"I have to," she told him. "I still have those loan payments to make. As it is, even if I sell the thing tomorrow, I'm going to be late with the first payment."

"So . . . are you going to . . . Do you . . . intend to move in to my place? With me?"

His voice sounded funny, and Chelsea was instantly anxious. "Not if you don't want me to. I guess I thought, since we're going to be married for a whole year . . ."

"Are you kidding? Where else would you live? It would be weird if you lived anywhere else. I mean, you're my wife, right?" He laughed. "I know because Jean-Paul said so, and he's French, and everyone knows the French know everything. I just thought you'd probably want us to live at your place."

"No, I've got to sell it," Chelsea said. "I need the cash, and besides, it's too far away from the office anyway. I've actually been thinking about selling for a while."

He snorted. "What a liar. You told me you just finished renovating the bathroom."

"Well, it turns out I don't really like the color tile I chose for the floor, so—" She broke off, realizing she wasn't fooling him—or herself. "It sucks. But the alternative is to borrow money from my father, and the fact is, I'd rather try to sell my condo first."

"Because you think asking your dad for money will be admitting you failed."

"Are you going to tell me where you live, or will I have to track down your address through the phone company?"

"You're changing the subject," he noted.

"Give the man a cigar. Come on, I've got my pen ready. Stop psychoanalyzing me and tell me how to get to your place."

She quickly wrote down the directions Johnny gave her.

"Look, I've got to get back to work," he told her then. "I'm trying to speed things along so I can get out of here at a reasonable hour. The way it looks right now, I'll definitely be able to leave by ten."

"So . . . I guess I'll see you at, say, ten-oh-one . . . ?"

Johnny laughed. "How about ten-thirty? I'll want to take a shower right away and maybe vacuum the living-room rug."

"You don't have to do that."

"Yeah, well, it's not every day that your wife comes over to your condo for the first time. First impressions count, you know."

Chelsea laughed.

"No rude comments about silly T-shirts, please," Johnny continued. "Look, I've got to run. You know I'd love to talk to you more. . . ."

"Go," Chelsea told him. "And call me if you think you'll be done sooner."

"Oh, I will." He paused, and when he spoke again his voice was huskier than usual. "I'll see you later."

"Bye, John." Chelsea hung up the phone and looked at her watch: 2:30. Eight more hours. She rolled her eyes in exasperation.

God, would this day *never* end?

There was a pair of boxer shorts hanging from the back of one of Johnny's dining-room chairs. He scooped it up as he breezed past on his way upstairs, taking off his shirt and kicking off his shoes and pants as he went.

He took the quickest shower in the history of Western civilization and vacuumed the living-room rug as he dried himself off.

He slipped into a clean pair of jeans and a plain red T-shirt, and then quickly set the table.

He'd turned on the oven the moment he came through the door, and it was preheated enough now to put in the still-warm containers of food he'd brought home from the restaurant.

He'd made a lamb stew early in the afternoon, and it had simmered all day, along with his buzzing anticipation, constantly reminding him of the night to come. Now the meat was so tender it seemed to melt from the pressure of a fork.

The sauce was up to his usual near-perfection standards, delicate and light, with a flavor that added to the richness of the lamb rather than covering it up. This was going to be a five-star meal. He couldn't wait to see Chelsea's face as she tasted it. He couldn't wait to watch her eyes as she realized the man she'd married was well on his way to becoming a master chef. He knew she hadn't asked him about his work because she'd been embarrassed for him—working in a restaurant. She probably thought he was a glorified waiter or a sous chef at best.

The water he'd put into a pot when he'd first come in finally reached a rolling boil, and he quickly rinsed a cupful of basmati rice and tossed it in with a dash of salt and a pat of butter. He stirred once, then put the lid on and turned down the heat. The rice's fragrant aroma soon filled the house.

He'd brought fresh lettuce and vegetables already cut for a salad from the restaurant, and he tossed them together in a cut-glass bowl and placed it on the table along with a small bottle of his own apple-cider vinaigrette dressing.

As he lit the candle in the center of the table, the doorbell chimed. Hoping he hadn't missed picking up any of the stray laundry that magically seemed to appear around the house, he went to open the door.

He took a deep breath before he pulled it open, but still, the sight of Chelsea standing on the steps outside nearly knocked him over.

His wife. Her blond hair was loose around her shoulders, and underneath her jacket she was dressed as he was, in jeans and a T-shirt, a gold wedding band around her left ring finger, and a matching blaze of desire in her eyes.

"Honey, I'm home," she said, in a decent enough imitation of Ricky Ricardo.

He laughed, but then stopped, afraid he sounded as giddy as

he felt. He opened the door wider to let her in. "Did you have any trouble parking?" he asked, trying to sound casual, knowing that grabbing her and pulling her inside, tossing her over one shoulder in a fireman's hold and carrying her up to his bedroom to tear off her clothes and bury himself inside of her would not be good form.

"No," she told him. "I took a cab."

Neither would pinning her to the wall with a soul-shattering kiss as his fingers found the zipper of her jeans and . . .

She was carrying a leather gym bag over one shoulder, and he took it from her as he closed the door behind her. His fingers brushed the warmth of her shoulder as an intimate whiff of her sweet perfume invaded his senses. He had to close his eyes briefly in an attempt to steady himself.

He watched her glance around the small entryway, taking in his somewhat eccentric collection of mismatched watercolors on the walls, and the soft—and recently vacuumed—beige carpeting underneath her feet. She looked at the stairs going up to the bedrooms, at the old-fashioned coatrack and umbrella stand in the corner, and the rather battered antique that served as a table for the telephone.

She stood back, slightly ill at ease, waiting for him to lead the way. This was going to be her home for the next year, but right now she was a guest here. "Something smells great."

"Yeah. I thought we could have a late dinner. Did you eat?"

For a moment she looked a little odd. "No," she said. "But I'm not very hungry—I haven't had much of an appetite lately, and . . ."

He set her bag down by the stairs and walked backward into the great room, unable to turn away from her for even a moment.

Chelsea looked astonished, then confused as she took in the huge single room that served as living area, dining room, and kitchen combined.

"This is beautiful," she murmured, looking at the vaulted

ceiling, the sliders that led out to the deck that had a million-dollar view of the harbor, and the sparsely furnished yet comfortable-looking living area. She turned to look at him, narrowing her eyes accusingly. "You have money."

"Not really," he said, moving into the kitchen and checking the rice. "Not the way your family has money."

"But this place must've cost—"

"It was bequeathed to my mother by one of her patients."

"I thought you told me she had a clinic near the Projects. How could one of her patients . . . ?"

"His name was David Hauser," he told her. "He was about a million years old. He lived next door—we had no idea he owned prime real estate all over town—and my mother always made a point to stop in and see him after she came home, no matter how tired she was."

Johnny took a pair of wineglasses down from the cabinet as Chelsea perched atop one of the bar stools on the other side of the counter that separated the kitchen area from the rest of the room. She was watching him, her eyes following him as he moved around the kitchen.

"She always made me cook a little extra at dinner," he continued, "and take a plate over to Mr. H, even on the days we were stretched a little thin for cash. Sometimes, if I knew she was going to be really late, I'd take my plate over, too, and eat with him. He was very cool. He was born in 1875, so he could tell the most incredible stories about Boston, before the advent of the automobile. He'd lived through the turn of the century and both world wars. He was amazing. My mother was convinced he was going to live forever—and he damn near outlived her."

He took a deep breath. "After my mother was gone, I thought about selling, but I'd lived here with her the last year before she died, and I liked it here too much, you know? There's a little bit of Davey and my mom still here. Their spirits linger—and I don't mean in a bad way," he added hastily.

"I know what you mean," she murmured, resting her chin in the palm of her hand, still watching him with those impossibly blue eyes.

"I never had a place like this before," he told her, losing himself in the ocean of her eyes. "I always lived in crappy little basement apartments or fifth-floor walk-ups with a courtyard view of the neighbor's bathroom window. So I decided to stay and see what it was like to have a real home. That's when I put in this kitchen and did the rest of the renovations—I tore down the walls and opened this area up."

"Your mother and Davey would've approved," she told him. "It's gorgeous."

She was gorgeous, with the overhead light from the kitchen glinting off her golden hair as she turned to look out at the dimly lit dining area, the living space beyond that, and the harbor lights twinkling on the other side of the sliding glass doors. Even dressed down in jeans and a T-shirt, she looked glamorous.

"How about a glass of wine with dinner?" His voice sounded raspy, and he cleared his throat.

She turned to look at him. "Dinner?"

"Yeah. The rice is just about ready. What do you say we eat?"

She looked uneasy. "John, I realized when I walked in here that there's something kind of important about myself that I haven't told you. I mean, I didn't *think* to tell you, and it hasn't come up when we've talked, which is odd, because it usually does, but..."

Chelsea took a deep breath. "I'm a vegetarian."

As she watched, her words sunk in. Johnny first laughed at the absurdity, then gazed at her with questioning disbelief, then looked incredibly disappointed. Finally he tried to hide his disappointment with a smile.

"Well, damn," he said. "If I'd known, I'd have made something with chicken or fish."

She shook her head at his common mistake. "I'm a *vegetarian*. I don't eat chicken *or* fish. I follow the face rule."

"The what?"

"The face rule: If it used to have a face, I don't eat it. I also don't eat any milk or dairy, although I will eat eggs if they're cooked into a bread or a cake—John, I'm so sorry. You went to all this trouble to make this nice dinner...."

He definitely didn't look happy. "So what *do* you eat?"

"Lots of things. Beans, salad, pasta, tofu, vegetables—*lots* of vegetables ... Just not meat of any kind."

"I'm not a vegetarian," he told her. "Obviously. Is it going to bother you to have meat around the house?"

"Not if you keep it in the kitchen."

He forced a smile as he crossed the kitchen and turned off both the oven and the burner under the pot of rice on the stove and made his own attempt at humor. "At least I found out before our appearance on *The Newlywed Game*. We would have lost big points, me not knowing this one."

"There's still so much we don't know about each other," Chelsea mused. "Yet here we are, about to live together as if we're really married for a whole year."

She found herself watching the loose-fitting cut of his jeans and the more snug fit of his T-shirt, the red cotton hugging his muscular chest and shoulders. His hair was still damp from his shower, combed back from his face and curling around his neck. He looked unbearably delicious.

"We *are* really married," he said quietly.

She looked up and into the midnight brown of his eyes, and the entire world seemed to tilt around her. He was right. They *were* really married, with rings and a marriage license and everything. And in just a few minutes—if she could make her rubbery legs work well enough to climb down off this stool—they were going to go upstairs together and consummate that marriage.

He turned and took a bottle of white wine from the refrigerator, and poured some into one of the glasses. He paused and looked up at her, bottle poised, ready to fill the second. She couldn't begin to interpret the look in his eyes. "Do you drink wine?"

"Not usually. No. It's not . . . I . . . No, I don't."

He nodded, setting the bottle down beside the empty glass as he took a generous sip from the other, swirling the wine around his mouth before he swallowed.

"I'm sorry," she said again.

He looked at her. "*I'm* the one who should be apologizing. It never even occurred to me to ask if you were a vegetarian." He forced another smile. "I guess we could send out for pizza—" He swore sharply. "Except you don't eat cheese, right?"

Chelsea slid off her stool and moved toward the end of the counter. "I'm not hungry right now. I'd rather see the rest of your condo anyway. What's upstairs?"

Johnny looked at her, standing there, leaning slightly against the edge of his kitchen counter. She knew damn well what was upstairs. The bedrooms. His bedroom. His bed.

Heaven. Heaven was upstairs.

She smiled at him, a smile that was bewitchingly sexy, and he instantly released his disappointment. Just like that, it was filed away, to be worked through at a later time. She was a vegetarian, and he was well on his way to becoming a master chef, specializing in dishes made with veal and lamb. By choice, his own wife would never taste his most magnificent creations. Of course, she would only be his wife for one year. But he refused to think about any of that now.

She held out her hand to him. "Will you show me the rest of your condo?"

She wanted to go upstairs.

He may have totally blown the chance for a romantic dinner

through his ignorance, but there was no way he could possibly blow this. He'd wanted her for far too long.

Still, he couldn't seem to do more than whisper, "I'd love to." Her fingers were cool as he took her hand and led her back down the hallway. As they passed he grabbed her gym bag with his free hand and carried it with them up the stairs.

He tried to stop at the first door off the upstairs hallway. "This is my home office."

But Chelsea only glanced in. "Which one's your bedroom?"

"The door on the left."

She slipped free from his grasp, and pausing only to glance back at him with another of those incredible smiles, she disappeared into the darkness of his room.

He followed her in, setting her bag down near the door.

The curtains were open, revealing more sliders like the ones downstairs and a similar view of the harbor. The moonlight streaming in gave the room a ghostly glow, and Johnny didn't switch on the overhead light.

He watched her make her way around the big room. His closet door was open, and as she passed she fingered one of the shirts hanging there. She trailed her hand along the polished wood of his dresser, along the huge bookshelf that lurked against one wall, along the metal frame of the NordicTrack system he had set up with other exercise gear in the corner of the room, working her way around to his bed.

She turned to face him then, across the wide expanse of his bedspread. "I was thinking that right about now would be a really good time for you to kiss me."

He took his time walking around the bed, each step filled with the pleasure of his anticipation. She met him halfway, impatient with his pace, and kissed him, instead.

Her lips were so soft, her entire body melting into his. Johnny laughed aloud and heard her join in.

"This is going to be really good, isn't it?" she whispered, looking searchingly into his eyes.

He could feel her heart pounding, feel his beating an answering tattoo. "Oh, yeah." He kissed her again, harder this time. This was going to be beyond good.

He felt her hands sliding up underneath the edge of his T-shirt, her palms gliding along his bare back, and he knew, despite his intentions to make love to Chelsea slowly, he couldn't wait a second longer.

He tugged at her shirt, pulling it free from the waistband of her jeans, filling his hands with the soft weight of her breasts as she fell back with him onto the bed.

Her legs were around him, and she kissed him fiercely. She tugged at his T-shirt, and he helped her pull it over his head, then did the same with her shirt. His fingers fumbled with the front clasp of her bra, and she quickly unfastened it for him.

He pulled back then, wanting to look at her, wanting to see her desire for him in the tautness of her nipples and the swell of her perfect breasts, in the way she lay there on his bed, half-naked and waiting for him, in the heat in her eyes.

"Touch me," she whispered, and he did. With his hands, with his mouth. He buried his face in her incredible softness.

He could feel her unfastening her jeans, and he helped her pull them off. Her legs were long and smooth and gracefully shaped and he laughed again because he couldn't believe he was actually running his hands along them.

Chelsea smiled at Johnny's laughter as he slid her panties down her legs.

She pulled him down on top of her, and before he kissed her, he gazed into her eyes and gave her a heart-stoppingly gorgeous smile. "I'm overcome by the need to spout a cliché," he told her.

"Such as?" Chelsea's heart kicked into overdrive. Was he going to tell her that he was falling in love with her?

He gave her a kiss that rocked her as he ran one hand up her leg, all the way up her thigh and even farther. He touched her, gently at first, slowly, softly, and all coherent thought vanished from her mind. She found herself reaching for the button of his jeans, wanting to feel his skin against hers.

"Such as, you're so incredibly beautiful, just looking at you makes me dizzy," he murmured, trailing kisses from her mouth down to her breasts.

He didn't mention whether or not he loved her and Chelsea didn't know whether to feel relieved or disappointed. And then she didn't feel anything but desire as he shifted his weight to allow her better access to the zipper of his jeans, as still he touched her, stroked her, harder now, deeper.

It was her turn to laugh aloud as she wrestled the zipper down and discovered he was wearing no underwear—just the way she'd described that night on the phone. And, as she'd also described, his arousal gave her powerful proof of his desire. He was totally, incredibly male.

She looked up into his eyes and he caught his breath as she touched him.

As she gazed at him something seemed to explode, and the passion they had kept buried between them for so long fireballed. He kissed her almost savagely, possessively, and she kissed him back just as ferociously. She'd never felt anything so intense ever before, and it terrified her, bringing tears to her eyes, but she couldn't have stopped had her life depended on it.

His hands were everywhere, touching, stroking, driving her wild with need. He paused only to cover himself and protect them both, and then he was on top of her, between her legs, and she was lifting herself up, seeking him, wanting him, needing to feel him, *all* of him, inside her, possessing her.

Owning her, body as well as heart and soul. No, *no*. She couldn't think that way. She *wouldn't* think that way. . . .

"Look at me," he whispered. "Chelsea, open your eyes."

She did, looking up into his beautiful, familiar, lovely eyes.

He watched her face as he filled her, his satisfaction evident in the hot, fierce smile he gave her. "Now you're *really* my wife," he said.

For a year. Only for a year. She pressed her hips up, pushing him deeply inside of her, in an attempt to show him that she was still in control. But she was the one who cried out.

And when he began to move, setting a rhythm that made her heart pound, she knew that when it came to Johnny, she hadn't truly been in control since the morning she asked him to marry her. Ever since that moment she'd been careening down a hill toward a cliff, in danger of falling crazily in love with this man, destined to crash, her life as she knew it shattered into a million irreparable tiny pieces.

But as she went over the edge, as her heart as well as her body was engulfed in waves of sheer, tempestuous, exquisite pleasure, she found a pure, uninhibited freedom in her lack of control. The fall would probably kill her, but dear God, all she was feeling was well worth it.

She felt Johnny's release, heard him cry out her name again and again, his voice like velvet, both smooth and rough against her sensitized skin, as he drove himself deeply inside of her one final, delicious time.

She heard him sigh, a deep exhale thick with satisfaction, and she closed her eyes, waiting to fall like a stone back to earth, preparing for the shock of impact.

But Johnny's arms were around her, holding her, keeping her safe. And she realized she wasn't going to crash.

At least not for a year.

twelve

THE PHONE RANG AS THE FIRST STREAKS OF dawn were lighting the sky outside the bedroom windows.

Chelsea felt Johnny reach for the receiver. "'lo?" He spoke softly, trying not to wake her. She heard him swear softly. "Did you try calling Carlos?" Another pause. "Yeah, I figured you did, but . . . How about Bobby?"

With his hair rumpled, his eyes sleepier than usual, and a night's growth of beard on his face, he looked impossibly sexy. He looked like someone she would wake up next to in bed only in her wildest dreams.

"It's me or no one, huh? Can you get the truck loaded for me?" He sighed and ran his hand through his hair. "Look, Doreen, I know you've got stuff to do in the office, but last night was my wedding night, and my bride's not going to appreciate me deserting her this morning for any longer than I absolutely have to, and—Yes, I said bride." He laughed softly. "Yeah, I'm married. Wild, huh? She's incredible, and I'm going to be in a big hurry to get back to her, so if you guys in the office can at least load the truck—"

Chelsea shifted, stretching her legs, and he turned to look at her, an apology in his eyes. "I'm sorry, I was trying not to wake you." He spoke into the phone. "Hold on a second, Doreen."

He covered the receiver, leaned forward, and kissed Chelsea on the mouth. "Good morning."

She smiled at him, snuggling closer and sliding her leg across his. "Rumor has it I'm incredible."

"Oh, yeah." He kissed her again, longer this time, and she could feel his body's instant response. "It's no rumor—it's the cold, hard truth. You're totally off the scale."

"Do you often get phone calls from women at dawn?"

He grinned. "Only from women named Doreen, who work at Meals on Wheels."

She ran her fingers lightly across his chest, delighting in the feel of his muscles and the soft, springy hair that covered them. "She wants to take you away from me, huh?"

"Just for a couple hours. I'll be back before you know it."

"Do you really have to go?" She let her hand drift lower, and he closed his eyes.

"If I don't, some of these people won't eat for a day." He opened his eyes and smiled at her. "But I sure as hell can be late." He brought the phone back to his ear. "Doreen? I'll be there. In forty-five minutes." He laughed. "I *know* it usually takes me ten minutes to get over there, but today it's going to take me forty-five, *capisce*?"

As he reached to hang up the phone Chelsea straddled him and lightly ran her cheek against his morning beard as she kissed her way to his mouth. "Since I'm the one who's making you late, maybe I should come along and help you with your deliveries."

He lifted her chin with one hand and looked searchingly into her eyes. "Really?"

"I'd like to—if it's all right with you . . ."

There was a softness in Johnny's eyes as he gazed up at her. "You *are* incredible."

Chelsea shook her head. "No, I'm not. *You* are. *You* want to make sure the people on that route get their food today. *My* motives are purely selfish. I want to get you back here, in bed, as soon as I can."

He kissed her and she closed her eyes, aware that she had nearly revealed too much. She'd nearly told him the real reason she wanted to make his deliveries with him. She'd nearly admitted that she wanted simply to be with him. It was better to let him think her reasons were based on sex rather than some deep emotion she couldn't even begin to identify—some deep emotion she *refused* to identify. And it would be better for *her* if she kept her straying emotions securely out of Johnny's reach and firmly in control.

She kissed him again, closing her eyes, knowing that when it came to Johnny, her control was in short supply.

"You're late."

Johnny turned to look at Chelsea and smiled. "I know, Mr. Gruber. But Evan got sick, and I was called in to drive the truck at the last minute. I got here as soon as I could."

They'd made over a dozen stops, and almost every person they'd brought food to had informed Johnny that he was late. And every time they told him that, he'd looked at Chelsea and smiled, and she knew he was remembering, in detail, exactly *why* he'd been late.

She could hardly wait to go back home and make him late for his work at the restaurant too.

The old man squinted at Chelsea. "You training a new girl?"

"No, sir," Johnny told him. "This is Chelsea. My wife." He still laughed whenever he said that. "I brought her over here to meet you."

Chelsea shook Mr. Gruber's hand. At one time he'd been remarkably tall, but time had made him stooped and thin, and now he was a narrow tower of a man. His hair was pure white and it grew thick and full. The thick lenses of his glasses made his eyes seem huge in his wrinkled face, but they were still a vivid shade of blue.

"I'm pleased to meet you," she said.

"Pretty girl," the elderly man told Johnny, shuffling into the kitchen, leaning heavily on a thick, wooden cane. "Your wife, huh? How'd you manage that one?" He laughed, a dry wheezing cackle.

"Wow, you're really a laugh riot today, Mr. G," Johnny said good-naturedly as he put a wrapped sandwich and a plate of microwave-ready food into the refrigerator.

"No, no, I'm just teasing, just teasing. Can't think of anyone more deserving of such a pretty girl's love." He turned to Chelsea and shook one finger at her. "You take good care of my friend Johnny."

"I will."

My friend Johnny. At every delivery stop, there had been someone—someone elderly or someone ill—that Johnny had made smile with his cheerful banter and friendly jokes. It was clear to Chelsea that he brought them far more than nourishing food.

He brought color into the grayness of their lives—the same way he'd splashed a psychedelic swirl of emotions and sensations onto the monochromatic sameness of her own life.

"What've we got for breakfast today?" Mr. Gruber asked Johnny.

"Standard fare, Mr. G. Cornflakes, bran flakes, crisp rice, or—drumroll please—instant oatmeal!"

"I think I've got some fresh eggs in the icebox. If I ask very nicely, might you scramble me a pair of eggs?"

Johnny laughed. "You know I will, Mr. G, but you also know as well as I do that what you really want is a bowl of instant oatmeal with brown sugar on top."

"Come to think of it, you're right," the old man mused. He grinned at Chelsea. "I've got a bit of a sweet tooth."

"You have an entire mouthful of sweet teeth, old man," Johnny teased, setting about making the oatmeal.

"At my age, it's a wonder I have any teeth at all!"

"At *your* age? What, do you really think eighty-four years is some kind of accomplishment or something, Mr. G? You want to boast about your age, you should wait until you hit a really big number, like one hundred. Then you can say things like 'at *my* age.'"

Chelsea smiled, recognizing that this conversation was one the two men had probably had every time Johnny came to visit.

"Do you know, Chelsea works just a few blocks away from here, Mr. G," Johnny said.

"Oh," the old man said darkly as he sat down to eat his bowl of oatmeal. "That's not good." He turned to look at Chelsea. "This neighborhood isn't what it used to be. I've lived here thirty years—no, forty years now—and I don't go out at night anymore. It's not safe."

"Fifty-four years," Johnny reminded him. "You moved in right after World War Two, remember? You were just out of the service."

"That's right. Martin was just a baby, and—" He broke off, a look of confusion crossing his face. "I don't know why he won't write. I told him to write when he's away at camp. . . ."

"How's the oatmeal, Mr. G? Did I put enough brown sugar on, or do you want to add a little more?"

"This is delightful, thank you."

The old man ate quietly, suddenly subdued. Whoever Martin was, he deserved to be strung up for not writing or visiting.

Johnny kept up a steady stream of conversation as he made short work of a pile of dirty dishes in the sink. But nothing he said seemed to bring Mr. Gruber out of his introspective mood.

"Ready for a quick game of cards?" Johnny asked, when Mr. Gruber had scraped his bowl clean.

Mr. Gruber carefully set his spoon down next to the empty bowl. "Not today, I don't think. I'm a bit tired. If you don't mind, I'll head in for a nap."

In the course of the past few minutes the old man had seemed to age a dozen years.

"How about I give you a hand into the other room?" Johnny asked quietly.

"Thank you."

As Chelsea watched, the older man let Johnny help him out of his chair, and together, they walked slowly down the hall to the bedroom.

"I'll give you a call later to remind you to put that dinner in the microwave," she heard Johnny tell Mr. G.

"All right, Martin."

"Should I pull down the shades or do you want to be able to look out the window? I know you like to watch the clouds. . . ."

"Leave them up, thank you."

"Okay, I'll see you later—probably not for another few days, so be nice to Bobby or Carlos or whoever comes out here. No fair trying to win their paychecks with your card games."

"All right, Martin."

"It's Johnny, Mr. G," Johnny said softly. "Johnny Anziano from Meals on Wheels. Remember?"

Johnny headed down the hall toward Chelsea, and she could hear the old man's voice, quavering now, calling after him, "Martin, call me if you're going to be late. . . ."

Johnny briefly closed his eyes and shook his head very slightly. "It's Johnny," he called back. "And I *will* call you later."

Chelsea followed Johnny out the door and waited while he carefully locked both bolts. He stood there for a moment, just staring at his keys, and when he finally glanced over at her, he looked impossibly sad.

"He seemed like he was having a good day, but . . ."

"Why won't Martin visit?" she asked softly.

"Because he died when he was fourteen years old." Johnny sighed, shaking his head slightly. "I can do everything for Al Gruber but the one thing he truly wants. I can't be Martin."

Chelsea knew at that moment, as she gazed into brown eyes made even darker with compassion, that she had been fooling herself for days now. She knew with a certainty that rocked her to the core that despite her pretending otherwise, she had fallen desperately in love with her husband.

"Johnny, will you kiss me?" she whispered.

He smiled then. It was a small smile, but it was real. "Always," he murmured, pulling her into his arms.

He tasted like coffee sweetened with sugar and cream. He was both gentle and demanding, both sweet and full of passion, both powerful and yielding. He was smart and funny and kind and sexy. She loved the sound of his voice, the husky catch to it when he was turned on. She loved the way his smile could light up an entire room. She loved the way he watched her when she talked, the way he listened to her so intently, every cell in his body alert as if what she had to say truly mattered. She loved the way the laughter in his eyes could dissolve into instant, searing heat. She loved everything about him.

She loved him.

"Come on, let's get out of here," Johnny breathed into her ear. "I have to be at work in a couple of hours."

Holding his hand, Chelsea let him lead her down the four flights of stairs and out to where the Meals on Wheels truck was illegally parked in a loading zone.

"I've been thinking about what Mr. Gruber was saying," he told her as he unlocked the truck. "About this part of town being dangerous at night." He helped her up into the passenger seat, then crossed around in front of the truck.

Chelsea reached over and unlocked his door.

"Thanks," he said, climbing in. "So I was thinking, if you ever want to work late, you know, past dark, maybe you could call me at the restaurant, and I could pick you up on my way home."

"I work late almost every night," she told him.

"Then I'll meet you over there almost every night," he told her as he pulled out into the traffic.

"You don't have to do that." She didn't *want* him to do that.

"Yeah, I know—but I want to."

"It's out of your way."

"It'll take me an extra ten minutes. Big deal. Your safety's worth that to me."

"If it's late, I call a cab, and wait to unlock the door until I can see it out the front window," Chelsea said coolly. She was a grown woman, and she could take care of herself.

He glanced at her and laughed. "Uh-oh, I've conjured up the Ice Princess. I'm in trouble now."

"That's the second time you've called me that," Chelsea told him, exasperation tingeing her voice.

"I'm just teasing," he said. "You sometimes get a certain tone in your voice, and you start shooting icicles out of your eyes. It's just really different from the way you are the rest of the time, it's kind of funny, that's all."

Icicles from her eyes . . . She'd always thought that her father had had what she called "Siberian eyes." At times colder than cold. Was it possible that she did the same thing? "God, do I do it a lot?"

"No. Just when you're mad. Or scared—you know, when you're feeling threatened." He glanced at her again. "Like right now."

Chelsea nodded. "I don't want you to pick me up every night after work, as if I'm a child that needs to be taken care of. I don't want that kind of relationship."

"I've noticed your resistance to the idea," he said dryly. He pulled up to a red light and turned to look at her appraisingly. "Promise me you'll do the thing with the cab?"

She looked back at him. "I promise you that I'm smart enough and old enough and experienced enough to take care of myself."

"That's not quite the promise I wanted, but I guess it'll do," he said with a smile.

Chelsea found herself smiling back at Johnny, marveling at the way he'd taken a potentially volatile situation and defused it. Of course, the fact that he'd backed down had surely helped. If he had insisted on picking her up and driving her home every night, there would have been figurative bloodshed.

But he respected her enough to recognize that she *could* take care of herself. And he seemed to know that when it came to protecting her independence, she would not negotiate.

Chelsea watched the morning sunlight reflecting off his face, accentuating his rugged features, making his dark hair gleam. On the other hand, maybe she *would* negotiate. In fact, it was entirely likely that if she wasn't careful, she would find herself giving in.

Because she loved him that much.

She was hit with a wave of panic, and she tried to calm herself, taking a deep breath and letting it slowly out. It could be worse. She could very well be in love with a man who insisted on imposing his rules upon her.

But she was lucky—Johnny wasn't like that. And maybe, just maybe, he was the one man she could live with as equal partners, both giving and sharing. Maybe, she could stay strong and refuse to let herself love him so much that she would give up her self and her dreams just to be near him. And maybe—and she knew that she was asking for an awful lot of miracles here— if she were really lucky, over the course of the next year he'd come to love her too.

"Can we go home now?" she whispered.

Johnny smiled, and he put the truck in high gear.

It was after seven before Johnny could get away from the stove and give Chelsea a call. It was time for a break, and he took a cup of coffee into his office, closing the door behind him. There was a stack of papers that needed his signature in his in-basket, and as he dialed the phone he set to work skimming them quickly then signing his name.

He tried Chelsea's number at work, assuming since she went in late, she'd be there still, working late.

He was right—she picked up on the first ring. He paused in his signing, afraid the sound of her voice would make his hand shake.

"Spencer/O'Brien," she said shortly. She sounded over-worked and overstressed and not very friendly.

"Hi, it's me. Is this a bad time to talk? I can call you later if you want. . . ."

"John. Hi." Her voice warmed up considerably. "No, it's no better or worse than any other time. God, I'm glad you called."

Johnny took a sip of his coffee, feeling the jolt of the caffeine mingling jazzily with the electric feeling he got just from talking to Chelsea on the phone. Talking to his *wife* on the phone. She was his *wife*. He laughed aloud in pleasure at the bizarre thought. "I was wondering if you had plans for later. I figured since we only had lunch at three, you wouldn't have eaten yet."

"Are you asking me to dinner?"

The next stack of letters were form letters to their food sup-pliers, and he could sign them one after another without having to read each one through.

"You bet," he told her. "Do you think you can catch a cab over to the restaurant in a few hours? I promise I won't make you eat anything that ever had a face."

Chelsea laughed then lowered her voice. "I'd rather meet you at home. Right now."

Home. This wasn't the first time she'd referred to his condo as "home." Johnny felt a rush of happiness. His condo was their *home*. And she wanted to meet him there. Now. It seemed almost too good to be true. "I can't get away right now, but you know I would if I could."

"Are you absolutely sure you can't just sneak off? I've had a truly awful afternoon, and . . ." She sighed, and when she continued, her voice suddenly sounded so sad. "All I want is for you to hold me."

Johnny's heart lurched. "Chelsea, if I worked for myself, I'd be at your office in an instant, but I don't. I work for a really nice guy named Rudy, who would be very unhappy if I left in the middle of the dinner rush." He glanced at the clock on his desk. As it was, he had to get back to the kitchen pretty soon. "Did something happen at work?"

She drew in a deep breath. "My father called. He didn't say anything directly, but it was a little obvious that he's waiting for me to come crawling, asking for money to pay back that bank loan."

He signed another letter. "Maybe he called because he thought by initiating a conversation, he might make it easier for you to ask him for the money."

She sighed again. "Well, whatever his motivation, I couldn't do it. Not over the phone. If I'm going to beg, at least I'm going to hang on to some shred of my pride by doing it in person. My parents are having some sort of party Sunday afternoon. I thought it would be a good time to corner my dad and grovel. I can get it over with, and he'll have all his party guests to distract him afterward, so I won't have to spend an hour or two listening to him lecture me on poor business decisions. I know it's your day off, and if you want, I can make up some kind of excuse for why you can't—"

Johnny put down his pen. "Don't be ridiculous. I want to go with you. I'd love to go with you."

She drew in an unsteady breath. "You're so sweet."

"I *insist* that I go with you—that is, unless you absolutely don't want me there?"

Her voice broke slightly. "I do want you there. Badly."

"Then I'm there."

"I think I'm going to cry. Say something to make me laugh, will you?"

"If you want to know the truth, I'm not sweet at all. The real reason I'm dying to go to this shindig is because I want to live out a certain fantasy I have of getting it on with you in your parents' guest bathroom—with a highclass party in full swing on the other side of the door."

Chelsea laughed breathlessly. "Oh, my God. That did it. Thank you."

"I'm serious."

"No, you're not."

"Wait until Sunday. You'll see." Johnny finished signing the last of the ordering invoices, and with unerring aim tossed the pen back into the coffee mug that held a variety of pencils and pens. "You know what? I need a picture of you for my desk. I'm sitting here, and I'm wishing desperately that I had a picture of you."

"You have a desk?" There was a trace of disbelief in her voice.

"I do. I have an office, too, with a door and everything. If you come over here, I'll show it to you. We can lock the door and live out my *other* fantasy about—"

"Very funny."

"This time I *am* kidding. Come on out here and have dinner with me, Chelsea. Please?"

"When do you want me over there? And where exactly is it?"

"Nine-thirty, quarter to ten." He quickly gave her the address.

"I'll be there."

"Take a cab."

"Right this way, madam."

Chelsea followed the maître d' through the hushed formal dining room at Lumière's.

Lumière's. Johnny worked at Lumière's. She remembered now that he'd told her that one of the first times they'd met. But she hadn't expected it, and therefore hadn't connected it to *this* Lumière's, which was, of course, *the* Lumière's on Beacon Street—Boston's premier gourmet restaurant.

She'd read a recent *Boston Globe* review of the restaurant, commending it on its ability to keep pace with the times and yet still consistently provide first-rate, four-star fare. They credited the restaurant's head chef and his young, capable staff—one of which surely was Johnny.

The stony-faced maître d' held open a door for her. "After you, madam."

"Thank you." There were plushly carpeted stairs on the other side of the door that led upward, and Chelsea climbed them. She turned back to glance at the maître d', who was now following her. "Where are we going?"

"To the private dining room, madam."

Lumière's fabled private dining room? Even Chelsea's father had never managed to get a reservation for Lumière's ultraexpensive, ultrachic private dining room.

It was a medium-sized room, decorated in tastefully muted colors, and only dimly lit by candles, both on the table and in candlesticks, scattered around the room. One wall was window, and it looked out over the street and the Boston Common below.

The table was set for two, with the simple elegance of a plain white linen cloth and shining black china. A bottle was chilling in a champagne bucket. Two tuxedo-clad waiters were standing attentively nearby, and at the maître d's nod, one of them picked up a telephone and discreetly dialed a number. The other held back a chair for her, then slipped the cloth napkin onto her lap.

"Mr. Anziano will be right with you, Mrs. Anziano." The maître d' bowed and quietly headed back down the stairs.

Mrs. Anziano. Funny, she kind of liked being called that. It was against all she believed in, as far as choosing to keep her own name despite being married, but it made her feel good.

Mrs. Anziano. It brought to mind images of a certain *Mister* Anziano lying next to her in bed, his heavily lidded eyes sleepy and warm as he held her after making love. It brought to mind images of him joining her in the shower, water streaming around them as they freely gave in to passion and desire. . . .

The waiters had resumed their soldierly stances near a door that no doubt led down a back staircase to the kitchen, and Chelsea smiled at them, hoping that neither was capable of mind reading. But they were like the guards to Buckingham Palace, and they didn't smile in return.

She smoothed down the skirt of her business suit, feeling much too underdressed for Lumière's. *Lumière's.* She still couldn't believe Johnny worked *here.* . . .

The door opened beside the waiters, and Johnny stepped into the room.

He was wearing a brown suit, and again, as on the day they'd met with the lawyer, his shirt and tie were shadings of the same color. Johnny smiled at her as he breezed toward the table, and before she could rise to her feet, he bent over and kissed her.

His hair was slightly damp and his cheeks were baby soft, as if he'd just shaved. He was wearing the slightest hint of a deliciously exotic-smelling cologne.

"Don't get up," he told her. He dragged the chair around from the opposite side of the table so that he was sitting next to her rather than across from her. The waiters scurried instantly to move the plates and silverware and countless wineglasses around. "Are you hungry?"

She couldn't believe how good he looked. "Did you go home to shower and change? You should have told me you were going to do that."

"No, I didn't, actually. I keep a couple of suits here at work," he told her. He nodded to the waiters and they disappeared. "I take a quick shower and put one on just about every night before I come up to the private dining room."

Chelsea didn't understand. "Why do you come up here?"

"When people pay as much as they do to eat in Lumière's private dining room, they usually want to meet the chef."

"The chef?" She was stunned. "You mean the *main* chef? The chief chef? The four-star review in *The Boston Globe* chef?"

Johnny was laughing at her. "That's me. The head honcho, top of the pecking order, I-give-the-commands, don't-mess-with-my-special-sauce chef."

He was watching her, gauging her reaction. He'd known full well that she hadn't thought he was anything more than one of the lowly kitchen staff. She judged him and made incorrect assumptions based on the way he looked and the neighborhood he'd grown up in. She was as narrow-minded as her father.

"God, you must think I'm a jerk," she whispered. "You told me you worked here, and I assumed the worst instead of the best."

He touched the side of her face, his eyes as gentle as his fingers. "Hey, come on. I didn't plan this dinner to make you feel bad. I thought you would think it was funny. When we met

I was driving a truck and wearing jeans. It's natural you wouldn't have expected me to be the head chef of a gourmet restaurant."

"It's natural, but it's also close-minded. Johnny, I'm so sorry."

He kissed her. "Apology accepted. Now lighten up, okay?" She didn't answer, and he kissed her again. "Okay?"

Chelsea nodded, and he kissed her one more time. "Good."

Johnny turned toward the champagne bucket, and one of the waiters appeared instantly, holding the bottle out for him to see. Johnny took it from him, holding it in turn for Chelsea.

"Oh," she said, shaking her head, "I don't—" But then she saw the label. It was nonalcoholic. It was sparkling grape juice.

"Does it have your approval?" Johnny asked.

She nodded.

Johnny handed the bottle back to the waiter, who opened it and poured them both a glass.

Chelsea couldn't speak through the lump in her throat. He'd gone to a lot of trouble to get that bottle specially for her. And she suspected getting that bottle had been the least of his efforts. She suspected that she was in for the meal of a lifetime. She knew for dead certain she was in for the year of her lifetime.

Johnny lifted his glass. "What should we toast?"

She shook her head, hoping that he'd want to toast the new level of their relationship, hoping he'd say something, *anything* that would give her hope to believe that he loved her too.

"I know what we can toast." He lifted his glass even higher. "Here's to never having to ask your father for money ever again."

Chelsea groaned. "Please. I don't want to have to think about that right now."

"You don't have to think about it ever again," Johnny told her, clinking his glass against hers and taking a sip. He set his wineglass down and reached into the inside pocket of his jacket.

He took out an envelope and handed it to Chelsea. "I think there's probably enough in there to cover the first six payments of your loan."

For the second time that evening Chelsea was stunned. She stared at him. Just stared at him. "What did you just say?" she finally breathed.

Johnny tapped the envelope. "There's a bank check in here," he said. "I wasn't sure I'd be able to get the money out—I had it in a long-term CD—so I didn't want to say anything to you until I talked to the bank officer. But I went over there this afternoon and the penalties weren't that high, so . . ." He shrugged and smiled. "You don't need to ask your father for anything."

Chelsea lifted the envelope's flap and peeked at the dollar amount written on the check. "This is your savings," she said softly, her eyes filling with tears as she looked back at him.

"Part of it."

"Why are you doing this?"

"Because you're my wife."

"I'm not *really* your wife, Johnny. Not *really*."

Johnny glanced up at the two waiters. "Can we have some privacy, please?" When the two men vanished, he looked back at Chelsea and took her hand. "We're married. From now until the day it's over we're really married. You're *really* my wife and you need this money. So, I'm giving it to you."

"But I thought . . ." She lowered her voice as if the walls might have ears. "I thought you were saving to open your own restaurant."

"Twenty-five percent of your grandfather's trust will more than pay me back," he told her, putting the situation in terms he knew she would understand. "In a year I'll have more than enough to open my own place." He smiled. "At the rate I was saving, that puts me about five years ahead of schedule. You're making my dreams come true. The least I can do is return the favor."

Chelsea gazed at him. Money. This was about money. For a moment she'd almost forgotten that their marriage was first and foremost a business deal. He was merely making a wise investment, using his savings to ensure her happiness, in turn ensuring that their sham of a marriage would survive an entire year, which would enable him to receive his share of her inheritance.

Silly her. She'd been sitting here hoping that he would gaze at her with those soulful brown eyes and tell her he was giving her this money because he loved her.

She took a deep breath and forced a smile. "Well, you're full of surprises tonight." She handed the envelope back to him. "I'd like it if you could hold on to this—at least until we get . . . back to your place." Home. Lately she'd caught herself calling Johnny's condo "home." She had to stop doing that, because it *wasn't* her home. It was merely her temporary residence until . . . How had Johnny put it? Until the day it was over. She had to remember that it *was* going to be over. And soon. A year would fly past more quickly than she could believe.

"I'll have my lawyer draw up a loan agreement," she added.

"That's not necessary."

"I'd prefer it," she told him.

He nodded. "As you wish."

Chelsea forced herself to stop wishing for things she couldn't have. She forced herself to stop thinking about the money and the future. She was with Johnny right now, and dammit, she was going to enjoy every minute of it. "So . . . what's for dinner?"

Johnny smiled.

"You would not *believe* what this man was able to do with a pile of vegetables, a chunk of tofu, and some spices," Chelsea told Moira. She shook her head, still disbelieving. "I've never tasted anything like that dinner in my entire life. He's some kind of culinary genius."

Moira was watching her, chin in her hand, eyebrow raised.

Chelsea had to look away. "I'm gushing, I know. Isn't it awful?"

"Sounds to me like Johnny Anziano should change his last name to Right—as in Mr. Right. Gee, and he's already your husband. How convenient."

"He's my husband for a year. *Only* for a year."

"So when the year end approaches you renegotiate—"

"He's got plans." Chelsea hated the sound of pure, aching despair in her voice. "He's going to use his share of the trust to open his own restaurant, but before he does that he wants to go to Paris, to study with some kind of famous master chef for three months." She rushed to explain before Moira could interrupt. "You see, after dinner, we went downstairs into the kitchen, and he showed me his office—Moira, he's got this huge, gorgeous office, and the walls are *covered* with newspaper and magazine reviews and awards—and I just happened to look on his desk and see this application that was half filled out for a special advanced cooking program in Paris being offered by the International Culinary Institute."

"You just *happened* to see it." Moira grinned. "And you being you, you couldn't just mind your own business."

Chelsea slumped over her desk, resting her forehead on her arms and closing her eyes, reliving the dread she'd felt when she'd spotted the word *Paris* on the application. "He lived with a woman for nearly three years, and she still lives in Paris. I couldn't *not* ask about that application."

"And he said?"

"He didn't mention Raquel, of course. But he told me getting accepted to this program was the ultimate nod from the international gourmet community. Only seven chefs are accepted each year. He told me his chances of getting in are extremely slim, and he reassured me that if he did get in, he wouldn't leave for Paris until next May."

"So maybe by next May we'll be doing well enough with the business that you can take a three-month leave of absence and go to Paris with him."

"He didn't ask me if I wanted to go."

"Give the man a chance. He hasn't been accepted into the program yet."

"And what if the business needs me here?"

"Then you're going to have to make some choices. Chels, if you love this guy—"

"No," Chelsea said, trying hard to convince herself that her words were true. "I don't love him that much. I refuse to love anyone that much."

"There are a million options. We could hire someone to fill in for you temporarily—"

"Do you know what John's specialty is?"

Moira snickered. "I can guess, but then again, you probably don't mean *that*. You probably mean his specialty as a chef."

Chelsea threw a telephone notepad at her friend. "Of course I mean his specialty as a chef."

"No, I don't know. Why don't you tell me?"

"Veal and lamb. Baby cows and baby sheep. I will never eat the food that *The Boston Globe* describes as 'culinary heaven,' and 'edible art.' I *can't* eat it, Mo. I *won't* eat it. And just how long do you really think he's going to want me hanging around, *not* eating his specialty?" Chelsea put her head in her hands again. "And the really stupid thing is, I keep finding myself thinking, well, maybe I can be a vegetarian only part of the time. Maybe I could eat his veal dishes every now and then." She lifted her head and looked miserably at Moira. "I'm actually considering giving up being a vegetarian—something I truly, honestly believe in for health reasons and for humanitarian reasons—just to please some guy who's good in bed."

"Some guy who's good in bed, whom you happen to be in love with," Moira pointed out.

"What am I going to do?"

"Whatever you do, *definitely* don't tell *him* how you feel," Moira said sarcastically, then ducked to avoid being hit with more flying office supplies.

thirteen

CHELSEA'S FATHER DEFINITELY KNEW.
Johnny had known from the look in his eyes when the man shook his hand, right when he and Chelsea had walked in the door of the stately Tudor-style house.

So it was no real surprise when Howard Spencer pulled him away from the other guests to ask, "So, who are you, really?"

"Giovanni Anziano," Johnny said. "My friends call me Johnny."

"And from where exactly did Chelsea dig you up?"

Johnny tried to smile pleasantly despite the rude tone of Mr. Spencer's voice. He could understand how a father might be a little bit upset to find out his daughter had married a man who was a complete stranger to her family. "Actually, we met as a result of Chelsea getting her purse snatched."

"Her purse . . ." Something flickered in Spencer's eyes. "She never told me about that."

"I'm sure most children don't tell their parents about a lot of things."

"And she met you when?"

"No, I wasn't the one who mugged her," Johnny said, his

words only half-joking. "I got her purse back for her and helped her get cleaned up."

"So naturally, in gratitude, she married you."

Johnny laughed. "Hey, that's a good one, Mr. S."

"I wasn't joking."

Johnny gave up trying to play nice. He lowered his voice and stepped closer to the older man. "Look, the fact is, I'm married to your daughter. I *like* being married to your daughter, and I intend to treat her really well, so you don't have to—"

"The *fact* is," Howard Spencer interrupted, "Chelsea married you solely to acquire her inheritance. I applaud her ingenuity but question her choice of . . . business partners. I'm just warning you, in one year, when this farce of a marriage is over, you will take whatever deal she's made with you and quietly slink back to whatever hole you came out of. If you don't attempt to stay married to her, or to contest the divorce in *any* way, I'll triple whatever payment she gives you. And I'm prepared to make you that offer in writing."

Triple. Just like that, one truckload of money could become three. But what good would three truckloads of money be without Chelsea to share it with him?

"You know where to reach me when you decide to take the money," Mr. Spencer said with smug certainty, then walked away.

Johnny's heart was pounding and his mouth was dry. God, what he would have given to deck that guy. Just one punch, that's all he wanted. Of course, that guy was his father-in-law, and in most circles, decking your father-in-law was considered bad form. But, damn, he wanted to. He'd also wanted to shout that if in a year Chelsea wanted him to stick around, dammit, he was going to stick around, and there was *no* amount of money in all the world that would convince him to do otherwise.

He grabbed a glass of champagne off a tray as a server went past, then turned to look for Chelsea.

He found her almost instantly. She was standing out on the sundeck, leaning against the railing, sipping a sparkling water and talking to Benton Scott.

"They look good together, don't they?"

Johnny glanced up to see Chelsea's brother Troy standing next to him, watching his friend and his sister through the glass in the French doors. They did look good together—both slim and blond and elegant.

"Bent told me just yesterday that he and Nicole have finally called it quits. He filed the divorce papers last week." Troy looked questioning at Johnny. "I'm sorry—what was your name again?"

"It's Johnny," he answered flatly, then added, "Does everyone know?"

"That you're not Emilio? Pretty much. It's hard to keep a secret in this family, especially one of that magnitude." Troy laughed. "It was funny how it slipped out, actually. The real groom—I mean, the *former* groom—had a mutual friend who knew my brother Michael, and that friend kind of let slip the news that Emilio was getting married next month to a girl from Greece, and Michael thought, gee, that's odd, this is the same guy who just married my little sister. Not long after that the cat was totally out of the bag." He paused for breath. "So I hear Grandpa went overboard with the amount he left for Chelsea. What's your share?"

"That's not your business," Johnny said evenly.

"I'll find out sooner or later, but suit yourself." Troy turned to look at Chelsea and Bent. "I think those two are going to end up together—you know, after she divorces you."

Johnny tried to stay cool despite the fact that with every beat of his heart, rage-heated blood was surging through his veins. Somehow, again, he managed to stay silent, and after a moment Troy faded away.

As Johnny watched, Chelsea gave Bent a smile and walked

toward the house. The man's eyes followed the soft sway of her hips, and Johnny knew that if it were up to Benton Scott, he'd steal Chelsea back in a heartbeat. He swore silently. Could this situation possibly get any worse? Chelsea's family obviously thought Johnny was beneath her, her father had tried to buy him off, and now the man whom she confessed had at one time been the love of her life was clearly interested in rekindling their romance.

He had a sick feeling that when he got home and finally went through yesterday's mail, he was going to find a notice of an impending IRS tax audit. The day was going *that* well.

But then Chelsea spotted him, her eyes warm with pleasure. She hadn't looked at Benton Scott that way, had she?

But instead of coming over to him, she took a left turn as she approached, veering away from him and toward the front hallway. She glanced back over her shoulder, gesturing slightly with her head for him to follow her.

Johnny set his glass down on a passing server's tray and trailed slightly behind her. In the entryway, she went quickly up a flight of thickly carpeted stairs, glancing back again to see if he was following.

"What's up here?" he asked, taking the stairs two at a time to catch up with her at the top landing.

She put her finger on her lips in a gesture of silence and looked carefully down the hallway in either direction. She glanced back down the stairs, then she stepped into a dark doorway, pulling him with her and shutting the door behind him.

Johnny laughed as she locked the door, and just like that, his unpleasant conversations with Chelsea's father and brother were instantly worth it. Johnny literally had to hold his tongue between his teeth to keep from telling her, right then and there, how deeply he loved her.

Because they were in the bathroom. Out of all the places they could have gone to talk privately, Chelsea had chosen this one because she knew it would make him laugh—and make him wonder if she was bold enough actually to make love to him with the party going on downstairs. He was wondering. Boy, was he wondering. He pulled her into his arms and kissed her, but she pulled away.

"My sister told me everyone knows you're not Emilio," she told him, "but my father hasn't said anything to me yet."

"He said something to me," Johnny told her.

Chelsea winced, her blue eyes filled with worry. "I'm so sorry. Was it awful?"

"It was . . . educational," he said diplomatically, deciding not to tell her about her father's offer of money. He didn't want to talk about what was going to happen when this year was over. He didn't want Chelsea even thinking about it until she had a real chance to see that being married to him wasn't a threat to her independence. He didn't want to talk about it until she'd gotten used to him being around, and maybe—please, God— even loved him a little. "But I survived intact."

Chelsea ran her hands up his chest and down his shoulders. "Maybe I should check, just to make sure."

Her touch had the power to make him crazy, so he pulled away slightly, needing to look into her eyes as he asked a question he knew he shouldn't ask. "I saw you talking to Benton Scott. Did he tell you he's getting divorced?"

She gazed back at him. "He did. Apparently it's been rather nasty. He wanted to have lunch sometime this week to talk about it."

Johnny felt his insides twist. He kept his face and his voice carefully neutral. "Oh?"

"What do you think?" she asked. "Should I go?"

Both her voice and the pure wideness of her eyes were far too innocent, and Johnny realized she had worked very hard to hide the smile that now slipped out.

"Only if you want me to kill him," he told her.

Her smile turned into a laugh of disbelief. "Oh, my God, you *are* jealous!"

"I can't help it," he admitted. "I know your history with this guy and . . ." He caught her beautiful face between his hands and looked searchingly into her laughing blue eyes. "I need to hear you tell me you don't want him anymore."

"I don't want him anymore," Chelsea said. "I stopped wanting him the first time you kissed me." She smiled at him, bewitchingly. "I think you know what I do want, though. It has something to do with you and me and the guest bathroom during one of my parents' parties . . ." Her smile turned to a grin, heat and devilment sparkling in her eyes. "I believe the expression is: Put up or shut up."

Pulling her into his arms, giddy with relief and desire, Johnny did both.

"He was really jealous of Bent. That's a good sign, isn't it?"

Moira looked at Chelsea in obvious exasperation as she poured the grounds for their morning pot of coffee into the filter. "Have you asked him how he feels? When grown-ups want to know how other grown-ups feel, they usually *ask*."

"I *know* how he feels. He likes me. He *really* likes the physical side of our relationship. But the biggest attraction for him is the money he's going to get when the year is over." Chelsea closed her eyes. "Sierra called to tell me that Daddy offered Johnny a huge amount of money—provided that at the end of the year he really does divorce me and disappear."

"And Johnny didn't mention that to you?" Moira added water and clicked the coffeemaker on.

"Nope."

"Ouch."

"Yeah."

"In that case, okay, I can understand why you might not want to take the risk of telling him that you love him."

Chelsea sighed, gazing out her window at the early-morning sunshine already warming the city street. "I have a year to figure out how to make him fall in love with me."

"A lot can happen in a year," Moira said reassuringly.

"Maybe if I offer him even *more* money, he'll stay," Chelsea said morosely. "God, I can't believe I just said that."

In the outer office, the bell tinkled. Someone had come in.

"Hey, how'd they get in without buzzing?" Moira asked, frowning. The building had an outer door that locked. People coming into the offices had to be screened through an intercom before they were buzzed in.

"The lock's not working again," Chelsea said. "At least it wasn't when I came in. I already called the landlord."

"Are you expecting a client?" Moira asked.

Chelsea shook her head. "No." Her heart leaped. Maybe it was Johnny, stopping in after his Meals on Wheels rounds. It was still a little early, but maybe . . . Eagerly, she pushed herself out of her chair and followed Moira into the outer office.

"Hey!" she heard Moira say in outrage. "What do you think you're doing?"

The man rifling through the drawers of Moira's desk definitely wasn't Johnny.

He was ragged and dirty, his short hair matted against his head, his face streaked with grime as if he'd slept, facedown, in the back alley. His hands were shaking and his eyes were red and tearing. He looked up, teeth bared in a growl of anger and frustration that made him seem more animal than human, an enormous handgun tightly clenched in one trembling hand. "Where the *hell* is your cash register?"

Chelsea's heart was pounding, but she spoke calmly as she gently took hold of the waistband of Moira's pants and slowly, an inch at a time, began backing them both away from that deadly-looking gun. "We don't keep any money here. This is an *office*, not a retail store. We don't have a cash register."

"You're lying," he bit out. He needed both hands to hold the gun steady, he was shaking so badly. He turned suddenly, and fired three fast, deafening shots that shattered the front window. Chelsea couldn't hold back a scream as Moira crumpled in a dead faint.

"Show me where the freakin' cash register is, or I'm going to freakin' *kill* you!" the man shouted.

Finding a big enough parking spot around the corner from Chelsea's office, Johnny pulled the Meals on Wheels truck into it, feeling particularly triumphant. His luck had been right on all day. Even Mr. Gruber had seemed much better, upbeat and cheerful for all of Johnny's visit.

And now he was going to drop in on his wife, see if he couldn't talk her into going home with him for an early lunch. Lunch, and maybe a little nonfood refreshment . . .

He rounded the corner, a definite jaunt in his step, but then stopped short.

There were three police cars and an ambulance haphazardly parked in the middle of the street, as if they'd arrived in a big hurry and skidded to a stop. Uniformed officers were crawling all over the place, going in and out of the building.

A crowd had gathered, and someone had put out yellow crime-scene tape, keeping them back—away from the main door to the building Chelsea's office was in.

It was the yellow tape that did it, the yellow tape that sent Johnny's heart into his throat and twisted his insides into a knot. He'd grown up in a part of town where he'd seen that yellow tape too often, and nine times out of ten, when that yellow tape appeared, there was a dead body or two to go with it.

Johnny broke into a run, and as he got closer the fear that was gripping his chest tightened its grasp as he saw the entire front window of Chelsea's outer office had been broken from the inside out. Jagged shards of glass littered the sidewalk.

He pushed through the crowd and slipped under the yellow tape, only to come face-to-face with a cop the size of a professional wrestler. "Where do you think you're going, pal?" the man demanded roughly.

"My wife works in there." Johnny pointed to the office beyond the broken window. He could barely get the words out, his throat felt so tight. "What happened? Was anyone hurt?"

"I don't know yet," the cop told him, sympathy in his eyes, moving aside to let him pass. "I'm just working crowd control. All I know is gunshots were fired and someone called the ambulance."

Gunshots fired. Ambulance.

Johnny took the stairs up to the door three at a time, bracing himself for the worst, preparing for the scenario that he dreaded finding—the woman he loved, her life snuffed out, lying in a pool of blood.

For the first time since his mother had died, Johnny found himself praying.

Several plainclothes detectives were standing and talking with several uniformed officers. But there was no sign of Chelsea—dead or alive.

"I'm Chelsea Spencer's husband," he nearly shouted at one of the police officers. "Where is she? Is she all right?"

"She's one of the women who worked here?" the policeman asked.

"Yes."

"Then she's with the paramedics," the policeman told him, "in the back office. Someone was hurt, but I don't know who. Junkie came in, needing a fix, went ballistic with a gun."

"Oh, my God." The door to Chelsea's office was closed, but Johnny went toward it anyway, intending to knock it down if he had to, imagining Chelsea lying there, in her office, bleeding to death while the paramedics stood nearby, unable to save her.

But he didn't have to knock the door down, because before he got there, it swung open.

And Chelsea was standing there. "Johnny? I thought I heard your voice."

She was alive. She was whole. Unbloodied. Unhurt.

Johnny reached for her, holding her tightly, unable to breathe, unable to hear from the rushing of the blood in his head, unable to see from the blur of tears that filled his eyes, unable to say anything but her name.

She held him just as tightly as he lifted his head and kissed her.

It wasn't a kiss of desire, although there was always a spark of passion each time their lips met. It was more a kiss of affirmation, a kiss of possession, a kiss of gratitude. It was a kiss that drove home to Johnny all that he would have lost had Chelsea been killed today, and it pushed him beyond his limit.

Holding tight to Chelsea, Johnny wept.

"Johnny, my God..." He could hear the surprise in her voice.

"I'm sorry," he said, laughing at himself, but unable to stop the flow of tears. "God, when I saw that yellow tape, I thought..." His laughter became a sob and he kissed her again, harder this time, molding her body against his own, uncaring of who saw them kissing, and who saw him crying.

He let her pull him into her office. Moira was there, lying on the sofa, an ice pack on her head and a paramedic sitting at her side, taking her blood pressure and pulse.

Chelsea pushed him down into the chair behind her desk and then sat on his lap.

Johnny took a deep breath, closing his eyes and letting his head rest against the softness of her breasts. He felt her hands in his hair, her fingers soothing. God, talk about losing it.

When he finally opened his eyes, she was looking down at him, her expression so sweet, her eyes so tender. Yeah, he'd lost it, but she didn't seem to mind.

He wiped his face with his hands, took a deep breath, forced a smile and tried to joke. "Let me get this straight. *You're* the one who was face-to-face with a strung-out gunman, but *I'm* the one who's being comforted. What's wrong with this picture?"

"Excuse me, Ms. Spencer." One of the plainclothes cops was standing in the door and Johnny and Chelsea both looked up. "If it's possible, we'd like to ask you some questions now."

"I have a few questions of my own." Chelsea slid off Johnny's lap. "I thought I overheard someone say you caught the man with the gun—is that true?"

"Yes, ma'am. A suspect similar to the one you described to the 911 operator was apprehended carrying a firearm." The police detective stepped into the room. He was an older man, slightly overweight, with thinning hair combed futilely over a bald spot. But his eyes were sharp as he gazed at them and around the room, seeming to miss no detail. "What we'd like is to get your statement, and then take you down to the station, to ID the suspect in a lineup."

"Will that take long?" Johnny asked.

The detective focused a pair of cool gray eyes on Johnny. "Are you the husband?"

Johnny stood up, holding out his hand. "Yeah. Giovanni Anziano."

The detective clasped his hand. "Detective Paul White. It shouldn't take more than fifteen minutes, tops."

But Chelsea was shaking her head. "I can't just leave Moira here. And what about the broken window? Anyone could just walk right in and take our computers."

Moira's voice drifted thinly from the couch. "My brother's on his way over. He's going to drive me home. I could ask him to come back and make sure the window gets boarded up."

"I can take care of that," Johnny volunteered. "No problem. But before you go anywhere, I want to know what the hell happened."

"The lock on the outer door was jammed again," Moira told him, "and this guy just walked right in. We heard the bell when the door opened, and when we came out into the outer office, he was searching through my desk, looking for money."

Chelsea spoke up. "He had one of those giant Dirty Harry guns."

"The perp we picked up was carrying a .44 Magnum," Detective White murmured.

"He kept asking where we kept the cash register," Moira said. "And when we told him we weren't a retail store, that we didn't have a cash register, he freaked, and fired at the windows, and started really screaming at us. That's when I did my Perils of Pauline routine and fainted. But Dudley Do-Right wasn't around to catch me, so I hit my head on the way down."

"I'm sorry I didn't catch you," Chelsea told her friend.

"You were a little busy trying to figure out how to keep the wacko from slaughtering us," Moira said dryly. "Personally, I think you made the right choice by ignoring me."

Johnny gazed at Chelsea, unable to keep from picturing her standing there, all alone, one-on-one with a man who probably wouldn't have hesitated to kill to get the money to buy him the drugs he needed.

"I was standing there, looking down the barrel of that enormous gun," Chelsea said, her voice very soft, "knowing that this guy was going to kill me because we didn't have a cash register that he could rob. And then I remembered—the petty-cash drawer. I keep a purse in the bottom drawer of my desk with about two hundred dollars in cash for emergencies or COD deliveries or whatever. I told him the money was in the other office, and that there was also a back door he could use to get out of the building."

Chelsea took a deep breath. "I knew there was a good chance he was going to get all paranoid about being caught, and that he would shoot me even if I gave him the money, but I was hoping that if I closed the door as we went into the back office, he would forget about Moira. So I gave him the money, and then I pretended to faint—I guess I figured maybe if I was lying on the floor, he might forget that he hadn't already shot me. I don't know, it just seemed like the right thing to do at the time, and when I opened my eyes again he was gone. That's when I called 911."

The police detective was taking notes on a small pocket pad. He looked up. "You were smart," he said. "And you were extremely lucky. This man's MO is almost identical to a robbery homicide that took place in Dorchester a week ago. Front window of the store shot out . . . Of course, three people were killed that time. Still, my money's on him being the same guy. We have prints from Dorchester—with any luck they'll match."

Johnny reached for Chelsea, pulling her into his arms. "God," he murmured. "My God."

Chelsea's voice shook. "May we go to the station now? I want to do this quickly so I can come back here and have my husband take me home."

Johnny didn't want to let go of her. "Sure you don't want me to come with you?"

She shook her head. "I need you to stay and take care of that broken window. I should probably call the landlord and—"

"Don't worry," he told her. "I'll take care of it. I'll take care of everything."

fourteen

CHELSEA COULDN'T BELIEVE HER EYES.

Two workmen were on the sidewalk and two were inside the office, carefully lining up a pane of glass to replace the broken window.

She glanced at her watch as she got out of the police car that had driven her back. True, she'd been gone longer than she'd hoped, but it really hadn't been much more than an hour since she'd left Johnny to deal with the mess in the office.

Identifying the man who'd robbed her hadn't taken long. She'd picked him out of the lineup without hesitating. It had been the paperwork afterward that had taken forever.

The lock *still* wasn't working on the outer door as she went into the office. Johnny was on the phone, sitting behind her desk, and he quickly rang off when he saw her.

Chelsea pointed out toward the outer office and the window. "How on earth . . . ?"

Johnny smiled at her. "Rudy—you know, my boss at Lumière's—his brother-in-law is best friends with a guy whose son owns a glass-replacement company. We got lucky, both that they had a truck in the neighborhood, and that this is a pretty standard-sized window." He stood up. "Let me see how long these guys think they're going to be. If they're going to be here for a while, I'll take you home and then come back."

Chelsea followed him out into the outer office. There were two police detectives dusting Moira's desk for fingerprints, and a uniformed cop standing nearby, chatting with them. This office had never been so busy. "Don't you have to be at the restaurant pretty soon?"

Johnny shook his head. "I told Rudy I wouldn't be able to get in until five at the earliest. I'll call in later and tell the guys what to start chopping for the evening's special."

Chelsea looked at the window and the men working. "They're going to be done in just a few minutes. Why don't we just wait, that way you won't have to come back?"

"I'm going to have to come back anyway," Johnny told her, putting an arm around her shoulder and giving her a hug. "Someone needs to be here when the truck arrives."

"Truck?"

"Yeah. I arranged for a moving company to come out and pick up your computers and all the stuff in your desks and on your shelves," Johnny told her.

"What?" Chelsea was shocked. "And move them where?"

"To my condo. I figured we can bring the dining-room table into one of the spare bedrooms and set up a temporary office there and—"

"No way." Chelsea pushed away from him. "Absolutely not. That's *crazy*—"

"It would only be temporary," he said. "Until you found office space in a better part of town."

Her voice rose. "Johnny . . . God! We can't afford to be in a better part of town."

"You can't afford *not* to be."

"I can't believe you would just go and call movers without even asking me."

His voice rose too. "I can't believe you're even *thinking* about staying here after what happened!"

"Well, I *am* thinking about it. And the more I think, the more I'm convinced that we have to stay. We have a lease. If we leave we'll be breaking the lease, and we'll not only have to pay a higher rent, but we'll be slammed with a lawsuit and forced to pay the rent on this place too. Not to mention all the time we'll waste searching for some mythical office that's both safe *and* affordable."

Johnny's eyes were bright with anger. "Money," he said. "That's what it always comes down to for you, Chelsea, doesn't it? What's it going to cost you? Well, let me tell you something, babe. There's no dollar amount in the world that's worth you risking your life for. If you get sued by this scumbag landlord, *I'll* pay. And *I'll* pay the difference between what you're paying now and the higher rent on a place with a doorman and real locks on the door. Jesus, in a year we're both going to have more money than we could spend in a lifetime! As far as I'm concerned, whether or not you should move your office was not a question that required any asking. You're outta here, as of today. I don't give a damn what your landlord says, or even what *you* say, for that matter."

Chelsea couldn't believe what she was hearing. "I'm not going anywhere, so you can just call those movers back." She looked around, suddenly aware of the police officers and the window repair crew who were listening with unabashed curiosity. "This is obviously not the time to discuss this," she said icily.

Johnny was furious, and the sudden appearance of the Ice Princess didn't help calm him any. "When will it be time to discuss it?" he asked. "After the next guy with a gun breaks in and this time blows a hole in your head?"

"I will not talk about this now." She stalked haughtily back toward her office, and he caught up with her, pushing open her office door and holding it for her.

"You want privacy? Fine. Let's go in here, close the door, and talk about how much of your precious money you plan to spend on security to make this place safe enough." Johnny closed the door behind her, watching as she stiffly moved to stand with her arms folded across her chest, staring out the window. "Let's talk about the fact that this guy didn't stumble in here in the middle of the night. Let's talk about the fact that it was ten o'clock in the morning when he held that gun in your face."

She turned to face him and her eyes were cold, her expression carefully distanced. "I'm sorry, this decision is not yours to make," she said icily. "It's my decision, and I'm not going anywhere."

Johnny wanted to scream. Didn't she know that just the thought of her coming back here to work tomorrow made him sick to his stomach? Didn't she know that the fear he'd felt when he'd first seen that yellow tape was not something he could just forget overnight? Didn't she know that he loved her more than any dollar amount, more than his own life? "Wanna make a bet? I already made the decision—the movers are on their way."

Two bright spots of pink appeared on Chelsea's cheeks, but she covered her anger with a thick layer of frost and spoke more softly rather than shouting. "Your name's not on this lease along with mine—"

"No, but my name's on a marriage license along with yours." It was the wrong thing to say. Johnny knew that it was the wrong thing to say, but once he started he couldn't seem to stop. "You're my wife, and I *will not* allow you to come here anymore. Why am I even bothering to talk to you about this? This is *not* a topic that is open for discussion."

The Ice Princess facade wavered, then crumbled as Chelsea's anger became too strong to hide. "You won't *allow* me to stay?"

"Damn straight."

"Just because you think you're my husband, you're ordering me to just pack up and run away—"

"I don't just *think* I'm your husband. I *am* your husband."

"Like hell you are." She was shaking, she was so mad. "Get out."

"I'm not going anywhere. I'm waiting for the truck, remember?"

Her movements jerky, Chelsea gathered up her purse and jacket, her laptop and her briefcase and started for the door. "Fine. Then I'll get out. You'll hear from my lawyer. This stupid game has gone far enough."

"Oh, so now it's a stupid game?"

She turned to glance at him over her shoulder as he followed her quickly down the hall, out of the office, and onto the side-walk. "Marriage has always been a stupid game. And I was a fool to think you'd play by smarter rules."

"Smarter rules. *Your* rules, you mean. What about *my* rules? What about what *I* need?"

There were tears in her eyes as she lifted her hand to hail a cab. "You need my money. And my father's money. Don't look so surprised. Did you really think I didn't know he'd sweetened our deal? Between the two of us, you'll have enough for your restaurant. That's all you really want, anyway."

And just like that Johnny's anger was deflated. "Is that really what you think?"

A taxi pulled to a stop in front of her.

"I can't talk to you right now," Chelsea said with a sob, opening the cab door. "I have to go home."

"Let me drive you."

"No." She closed the door.

He leaned in the window. "Chelsea, we need to talk more. If you think all I need is that money, then we have to—"

"Go," Chelsea told the driver.

The taxi pulled away, taking with it Johnny's heart.

His condo was as silent as a tomb. Johnny knew before he even shut the door behind him that Chelsea wasn't there.

She'd gone home. To *her* place. *Her* home.

Dammit, he'd handled that all wrong.

After Chelsea had left he'd called and canceled the movers. He wanted her to move, but now that his anger had faded, he knew that making demands and doing it against her will was not the way to go. She had to make the decision to move on her own, not have it forced down her throat.

Johnny picked up the phone and dialed her number in Brookline. No answer. He was about to leave a message on her machine when he heard the sound of a key in the lock.

As he hung up the phone the front door opened, and Chelsea came in. She was dressed in jeans and a T-shirt, her hair back in a ponytail. She looked like a teenager, sweet and impossibly young. She stopped short at the sight of him, glancing quickly at her watch.

"No," he said. "You're right. It's after five. I'm supposed to be at work."

She was clearly ill at ease. "I just, um . . ." She moistened her lips. "I wanted to get my stuff."

Johnny felt his heart break. "That's it? You're just gonna pack up your things and leave?"

"This whole thing was such a big mistake, and—" She turned back to the door. "I don't want to talk, John. Not now. You're already late for work—"

"I went in earlier," he told her quietly. "I got everything set up and ready to go. I told Rudy I needed the night off—to try to save my marriage."

She looked up at him at that, her eyes bruised looking in the paleness of her face. "Johnny—"

"I know. You don't want to talk. You don't have to talk—you just have to listen, okay?"

"I heard more than enough this morning," she said softly.

"No, you didn't. You heard too much and too little, all at the same time. Chelsea, look, I know I was wrong to make the demands I did." He held her gaze steadily, praying that she would believe him. "I said some things I shouldn't have, I went a little crazy on you, and I'm sorry about that. But I need you to give me a chance to explain why finding office space in a safer part of town is so important to me."

Johnny took a deep breath. So far, so good. So far she was listening, and that's all that he could ask. He glanced at Chelsea's watch, reading the time upside down and backward. It was five-fifteen. The timing was perfect. He couldn't have planned this better if he'd tried. "I'd like to show you something," he continued. "Will you go for a ride with me?"

But Chelsea was shaking her head no, opening the door, about to walk out of his life, maybe forever. "I can't."

"Please," he said. "Chelsea, I heard you out. That day you asked me to marry you? I could've walked away from you, but I didn't. I listened to what you had to say. All I'm asking is for you to give me the same chance."

She closed her eyes in defeat. "Oh, God." She took a deep breath and looked up at him. "I'll give you fifteen minutes."

Johnny nodded. "That's all I need."

Chelsea sat in the front seat of Johnny's VW Bug. "Where are we?"

"We're in a part of Boston you've probably never been to before," he told her with a wry smile. "We're a few blocks away from the Projects. This is where I grew up."

Chelsea gazed out the window. The dreaded Projects. Funny, she'd always imagined a bombed-out, burned-down landscape with deserted buildings and trash in the streets. But this neighborhood was nice. There were flowers growing in window boxes, the sidewalks were swept, and a carefully tended playground where children played and laughed was nestled between two apartment buildings.

Johnny pulled over to the side of the road, squeezing the little car into a tiny parking spot. "I can't come down here without thinking about my mother," he continued. He got out of the car and came around to open Chelsea's door. "She was an advocate against urban violence. She was one of the leading forces in the community pride program too."

He led her down the sidewalk, toward the corner, where they stood, waiting for the light to change. "She started all kinds of neighborhood watch programs, and cleanup programs, and afterschool programs. She helped clean out the basement of her health clinic and turn it into a rec center for teenagers. I spent a lot of time there myself."

The traffic slowed before the walk light came on, and Johnny stepped out into the street. Chelsea hurried across after him, wondering if her nervousness at being in this part of the city showed. Didn't drive-by shootings happen down here regularly?

But Johnny didn't seem to notice her nervousness. He was still talking about his mother. "But there was one program she started that she wished to God she hadn't had to set up. They had their first meeting more than fifteen years ago, and they're still meeting once every two weeks, here at the church."

Chelsea looked up and realized she was climbing the steps that led up to the front doors of a stately-looking brick church.

Johnny fell silent as he opened the door for her and they went inside. She followed him down a flight of stairs to the cool mustiness of a church basement. He led her down a long, dimly lit hallway, where there were a number of little darkened Sunday-school rooms off to either side. She could hear voices coming from a room way down at the end, but that room, too, seemed dark.

As they approached the double doors she saw that the room

was quite large. The overhead lights had been turned on only for the far side of the room, creating an area of light bordered by the late-afternoon dimness.

A group of about thirty people sat in a circle illuminated by that light. One of them was speaking as the others listened. The mood was solemn and the tone of the voice speaking was sad.

Chelsea stood next to Johnny, in the shadows. "What is this?" she whispered.

"It's a support group for people who've lost a child or a parent or a spouse to urban violence," he whispered. "Listen, okay?"

"I should have been home," a woman was saying, her voice tearful. "Or I should have somehow taught her not to open the door for anyone. Not for *anyone*. I should have spent more time with her, teaching her things like that. And I keep thinking about all those times I was too tired or too busy or too wrapped up in figuring out how to pay the bills to play with her. I keep thinking about all those times that I didn't take the time to give her a hug and tell her how much I loved her. . . ."

"I think that's something we all feel," another woman said, her voice stronger, clearer than the first. "This sense of wasted opportunity, this sense of wishing we'd been a little more aware of how precious life is, and how quickly it can be taken from us. I think we all wish we had one more chance to tell our loved ones that they were, indeed, loved."

A man spoke up. "My wife was killed four years ago by a car being chased by the cops. As I was watching her casket being placed into the ground, I couldn't remember the last time I told her that I loved her. I tried, but I just couldn't remember. It may well have been years. And I remember thinking, sweet Jesus, I'll never have another chance. So now I tell our daughter and son how very much I love them every single day. And I like to believe that somewhere up in heaven, LaRae can hear me." He laughed, but it was laughter filled with sorrow. "She always did have good ears, that woman. I like to believe she knows I'm talking to her too."

"I love you, Chelsea," Johnny whispered.

Startled, she turned to look at him. Despite the shadows, she could see the shine of tears in his eyes.

He tried to smile. "That's why I want you to move your office out of that part of town," he told her softly. "That's why it's so important to me that you're safe. I know damn well that you could've died today, and then I would've spent the rest of my life sitting in a group like this one, filled with regret that I never told you that I love you."

He loved her. Johnny Anziano *loved* her.

"Oh, my God," she said, forgetting to be quiet, and across the room, a number of heads turned toward them.

"May I help you?" one of the women called out.

"No," Johnny said. "No, thank you. I'm sorry we disturbed you."

"Johnny Anziano, is that you?" another woman asked.

"Yeah," he said. "How are you, Mrs. Samuels?"

"It's Dr. Anziano's boy," Mrs. Samuels told the others. "Who's that with you, Johnny?"

"This is my wife. Her name is Chelsea," Johnny told them.

"Your *wife*!" a man called out. "Congratulations, young man!"

"Thanks, Mr. Hart."

"What are you doing out this way?"

Johnny hesitated. "I wanted to . . . show Chelsea the church."

"The sanctuary's open, sweetie," Mrs. Samuels said. "Just go on up."

"Thanks, Mrs. S. Sorry to interrupt your meeting."

Chelsea let Johnny lead her out of the room and up a flight of stairs. He loved her. He *loved* her. "Everybody knew you." Somehow her voice sounded normal when she spoke. How had she managed to do that?

"About ten years ago I was tapped to join a gang," Johnny told her, "and when my mother found out, she made me sit in on these meetings. Needless to say, it was an eye-opener."

Johnny opened a set of doors and they stepped into the church.

The late-afternoon sun was shining through the stained-glass windows, giving the sanctuary an otherworldly, shimmering glow.

She followed him down the aisle and up toward the altar.

"I always thought if I ever got married, I'd be married here, in this church," Johnny said. Even though he spoke softly, his voice seemed to echo in the stillness.

He turned to look at her then. The ghostly light cast shadows, but even they couldn't disguise his face—a face she'd come to know so very well over the past few short weeks. His eyes were lazily hooded, as ever, and, as ever, they seemed to gleam with an intensity that was far from lazy.

"I don't want to join one of those support groups, Chelsea," he told her. "I don't want to sit in that circle and cry while I talk about losing my wife. I know I said some things to you this afternoon that I shouldn't have. You're right. Even though you're my wife, even though we're married, I don't have the right to tell you what you can or can't do. But I do have the right to ask. So I'm asking. Please, *please* move your office to a better part of town. I'll beg, if you want. I'll crawl if that'll make you understand how important this is to me. I need to know you're as safe as you can possibly be."

Chelsea couldn't speak. Her heart was in her throat.

"I know you were surprised when I told you that I love you." He cleared his throat. "And I don't have a clue what you're thinking, but don't freak out, because I know that falling in love wasn't part of our deal, and I know that you're in this marriage thing for only a year, and I swear, I'd never hold you to anything more, and even if you don't want to stay with me, I'm not going to take that money from your father and . . . Okay, now I'm babbling." He took a deep breath. "At least tell me you forgive me."

"I forgive you," she whispered. "Promise you'll try not to do it again?"

He nodded, tears again gleaming in his eyes. "Please," he said again. "Let me help you move your office somewhere safer. Please, Chels. If you care for me even just a little bit . . ."

"I do," she said. "I will. Move the office. But I *will* need your help—"

He stepped toward her. "You know you've got it. I promise."

"What I really want you to promise me . . ." Chelsea had to stop and blink back her own tears. "Promise me you'll love me forever."

She saw disbelief flash in Johnny's eyes. "Do you want me to?"

"Yes," she whispered. "More than anything."

The disbelief turned to sheer joy. He laughed aloud, then raised his voice so his words rang out in the church. "Then, yes, I promise."

"For richer or poorer?"

Johnny held out his hand to her, again letting his words echo. "I do promise."

"For better or for worse?" She slipped her hand into his, and it felt like coming home.

The look in his eyes was one she'd seen there before. When she'd woken up in the middle of the night and found him gazing down at her, when he thought she didn't see him watching her from across the room—that was love she'd seen in his eyes. He truly loved her.

"I do," he told her.

"In sickness and in health?"

"Yes. For as long as we both shall live," he said.

"I love you, Johnny," Chelsea said. She smiled at him through her tears. "I think you better kiss the bride."

Johnny was nervous. He knew he shouldn't be. He knew he held the upper hand, along with the element of surprise.

He stood up as Howard Spencer came briskly out into the waiting area.

"Why don't you come on back into my office," the older man said, leading the way to a huge corner office with a gorgeous view of downtown Boston that was almost as good as the view from Johnny's condo. "I have the contracts all drawn up for you to sign."

Johnny waited until Mr. Spencer had closed the door behind him. "Actually, Mr. Spencer, I have no intention of signing your contracts, because I have no intention of taking your bribe. As a matter of fact, I came here today to tell you that your daughter and I have come to a new agreement. We've removed the end date from our relationship and hope to have as long and as happy a marriage as you and Julia have had."

Howard Spencer was not the kind of man who sputtered, but he was as close to sputtering now as he ever had been.

"Also—for your information—I've made Chelsea sign an addendum to our prenupt, saying the financial deal's off. I made her sign an agreement saying that her money is her money, and my money is *our* money." Johnny smiled. "I know, I know, you're thinking, if she ever leaves me, I'm going to get royally screwed, but you know what, Mr. S.?"

Howard Spencer seemed unable to respond.

"She's never going to leave me. I'm going to do my damnedest to see that Chelsea stays madly in love with me for the rest of our lives. Because I love her that much. Look at me and read my lips, Mr. S. I love your daughter. There's no amount of money in the world that would make me walk away from her. I'm going to make her happy—and that's what you want for her, right? For her to be happy? Nod your head. Yes."

Howard Spencer managed to nod his head. Yes.

Johnny smiled again. "Then I'm your man. We're on the same team now, Howie."

He turned to leave, but then turned back. "Oh, I almost forgot." He lowered his voice conspiratorially. "This conversation? And the one we had previously? They never happened."

Johnny walked out of the office, but then stuck his head back in the door. "One more thing. Chelsea and I would love for you and Julia to join us for dinner Friday night—in Lumière's private dining room. Chelsea tells me you haven't had any luck getting a reservation for the private room—I don't know why. But from now on, when you call, tell 'em you're Johnny Anziano's father-in-law." He winked. "*That'll* get you in."

epilogue

CHELSEA COULDN'T BELIEVE WHAT SHE'D
found.

She'd been looking for a spare book of stamps in Johnny's
desk, thinking if she found one, she wouldn't have to pull on her
boots and trudge out into the snow, shovel out her car, and drive
through the slushy streets to the post office vending machines.

She hadn't meant to pry. But the envelope was right there,
top slit open, sitting next to the computer. The return address
said it was from the International Culinary Institute in Paris.

Johnny had told her he'd get a response to his application
for the Paris study program by December. And it was definitely
December.

Chelsea picked up the envelope and held it up to the light,
which of course revealed nothing. She put the envelope down
and picked up the phone, pressing the speed dial for Lumière's.

Johnny answered on the fifth ring. "Anziano."

"Hi," Chelsea said. She held the envelope up to her nose and
smelled it. It smelled like paper. "Are you busy?"

"For you? Never. Well, almost never. What's up?"

"That's what I was going to ask you," Chelsea said, tapping
the envelope on the edge of his desk. "What's up?"

Johnny laughed. "Didn't *you* call *me*?"

"Yes, but, I was just..." Chelsea sighed. "We've both been so busy lately, we haven't had as much time to talk, and..."

"Well, let's see. Jean-Paul's wife is pregnant again—have I told you that?"

"Yes," Chelsea said. "Yes, I think you mentioned that last week." She tapped the envelope on her teeth.

"Your father called me again—he wants to back me in whatever kind of restaurant I want to open."

"Don't even *think* about—"

"I made polite, vague noises. Don't worry about that. Let's see.... You knew that my latest tofu recipe was getting a huge write-up in *Vegetarian Times*. I saw the article today—it's *great*. I'll bring it home for you. They're calling me the 'Tofu Gourmet.' There's been a huge demand for the dish here at the restaurant—I just wish tofu weren't so damn *ugly*. But that's all I can think of. Nothing else is new. Hang on a sec." There was a pause, and Chelsea heard muffled voices, as if Johnny had put his hand over the mouthpiece of the phone. "I'm sorry, Chelsea, I gotta go. I'll try to get home early tonight, okay?"

"Johnny—"

"I love you, Chels."

"Wait!"

But he'd already hung up.

Chelsea slowly put the handset back in the cradle of the telephone and looked at the envelope she was still holding. Nothing else was new?

She couldn't help herself. She pulled the letter out and opened it and...

Dear God, he'd been accepted.

She skimmed the page, then went back and read the next-to-last paragraph. Dear God, he'd not only been accepted, but he'd been asked to *give* a seminar on his new specialty—gourmet cooking with tofu. It was an honor beyond compare.

The letter was dated October 25. Even if it had been sent via surface mail, Johnny must have gotten it weeks ago. Longer.

Yet he'd said nothing about it to her.

Feeling a total sneak, Chelsea turned on Johnny's computer and accessed his word-processing program. It didn't take her long to skim his list of files and find one labeled Paris.ICI. She clicked on the job and, saying a silent pray asking forgiveness from the God of Nosiness, opened it.

> *Dear Admissions Committee,*
> *It was with great pride that I received your letter requesting my presence as part of your Paris study program this May. And it is with great regret that I inform you that I am unable to attend for the full three months. I understand that—*

Chelsea clicked out of the job. She'd seen enough.

Unable to attend. Regret.

Oh, God, Johnny was turning down the chance of a lifetime—because of her.

Oh, God, this was her worst nightmare come true. There was no way she could leave Spencer/O'Brien Software in May for three months.

But it didn't matter anymore. He'd turned the opportunity down. Without even *talking* to her.

Chelsea turned off Johnny's computer and went to pull on her snow boots.

Johnny was preparing the fourteenth order that afternoon for his tofu dish when Chelsea burst into the kitchen.

"I need to talk to you. Now." She then added the word they'd promised each other they'd always use, even when they were upset. "Please."

Johnny nodded to Philippe, who took over his pan of sautéing vegetables. "Let's go into my office," he said, but she was already heading there. What had he done? He couldn't think of a single thing. Maybe it had something to do with that weird phone call she'd made just a little while ago. He closed the door behind him. "Are you mad at me?"

"Yes, I'm mad. And I'm hurt, and upset, and disappointed and sad and—"

"What? Why? Chelsea, wait a sec, I'm clueless here. What's this about?"

She smacked him in the chest with an envelope. Johnny fumbled, but caught it before it hit the ground. He recognized it immediately.

"How could you not talk to me about this?" Chelsea looked ready to cry. "How could you just turn down their offer without even telling me?"

"How do you know I turned down their offer?"

"I searched for your return letter on your computer." She was too upset to be embarrassed.

Johnny had to laugh. "But you didn't read the whole thing, did you?"

"I read all that I needed to."

Johnny pulled her into his arms. "Chels, if you're going to be nosy, don't be nosy halfway—or you'll get only half the story. The letter I faxed them said that *at this time* I couldn't stay the full three months, but I proposed that I attend for a few weeks to give the seminar they requested. I asked if I could postpone taking part in the full three-month program until next year. I'm waiting for their response."

She looked sheepishly up at him. "I didn't read that far."

He kissed her. "No kidding."

"Johnny, why didn't you tell me about any of this?"

"I was waiting to hear back from ICI before I told you. It seems like a good compromise, don't you think?"

"What if ICI says it's now or never?"

Johnny shrugged. "By May, you'll have the money from your trust. You can fly me home for weekends—I don't know. We'll figure something out."

"We can compromise," Chelsea said. "You can fly home for some weekends, I can fly to Paris for others. We can definitely make this work."

As Johnny gazed into Chelsea's ocean-blue eyes he knew she was right. Together, with compromise, they were unstoppable.

Johnny smiled, and then kissed his wife.

Time Enough
for Love

For my Gram & Gramps, Fred and
Tilly Brockmann, on their 68th
wedding anniversary, with all my love.

---

one

THERE WAS A NAKED MAN POUNDING ON
Maggie Winthrop's back door.

She did a double take as she looked out her kitchen window
and realized that he was covered with dirt, as if he'd been crawling around in her garden. Dirt and . . . could that possibly be
blood? Streaks of something that looked like blood were on his
shoulder and arm. He was wild-eyed, with dark, shaggy hair
that exploded around his face, looking as if he'd just been ejected
from a wind tunnel.

And yes, he was definitely, undeniably naked.

Somehow he knew her name. "Maggie!" he shouted, ham-
mering on the door. "Mags, let me in!"

It was locked, thank God, and Maggie ran to be sure the
front door was locked as well.

She had her cordless phone in her hand, ready to call the police when he called out again.

"Maggie! God, please be home!" There was such anguish in
the man's voice. Anguish and something that stopped her from
dialing the phone. Something oddly familiar.

Maggie took the stairs to the second floor of her house two
at a time. She set the phone down on the vanity of the sink as she

used both hands to open the bathroom window and push up the screen.

The man heard the noise, and he stopped pounding on the door. He looked up at her expectantly as she peered down at him.

"Maggie." There was such relief in the way he said her name. But despite the strange flash of familiarity that she felt once again, she didn't recognize him. The naked man was a total stranger.

Maggie definitely would have remembered meeting a man like this one before—even *with* his clothes on.

He was tall and almost sinfully well built, all hard muscles and not an extra ounce of fat on him anywhere. And in his current state of undress, she had an extremely accurate view of all of his anywheres. He had extremely broad shoulders and powerful-looking arms. He had one of those sexy washboard stomachs leading down into narrow hips, a perfect butt, and lean, long legs.

He had thick dark brown hair that he now ran his fingers through, taming it somewhat as he pushed it back from his face. He had dark hair on his chest and other places as well.

Maggie hurriedly brought her gaze back up to his face. His nose was gracefully shaped with almost elegant nostrils. His cheekbones were prominent, too, as was the firm set of his jaw and chin. He had a scar on his cheekbone, underneath his left eye, making him look faintly dangerous. But it was his dark brown eyes that held her attention. They seemed to burn her with their intensity and fire.

Without question, he was the most gorgeous naked madman she'd ever come face-to-face with. Not that she'd come face-to-face with many madmen, clothed or otherwise, in her life.

"It's me," he told her, holding out his arms as if that would make her recognize him. "Chuck."

"I'm sorry," she said. "But . . . I don't know you."

He stared at her, confusion in his eyes. "You don't?"

"Maybe you have the wrong house," she suggested hopefully.

The man shook his head. "No. Maybe I have the wrong—" He interrupted himself. "What's the date?"

"Thursday, November twentieth."

"No, the year. What's the *year?*"

She told him.

He swore sharply, clearly upset, and Maggie reached behind her for the telephone, ready to dial 911 at the least little eruption of violence.

"The damned prototype overshot my mark by three years," he muttered, talking more to himself than to her as he paced back and forth on her patio. His words didn't make sense, but he was insane. His words weren't *supposed* to make sense. "Okay. Okay. So here I am. Better early than late."

As Maggie watched he took a deep breath and seemed to pull himself together then looked up at her again.

"I'm Chuck Della Croce," he introduced himself. "And you don't know me, and . . . I'm naked." There was a flash of chagrin in his eyes, as well as something that might have been amusement. "God, talk about making a good first impression."

"Is there someone you want me to call to come and get you?" Maggie asked, trying to remember what she knew about insanity. Was she supposed to back slowly away, speak softly, and keep from looking directly into his eyes? Or was that what she was supposed to do if she encountered a wild animal? Something about this man was wild, that much was for sure.

The man shook his head, again trying to tame his hair, combing it back with his fingers. "No, I'm right where I want to be." He snorted. "Give or take three years." He took another deep breath. "I could sure use a pair of pants, though." He seemed to notice the gash on his shoulder for the first time, along with the dirt that covered him, and he swore again, softly this time. "And maybe the use of your garden hose to wash up?"

Maggie hesitated.

"Please?" he added, gazing up at her.

What *was* it about him...?

"I don't think I have any pants that will fit you," she told him. "But I'll look. And yes. Use the hose. It's in the—"

"I know where the hose is, Mags." Sure enough, he seemed to know that the hose and the spigot it was attached to was inside the little garden shed built onto the side of her house.

Maggie felt a chill run up her spine. How did he know that the hose was there instead of outside, the way it was for most houses? And how did he know her name?

Mail. He could have checked her mail. Or looked in the phone book. There were a zillion ways he could have learned her name. And she'd used the hose to water her fig tree just the night before, after the searing southwestern sun had set. He could have been watching. He might well have been watching for days.

The thought was a creepy one, and she shivered again as she shut and locked the window. Why was she doing this? She should just call the police and have this man removed from her yard. There was surely some Phoenix city ordinance that prohibited people from walking around naked in other people's yards.

She carried the phone with her as she went into the guest bedroom and opened the closet door. The small space was jammed with boxes of Christmas ornaments and Halloween decorations and a rack of clothing that she couldn't bring herself to throw out. But there was nothing inside that would fit a tall, solidly built man.

Maggie had a muscle or two herself from taking long bike rides around the city, but at five feet two, she was seriously height-challenged. She bought her clothes from the petite rack at the store. No, nothing she owned would even begin to cover the handsome, naked, extremely tall madman in her backyard.

Her bathrobe. That might at least cover him. Of course, it was pink with little flowers on the lapels. A friend had bought it for her, as a kind of a joke. Maggie was not and never had been the pink-with-little-flowers type. She would be embarrassed even to show it to him.

Still, it was the only thing she had that would fit him.

And hey. He was crazy. Maybe he'd like it.

Unless . . .

Maggie quickly pulled one of the boxes down from the shelf. It was the wrong box, but there were only two others marked CHRISTMAS, so she knew she didn't have far to search.

She found what she was looking for in the second box she took from the closet.

A Santa Claus suit. Huge red pants with a drawstring waist and a red jacket with fluffy white trim and a black plastic belt sewn directly onto it.

It was big enough, that was for sure.

She carried it back to the bathroom window. Out in the yard, Chuck What's-his-name had somehow hooked the hose to the old clothesline. He'd also managed to make the water come out in a spray. He stood underneath it, as if it were a shower, water streaming onto his head and down his face. The water made his muscles glisten and shine.

Maggie felt like some kind of voyeur, watching him like that. She was grateful her yard was enclosed by solid wooden fencing and that none of her immediate neighbors in this little Phoenix development had more than a single-story house. No one could see the naked man taking a shower in her backyard.

Except for her.

He opened his eyes and looked directly up at her—catching her staring at him.

Quickly, she turned away from the window, rummaging through her linen closet for one of her older towels. She found one that was worn and tossed it down, directly onto the center of the sun-blistered picnic table on her patio. She tossed the Santa suit down too.

"Thanks." He grabbed the towel as he moved to shut off the water.

Maggie tried not to watch him as he dried himself, but it proved impossible. She had to move away from the window and gaze up at the bathroom ceiling to keep herself from staring.

What *was* it about this guy? she found herself wondering again. The man was matter-of-factly casual about his nakedness, but so would she be, if she were as physically fit as he was.

"Hey, Maggie?"

She peeked out the window, relieved to see that he had pulled on the bright red pants and tied the drawstring around his waist. They were baggy and much too short, but at least they covered him.

He was holding the Santa jacket up, looking at it with barely concealed horror.

"Don't you have a T-shirt I can borrow?" he asked her. "I'm going to roast if I have to put this on."

Actually, she had a number of oversized T-shirts that she wore to bed as nightshirts. "Hang on," she told him, and carefully closing and locking the window, she went into her bedroom. She grabbed one of her T-shirts from her drawer. On second thought, she took a comb from the top of her dresser as well.

He was sitting on the edge of the picnic table, drumming the fingers of both hands on the rough wood, waiting for her when she returned to the bathroom window. She tossed down the T-shirt and comb, and again, he thanked her politely.

He was clean now, and while the lack of dirt and blood made him look slightly less certifiable, the Santa pants took him well in the opposite direction.

But as he ran the comb through his dark hair, he looked up at her again and his eyes were clear and sharp. "Will you take a walk over to the park with me?" he asked. "I'd like to talk to you about—"

"I'm sorry," she cut him off. "I have to get back to work."

He saw right through her excuse. "We could go somewhere less deserted," he suggested. "That restaurant around the corner—you know, the place you like to go for Mexican food."

"Tia's?"

"Is that what it's called? The place that makes that killer black-bean soup?"

How did *he* know black-bean soup was her favorite? This was getting downright weird. "That's Tia's. But you'll never get in without shoes on."

"I'll improvise."

Still, Maggie shook her head. "I'm sorry, I really can't—"

"Look, you don't have to walk over there with me. I'll go first. You can meet me there in twenty minutes. In the bar. In public. I won't get near you. No tricks, I swear."

"Why do you need to talk to me so badly? And how do you know my name?"

Chuck Della Croce gazed up at her silently for a moment. Then he dropped his bomb.

"I'm from the future," he told her almost flatly, matter-of-factly. "And in the future, we're friends. I'm a time traveler, Mags, and I need your help to save the world."

Chuck watched as Maggie took a fortifying sip of her beer.

"Okay," she said. "All right." She pressed her palms flat against the table in the bar in Tia's restaurant, as if needing to feel the solidity of the wood beneath her hands. "Let me see if I've got this straight. I'm supposed to believe that you're some kind of a rocket-scientist genius type who's invented a time machine. Despite the fact that you look like some crazy, homeless guy wearing Santa pants, a Phoenix Film Marathon T-shirt, and ugly cardboard shoes."

Chuck glanced down at the cardboard and string sandals he'd made. He didn't think they were *that* bad—considering the choice of materials he'd had to work with.

"I'm supposed to believe that you've zipped back here in your little Runaround time-travel pod—"

"Runabout," he corrected her.

"—from seven years in the future, where you and I just happen to be friends."

She didn't believe him. Why should she believe him? Time travel. It seemed so science fiction. She was gazing at him with such cynical disbelief in her eyes, he couldn't help but smile.

He smiled as he hid his trembling hands, as he fought to keep these waves of emotion from overpowering him.

God, three hours ago, he hadn't thought he'd ever smile again. Three hours ago, the woman sitting across the table from him had bled to death in his arms. Three hours ago, she'd used her own body as a shield, taking bullets meant to kill *him*. Three hours ago, he'd escaped through the ventilation system in the Data Tech building, running for his life.

The pungent odor of gunpowder and blood still lingered in his nostrils despite the shower he'd taken underneath Maggie's garden hose. Boyd was dead. Maggie had seen Chuck's best friend and security chief take a bullet in the back of the head. She'd told him about it before she, too, had died. He was still shaking from all that he'd been through, all that he'd seen. Destruction of his lab. Death on a massive, global scale in the form of a bomb taking out the White House, and with it, the President of the United States. And death on a smaller, far more personal level too.

Chuck gazed at Maggie, shifting slightly in his seat, trying to rid himself of the disturbing memories of death on an extremely personal level. He took a deep breath.

None of that had happened yet. And he was here to make damn sure it wouldn't happen again. This time around was going to be different. He'd never tried to tamper with time before, not to this degree. He had no idea how easy or hard it was going to be. But easy or hard, it didn't matter. He was determined to set things right and keep innocent people from dying.

But for right now, all he wanted to do was gaze into Maggie's light brown eyes. He didn't care that they were filled with skepticism. He didn't care that one graceful eyebrow was lifted in disbelief. He'd expected as much from her. She was so straightforward, so honest and down-to-earth, he would have been surprised had she believed him without an argument.

Chuck was ready to argue with her all night, if she wanted. He didn't care. He just wanted to look at her. She was just so beautifully alive.

His hand was shaking as he picked up his mug of coffee, so he set it back on the table without taking a sip. He wanted to touch her hand, or the soft smoothness of her cheek, but he didn't dare.

She thought he was nuts.

"So if what you're saying is true, there's some kind of time machine—this Runabout thing—sitting in my backyard?"

Chuck shifted in his seat. "Actually, no—"

"No."

The look in her eyes made him want to laugh, but he was afraid if he started, he wouldn't be able to stop.

"Of course not," she continued. "Come on, tell me why it's not still there, and make it a really good one."

"I had to program the return jump in my lab, before I left, and since I knew this was going to be a one-way trip, I set it up to self-destruct," Chuck told her. "See, there's a long recharging delay between jumps. If the mechanism is engaged too soon, the device malfunctions, and the Runabout is destroyed."

"Of course," she said. "I should have known."

"It's the truth."

"It sounds like anything but. I mean, *really*, Chuck. You've traveled back in time because some evil government agents from some ridiculous-sounding organization—"

"Wizard-9," he supplied.

"Yeah. Right. These guys from Wizard-whatever got their nefarious hands on your time machine and managed to plant some kind of bomb in the White House that killed the president and his entire staff, including the Speaker of the House, in order to trigger a political coup." When she said it that way, it sounded like the bad plot of a comic book.

"The coup is just my theory. I didn't stick around long enough to find out if I was right."

"So you've come back in time to stop yourself from developing time travel, in order to prevent this assassination. Have I left anything out?"

"That's about it in a nutshell," he told her.

"Why not just go back in time and warn the people at the White House about the bomb? Why stop the entire project before it even starts?"

He answered her gravely, as if her question were serious. "I figured if I did only that, the door through time would still be left open. This way, the problem of unauthorized time tampering is solved once and for all."

Chuck had actually considered going back to his childhood, back before the time when the idea of time travel first flashed into his head. But he couldn't be sure that a change made that far in his past would be enough to alter his entire future. He knew he had only one shot, and he had to be damn well certain it would work.

Maggie sat back in her chair. "Meanwhile, while all this was happening in Metropolis, Superman couldn't do anything to stop the evil Wizard-9 agents, because he had been struck down by a bullet made of kryptonite."

Chuck had to laugh. "I'd almost forgotten how sarcastically funny you used to be."

"What, I'm not as funny seven years from now?"

He couldn't quite meet her gaze, unwilling to tell her the truth. He realized he was nervously drumming his fingers on the table and he forced himself to stop, to sit calmly, without moving.

She leaned forward. "Come on, Futureman. What am I like seven years from now? Does my freelance-writing business finally earn enough to pay my mortgage? Do I move into one of those big houses on Camelback Mountain? Do I have any kids? A rich, handsome husband? No, wait a sec. Don't tell me. *You're* my husband, right?"

"Wrong." He looked across the table at her. She was incredibly pretty, but she didn't know it. She'd probably never know it.

Her hair was brown and from a distance it seemed to be nothing special. It was only up close that one could see that it hung in shining waves around her face, long and thick and glistening. Her eyes, too, were an average shade of brown, but they sparkled and danced when she smiled and laughed. Her face was long, with a delicate cleft in her chin, her jaw strong and almost square. Her nose turned up very slightly at the end.

She was gorgeous in a girl-next-door kind of way, with a brilliant smile that could light up the darkest night.

She was funny and smart and sweet. And incredibly sexy.

He'd been wildly attracted to her from the very moment he'd first set eyes on her—seven years ago, his time. And she'd been attracted to him. It had happened this time around, too, despite the fact that she doubted his sanity. He could feel the familiar sexual pull, even now, each time she looked into his eyes.

If history was going to repeat itself, she would learn to hide that attraction from him, letting him see only friendly warmth in her eyes. But he was here to make sure that history *didn't* repeat itself.

"Two years from now you'll marry a man named Albert Ford," he finally told her. "An accountant. It won't work out. One of the last times we spoke, you told me you were waiting for the divorce papers to arrive. I think the whole thing was pretty nasty. So, yeah, it's been a while since you've made very many jokes."

Maggie stood up. "Well, this was more fun than I've had since the last time I played with my Magic Eight Ball."

He stood up, too, and Maggie felt a flare of panic. Shoot, she'd forgotten how big this guy was. When she'd come into the bar, he was already sitting down. But now he towered over her.

He sat down quickly, as if he could read the sudden fear in her eyes. "I'm sorry," he murmured. "I didn't mean to—"

"I have to go," she told him. It was the truth. She'd already lost more than an hour of her workday thanks to him, and she had a deadline to make, writing copy for an upscale landscaper's brochure. She should be thinking of ways to describe mulching and privacy shrubbery instead of wasting her time with incredible tales of presidential assassination and Wizard-9 agents told by a too-handsome escapee from a mental hospital.

She was a fool for coming in the first place. It was her attraction to this man that made her meet him here—and that made her an even bigger fool. What did she honestly think? That he was potential boyfriend material? A lunatic who walked around naked and thought he came from the future?

She'd never considered herself a particularly good judge of character when it came to men, but this situation was a no-brainer.

He was trying to hide his desperation the same way he'd tried to hide the fact that his hands were shaking. He was good at hiding things. When he spoke, his voice was calm, and when he looked up at her again, his manner was cool, almost distant. He'd even managed to lose some of the heat in his liquid brown eyes. "Maggie, what can I say to make you believe me? To make you stay?"

He was remarkably attractive with the restaurant's dim mood lighting casting shadows across his rugged features. He was good-looking despite the grim set to his mouth and the clenched tightness of his jaw.

It was funny, she'd never found the Clint Eastwood type of man so attractive before. She usually preferred a Tom Hanks. Sensitivity with a healthy dose of good humor usually won out over ominous, smoldering danger any day.

And this man sitting across from her *did* exude danger with the start of a five o'clock shadow darkening the lower half of his face, his damp longish hair swept back from his forehead, and blood from his wounded shoulder seeping through the thin cotton of his borrowed T-shirt. Fortunately, from where she was sitting, she couldn't see the Santa pants.

She pulled the strap of her handbag over her shoulder. "Well, you might've tried telling me that I'm going to win the lottery next year rather than all that doom and gloom about a failed marriage."

He shook his head. "But that wouldn't be true."

Maggie felt a flash of pity. Poor crazy guy. He actually believed all that he'd told her.

"I really have to go." She looked down at her half-empty glass of beer and his barely touched coffee. "I don't suppose you have the money to pay for this."

He looked embarrassed. "Not at this time, no. I used an early prototype to make the leap back. It was in my basement—the Wizard-9 agents didn't know about it. It was less sophisticated than the final version of the Runabout, and because of that I could take nothing with me—not even my clothes."

"Well, *there*'s a convenient explanation for why you were walking around naked." Maggie opened her purse, took a twenty-dollar bill from her wallet, and set it down on the table. "Keep the change, Nostradamus, all right?"

"I'll pay you back."

"Don't bother."

"I will. I'll bring it to you tomorrow."

His quiet words stopped her, and she turned to look back at him. "I'd rather you just stayed away from my house. In fact, if I see you again, I'm going to have to call the police and—"

"Then maybe I better warn you. We're going to meet for the first time in just a few days," he told her. "At Data Tech's Thanksgiving party."

Maggie took a step back toward him, startled. Data Tech. She'd recently signed a contract with Data Tech to write a prospectus for a public offering. And the ink on a second contract with the software giant—this one for editing an annual report—was barely dry. And she *had* received an invitation to the annual Thanksgiving party at Data Tech. She'd already decided to go to the Tuesday-night affair, to schmooze with her new clients and to sniff around and see if there were any other potential projects requiring her talents.

"You won't meet me," Chuck told her. "At least not exactly. You'll meet my younger self—Charles. Dr. Charles Della Croce."

"Your *younger* self..." Maggie had to laugh. "Of course. If you're from the future, then it stands to reason that there's another you—a younger you—running around somewhere."

He didn't crack a smile. "Look, I know this sounds crazy to you."

"Well, there you go," Maggie said. "We've finally agreed on something."

"I really need your help."

"Chuck, you need help—that's for *sure*, but I'm not the one who can give it to you." Silently she cursed herself for not just turning and walking away. Instead she sat down across from him again, knowing she was going to kick herself over and over as she was forced to work late into the night to make up for this lost time. "Let me make some phone calls, call a few friends, find you a doctor who can—"

His fingers started drumming impatiently on the table again. "Nostradamus," he said suddenly.

"Excuse me?"

Chuck realized he was doing it again. He was tapping his fingers, and he stilled them, consciously trying hard to rein in his impatience. "You called me Nostradamus," he told Maggie, gripping the edge of the table instead. "And you're right—I know your future. All I have to do is remember something...I don't know, some newsworthy event that happened after November twentieth this year."

Maggie closed her eyes as she pressed one hand against her forehead, as if she had a headache. She sighed and opened her eyes again. "I'm going to have to go," she said again. "I can't worry about where you're going to spend the night or what you're going to eat or—"

"There was a plane crash," Chuck suddenly remembered. "I think it was November. Yes—it was about a week before Thanksgiving. It hasn't happened yet, has it?"

Maggie threw her hands into the air. "Jeez, I don't know. Maybe. Where was it? A private plane went down a few days ago in the Rockies."

"No," Chuck said. "This was major. This was a commercial flight out of New York, heading to London. A terrorist's bomb went off when the plane came in for a landing. It was awful—hundreds of people died."

Maggie pushed back her chair and stood up, opening her purse one more time. "God knows I can't afford this, but..." She put another two twenties on the table. "Stay someplace warm tonight, Chuck. And think about getting some help."

He picked up the money and held it out to her. "Maggie, I don't need this. Honestly. I've got access to a bank account."

But Maggie was backing away. "Good-bye, Chuck."

"I'll be here at Tia's, every afternoon at this time." He didn't raise his voice to call after her, but it carried to her just the same. "If you change your mind, you can find me here in the bar."

Maggie pushed open the door and stepped out into the late-afternoon heat, resisting the urge to turn one last time and look back.

two

IT WAS AFTER FIVE O'CLOCK ON FRIDAY WHEN
Maggie finished her meeting with the Data Tech vice-presidents.
There were four of them, and each had had his own idea about
how the company's current prospectus should be written.

Working for more than one boss was a potential nightmare,
but she'd learned a long time ago simply to smile, nod, take
notes—and then write the darn thing the way *she* envisioned it.
She'd give each of them an individual call to tell them how she'd
incorporated their personal suggestions into her final draft.
With any luck, everyone would be happy.

More than one of the VPs had hinted that if this project
went well, she'd be offered a salaried position with the company.
After three years of self-employment, the thought of a steady
paycheck, employer-paid benefits, and scheduled vacations was
tempting.

The Data Tech headquarters was an easy commute from
her house. The company was a fairly affluent one, and it showed
in the design of the building. Tasteful Southwestern decor
graced the spacious three-story lobby, allowing office workers,
clients, and guests three different views of the magnificent metal

sculpture of a flock of birds taking flight that seemed to lift off from the lobby floor.

As Maggie joined the small crowd of people waiting for the elevator going down, she turned to look back at the sculpture. The people she'd met here were friendly and happy. She'd been told about a workout room in the basement, and that the food in the cafeteria was near gourmet quality. And salary raises were regular and generous. No, she wouldn't mind working here at all.

The elevator door slid open, and she turned to see that it was already crowded. Only a few people got on—there was no room for her.

The crowd shifted slightly, and then she saw him.

Chuck Della Croce. The gorgeous madman.

He was standing in the elevator, fully dressed in a respectable-looking business suit. His hair was shorter, his mouth less tight and grim, but it was him, wasn't it? He was facing her, and as she stared at him he briefly met her gaze.

There was nothing there. No flicker of awareness, no sign of recognition. Nothing.

Because it wasn't Chuck Della Croce. It was his "younger self," Charles. And this younger man hadn't met her yet.

The door closed, and he disappeared from view.

Of all the ridiculous, silly thoughts! Of *course* it wasn't Chuck Della Croce or even *Charles* Della Croce. It was simply someone who looked a lot like him.

She was losing it, big time. As if time travel really existed. As if she actually believed Chuck's delusional ravings.

Still, Maggie moved quickly to the railing and looked down into the lobby. As she watched, the tall dark-haired man who may or may not have been Charles Della Croce came out of the elevator and walked across the tile floor, past the flying birds, talking to another man.

Both men were pulling off their ties, and Chuck...

Charles—whoever he was—shrugged out of his jacket in preparation for heading out into the late-afternoon sunshine.

From this angle, this height, the top of his head sure looked familiar. Too bad he wasn't naked—that would have clinched it. If he hadn't been wearing his clothes, she would have known without a doubt whether or not this was the same man who'd pounded on her door the afternoon before.

And then he laughed at something the other man said. Maggie caught only the briefest profile of his face, but it was enough to make her heart nearly stop beating. Whoever he was, when he smiled like that, he was impossibly handsome.

As she watched, the man pushed open the heavy glass doors and headed toward the parking lot.

By the time Maggie reached the lobby herself, he was long gone, and she'd nearly succeeded in convincing herself that seeing this man was a mere coincidence. So this guy looked like her gorgeous madman. A lot of men did. The phrase *tall, dark, and handsome* hadn't become a cliché without reason.

Still, she couldn't keep herself from stopping at the main reception area. "Excuse me, is there a Charles Della Croce working here?"

The woman behind the reception desk keyed the name into her computer. "Yes," she said. "Dr. Della Croce. He's upstairs in research and development. Oops, I'm sorry—I see he's just left the building. Would you like to leave a message for him?"

But Maggie was already backing away. "No. No, thank you."

Okay. There had to be a reasonable explanation for this. Such as, the madman knew he looked like this scientist and had borrowed his persona. She knew nearly all there was to know about Data Tech, after all. Most of the work done in their R&D labs dealt with computer software, not time travel. In fact, there was no mention of time travel in any of the information Maggie had been given about the corporation.

She headed quickly out to the parking lot and unlocked her little car.

It had been sitting in the sun for hours, and the temperature inside was ovenlike. Maggie pulled down all the windows and turned the AC on full power as she headed onto the main road.

What if he were telling the truth?

The thought was a tiny one, but it niggled at the back of her mind obstinately.

He wasn't telling the truth, she told herself firmly. He was insane. And she would be, too, if she started believing him.

The air coming out of the vents was starting to feel cooler, so she closed the windows. She turned on the radio, too, determined not to think about anything at all until she got home. Then she'd think only about dinner. And after dinner, she'd finish up the copy for that landscaping brochure and—

"... reports now say that the airliner carrying over three hundred passengers went down around two A.M., London time, over the Atlantic." The normally ebullient country-station DJ sounded sober and solemn. "I repeat, World Airlines flight 450 from New York to London exploded in midair over the Atlantic Ocean around two o'clock this morning. There are believed to be no survivors."

She was only a block away from her house, but Maggie had to pull over to the side of the road. She could barely breathe despite the fact that the air conditioner had fully kicked in.

How could Chuck have known? Somehow he'd *known*....

"The investigating agencies have issued a short statement saying that the explosion was the result of a terrorist act. Apparently attempts were made to negotiate with the terrorists onboard. A tape of those conversations will be released at a later date."

Terrorists. A terrorist's bomb brought the plane down. Chuck had told her about it. He'd warned her. But she'd done nothing. She'd called no one.

And over three hundred people had died.

Maggie did a U-turn, tires squealing, heading for Tia's.

Chuck saw Maggie pull up outside of the restaurant. She was driving much too fast, and he knew she was here because she'd heard the news reports about Flight 450.

He went out on the sidewalk to meet her.

As he moved into the late-afternoon sunshine he was struck again, as he had been repeatedly since yesterday, by the sense of freedom he felt. For the first time in years he was able to go wherever he pleased without a pair of bodyguards watching his back.

"I tried to warn them," he told Maggie before she could say even a word. "I remembered it was World Airlines, and I called them right after you left last night, but the jet had already departed from Kennedy Airport. I was too late."

"How did you know?" she asked. There was suspicion in her eyes, and her face was almost ashen.

"I told you how I knew," he said quietly, aware that the clerk from the nearby convenience store had come out onto the sidewalk to have a cigarette and was eyeing them curiously. "Why don't you come inside, and I'll buy you a drink. You look as if you could use something."

She backed away from him. "You knew because you're one of them. You're one of the terrorists who planted that bomb."

"Oh, come on. You don't believe that. That's ridiculous."

"And your claim that you're a time traveler isn't . . . ?"

She did a double take then, as if really looking at him for the first time. The Santa Claus pants and makeshift sandals were gone. Her eyes were wide as she took in his jeans, his nearly brand-new polo shirt, and the expensive leather of the new cowboy boots he'd picked up just this morning. He knew he looked a lot different from the wild-eyed man who'd pounded on her door just over twenty-four hours ago.

"Where did you get those clothes?"

"I'm not a terrorist," he told her. "In fact, my phone call to World Airlines saved lives. The way it really happened—the way I remember it happening the first time around—the bomb didn't go off until the plane was coming in for a landing. It took out an entire terminal at Heathrow. Five hundred people on the ground died, as well as the three hundred and forty-two passengers on the plane."

"Where did you get those clothes?"

He could tell from the look in her eyes that she wasn't buying any of this. Okay. They'd start small. They'd start with his clothes.

"That was easy. I went home. To *Charles*'s home. I know where I used to hide the key, and his clothes are all my size—because I'm him. This shirt is a color I never liked—I won't miss it. The jeans I've already missed. I remember that I wondered what happened to them. See, there's this strange memory thing that happens when you change the past. You get something called residual memories and—"

"Just stop!" she said fiercely. "Stop with the time-travel crap. I want to know who you really are. I want to know the *truth*."

"Maggie, I swear, I've told you nothing but the truth."

Maggie spun away from him, heading toward the pay phone that was under the overhang of the convenience-store roof. "That's it. I'm calling the police."

He caught her arm. "Don't. Please. I didn't have anything to do with that plane crash. I was just trying to show you that I *am* from the future by telling you what was going to happen."

Maggie was scared. She didn't know what to think, what to do. She wanted this out of her hands. This man looked so normal, dressed in jeans and a casual faded-green polo shirt. His hair was neatly combed and his chin was smooth from a recent shave. He didn't look like any kind of a madman today. He looked like the kind of man who would stand out in a crowd—the kind of man she'd make an effort to meet face-to-face.

Well, she was face-to-face with him right now, all right.

"Let go of me or I'll scream," she whispered.

"Two more days," Chuck said. His gaze was steady but no less intense as he looked into her eyes. "Please, Mags. Give me just two more days to change your mind."

She shook her head. "Two days isn't going to make a difference in the way I feel."

"Yes, it will. I remembered something else that happened. The news came just two days after the reports of the downed jet."

She closed her eyes. "Oh, please, don't tell me anyone else is going to die—"

"Not if I can help it," he told her. "I already called the seismology center in California, telling them to release a warning. There's going to be an earthquake—a pretty bad one. The epicenter's in Whittier. The reports should be coming in right about this time on Sunday." He smiled then, a slight twisting of his lips. "Even *you*'ve got to admit that there's no way I could be responsible for an earthquake."

Maggie stood in her living room, staring at the television.

An earthquake. The TV news anchors were reporting an earthquake, just the way the madman had said. *Exactly* the way he had said.

The epicenter *was* in Whittier. The quake registered a 6.2 on the Richter scale.

Amazingly, the news anchors reported, as far as they knew at this point, no one had been killed or even badly injured. Apparently, an unidentified caller had predicted the quake. Since this was California, they said with a smile, and conditions for an earthquake had been right, the caller had been taken seriously enough for them to use the emergency broadcast system to warn the city's residents.

Oddly enough, the call was traced to a pay phone in downtown Phoenix, Arizona, of all places.

Maggie slowly sat down, right in the middle of her living-room floor.

She'd spent the entire weekend trying to work, but barely able to. She'd kept coming back to the TV and the news reports of the plane crash. To the pictures of the people who had lost their lives when the terrorists' bomb had gone off.

But now the screen was filled with live video footage taken during the earthquake.

The madman had accurately predicted the future not once but twice.

The madman very likely wasn't mad at all.

The telephone rang. Maggie wasn't a time traveler from the future herself, but she knew exactly who was on the other end.

She crawled across the carpeting to her coffee table and pressed the mute button on the remote control as she picked up her cordless phone.

"Where are you?" she asked. "We need to talk."

"I'm at Tia's," Chuck's soft baritone voice told her. "I was hoping you'd let me come by."

Maggie looked at the soundless pictures of the earthquake's destruction on the TV. A road had been nearly ripped in half, the blacktop crumpled and folded.

"I'd rather meet you at the restaurant," she told him.

He didn't hesitate. "Fair enough. I'll get a table for dinner."

"Order me a tequila," Maggie said. "I think I'm going to need one."

"I called it the Wells Project," Chuck said.

"As in H. G. Wells?"

He nodded. "Yeah. I'd been working on the theory for years—literally since I was a kid. But it wasn't until a little more than three years from now that I came up with the breakthrough equation.

"I got approval from Data Tech to run with it, but when the time came to actually build the Runabout, we had to look outside the company for funding." He frowned down at the last of the refried beans that remained on his plate. His cheese enchilada was long gone. "That's when I was approached by Wizard-9."

"They're *really* called Wizard-9?"

Chuck had to smile at Maggie's expression of disbelief. "Yeah, they're really called Wizard-9. It's a pretty powerful organization. Covert too. And dangerous as hell. Not even the president himself knew about this group. Or if he knew about them, he didn't know what they had planned, that was for sure."

He took a deep breath. "Anyway, they provided Data Tech—and me—with the money necessary to build the Runabout in return for the right to regulate use of the device. They told me that time travel could be a deadly weapon, and without regulation, there was always the possibility that terrorists or criminals could get their hands on the Runabout and change the course of history. I suspected they were interested in more than regulating the project, but I let myself be blind to that. All I cared about was making the Wells Project a reality."

He stopped himself from drumming his fingers on the table before he even started. All this was his fault. He'd let Wizard-9 get involved. He was responsible for everything that happened as a result of that. He was responsible for all those deaths, for Maggie's death. . . .

"Turns out that the agents from Wizard-9 *were* the terrorists," he told her grimly. "They used the Runabout without my authorization to go back in time and set a bomb at the White House. The president, the vice president . . . everyone was killed."

"How did you know?" Maggie frowned. "I mean, if the agents from Wizard-9 didn't tell you they were going back in time, how could you even know that everything didn't happen the way it was supposed to happen? How did you know they were responsible?"

"I probably *wouldn't* have known, if I hadn't been doing experimentation in something that I called 'double memories.'" Chuck pushed his plate forward as he explained. "I just ate a cheese enchilada, right?"

She glanced down at his plate and nodded.

"You have a memory of me eating that cheese enchilada. If you were paying close attention, you probably have a memory of me burning my tongue. You have a memory of sitting across from me, eating your black-bean soup and a salad. You remember the waitress—the scent of her perfume, perhaps. You have memories of all those things, right?"

She nodded again, her gaze never leaving him as she tried to follow where he was leading. He liked having her full attention. It had been a long time. The Maggie from his time had been distracted and unhappy for the past few years as she struggled to make her failing marriage work. But this was before all that. This was before she married that fool. This was before she discovered that the sizzling attraction that sparked every time she looked in Chuck's eyes wasn't what she wanted.

"Now, suppose I were to go into the men's room and sneak out the window to the alley where I supposedly keep my Runabout. And suppose I were to travel back in time just an hour or so," Chuck told her, "where I would intercept you on your way into Tia's and take you somewhere else—like up to the Pointe—for dinner. Suppose I order a couple of steaks and baked potatoes and we eat that. I changed history, right? Steaks and potatoes replaced enchiladas and black-bean soup. *But.* Here's the strange part.

"I've found that when time has been tampered with—and my going back in time and changing these things, as inconsequential as they seem, *is* time tampering—people are left with residual memories. These residual memories—or memories of how it actually happened the first time around—provide time travelers and those people affected by the time travel with *double memories*.

"Your most vivid memory would be of your steak and potato, but you would *also* remember the black-bean soup. It'd be foggy almost as if it were a dream, but it'd be back there. Double memories. Of course, since I'm the person who did the actual time traveling, both of my memories will be clear and vivid, because both events actually *happened* to me."

She nodded. "That makes sense."

"If you concentrate, you may be able to find a residual memory of what you did immediately after you heard about the earthquake the first time around."

Maggie closed her eyes for a moment, frowning slightly. When she opened her eyes, they were wide with surprise. "I stayed home and watched the news all night," she said. "Oh, that's so *weird*."

"That's right." Chuck gestured around them at the restaurant. "This isn't the way it originally happened, so you have double memories both of being home alone, and of spending the night with me."

Her eyes flashed as she met his gaze, but she looked away immediately, and he realized the implications of what he'd said. He'd meant evening, not night. Spending the evening with him. Still, she didn't seem overly averse to his inadvertent suggestion that they spend the night together, and he felt a familiar hot flare of desire at the thought. God, he'd wanted her for so long.

He had to clear his throat before he spoke again. "A double memory can be so distant and dreamlike, I might not have noticed it if I hadn't been researching the phenomenon. But I knew something was wrong the morning that I woke up and turned on the TV and heard the first of the news reports about the White House bombing. I had a residual memory of that same morning that was very different. I could remember that I got up, turned on the TV while my coffee machine did its thing, and I felt disgusted by the lack of hard news. The biggest story even on CNN was the birth of some pop singer's baby. I still had that memory, and that's how I knew that time tampering was responsible for the assassination. And I knew it was the work of Wizard-9. They were the only ones besides me who had access to the Wells Project."

She was still watching him intently, her chin tucked into the palm of one hand. "So, okay," she said. "You've come back in time to change events that are going to occur in my future. But since you're *from* the future, all of the changes that you're going to make have already happened in your past. Shouldn't you already remember them?"

Chuck shook his head. "I understand what you're saying, but it doesn't work that way. I can't make one little change and know instantly how it's going to turn out unless I return to my own time. If I were to go back to my time after making a change, I'd have a sudden rush of very vivid double memories. I'd remember all the things that had happened differently in the seven years between now and then."

"So how will you know when you've made the changes you need to make?"

He gazed into her eyes. "I'll know."

"How? Because if you don't know the outcome, maybe you *have* done all you need—"

Chuck shook his head. "Simply coming back in time isn't enough. I need to create an event that will affect the life of my present-day self—of Charles. And as Charles does things differently, I'll have those new double memories—but only one by one as they happen in real time."

"Wait, you lost me. . . ."

Chuck shifted in his seat, leaning across the table, trying to make her understand. "Think of it on a physical level," he said. "Look at me. I'm here, I'm whole, right? If you were to X-ray me, you'd see I've never had a broken bone. I've lived to be forty-two years old and I'm still in one piece. But if I convinced you to go and push Charles—not me, but Charles—off the sidewalk and into oncoming traffic, my own X rays would suddenly be very different. You'd probably see multiple signs of healed fractures. And I'd probably have a couple more scars to show for it, even though it didn't happen to me. But think about it. It *did* happen to me, because he's *me*."

He sat back in his seat, uncertain if she understood. "Memories, even double memories, work the same way. Until I actually change the past—until I convince you to actually push me into traffic, to continue with that rather grim example—I won't have a clue as to what's going to happen."

Her eyes didn't leave his face, her gaze sharp and probing. "Most people die when you push them into oncoming traffic. You're not here to ask me to help kill you, are you?"

Chuck considered trying to laugh her words off for about a tenth of a second, but the look in her eyes convinced him to be honest. This was Maggie he was talking to. She'd always been able to see right through him. "Actually, that's a solution I've considered," he told her seriously. "If Charles is gone, all those theories about time travel are gone too. It's a quick and easy fix. But remember what I just told you. What happens to him affects me. If he's dead, I'm dead too. I'm hoping to find another way."

Maggie took in a deep breath, letting it out in a burst of air. "Oh, man."

"I'm *going* to find another way," Chuck told her. "The agents from Wizard-9 tried to kill me. I don't want to give them the satisfaction of seeing me dead—even if the only way they'd remember me was in the faintest of double memories."

"That day you came," Maggie said. "There was blood on you. Your shoulder . . ."

His shoulder had only been scraped. Most of the blood had not been his own. Chuck took a sip of his soda. "I went to Data Tech that morning breathing fire, intending to use the Runabout to go back in time and prevent the bombing, but they were waiting for me."

He reached across the table for her hand, needing to touch her to eradicate the memories. He could still see her eyes, dimming as the life seeped from her body. He couldn't tell her all of it, but that didn't matter. He was going to make damned sure that it happened differently this time around.

"You were there," he whispered, "and somehow you knew they were gunning for me. You tried to warn me. You saved my life."

"Yeah, well, saving people's lives is one of those things I just happen to be good at—along with finding clothes for the naked time travelers who show up in my backyard." She was trying to make light of it, but he knew she was not unaffected by the touch of his hand.

He was not unaffected either. He laced their fingers together as he took a deep breath. "I need you to help me, Maggie."

She looked down at their hands, and then up, back into his eyes. "Okay." She nodded. "I'll help."

three

"CHARLES NEEDS TO BE CONVINCED TO give up time-travel research," Chuck said. "I've been thinking about the best way to do this, and I keep coming back to you."

Maggie took a sip of her drink, feeling the warming kick of the tequila.

This seemed so unreal. She was sitting here, across this restaurant table from one of the most attractive men she'd ever met—discussing his plan for changing the future. He was going to tamper with time and change his own destiny in order to prevent Wizard-9 agents from overthrowing the U.S. government. She took another slug of her drink.

"Why me?"

"It's not going to be easy," he told her. "Developing time travel was always something of an obsession for me. What you'll need to do is to talk Charles into going back to school and getting his medical degree. You'll need to convince him—me—that there's plenty of work to be done in AIDS research. Charles needs to be talked into leaving Phoenix, into leaving Data Tech. And all his—my—research notes on time travel need to be destroyed."

Maggie shook her head. "I don't get it. Why do you need

me? Why don't *you* just go to Charles and tell him everything that happened, convince him to give up his research that way?"

Chuck silently gazed at her. When he finally spoke, his voice was soft. "Because I remember how badly I wanted to develop time travel. And I'm not sure that loyalty to a president whose name he's never even heard is enough to make Charles give up his dream. Yeah, over a hundred people were killed in the bombing, but I know what he'll say. He'll say, think of the thousands who could be saved if time travel exists. He's never met anyone from Wizard-9. He won't understand the danger."

As Maggie looked into his eyes she knew he wasn't telling her everything. There was more, but he was leaving it out.

"But why me? Why should *I* be able to get through to him?"

He didn't answer right away. "Because there's something between us," he finally said quietly. "I feel it right now. I felt it the first time we met too. And Charles is going to feel it when he meets you at that Data Tech party on Tuesday."

Chemistry. He was talking about the sexual attraction that simmered between them. He was talking about using that attraction to knock his past self off his predestined path. If he really thought she could do *that*, he must be experiencing one hell of a powerful attraction.

Maggie was glad she was sitting down. She felt slightly weak in the knees. She hated to admit it, but she was feeling that attraction as well. Every time their eyes met. Every time their eyes *didn't* meet. It was always there, snapping and crackling around them like a live wire.

If you weren't careful, a live wire could kill you.

But what was he asking her to convince Charles of, really? Leave Phoenix, Chuck had said. Leave Data Tech. Did he expect her to leave Phoenix and Data Tech too? Did he expect her to do something like *marry* him? No, not him—Charles.

This was way too weird.

"Why do you call him Charles?" she asked. "I mean, he's really just you, only younger."

He shifted in his seat for about the thousandth time that evening. It was just one of the many ways his relentless energy slipped through the cracks of his self-control. Maggie knew well—even just from the few times she'd met him—that Chuck Della Croce was not a patient man. He didn't like to sit still, he didn't like to move slowly. Yet his intensity burned deeply, and he seemed to focus every ounce of his attention on every word she spoke and every move she made.

It was kind of scary actually—having him look at her that way.

What would it be like to make love to this man, to have that focus and attention in a purely sexual context? The thought made her mouth go dry, and she had to take another sip of her drink.

"Up until recently—this year in fact, your time," he clarified, "nobody ever called me anything but Charles." He smiled. It was really only a half smile, a slight twisting of one side of his mouth, yet it made him look even more handsome. Thank God he didn't give her a full grin. The force would've knocked her clear out of her chair.

"But when I met you at that party," he continued, "you decided right then and there that Charles was too formal, and you started calling me Chuck."

Wait a minute. . . . "*I* did?"

"Yeah. Even though we didn't do more than date a few times, you had a rather strong influence on my life."

She sat even farther forward. "We *dated*?"

"After we met at that Data Tech party, yeah, we went out once or twice."

"Just . . . once or twice?"

He was cryptic. "At the time I didn't think we were compatible, so I didn't pursue a relationship beyond friendship."

She didn't get it. "But at that time you were Charles, weren't you? I mean, you were more Charles than you are now, seven years later. So if you didn't think we were compatible then, why would Charles think we're compatible now? And what is it *exactly* that you want me to do? All this talk about compatibility is making me a little nervous."

"All I want you to do is meet him—me—*Charles*—at that Data Tech party and let things happen as they're supposed to. Only this time around, don't be so quick to quit."

Maggie blinked. "Quit?"

He was drumming his fingers against the table and—as she'd seen him do before—he seemed suddenly to become aware of the sound, and forced himself to stop cold.

"Yeah," he said. "You were the one who broke it off between us."

Maggie had to laugh. This was too absurd. "Okay. Now we're getting into the really unbelievable stuff. The time travel I'm starting to be able to handle, but this . . . Nuh-uh. You're telling me that I broke up with you. That's insane. Why would I break up with you? You're brilliant, you're nice, you're polite—you seem socially adept—not too many eccentricities, give or take the finger-tapping thing. Your sense of humor needs a little work, but, you know, it's back there. It's hiding, but it seems solid enough. And, okay, maybe you need to work on being just a teeny bit warmer—maybe you need to practice stretching those lips into a smile in front of a mirror a few times a day. And speaking of mirrors, have you looked into one lately? You're gorgeous, Chuck. You're a twenty on a scale from one to ten. So what you're telling me is that you're perfect and *I* broke up with *you*. I don't think so, bub."

"It's true."

"And that's just you," she continued. "I haven't even started on *me*. I'm always the one in a relationship who hangs on until the bitter end, hoping for a happy ending. And oh, will you

please look at me a little more closely? Maybe the light's not
bright enough in here. You keep hinting at this instant animal attraction, love-at-first-sight doody, and—believe me, I know—
I'm not the love-at-first-sight type. I mean, look at me. I'm
just . . . not."

"Sorry, you're wrong," he said coolly. "Have *you* looked into
a mirror lately? You're beautiful, Mags. This time around, I'm
going to make damn sure you believe that."

Maggie rolled her eyes. "Oh, please."

He leaned forward, the intensity in his eyes sparking even
hotter. "As far as I was concerned, the attraction factor alone was
enough to keep us together for years, but you didn't agree."

"Are you sure you're talking to the right person?" she asked.
"Because that doesn't sound like anything I'd ever say."

"I remember what you said." Chuck sat back and stirred the
ice in his glass, his body language suddenly distant and closed.
He glanced at her only briefly, keeping his eyes for the most part
trained on his glass. "After we went out a few times, you told
me . . . how did you say it? That you weren't interested in being
physically intimate with a man who wouldn't be emotionally intimate with you—a man who wouldn't even talk about his day-
to-day life, let alone his feelings."

"That sounds like me," Maggie conceded. Suddenly it all
made sense. Chuck was attractive and intelligent and as sexy as
hell, but he wasn't exactly the warm, fuzzy, sharing type. Even
the level of intimacy needed for this conversation was difficult
for him to handle—she could tell that from the way he was sitting, the way he wasn't meeting her gaze.

"There are some things I'm not sure I'm going to be able to
do any differently this time around," he said quietly. "And yet
I'm asking you to do nearly everything differently." He forced a
smile. "After seven years of friendship, I know you pretty well,
Mags. I know you don't want me. If I could think of another
way, short of kidnapping my own self . . ." He shook his head.

I know you pretty well, Mags.

Maggie was shaken. She was sitting and talking with a man who knew her far better than she knew him. How much better, she didn't know. She took a fortifying sip of her drink.

"So," she said, taking a deep breath. "Tell me honestly. Did I ever sleep with you—in my future and your past . . . ?" She rolled her eyes again. "Whoa, this is definitely Twilight Zone stuff."

He answered her seriously, quietly. "No. We never made love."

But he'd wanted to. He didn't say it in so many words, but she could see it in his eyes. He *still* wanted to.

"I have to go home now," Maggie told him. "I think my brain has just absorbed all the weirdness it can hold for one night."

She stood up, but then she stopped, looking back at him. "Do you have a place to stay tonight?"

He gave her another of those half smiles. "I don't suppose that's an invitation."

Her laughter sounded slightly hysterical. "Not a chance. But if you need some money for a motel room . . ."

"I'm fine. I know where Charles kept his extra bankmachine card. I'm all set for cash." He hesitated. "Can I walk you home?"

"Please don't."

Chuck nodded. "May I call you tomorrow?"

"Yeah. Call me." Maggie hurried away.

Maggie had three different work deadlines approaching at the rate of a speeding train, but she simply could not concentrate.

She couldn't stop thinking about Chuck.

His story was impossibly absurd. Time travel. A covert agency with plans to overthrow the government. It was insane.

Still, she found herself believing him.

And she found herself drifting out of focus as she sat in front of her computer, thinking not about his story, but about his eyes. About the way he looked at her, as if she were a tall glass of water and he was dying of thirst.

Getting involved with this man would be crazy. If everything he'd told her was true, he was from the future. He didn't belong in this time. There was already another one of him here. If he couldn't get back to his own time—and he'd implied that was true—he'd probably have to take on a new identity and . . . And if everything he'd told her *wasn't* true, if this all was some kind of giant con or scam, well, then she'd be twice the fool.

No, she was going to have to keep her emotions out of this. Friends. She was going to have to work to be sure they became nothing more than friends.

She closed her eyes tightly, trying to banish the picture of him standing naked in her yard.

The intensity in his liquid brown eyes was even harder to forget.

Unable to write an intelligible word, Maggie grabbed her purse and her car keys and headed over to Data Tech. She had to pick up a file she needed, and as long as she wasn't getting anything done, she might as well do it now.

This didn't have anything to do with wanting to get another look at the man Chuck had called Charles. She *wasn't* going to Data Tech to do something as asinine as to spy on Chuck's younger self.

As she made the turn into the Data Tech parking lot, she saw him. Charles Della Croce. Sitting behind the wheel of a gleaming white Honda, he was slipping on a pair of sunglasses as he braked to a stop before leaving the lot.

As he took a right, heading out toward downtown Scottsdale, Maggie made a quick U-turn, her tires squealing slightly on the hot asphalt as she followed him.

This was insane. This was not "picking up a file."

There were two other cars between her car and Charles. That was good. Not wanting him to notice that she was following him, she hung back slightly as he took another right turn.

He drove into the old-fashioned part of Scottsdale that was filled with quaint little shops and cafés and four-star restaurants.

Modern Phoenix and Scottsdale were made up of enormous shopping malls—places where, once inside, shoppers didn't have to face the fiery heat of the Southwestern sun as they went from store to store. But the older section of the city dated back to the days before air-conditioning, to the time of small-town America. The sidewalks here were no less busy because they were outside. They were crowded with tourists and the usual lunchtime business men and women.

Charles pulled into a parking space on a side street, and Maggie did the same, parking some distance away from him. He headed back toward the shops and restaurants on foot, and Maggie ran to keep up as he disappeared around the corner of a building.

The noontime sun was unseasonably warm for November, and even a brief sprint made her shirt stick uncomfortably to her body. As she rounded the corner she felt a rush of relief as she spotted Charles, his dark head a good four inches above the rest of the crowd. As she watched he crossed the street and went inside a trendy-looking little restaurant called Papa John's Eatery.

He sat down at a table near the front window. Maggie tried not to look too conspicuous as she pretended to look into the window of a Native American art and jewelry store while glancing back over her shoulder at the restaurant.

She saw a waiter approach Charles and hand him a cellular phone. He spoke for a moment, then handed the phone back, decidedly displeased. He said something to the waiter, gesturing at the place setting in front of him. The waiter nodded, and removed the extra silverware and glasses. It didn't take the detective ability of a Sherlock Holmes to figure out that Charles's lunch date had called to cancel.

As Maggie watched, Charles glanced at a menu and ordered quickly and seemingly without much regard for what he would be eating.

She crossed the street, wanting to get nearer, needing to take a closer look. After all, she'd never seen Chuck and Charles in the same place at the same time. They could well be one and the same.

On a whim, she pulled open the door to Papa John's and went inside.

Charles was sitting at his table, paying no attention to what was going on around him, writing something in a small notebook.

Waving aside the waiter who was coming toward her, Maggie took a deep breath and headed for Charles, counting on the fact that she'd come up with some real-sounding excuse for being there when the time came to open her mouth.

"Hey, Chuck," she said, slipping into the chair next to his.

He looked up, startled.

Part of Maggie still hoped that this was one great big practical joke. He would meet her eyes sheepishly and grin and admit that Katy, Maggie's college roommate, had coerced him into playing this silly trick on her.

But there was absolutely no recognition in his eyes. None at all.

Dear God, he was Chuck—but he wasn't. His eyes were the same liquid shade of brown, his nose the same perfect shape. His hair was shorter, though, and the lines around his eyes and mouth were less pronounced. He looked younger. About seven years younger, she'd guess. *Exactly* seven years younger . . .

"I'm sorry," he said. His voice was the same too—a sexy baritone, resonant with a rich timbre. "I don't think we've . . . *Have* we met?"

His scar. The thin line that marked his left cheekbone, directly underneath his eye. It was gone. Or rather, perhaps more accurately, it hadn't yet appeared.

"Actually, no," Maggie said.

He was looking at her as if he were afraid she might be insane, and for a moment Maggie felt that could well be true. Sitting here like this, talking to him like this... This wasn't the way they'd met. Chuck had told her they'd first met at that party at Data Tech. She was probably messing things up royally, but now that she was here, now that she was face-to-face with Charles, she didn't want to leave.

She was fascinated. This *was* Chuck she was sitting across from. But he was a younger Chuck. A Chuck without that grim tightness to his mouth, without that tightly clenched jaw, and without that weary desperation in his eyes.

"I was being followed," she fabricated, praying that God would forgive her for lying, "by this really creepy guy—every time I turned around, he was right behind me. He was talking to himself, saying all kinds of really weird things. I saw you sitting in here all alone, and I thought maybe you wouldn't mind helping me out by pretending to be, you know, my significant other or something, so this guy will leave me alone once and for all...?"

His gaze shifted and he squinted slightly as he looked out the window into the glaring brightness of the crowded street. "Is he still out there?"

Maggie turned to look. "I...don't know." She hated lying like this. She was amazed that she could come up with a story so quickly with those disturbing brown eyes gazing at her. But there was no way she could tell him the truth.

"Well, just in case he's still watching..." Charles leaned forward and kissed her.

He kissed her.

On the mouth.

His lips were warm and soft and he tasted like lemonade.

Maggie was caught so off guard, she could do nothing but laugh.

He laughed too.

His smile was incredible, and Maggie realized she'd never truly seen Chuck smile. Sure, he'd made an attempt. He'd twisted his lips in a vague imitation, but it had been nothing like this. Something had happened over the past seven years to make him forget how.

"Maybe we better do that again," he suggested, his grin widening. "Make sure this man—whoever he is—really gets the message."

Charles started to lean forward again, and whether he was only teasing or not, Maggie would never know, because temporary insanity overcame her and she leaned forward, too, closing the gap between them.

And then he was kissing her again. Not a swift gentle brushing of lips like the last kiss, but a longer, deeper kiss. Maggie felt a jolt of disbelief as his tongue swept into her mouth. Not disbelief that he would kiss her that way, but that she would welcome such a kiss, that she would kiss him back with such abandon, and most of all, that she wanted that kiss to go on and on and on.

Forever.

It had to be insanity—she'd never do something like kiss a total stranger without having first lost her mind. Except he wasn't a total stranger. He was so much like Chuck. A Chuck who still remembered how to smile and laugh.

"Well," Charles breathed as he pulled back to look into her eyes. "Yeah. That was pretty damn territorial. I think if the man who was following you was watching that, he's probably convinced that you're not single and . . . are you, by any chance, single?"

His eyes were filled with a molten heat. Maggie had seen traces of the same fire in Chuck's eyes, but Chuck was quick to try to hide it, while Charles had no qualms against letting her see his attraction.

She cleared her throat as she straightened up, gently freeing herself from his grasp. "Yeah," she said, having some trouble catching her breath. "Yes, I sort of am. Single."

Chuck had told her that the physical attraction between them had been instant when they met. He hadn't been kidding.

Charles picked up on her evasive wording. "Sort of?"

There was no way she could explain that over the past day or so she had been fighting the totally insane urge to have a love affair with the man he would become in seven years. Fortunately, he let it go.

"Do you have a name?" he asked.

"Maggie," she told him.

"Maggie," he repeated. The way he said it, it sounded like a caress.

"Winthrop," she said, moistening her suddenly dry lips with the tip of her tongue. "Maggie Winthrop."

Charles held out his hand. "Pleased to meet you, Maggie Winthrop."

His hand was big and warm, with long, graceful fingers. Instead of shaking her hand as she expected, he lifted her fingers to his lips and kissed the back of her hand.

Maggie had to laugh again. Again, from knowing the grim and seemingly dangerous man he would become, she never would have dreamed he could be so utterly flirtatious. And smooth. He was *very* smooth, as if he'd had a great amount of practice using his considerable charms to seduce. And his charms were considerable, as he darn well knew. He didn't let go of her hand as he smiled at her again.

"I'm Charles—"

"Della Croce," she finished for him. "I know."

He froze for just a fraction of a second. "You do?"

"You work over at Data Tech," she explained. "I do too. Sort of."

He released her hand. "There's that 'sort of' again."

"I'm a freelance writer. I just signed a contract with Data Tech to do a couple of projects including the annual report. I'll be in and out over the next few months until all the jobs are complete."

He shifted in his seat, his gaze intense, sharp with curiosity and a hint of wariness. "As far as I know, I've got nothing to do with the annual report. What made you recognize me?"

"I've seen you around. That, combined with gossip heard at the coffee machine . . ." Maggie lied again. Still, this one wasn't a very big lie. She had no doubt that this man was talked about frequently as the women in the office took their morning coffee break.

He laughed. "If it's gossip, it's probably not true."

He was still gazing at her, and despite the warmth in his eyes, she was struck by his coolness, his reserve. It was odd, really. There was heat in his eyes—heat from desire and attraction. But at the same time he held himself aloof, keeping himself emotionally distanced.

Maggie had seen that same distance in Chuck, she realized, but it wasn't as glaringly obvious. With Chuck, it was hidden beneath his burning anger. It was dwarfed by his desperate need to set things right.

In a burst of nervous energy so much like Chuck's, Charles drummed his fingers on the table for the briefest of moments before forcing himself to stop. It was a gesture so like Chuck's because Charles *was* Chuck. Or rather, at one time, Chuck had been Charles.

"You called me Chuck," he remembered suddenly. "When you first sat down."

"I knew your name was Charles, I assumed Chuck was a nickname."

"I don't have a nickname. I've just always been Charles."

"Even when you were a child?"

Something shifted in his eyes, and Maggie got the impression of a drawbridge being raised and clanging shut with a metallic thud against the very private outer defenses of an impenetrable castle. "No," he said. "Not even when I was a child."

"No nicknames, huh? None at all?" she asked. "Come on. There must be something." She wanted to rock the foundations of that castle. "What do women call you when you take them to bed?"

For one short moment Charles dropped his guard, and Maggie could see honest emotion in his eyes. Surprise, and genuine amusement. But then heat sparked, drowning out all else. "I don't know," he murmured. "Want to try it and see?"

She was treading upon extremely dangerous territory.

Still she couldn't forget what Chuck had told her. She'd dated this deliciously sexy man, and because he wouldn't share more than the physical with her, she'd kept their relationship from becoming intimate.

She still wanted more from him.

"Can I talk you into having lunch with me?" he asked.

Maggie shook her head no, glancing at her watch. "I have to go. I have a one o'clock meeting." But instead of standing up, she leaned forward. "Charles, tell me something. Tell me just one thing about yourself that you've never told anyone before."

He hesitated just long enough so that for a moment Maggie thought he might actually do it.

But he didn't. "I hate carrot cake," he said.

She laughed to cover her disappointment. "The fact that you hate carrot cake is a deeply personal secret?"

"Actually, yes, it is."

Maggie shook her head in despair as she stood up. "Thanks for . . . helping me."

He rose to his feet, and once again she was struck by his height. "Wait—"

She started for the door. "I really have to go."

"Without giving me your phone number? I'd like to see you again, Maggie."

She turned and looked up at Charles Della Croce. "Oh, you'll see me again," she told him. "You can count on it."

four

MAGGIE GOT TO THE MALL AT SEVEN-THIRTY.
Chuck had left a message on her answering machine, asking
her to meet him there at six, but she'd had a dinner meeting
scheduled with a client. It was a meeting that she couldn't get
out of. Or maybe she simply didn't *want* to get out of it. Maybe
she was intentionally trying to keep her distance from this man.

Lord knows she'd let herself get a little too close to Charles
this afternoon.

As Maggie hurried into the air-conditioned coolness of the
shopping mall, she wondered if Chuck would still be waiting for
her. She hadn't had any way to contact him to tell him about her
meeting, and he hadn't called back.

He was sitting on one of the benches near the movie theater,
reading a book, just the way he'd said he'd be. Maggie felt a
surge of emotion at the sight of him. It may have been relief. Or
it may have been something else entirely.

He stood up as she approached.

"Sorry I'm so late," she told him. "I had a meeting that
couldn't be rescheduled."

"I figured it was something like that," he said. "Did you eat?"

"Yeah. Did you?" Why was she so nervous? Just standing

here talking to him, saying nothing of any importance whatsoever, was making her feel totally on edge.

"I grabbed something from the food court about a half hour ago."

Maybe it was the way he was looking at her, with his usual high-powered intensity. It was as if he were memorizing every detail of her—face, clothes, hair, everything. And all *she* could think about was that he was surely noticing every wrinkle in her denim skirt, every chip in the polish on her toenails, every scuff mark in the leather of her sandals.

"Come on," he said, slipping his book into the back pocket of his jeans. "There's something I want you to try on."

Maggie had to laugh. "Are you kidding? We're here to go *shopping?*"

One side of his mouth turned up in wry half smile. "You don't think I asked you to meet me at the mall simply for the atmosphere, do you?"

"Actually, I didn't think about it," Maggie admitted, hurrying to keep up.

"We're here to buy you a dress to wear to the Data Tech party."

Maggie stopped short. "I don't need a dress. I've already figured out what I'm going to wear—"

"Black pants with a tuxedo-style jacket," Chuck told her, "over a shirt made of some kind of shimmery material."

"Yeah," she said slowly. "That's what I'm going to wear. It's formal without being too feminine. It's businesslike. It's not too . . ."

"Sexy?" he supplied.

Maggie lifted her chin. "That's right. In order to compete in the male-dominated world of business, women have to be careful not to—"

"I happen to think it made you look incredibly sexy."

Maggie started walking again, trying to hide the way his

softly spoken words affected her. "Then why are we buying me a new dress?"

Chuck glanced at her. "Because over the past seven years there's been a time or two when you went all out and got really dressed up and wore a... I don't know, maybe you'd call it a gown. It was some kind of really fancy dress and you wore your hair up and..." And each time he had seen her dressed like that, it had damn near stopped his heart.

But he couldn't tell her that.

"Just trust me on this, all right?" he said.

She was silent, walking alongside him, carefully not meeting his eyes. Trust him, Chuck had told her. But he wouldn't blame her one bit if she didn't trust him. After all, in her mind he'd given her nothing of himself, nothing to make her think that he trusted her in return.

In her mind.

In truth, he had. In truth, he'd told her something he'd never told anyone before.

"Carrot cake," he said.

She stopped in front of a shoe store's window display to stare at him. "Excuse me?"

"The fact that I don't like carrot cake really was something I'd never told anyone." He could see surprise and confusion in her eyes, so he tried to explain as he pulled her closer to the window, out of the stream of pedestrian traffic. "When I was little, I went to live with my uncle, my mother's brother, and his housekeeper made me a carrot cake the first day I arrived. I really hated it, I mean, *hated* it—but I ate it because it seemed rude not to."

Maggie was still staring at him, her eyes wide.

Chuck cleared his throat. "I, um, I guess, you know, because I didn't want to be there, I had this sense that everything was destined to be awful, but I was stuck there until I was old enough to live on my own. I don't know, it seemed kind of appropriate that I choke down that terrible cake. So I did, and Jen, the housekeeper, got it into her head that I really loved her carrot cake, so she made it for me all the time. Every holiday, every birthday. She'd probably still be making it for me now, but my uncle finally died a few years ago, and she retired."

Maggie didn't say a word.

"I know I didn't manage to get that all out this morning, but that's what I was talking about when I told you that I hated carrot cake," Chuck told her.

"This morning..." The surprise in Maggie's eyes turned to suspicion. "Did you follow me today? Oh, my God. Did you somehow listen in on my conversation with Charles?"

Chuck had to laugh. It started as a chuckle but grew into a full laugh. He couldn't remember the last time he'd laughed this way. "Mags. You don't get it, do you? Think about it. Think about what you just said."

But her expression had changed again. She was looking at him now much the way she'd looked at him this morning. This morning, in her time. Seven years of mornings earlier in his.

He could see his own attraction for her mirrored in her eyes. And he could see something else, something warm and soft, something that made him nearly dizzy with longing.

"You don't do that often enough," Maggie told him quietly. "You don't laugh anymore. Or even smile."

She reached out then, gently touching the side of his face, and he remembered the heaven it had been to kiss her. Seven years ago she'd walked into that restaurant in downtown Scottsdale. He was supposed to meet Boyd Rogers for lunch, but Boyd had called and canceled. And then Maggie had appeared, telling him some ridiculous story about someone following her. He'd been so enchanted by her sparkling smile, by the way she seemed to look at him with something akin to wonder in her eyes, he hadn't been able to resist. He'd kissed her. Twice. God, he could remember the softness of her lips, the sweetness of her mouth as if it were yesterday.

Or more precisely, as if it were about eleven forty-five this morning.

"I didn't follow you," he told her. "I didn't have to. I was there." He saw the realization dawn in her eyes, and he said aloud the words she already knew. "I was there, because I'm Charles. Or rather, I *was* Charles."

He'd spent most of the day going to movies. It had taken him almost no time to find the perfect dress for Maggie to wear to the Data Tech holiday party, and then he'd had the entire rest of the day free.

He'd walked around the mall for a bit, delighting in his ability to take his time, to stroll without his crowd of bodyguards hurrying him along. It had been years since his experiments with time travel had been made public knowledge. And after that, as a target for terrorists and lunatics, he'd needed professional protection. He'd taken the time to learn to protect himself as well, and there was still a part of him that constantly checked in the glass windows and mirrors of the mall stores to make sure he wasn't being followed.

But of course he wasn't being followed. In this year, in this time, no one gave a damn about Dr. Charles Della Croce. He liked it that way.

That morning, he'd bought a ticket to the eleven-thirty showing of a movie whose name he couldn't even remember now, and halfway through he'd been flooded with memories—new memories, double memories—of meeting Maggie Winthrop for the first time not at the Data Tech party, but rather at a little restaurant in Scottsdale.

The memory was fuzzy at first, and he really had to work to

recall the incident. Even then, it didn't seem to gel until he remembered that kiss. Somehow that sweet sensation brought the entire encounter into sharp focus. Then he remembered the conversation he and Maggie had had almost word for word.

He hadn't bothered to watch the rest of the movie. He'd spent the time instead sitting there in the darkened theater with his eyes closed, replaying that second incredible kiss over and over in his mind, trying to make that memory stronger, willing himself to recall something that had happened seven years ago.

Something that had happened mere moments before.

But now Maggie was here, inches away from him, and he didn't have to rely on memories. Her gaze flicked down to his mouth before she looked searchingly into his eyes. She smiled then, very slightly, and he knew she was thinking about that incredible kiss too.

"That *was* you, wasn't it?" she whispered.

Chuck nodded. "Yeah. That was me."

Maggie held her breath, entranced by the way, once again, just like this morning, he took his time leaning closer and closer until his mouth covered hers. He kissed her, slowly, sweetly, almost reverently.

Then he reached for her, pulling her tightly against him, burying his face in her hair as he held her close. "I've been dying to do that again for the past seven years."

"Chuck—" Maggie lifted her head to look up at him, but instantly forgot whatever it was she'd intended to say. The heat in his eyes seemed to magnify all of the secrets revealed by the intimacy of their embrace. He wanted her. Badly. She couldn't help but know that.

And when he lowered his head to kiss her again, she kissed him back hungrily, desperately, reaching up to meet him on the tips of her toes. She pulled him even more tightly against her, running her fingers through the nearly unbearable softness of his hair. All of her senses seemed to explode as she kissed him harder, deeper, as if all of the emotions of the past few days stood up in unison and cried out to be heard.

Heard and harkened to.

Maggie had had complete sexual encounters that were far less powerful, and far less meaningful, than this single kiss.

He pulled back, pushing her away to arm's length, breathing hard, both alarm and elation written clearly on his face, as if he had been able to follow her very thoughts.

"Dear God," he breathed.

As Maggie gazed into his eyes she knew that with that kiss, she had given far too much away—she had revealed way too much of her feelings. She took no comfort from knowing that Chuck had done the same.

"That was a mistake," he told her.

She pulled free from his grasp so that he wouldn't see the disappointment she knew was on her face. "Yeah," she said. "You're probably right. A big mistake."

He *was* right. What was she thinking? What was she doing?

The last thing in the world she needed was to get involved with a man who took seven years to open up and tell her why he hated carrot cake. "Let's find that dress and get out of here."

"How's this?" Maggie's voice interrupted Chuck's reverie, and he turned to see her standing in The Dress.

It was the one. He'd known from the moment he saw it on the mannequin in the store. He would have bought it right there and then, at quarter past ten that morning, but when it came to women's clothing sizes, he was clueless. A fourteen seemed much too big, and a four was surely too tiny. Maggie was somewhere in between the two, but where, Chuck couldn't begin to guess.

"Please don't look at me like that," she said tightly. "It's making me nervous."

"I'm not sure I can be in the same room with you and *not* look at you like this," he admitted. "You look... amazing."

She'd pulled her hair up off her neck, holding it in place with one of those bear-trap-like clip things that she'd no doubt had in her purse. Several tendrils had escaped, hanging down around her shoulders, accentuating the sheer elegance of the strapless gown.

The dress itself was a rich shade of brown, made of some kind of fabric that managed to be both velvety and silky. It clung intimately to the soft curves of her breasts, yet fell smoothly, gracefully across her stomach and hips, cascading all the way down to her ankles.

It had a neckline that was shaped with the swell of her body, dipping down to meet between her breasts. And it had a slit up the side, all the way to her thigh. He couldn't tell it was there now, while she was standing still, but when she moved, he knew it would reveal tantalizing glimpses of her legs.

She turned away, going back into the changing room.

Chuck could see himself reflected in the store mirror. From a distance, he looked the same as he ever did, nearly the same as he did seven years ago. But he wasn't the same. The road he'd taken over the past years had been a rough one, fueled by his obsession to find a way back to the past.

He'd sold his soul for the chance to develop and test his theories. He'd danced with the devil that was Wizard-9, and soon he was going to have to pay the ultimate price.

Maggie came out into the store, dressed once again in her sleeveless blouse and denim skirt, the dress on a hanger, the long skirt looped over her arm. She didn't do more than glance at him, as if she were afraid to meet his eyes, and Chuck knew that his talk of mistakes had hurt her.

But it was true. Getting involved with him—physically or otherwise—was surely the last thing she needed.

Chuck followed her over to the cash register and took the

dress from her. She wandered around the front of the store as he used cash to pay, as the store clerk wrapped the dress in tissue paper and put it into a shopping bag with handles.

Maggie looked up as he headed toward her, and together they left the store.

"My car's over by Sears," she told him. "On the lower level."

They walked for a moment in silence, and then, as if she couldn't stand it another moment, Maggie spoke. "You know, it *wasn't* a mistake."

She was talking about that kiss. "Yes, it was," he said gently.

"Why?"

Chuck had to close his eyes briefly at the impossible irony. He'd wanted this woman for years. *Years*. He'd kept his distance when she dated and then married Albert Ford, but he'd never stopped wanting her. If anything, the years and their continued friendship had made him want her more. Yet now here he was, about to talk her out of the kind of relationship he'd only ever dreamed of having.

"Because I need you to help me change *Charles*'s future."

She forcefully pushed open the door and he followed her out into the warm night air. "But you're Charles, and Charles is *you*," she argued.

Yes, he was Charles, but Charles wasn't him. Charles hadn't made the mistakes that he'd made. Charles hadn't put an entire nation in jeopardy. Charles hadn't been tainted by his connection to Wizard-9.

"Here's what I think we should do," Chuck said to Maggie as they crossed the car-filled parking lot. "You take this dress and go home, and tomorrow night wear it over to Data Tech and . . ."

Chuck had seen the car approaching the moment they exited the mall. He'd been watching it out of the corner of one eye, his wariness a habit that was impossible to break. The car was moving too fast, bouncing jarringly over the speed bumps. But it was the fact that the windows were tinted and the front passenger's window—the side nearest them—was rolled slightly down that made the hair stand up on the back of his neck.

He was reacting even before he saw the slight movement at the window, even before his mind registered the fact that that was, indeed, the barrel of a gun being aimed at them.

He caught Maggie around the waist, pulling her down between two cars, dragging her to cover as an assault rifle was fired from the open window of the car. Bullets slammed into the cars around them, breaking windows and tearing into the metal with a terrible screeching sound.

And as quickly as it had started, it was over. The car was speeding away with a squeal of tires.

The explosive racket of a weapon being fired at close range still rang in Chuck's ears as he took one shaky breath and then another. He realized he had thrown himself on top of Maggie in a ludicrous attempt to shield her from the bullets with his body. He was probably crushing her, grinding her into the rough asphalt. But she didn't move beneath him, didn't protest, didn't make a sound.

A drowning wave of panic washed over him as he pushed himself off of her, terrified that the future was repeating itself. *Please God, don't let her have been hit. . . .*

But Maggie moved then, throwing her arms around his neck and clinging tightly to him. She was alive. His relief nearly knocked him over, and as he sat up he pulled her with him, cradling her in his arms. He ran his hands over her, reassuring himself that with the exception of a slightly skinned knee, she was all right.

She seemed only to want to hold him tightly. He could feel her trembling, or maybe that was him, he wasn't sure anymore. But then, God, she lifted her face, and just like that, he was kissing her. Kissing her as if the world were coming to an end.

In some ways, it was.

This was what he should have wanted more than anything

else in the world. Maggie, with all of her passion and joy and those smart-aleck comments that always made him smile. Maggie, with her million-watt grin, her husky laugh, and her sparkling eyes. Maggie, not just his best friend, but the keeper of his heart and soul—his lover, his only, his wife.

If only he had fought as hard for her as he'd fought to develop his theories on time travel . . .

But *what ifs* weren't any use to him now. Chuck had come too far down his own path ever to turn back. But Charles, Charles still had a chance to choose heaven over hell.

Only Chuck was finding out firsthand just how very hard it was to let go once he held heaven in his arms.

Especially since heaven was responding to each kiss he gave her with a fierceness and intensity that damn near took his breath away. She wanted him as badly as he wanted her. Chuck couldn't stop his feelings of elation. He wanted to sing, to dance dizzily with her in circles, spinning and jumping and whirling like crazy until they fell, laughing, together on the ground.

But what he had to do instead was stop kissing her.

It took everything Chuck had in him to pull back. And even then, it was only the fact that they were in danger that made him stop.

"We have to get out of here." His voice sounded hoarse.

"We can go to my place." He could hear her desire in her voice, see it in her eyes. God, she thought he was talking about . . .

"I mean, we can if you want," she added more softly, almost uncertainly.

I want, he wanted to tell her. *God, do I want. . . .*

"No, Mags," he said instead, "I meant whoever did this might come back. And if they do, I want us far from here."

"Who *was* that? Who would shoot at *us*?" Maggie started to get up, but he grabbed her wrist and kept her down, her head lower than the hoods of the cars surrounding them.

As Chuck got to his feet he stayed in a crouch, too, reaching around the car to grab the bag that he'd dropped. "Not us—me." Taking her hand and staying low to the ground, he started moving between the cars.

"But why?"

She figured it out herself, and as he answered they spoke in unison. "The Wells Project."

She was quick to add, "You said the men from Wizard-9 didn't follow you here. You said they couldn't."

"I didn't think they could. I *know* I disabled the prototype." Chuck frowned. "I also know they destroyed my lab at Data Tech. I assumed the working model of the Runabout and the other equipment were in there at the time." He glanced back at her. "And you know that old saying about the word *assume*."

"You mean, when you assume, you and me get a bullet in the ass?"

Chuck had to laugh. Somehow the direst, most serious thing that could have happened *had* happened. Wizard-9 agents had followed him into the past, using techniques he himself had written about to find him. The ripple effect. Or the displacement theory. It was possible to trace the Runabout as it traveled through time using either of those theories. Neither was one hundred percent accurate, but obviously Wizard-9 had been close enough.

But despite the danger, Maggie had still managed to make him laugh.

Still, the situation was extremely sobering. The latest working model of the Runabout could hold four travelers for each leap in time. The technology was still in its early stages, and for the first time since the Wells Project went on-line, Chuck was grateful for that. Even in this advanced version of the Runabout, the energy source required at least ninety-six hours for its various components to cool and reset before another jump through time could be made.

He had to figure it had taken the Wizard-9 agents a full twenty-four hours to track him here to the mall. It had probably taken them a whole lot less than that, but he estimated high just to be safe.

That left him only seventy-two hours. After seventy-two hours, he'd be a dead man. After seventy-two hours, Wizard-9 would be able to make another leap through time. This time, they'd arrive before him, and when he made the jump, when he arrived naked and disoriented in Maggie's backyard, they'd be there waiting. And they'd kill him.

Maggie tugged on his hand. "My car's over this way."

He shook his head. Seventy-two hours. God, the clock was ticking. "We can't risk taking it. If this *is* Wizard-9, then they've already found your car and rigged it with some kind of tracking device. Or a bomb."

"A bomb!" Even Maggie couldn't make a joke about that. "Like . . . a *bomb*?"

"A bomb," Chuck told her. "Like the one they planted that took out most of the White House."

"If they could find my car in this parking lot, then they've surely found my house," Maggie said.

"That's right," Chuck said, moving down the line of parked cars, looking quickly at each one they passed. "We can't go there."

"Where are we going to go?" Maggie asked. "An even bigger question: if we can't take my car, how are we going to get there? Wherever *there* is."

He glanced back at her. "We'll have to borrow someone else's car."

Maggie dug in her heels. "*Borrow* someone else's car? It's not as if we're going to find one with the keys in the ignition," she said. "What are you going to do? Hotwire it?"

Chuck nodded. "Absolutely."

---

five

"I CAN'T BELIEVE YOU KNOW HOW TO HOT-wire a car."

Chuck glanced away from the road and over at Maggie, his face dimly lit by the green dashboard light. "It's all a matter of understanding how things work."

It was obvious to Maggie from the ease with which Chuck had started the engine of this white, late-model Taurus with only the Swiss army knife he had in his pocket, that he had a clear understanding of how things worked.

It was obvious, too, that he had an understanding of how to *keep* things working when he not only switched license plates with the car next to the white Taurus, but stopped in another badly lit corner of the parking lot and quickly switched plates a second time.

It was likely that while someone coming out of the mall would notice that their car was missing, they probably wouldn't notice that their plates had been switched. And while the state police would be on the lookout for a white Taurus with the original plates, they wouldn't be looking for a white Taurus with this third set of plates.

Chuck glanced at her again, and Maggie realized she was

staring at him, but she couldn't seem to stop. His face looked angular in the shadows, his cheekbones in sharp relief.

There was more than mere age that made him look different than Charles. There was a hardness to his mouth, an edge to him that made her wonder with a shiver just where he'd draw the line in his quest to set things right.

They were traveling north on Route 17, heading up into the mountains, toward Sedona and Flagstaff. The tires of the car made a low humming sound on the highway as they moved at a speed slightly over the limit.

They'd made only one stop—right before they left the city limits. Chuck had pulled up to a roadhouse-style bar, and he and Maggie had gone inside.

They weren't there to quench their thirst. No, in just a matter of minutes after walking into the place, they were seated at a table in the back, across from a man who looked as if he hadn't bathed since Jimmy Carter was in office. As Maggie incredulously looked on, Chuck paid a hundred and fifty dollars cash for a deadly-looking handgun, a shoulder holster, and a box of ammunition.

The two men shook hands, and then—cool as a cucumber, as if he wore an illegally obtained, unregistered handgun underneath his jacket all the time—Chuck slipped the leather straps on over his shirt. Somehow he knew how to fasten it all together to make it work as a holster. He checked the gun—for what, Maggie didn't know; to see if it was loaded?—then slipped it into the holster, putting his jacket back on to hide it. The box of bullets went into his pocket.

Maggie didn't say a thing.

Chuck suggested they make use of the facilities before they hit the road again, and when she came out of the ladies' room, he was talking on the pay phone. He hung up as she approached. He didn't tell her who he'd called, and she didn't ask.

She didn't say a word as they walked back out to their stolen car. She still didn't speak as once more he used his knowledge of how things worked to restart the Taurus.

Now, though, she cleared her throat. "Where are we going?"

Chuck glanced at her. "Maybe you should close your eyes, try to get some sleep. We've got a long night ahead of us."

"Yeah, right. I always get the urge to take a nap after nearly being gunned down at the mall."

He looked at her again, longer this time. "I'm sorry," he said. "I'm sorry I got you involved in this. I should have stayed far away from you. If I'd been thinking straight, I would have realized that Ken Goodwin would never let something like the Wells Project be destroyed."

"Ken Goodwin?"

"Out of all the Wizard-9 agents I dealt with, he seemed to be the one in charge. If he's here, if he's behind this . . ."

"What?" Maggie prompted softly. "Talk to me."

His eyes seemed to flash as he shot her another quick look. "This whole situation has just gone from difficult to near impossible. Goodwin knows that I need to get close to Charles to keep him from developing those time-travel theories."

"Charles!" Maggie said suddenly, turning in her seat to face him. "Wizard-9 can get to you through Charles. If they kill him, you'll be dead too."

"No, that's not a problem."

"But the way you explained it to me—"

"They won't risk hurting Charles," Chuck reassured her. "They need him alive to develop the time-travel theory. My bet is they won't even get near him, for fear of interfering with the natural course of events. No, *I'm* the one Goodwin needs to get rid of. If I get within fifty feet of Charles, Wizard-9 is going to be there to stop me cold."

"What about me?" Maggie asked. "I could approach Charles—"

"No. They'll be looking for you too. They know who you are. They know what you did in the future."

She studied his profile. "What exactly did I do?"

Chuck was silent, his eyes fixed on the road ahead of him. When he finally spoke, his voice was almost unnaturally matter-of-fact. "I told you what you did. You warned me. You saved my life."

"How?"

He shifted slightly, impatiently in his seat, glancing briefly at her. "You said, 'Chuck, look out!' You know, Mags, when we're talking, I can't think, I can't plan. I need to think this through and figure out what Goodwin would expect me to do. And then I need to figure out if I should do that, or do the opposite, depending on whether or not he'd expect me to second-guess him and—"

"Okay, okay! You've convinced me. I'll shut up." Maggie's voice shook very slightly as she added, "I'm sorry."

"No." Chuck's voice was barely audible over the hum of the engine. "*I'm* sorry. I'm sorry for getting you into this. And I'm sorry I can't be the man you need me to be."

Maggie reached out, lightly touching his denim-clad leg. "I think if we want to stay alive—and I don't know about you, but I sure do—you're exactly the man I need you to be."

Chuck didn't say anything. He didn't even look at her. But he did take her hand, intertwining their fingers.

They headed north into the Arizona night in silence, holding tightly to one another's hand.

They had to walk from the bus station to the motel in the early-morning sunshine. It wasn't more than a few blocks, but to Maggie, it seemed like a thousand miles. It had been years since she'd pulled an all-nighter like this one.

They'd left the stolen car at the Flagstaff airport and had

taken a shuttle across town to the bus station. They'd had to wait nearly three hours for the next bus heading back to Phoenix.

As they'd snacked on candy and cans of sodas from the vending machines in the bus station, Chuck had explained why they were heading back south—doubling back on their six, as he called it.

They had to return to Phoenix because Charles was there, because he was the key to changing Maggie's future and Chuck's past. Ken Goodwin and his agents from Wizard-9 would expect them to return, but Chuck was banking on the fact that Wizard-9 wouldn't be ready for them to return this soon. Over the course of the next twenty-four hours Wizard-9 would set up roadblocks and spot inspections on the routes leading into the city in an attempt to intercept them.

But by then, Chuck and Maggie would have already returned to Phoenix.

Maggie had pointed out that it was possible Wizard-9 was as adrift and as out of place as Chuck was in this time frame. Maybe they wouldn't have the resources or connections needed to authorize the setting up of roadblocks. But despite their botched assassination attempt, Chuck seemed to think they were capable of anything.

He was determined to return to Phoenix as soon as possible.

The stolen car was left in the airport as a false lead. When they found it, the agents from Wizard-9 would waste valuable time and manpower attempting to pick up Chuck and Maggie's trail in the Flagstaff area.

But their trail would long be cold.

Chuck had briefly considered leaving Maggie safely hidden up in the mountains. But Maggie didn't even have time to protest before he told her he'd rejected that idea flat out. Apparently, where Wizard-9 was concerned, there was no such thing as *safely* hidden. The only way Chuck could guarantee her safety was if he was with her.

It was also there, in the late-night quiet of the Flagstaff bus station, that Chuck had told her that kiss they'd shared in the mall parking lot had been another mistake.

The clock on the wall of the motel lobby said 8:30 A.M. as Maggie watched Chuck fill out the motel registration form. He paid in cash, and a few minutes later they unlocked the door to a room.

One room.

A single, solitary room.

Chuck entered first, tossing the bag with the dress in it onto one of the two double beds before he turned to switch on the heater. The November night had been cold and a chill lingered in the room.

Maggie stood in the doorway as the old machine underneath the front window wheezed to life. "I don't think this is a good idea."

He knew she was talking about the fact that he'd gotten only one room. "I need to know that you're safe. There're two beds." He switched the heater on high, turning the knob to the warmest setting, then straightened up. "Come in and close the door. You're drawing attention to us."

Maggie stepped inside, leaning back against the door to shut it.

Two beds. He was right. There were two beds. But as far as Maggie could tell, there wasn't a brick wall with a steel-reinforced, heavily padlocked door separating them.

"I won't touch you," he continued, glancing at her in the dim light of the lamps. His face was grim, his mouth a tight line. "I promise."

It wasn't the idea of Chuck losing control that Maggie was afraid of. It was her own inability to stay away from him that frightened her. So far she'd failed rather miserably in her attempts to keep her distance from this man. Chuck may have been sure that the kisses they'd shared had been mistakes, but to

Maggie they had felt impossibly right. He may have been sure, but she wasn't at all certain she was strong enough to fight her attraction to him much longer.

She cleared her throat. "I'm just . . ." A deep breath and then she started again. "We've been together constantly all night. No offense, but I could really use some time away from you and—"

"No." He crossed to the sink that was on the wall outside of the bathroom and began washing the miles of travel off his hands and face. He met her eyes in the mirror. "I'm sorry. If we need to leave out the back window, we can be gone in a matter of seconds. But if you're in another room, even next door . . ." He shook his head. "We're toast."

The high window in back of the little room was not easy to access, but Maggie had no doubt that Chuck could get it opened if they needed to leave in a hurry. He was proving to be something of an expert at all kinds of unexpected things.

"What kind of scientist who works in an R and D lab knows how to get hold of a gun and hot-wire a car?" she asked. "Where did you learn things like 'doubling back on our six,' or whatever you called it?" She paused. "Isn't that some kind of military expression?"

"Yeah." Chuck dried his face with a hand towel, still watching her in the mirror. "You can pinpoint locations by using the numbers from the face of a clock." He pointed directly to his right. "The bathroom door is at three o'clock. The sink is at twelve. Right now you're standing at my seven—"

"And directly behind you—where you've already been before—is your six."

He gave her a slight smile. "Right."

"So, what, did you learn that in the Data Tech employees' manual or something?"

"Or something."

Maggie sat down on one of the beds. The mattress was soft and springy. Sitting down felt good, though. And lying down would feel even better. She sank down onto her back, her feet still on the floor as she stared up at the cracks in the motel-room ceiling. "Would it really kill you to be more specific?"

She heard the creak as Chuck sat down on the other bed, heard the double thuds as he took off his boots and tossed them onto the floor.

She was actually surprised when he finally spoke.

"Shortly after the news leaked out that I was working on the Wells Project, I started getting death threats. Some were just threats, but some were real. A few were near misses. At the time I had a friend who was thinking about retiring from the Navy. He was in the SEAL units, and he had some...skills that I thought would come in handy. I hired him as a security consultant. He taught me a bunch of nifty little tricks."

"Where was he when the Wizard-9 agents tried to ambush you in your lab?"

Chuck didn't answer right away, and Maggie turned her head to look at him.

He was still sitting on the edge of the other bed. His feet were bare, and his elbows were resting on his knees, his shoulders bent with fatigue. Or despair. He was resting his forehead in the palm of one hand, rubbing it slightly as if he had a headache. But he glanced up as if he felt her gaze on him.

"He was dead," he answered. "They shot him in the back of the head at close range before I got to the lab that morning." He paused. "You saw them do it."

Maggie's breath caught in her throat. "Oh my God."

He looked away from her, breaking the almost palpable connection that had shimmered between them. "I'm sorry. I shouldn't have told you that."

Maggie sat up. "No," she said. "Chuck, I want you to talk to me. I wish you would tell me *more*."

He stood up. "We should get to sleep."

Maggie felt a surge of frustration. Why wouldn't he talk to

her? She could see his pain etched into the lines of his face. He tried to hide it, tried to pretend it didn't matter. Nothing mattered but fixing the mistake he'd made.

But the desperation and anguish of the wild-eyed man who'd first pounded on her back door were not gone. All those emotions were still inside of him, despite being carefully locked away. He worked hard to stay in control, never to lose sight of his single goal.

His control had slipped only when he'd given in to passion. He'd dropped his guard only when he'd kissed her. He'd kissed her as if there could be no secrets between them, as if their hearts beat in perfect unison, as if they were two parts of a single whole.

But those kisses were wrong, or so Chuck said when he'd regained his precious control. They were mistakes that weren't meant to happen.

Maggie fought the frustration that rose up into her throat, choking her. Across the room, Chuck unwrapped the dress they had bought at the mall.

The mall. Maggie nearly laughed aloud. It had been hardly more than twelve hours since she'd met him outside of the movie theater. It had been hardly more than twelve hours since her life had been forever and irrevocably changed. But what had changed it most? The rain of bullets that had very nearly taken her life? Or that incredible, soul-shattering, heart-stopping kiss she'd shared with Chuck immediately after?

When Chuck had kissed her, she thought she'd found all of the answers she'd ever been searching for. But Chuck had only found that he'd made a mistake.

As he carefully hung the dress on a hanger, the fabric glistened in the dim light, an odd spot of elegance in the shabby room.

"Why bother?" she asked. Her voice sounded harsh in the stillness.

He turned to look at her, and she held his gaze pointedly, almost aggressively, as if daring him to look away from her.

He didn't look away, but his eyes revealed nothing of what he was feeling. "Why bother hanging this up?" he asked.

"Yeah. I'm not going to be able to go to the party tomorrow night—no, *tonight*. The party's tonight." Everything was happening so fast. Maggie took a deep breath. "If the guys in Wizard-9 are so smart, it won't be long before they notice that my name is on the guest list—"

"I'm sure they already know," Chuck told her. "And you're right. The party's no longer an option. But you can still wear the dress. I just have to figure out an alternative time and place for you and Charles to meet."

He spoke so quietly, so matter-of-factly, as if nothing about this insanity affected him personally. Well, shoot, maybe it didn't. *He* wasn't the one who was going to have to get all dressed up in a ludicrous attempt to catch the attention of a man she knew damn well wasn't interested—the seven-years-younger version of a man who had told her their kisses had been a mistake.

"I don't know how you think I'm ever going to be able to talk Charles into something as huge as changing his career." Her voice shook, but she couldn't help it. She didn't care, anyway. She had every right to be upset, dammit. She'd been shot at and dragged halfway across the state and back all in one night. She'd found everything she'd ever wanted, only to realize she hadn't found anything at all. Because the kind of love she wanted was a love that was returned.

"Just be yourself. He won't be able to resist you."

She rose to her feet as her temper blazed. "Resist what? What exactly is it you want me to do, Chuck?"

But he wasn't going to let her fight with him. He turned away, pulling back the covers of his bed. "Let's just go to sleep. It's been a long night."

He was so calm, so cool. Maggie wanted to see beneath his

facade. She wanted to get a rise out of him. She wanted to see *some*thing in him besides this grim determination. "You want me to sleep with him, right? Okay. You win. I'll do it. But I have to warn you. If I have sex with Charles, you'll have a memory of it too."

He stood quietly, expressionlessly. "Maggie, this isn't about sex."

"If it wasn't about sex, you wouldn't've cared if I wore a potato sack the next time I met Charles," she countered hotly, gesturing toward the dress hanging in the corner. "And *that's* no potato sack."

"You're right. It's about sex." His lack of emotion was driving her crazy. "But not entirely. It's more complicated than that."

"Complicated is putting it mildly." Her voice cracked. "I don't know why you think I have the power to make Charles change his entire life. You tell me he won't be able to resist me. But, hey! *You* have no problem resisting me. All you do is push me away—"

Chuck turned away with a forceful exhale of air halfway between laughter and a sob. And just like that, he wasn't standing still anymore. He was moving, using one hand to rake back his unruly hair as he paced toward the sink.

Maggie met his gaze in the mirror, and she knew from the blaze of heat in his eyes that something she'd said had managed to put a crack in his control. If he were ever going to open up and talk to her, it was now or never.

"Okay," she said as he turned to face her. "Okay. You said it's complicated. More complicated than just sex. Tell me what you mean. Make me understand!"

Chuck took several steps toward her, but then stopped, turning away and running both hands up his face and over his hair to grip the tensed muscles in the back of his neck. He swore, softly but steadily.

"Please?" She reached out to touch his arm.

He pulled away as if she'd burned him. "Maggie, Christ—I can't explain. Not without . . . Not easily."

"Not easily?" The way he'd jerked his arm away from her made her want to cry. "So it won't be easy. Do you think any of this is easy for *me*? Do you think it's going to be easy for me to put on some stupid dress and seduce some stranger who both is and isn't the man I *really* want to be with? I don't want to make love to Charles, I want to make love to *you*." Oh, damn, she'd gone and told him far too much. But now that she'd started, she couldn't seem to stop herself. "Except, he's you. He's part of you, and if I *do* make love to him, I'm making love to you, too, aren't I? And . . . and . . . it's *so* damn *confusing*!"

There were tears in his eyes as he stood there, just looking at her. "Dear God," he whispered, "I've done this all wrong."

six

MAGGIE SAT DOWN AND CLOSED HER EYES, feeling all of the fight draining out of her. He'd done this wrong. He'd made mistakes.

Not half as many as *she'd* made, obviously.

She felt the mattress sink as he slowly sat down on the bed. He didn't move to touch her, he just sat there, next to her.

"Mags, I... I've known you for seven years," Chuck said quietly, haltingly. "And I swear, I've wanted you in every way possible for every single second of that time."

She lifted her head, turning to look at him, uncertain of what she'd just heard. "What?"

He gave her one of his crooked half smiles. "Don't make me say it again. Once was hard enough."

Maggie turned toward him. "But..."

"I've been fighting like hell to stay away from you these past few days." He reached up with one hand, again as if trying to loosen the muscles in his shoulders and neck. "And yes, you were right. I was trying to set it up so that this time when you met me—Charles—at that party, you'd end up going home with him. See, I thought that might be a way to compress those seven years into just a few short weeks. But we don't have weeks anymore. We don't even have days. Only *hours*. I don't know, maybe it'll still work. See, I thought if I could make Charles feel the same way as I do about you . . ." He took a deep breath as he glanced at her, then shook his head. "I guess I just thought . . . I mean, *I* can't imagine making love to you and then letting you walk away. I guess I thought if I did this right, Charles wouldn't let you walk away, either."

Maggie was watching him silently, her brown eyes subdued. Chuck wanted to reach out and touch her cheek. Her skin looked so smooth and soft. But he knew that touching her was the last thing he should do. "I'm sorry. I said that badly."

"No," she said softly. "You did okay."

"You were right about my having double memories," he told her quietly. "If you and Charles . . ." He couldn't say it, but he knew from her eyes that she knew what he meant. "I guess I figured at least I'd have *that,* because you're right. I'd definitely remember. I haven't quite figured out what it is—maybe some kind of hormonal release that affects certain memory centers of the brain—but even a simple kiss is enough to make a residual memory extremely clear and—" He broke off. He was babbling now, and she was just watching him, her eyes so soft, so warm. He could drown in those eyes.

And still, she didn't speak.

"So now what?" He forced a half smile. "Which one of us locks ourself in the bathroom until checkout time?"

Maggie touched the side of his face. "How about neither?"

Chuck knew he should stand up and put some distance between them, but he had no strength left. Instead he closed his eyes, allowing himself the forbidden pleasure of her touch. He felt her move closer, felt the softness of her lips where her fingers had been mere seconds before.

He couldn't keep from touching her, too, from gently trailing his fingers down the smoothness of her arms. He felt her shiver and he knew he should stop, but he couldn't. God, he couldn't.

"Chuck?" she breathed.

He opened his eyes. Her mouth was mere inches away from his. At this distance, her eyes were more than brown. He could see dark brown and lighter brown mixed in with flecks of every gorgeous shade in between. She smiled, and even though it was a sad smile, it made her eyes shine. He couldn't keep himself from reaching up and lightly tracing the line of her jaw. She was so beautiful, it hurt.

He had to moisten his lips before he could speak. Even then, his voice came out little more than a whisper. "Yeah, Mags?"

"I want to be with you tonight."

He couldn't answer her. What could he possibly say to that?

"Tomorrow night I'll do what you ask," she told him. "But tonight I want you to make love to me." She kissed him lightly on the mouth, pulling back to look into his eyes and whisper, "Please?"

She kissed him again, and Chuck felt his resistance crumble in a flood of emotion so powerful, he nearly cried out.

And instead of backing away, he kissed her too.

He kissed her deeply, taking possession of her mouth, thrilling at the sound of pleasure she made as he pushed her back onto the bed with him.

Dear, sweet God, he wanted this. He wanted her. He *needed* her. He kissed her even harder and she met him with a fierce passion that took his breath away.

She molded her body around him, tightly gripping the leg he thrust up between hers, pressing herself against him. She was a dizzying mixture of softness and muscles, of sweetness and fire. She was everything he'd ever wanted, everything he couldn't truly have.

Chuck knew he shouldn't run his hands up underneath the

edge of her shirt. He knew he shouldn't cup the softness of her breast in the palm of his hand. And he knew the last thing he should do was to caress the tantalizingly erect nub of her nipple and arouse her even further.

But he did and the sounds she made deep in the back of her throat as she kept on kissing him set him on fire.

He knew he should stop. He knew he should back away. Maggie didn't belong to him. She never could.

But when she tugged at his jacket, he helped her pull it off. He unfastened the shoulder holster and that and the gun soon followed the jacket onto the floor. And when she pulled at his T-shirt, that, too, went up and over his head.

And then he kissed her again. The sensation of her hands gliding across the bare skin of his back combined with the soft eagerness of her mouth was dizzying.

Sixty hours. He only had sixty hours left, regardless of his own failure or success. His time was running out, and there was nothing he could do about it.

Except take this moment. He could take these few hours, steal this single taste of paradise.

And he *would* be stealing. Maggie had laid all of her feelings and desires out on the table, leaving herself open and vulnerable.

But he couldn't keep himself from taking advantage. He could no longer resist what he'd wanted for so long.

She'd unbuttoned her shirt and he pushed it off her shoulders, exposing the lace of her bra and the smooth expanse of her stomach. He kissed the tops of her breasts, ran his mouth and hands along all that glorious skin as she reached for the top button on his jeans.

Her fingers brushed against him and the reality of what they were going to do—of what they were doing—was too much. He lifted his head. "Maggie—"

She knew what he was thinking. "This is right," she told him. "We *need* this." She pulled him down on top of her, cradling him between her legs as she kissed him again. "*I need this. I need you, Chuck.*"

Her skirt was gone. Somehow she'd managed to free herself from it. She lifted her hips, pressing herself intimately against him, and Chuck knew he was only kidding himself. Even if he had wanted to, there was no way he could stop what they'd started.

And God help him, he didn't want to.

He kissed her, filled with that odd mixture of euphoria and despair as she reached for him again, unfastening his zipper. And then, God, she was touching him.

He pulled back, swiftly kicking his legs free from his jeans and his shorts, even as she unfastened her bra and skimmed her own panties down her legs.

He wanted to stop time, to freeze this moment, to step back and just look at her, Maggie Winthrop, lying naked on his bed, waiting for him, *wanting* him. It was his richest, dearest fantasy come true.

But he knew he couldn't hesitate, he couldn't risk taking the time to form any rational thoughts. Because if he were thinking rationally, he would know damn well that the right thing to do was to stop. To keep this beautiful insanity from going any further.

Maggie reached for him even as he lunged for her, and together they fell back on the bed, skin touching skin, soft flesh against taut muscle.

She was so tiny, so perfect. He felt as if he could crush her, as if it wouldn't take much for him to hurt her badly. Yet she pulled him even closer, as if the weight of his body on top of hers didn't alarm her, as if she trusted him completely.

Chuck wanted to touch her everywhere at once and he skimmed the softness of her skin with his hands and mouth, stroking, caressing, reveling in her sweet smoothness. He explored her most intimate place with his fingers; she was slick and hot and so ready for him. She pushed him over onto his back so that she was on top of him, straddling him, the softness of her belly pressing against his arousal. Her dark hair hung like a curtain around them as she leaned forward to cover his mouth with hers in a hot, sweet kiss. Then she shifted, leaving a trail of kisses along his neck, down his chest. The sensation was so exquisite, he heard himself groan aloud.

He grabbed her then, pushing her back against the bed. Her hair was spread out around her, dark against the white linen.

She smiled up at him with such delight dancing in her eyes.

He couldn't smile back at her, couldn't speak. He could only kiss her, only pray that the waves of emotion that were flooding him would subside before he broke down and wept like a child.

His heart clenched. God help him, God help him, he shouldn't be doing this. He had no right. . . .

"Do you have protection?" she whispered. "A condom?"

Chuck shook his head no. No, this had been the last thing he'd imagined actually happening.

Now they were going to have to stop. Now he would have no choice. He should have felt relief, but the rush of disappointment was so sharp, he had to close his eyes.

"I've got one in my purse," she told him, pushing herself up and off the bed, moving swiftly across the room.

She was back almost instantly, tearing open the foil-wrapped package and handing him its contents.

But it was too late. Sanity had returned. "Mags, we shouldn't do this." God, if only his body would listen to his own words of reason. He knew what he was saying would be far more believable without the extremely obvious proof of his desire for her.

He saw the flare of impatience in her eyes. Impatience, anger, and hurt. "Why not? Where does it say that you shouldn't get what you want? Who the hell are you to say what's wrong and what's right?

"*This* is right," she said, pushing him back against the pillows, straddling him once more, leaning forward to kiss him on the mouth. It was a hard kiss, a punishing kiss, but her lips softened almost instantly, and the rush of need that filled him was dizzying. It didn't seem possible, but he grew even harder with her stomach pressed against him.

"And *this* is right!" She shifted her hips, coming down on top of him, and with one smooth, incredible thrust, he was inside of her.

But the rolled condom was still in his hand.

"Maggie—God!"

Her head was thrown back as she sat above him, moving on top of him, setting a rhythm that echoed the sudden leap of his pulse, and he felt himself slipping toward the edge of a cliff, toward the unstoppable free fall of his own release. The sight of her, her breasts taut with need, her nipples tight peaks of desire, only fueled his desire, and he felt himself sliding faster and faster toward the point of no return.

Nothing, *nothing* had ever felt so good. . . .

He was bigger than she was, stronger, yet he was powerless to stop her, enslaved by his own needs. He wanted her, he needed her.

He loved her.

And he loved her enough to lift her up and off of him.

They couldn't do this. This *wasn't* right.

Maggie protested, and even fought him at first. "No! Chuck—"

He held up the condom he'd damn near crushed in his hand. "These things don't work too well unless you actually put them on."

She watched as he swiftly did just that, her smile tentative. She'd actually thought he'd intended to stop them, to keep them from going any further.

In one swift move, he flipped her onto her back. She

reached for him, opening her legs to him, ready to give herself to him so completely. He gazed into her eyes as he entered her slowly, slowly but so deeply she caught her breath at the sensation. Her lips were parted, her eyes dreamy, her lids half-closed as he held himself still inside of her.

And then she smiled, and Chuck knew that his entire life had been building to this one exquisite moment in time.

"This is right," he whispered. "*This* is right."

Her beautiful eyes filled with tears. "Yes," she whispered back. "I think so too."

He kissed her then. Her lips were so soft, so sweet. She lifted her hips, pressing him even farther inside of her, and they both cried out, their voices intermingling in the stillness of the dimly lit room.

He wanted to make love to her slowly, to make this moment last forever. But she urged him on, faster, harder, deeper. He drove himself inside of her, filling her again and again, as the world blurred around him, until there was only now, and only Maggie.

Only Maggie.

She cried out and he felt the beginning of her release. It was completely consuming, wildly overpowering. She clung to him, writhing beneath him, her fingernails sharp against his back.

Her release pushed him over the edge and he exploded in an eruption of pleasure that cannonballed through him. It was a pleasure so sharp and sweet, it seemed to burn him, incinerating him instantly. All coherent thought vanished, and there were only feelings, only warmth.

A sense of peace.

A sweet, perfect sensation of timeless floating.

The scent of Maggie's sweet perfume.

"I think I love you," Maggie whispered, her mouth brushing lightly against his face.

And just like that, he was back. His eyes opened, and reality clicked back in to focus. His scientist's brain was back on-line, and he felt a sinking sense of dread at her words.

She thought she *loved* him.

He rolled off of her, suddenly aware that he was crushing her. He felt her watching him, felt her light brown eyes studying his face, and he forced a smile. She didn't move closer, didn't try to nestle against him or snuggle with him.

He closed his eyes.

God, what he would have given to hear her say those words anytime over the past few years.

But now . . . She *couldn't* love him. She had to love *Charles*.

But he *was* Charles, he reasoned. Maybe this wasn't such a terrible thing. If Maggie could love him, as scarred and jaded as he was, then surely she could love Charles. It only made sense.

Except for the fact that love wasn't rational—love didn't make sense.

Still, perhaps this intimacy they'd just shared would work in his favor. Maybe this physical connection would help to bind Maggie to him—whether he was Chuck *or* Charles.

"Are you asleep?" she whispered.

Chuck opened his eyes to find her still watching him. "No."

"Are you okay?" There was concern in her eyes. Concern and uncertainty.

"Yeah." He reached for her, pulling her against him, molding her back against his front and covering them both with the sheet. Her head was nestled underneath his chin, and he held her close, his arm around her, one hand resting lightly on her breast.

He held her possessively, even though he knew she wasn't his to keep.

This *wasn't* right, what he'd done, what he was doing with her here, tonight. He'd tried to convince himself otherwise in the heat of passion, but now he was face-to-face with the truth.

Making love to her and holding her this way as she slept was wrong. But tonight was the only time with Maggie that he had—it was the only time he'd ever have.

And he was taking that time, even though he knew doing so was selfish and cruel.

He knew damn well he couldn't give her what she wanted. He couldn't bring himself to tell her his secrets. He wasn't any good at opening up, at expressing himself. God, he hadn't even been able to tell her that he loved her.

But that was the least of it.

Sixty hours. Fewer now. If he failed, in less than sixty hours he would be dead.

And if he succeeded . . . If his plan worked, if Maggie could convince Charles to switch his career to medicine, then time travel would never be invented. Wizard-9 would be thwarted, the White House wouldn't be blown up, the president wouldn't die.

And Chuck's current life and the path he'd taken to get here would be instantly erased. His life as he knew it would simply cease to exist.

And Chuck himself would vanish.

seven

LATE IN THE AFTERNOON, MAGGIE AWOKE
to find Chuck staring at the ceiling.

She lay there for a moment, studying his profile. His mouth
was set in its usual grim line, and the muscles in the side of his
jaw were jumping. No wonder he frequently gripped and
rubbed his forehead and neck—his constantly clenched teeth
probably gave him one incredible headache.

Maggie wished she had the power to read minds, to know
what he was thinking.

She didn't try to fool herself into imagining that he would
ever volunteer that information.

Her stomach rumbled hungrily and he turned his head.
"You're awake."

She nodded, wondering when he looked into her eyes if he
saw a still-smoldering echo of the love they'd shared in the early-
morning light.

Maggie had never experienced anything like that before in
her entire life.

It had been wild and raw—by far the best sex she'd ever
had. Ever.

But it had been so much more than that too.

She had never felt so connected, so in tune with another human being.

She had never felt so complete.

Except after they'd made love, after they'd exhausted their desire, after he'd pulled her into his arms and held her, he hadn't said a single word.

Maybe it didn't matter. Maybe she didn't need him to talk to her. Maybe his nonverbal skills would make up for his deficiencies in the more traditional types of communication.

She leaned toward him to kiss him, hoping to engage in more of that nonverbal communication.

But Chuck met her lips only briefly before he pulled away. He swung his legs over the side of the bed, sitting for a moment with his back to her. "It's nearly four-thirty. We need to start getting ready."

She sat up, touching his back. "Ready for what? I'm in no hurry to go anywhere." She pressed herself against him as she kissed his shoulder, encircling him with her arms, her hand encountering the muscles of his taut stomach, then sliding even lower. "Are you sure I can't talk you into—"

Chuck caught her hand. "Maggie, we need to go." He stood up, grabbing his jeans from the floor and pulling them on in one swift motion. "If you want to take a shower, you should do it now."

He wanted her, Maggie knew he did. He was far more than half-aroused. It was something of a challenge for him to zip his jeans.

"I want to take a shower—but I want you to take it with me," she said boldly. She stood up, too, making no move to cover herself.

For some reason, he was back to trying to resist her. She didn't know why, but if she had her way, that resistance was going to crumble, and soon.

But when he turned to look at her, the heat and desire that flared in his eyes was tempered with a profound sadness.

"I can't think of anything I'd rather do more," he told her quietly. "But we're running out of time. I need you to intercept Charles before he leaves for the Data Tech party."

He needed her to . . .

"Please, Mags," he continued. "Take a shower, and get dressed."

He turned away, taking the slinky dress from its hanger. As Maggie watched, he disappeared into the bathroom, and she heard him hang it on the back of the door. He came back out, stepping aside for her.

But she didn't move. *Get dressed*. He didn't seriously expect her to put on that dress and . . .

But he did. Maggie saw that fact in his face, in his eyes. He still expected her to use that sexy dress to try to seduce Charles.

No, she couldn't believe that. Not after the way he'd made love to her. She *wouldn't* belive it. He must have something else in mind.

"You said I wouldn't be able to go to the party—that the Wizard-9 agents would be waiting for me!" Her words came out in barely a whisper.

"You aren't going to the party," he told her. "*I* am." He took one of the bath towels and shook it open. He handed it to her as if hoping she'd use it to wrap around herself. But Maggie still didn't move. She couldn't move.

"But they'll kill you."

"No, they won't. They need Charles alive, remember? To develop the Wells Project. When I go to the party, they'll think I'm Charles."

"I don't understand."

"Ken Goodwin's men are probably watching Charles's condo, because they know that sooner or later I'm going to try to contact him," Chuck explained. "They're probably been following him wherever he goes, only this time they're not going to follow him, they're going to follow *me*. I'm going to get my hair cut and pick up a tux and—"

"You're going to sneak in the back door of the condo and come out the front, pretending to be Charles," Maggie realized.

"That's the general idea," Chuck agreed. "But Wizard-9 is surely watching both the front door *and* the back. There's no way I could get into the condo without being seen."

He took the towel from her hands and gently wrapped it around her. "I was trying to figure out how to make this work when I remembered I left for the party about ninety minutes early. I went into Data Tech to get some work done up in the lab before I had to make an appearance downstairs. But I'd been up late the night before, and before I got into my car, I stopped at the Circle K on the corner to get a cup of coffee to go."

"So Charles will come into the convenience store. . . ."

"And *I'll* come out. I'll take his car and go to Data Tech. The Wizard-9 agents will follow me."

"But if you're both in the Circle K, Charles will see you."

"No, he won't. He'll only see *you*."

This wouldn't work. There had to be a reason why this wouldn't work. Maggie grasped at anything. "How will you get Charles's car keys? If you don't want him to see you—"

Chuck's mouth twisted into a half smile. "You know I don't need keys to start a car."

Maggie drew in a deep sob of air. "So there I am, with Charles in the Circle K. What is it exactly that you expect me to do?" She knew. She just wanted to hear him say it.

His gaze was steady. "You can't go with him back to his place—Wizard-9 probably has the condo bugged. We'll get a suite at the Century Hotel. It's right around the corner. You can take him there."

"You want me to take him to a hotel room."

"Yes."

She hugged the towel tightly. "I can't believe you intend for me to go through with this!" Yes, she'd told him that all she'd wanted was one night, but she couldn't believe after the intensity of what they'd shared . . .

Chuck stood there, dressed only in jeans. Her scent still clung to his skin, his hair was still disheveled from her fingers, and his body was still responding to her nearness.

He was her lover. He was the man she had let steal her heart. But while her eyes may have been filled with tears, his were dry, his face set in an expression of determination.

"We have no choice," he said quietly.

"I'm not going to do it." Her lip was trembling, so she lifted her chin defiantly, hoping the one would cancel out the other and she would look as determined as he did.

He took a step toward her. "Maggie, he's *me*. It's not as if I'm asking you to be with some other man."

"He's *not* you. He's only a part of you. He doesn't even know me!"

He drew his hand through his hair in a gesture of pure frustration. "He *is* me. The same way you're still the same Maggie I've cared so much about for the past seven years."

That stopped her. Was she? Was she truly the same? Chuck had mentioned that the Maggie he had known had changed— that time and a lousy relationship had made her quieter, less sarcastic, perhaps more compassionate and understanding. When Chuck looked at her, did he see a mere shadow of the woman she was to become? Did he miss the maturity and growth that seven extra years of life had surely brought?

Was she nothing more than a poor substitute for the Maggie he truly cared about?

She sank down onto the bed. "Chuck, please. I don't want to be with Charles. I want to be with *you*. Why can't we simply let events play themselves out?"

Chuck didn't reach for her, didn't try to comfort her. Instead he slowly sat on the other bed. "We can't."

Maggie wiped at her face, trying to push away the flood of emotion that threatened to overwhelm her. "Why not?"

He gazed at her. "Because in approximately fifty-one hours, Wizard-9 will be able to reactivate the Runabout. They'll make another jump—to just a few days into the past this time. And this time they'll get here before me. They'll be waiting to kill me. And then you won't find a naked man in your backyard. You'll find a naked *dead* man."

"Oh, my God! Only *fifty-one* hours . . . ?" Maggie fought a wave of panic.

"The clock's ticking, Maggie. We've got to get moving."

"But . . ." She stared at him, her mind whirling. "Maybe we're going about this all wrong. Maybe instead of trying to keep Charles from developing the Wells Project, we should be trying to find where Wizard-9 has the Runabout. If we could destroy it—"

"That wouldn't be enough. If I'm allowed to continue with my work—" Chuck broke off, shaking his head.

She waited for him to explain, but he didn't say anything more.

She moved toward him then, taking his hands and kneeling on the floor at his feet, prepared to beg if she had to.

"Please. *Why* wouldn't it work? Tell me what you're thinking! Talk to me, Chuck! Tell me what you're feeling! I want to know."

His eyes were a blaze of intensity. "I can't. There are things you shouldn't know about the future."

"I don't give a *damn* about the future. It's all going to be different now anyway," she said, gesturing toward the bed where they'd shared such incredible love just a few short hours before. "I don't know about you, but *I'm* never going to be the same!"

The sadness in his eyes only deepened, and his words seemed to catch in his throat. If Maggie hadn't known better, she would have thought he was going to cry. "It's not going to be different enough."

Her towel fell off her as she moved up and onto his lap. She held on to him, needing to be closer to him, her arms locked around his neck. "I don't care!"

"Maybe you should." His voice was ragged as he clung to her, holding her as tightly as she held him. "Maggie, you should. God knows *I* care!"

He kissed her fiercely, taking her mouth, stealing her breath, touching her very soul. There were tears on his face. Chuck Della Croce was actually crying.

He seemed to draw strength from her as his hands skimmed the warmth of her body, as he cradled her close to his heart. He kissed her again, softly now, sweetly.

"The day I left my time," he said, his voice a hoarse whisper in the quiet of the room, "only an hour before I appeared in your yard . . . Maggie, I held you while you died."

Maggie couldn't say a word. She had died. She *would* die. Seven years in the future, she was going to die.

"I went to Data Tech," he continued. "You were there. Ken Goodwin didn't know it, but one of the lab cameras was on and you saw the Wizard-9 agents kill Boyd Rogers, my security chief, on the monitor in another lab. You knew I was next, and you tried to warn me.

"We tried to get away, but they started shooting. You stepped in front of me, Maggie, and you took a bullet meant for me." His voice shook. "I locked us both in one of the computer labs, and I held you while you died. Your heart stopped beating, and your eyes glazed over and you were gone. You were *gone!*" He took a deep breath, and when he spoke again, his voice rang with a hard certainty. "I will not let that happen again."

"We can run away," she whispered. "We can destroy the Runabout and then we can hide. You're good at hiding—no one will ever find us."

"We'd have to kill the Wizard-9 agents as well as destroy the Runabout," Chuck said quietly. "If we didn't, they'd simply wait seven years, and then warn themselves about me. They'd let their own selves know about the prototype in my basement, about their failed attempt to kill me. They'd get me before I even left my house that morning." He shook his head. "As long as Charles is out there, they can get to me. And once I'm gone, they'll kill you, too, just to be safe."

Maggie was silent.

"I've got to stop this before it starts." He kissed her gently. "I've opened a terrible Pandora's box," he told her. "Please, Mags, you've got to help me nail it shut."

eight

CHECKING TO MAKE SURE HIS CAR KEYS were in his pants pocket, Dr. Charles Della Croce stepped out of the front door of his townhouse condominium, locking it behind him.

The Thanksgiving party at Data Tech didn't start until seven. He was more than an hour and a half early. He was planning to go over now, spend some time in the lab, put in an appearance at the cocktail hour, then leave before the tedium of the actual dinner began.

Unless Maggie Winthrop showed up.

If she showed, without a date, he'd stay for dinner.

He hadn't been able to stop thinking about her since she'd appeared at his table in Papa John's Eatery. He'd done a little investigation and found out that she was, indeed, a freelance writer, hired by the corporation for several short-term projects. He'd dug a little further and found an address for her, and a phone number.

He'd even found out that she'd been issued an invitation to tonight's shindig. But whether or not she was going to attend was still a mystery.

He'd gone as far as calling her to find out if perhaps she'd want to go with him. But he'd only reached her answering machine, and she'd never called him back.

Maybe she was out of town.

Or maybe she wasn't as interested as she'd led him to believe at Papa John's.

Maybe that kiss they'd shared hadn't made her head spin the way his had. He hadn't been able to stop thinking about that kiss.

His car was parked on the street, and as he started toward it a wave of fatigue hit him. He turned, heading for the Circle K on the corner and the self-serve coffee inside.

He'd been up well until dawn the night before, working on his time-travel theories. He was close. He was *so* damned close, but it was still out of his grasp. He'd stayed awake until five-thirty, working the equations, again and again.

He'd slept only two hours before he had to get up and go in to work. He'd told no one at Data Tech about his work with time travel. His theories weren't ready yet for public scrutiny. But maybe soon . . .

He went toward the back of the convenience store, where the brewed pots of coffee simmered on burners. He poured himself a large cup and then turned, searching for the correct-size lid.

"Hello, Charles."

Charles nearly spilled the entire cup of coffee down the front of his tuxedo.

It was Maggie Winthrop. But instead of looking the way he remembered her, like a sparklingly pretty girl-next-door, the woman who stood before him was pure sensual elegance.

"Remember me? I'm Maggie—"

"Winthrop," he finished for her, setting his cup back on the counter and quickly taking the hand she extended. "Of course I remember you."

Her hair was up off her shoulders—delicately smooth shoulders exposed by the strapless neckline of her dress. And what a dress! It was the richest shade of brown and made of silky material that clung to her breasts. It swept down all the way to the floor, emphasizing her slender waist and the soft curve of her hips.

"I left a message on your home answering machine," he told her with a smile, fighting to keep his gaze properly above her neck. God, she was a knockout! She was wearing makeup—more, at least, than she had on the other time they'd met. It accentuated her soft lips and her gorgeous eyes and the delicate bone structure of her face.

"You did?" Her eyes lit up with genuine happiness.

Charles realized he was still holding her hand. She hadn't tugged it free from his grasp. He held on even tighter, lacing their fingers together, feeling a surge of pleasure. God knows their attraction was mutual. The connection that flowed between them was hot enough to make his coffee seem tepid. But in addition to that attraction, she honestly seemed to like him. As much as he liked her. And he did, he realized. He liked the sparkle in her smile and the amusement that danced in her eyes.

But tonight there was something else in her eyes as well. He could see a quiet sadness that seemed to linger.

"Yeah," he said. "I guess you didn't get my message."

"No, I haven't . . . been home for a while." As he watched she surreptitiously checked her watch. It was a sign that he was either boring her, or she needed to be somewhere. He couldn't believe the first.

"I called to see if you were going to the Data Tech party." He released her hand. "But obviously, you're heading someplace else tonight."

"No, I was planning to go to Data Tech, but not till a little later." She leaned back against the coffee counter, as if she intended to stay for a while. So much for his second theory. "So, what are you doing here? Do you live nearby?"

"Just down the street," he told her. "Are you meeting some-one at the party?"

"Actually, I'm supposed to meet *you* there."

Now, what the hell did she mean by that?

"I mean, I was hoping to see you there," she added. She held his gaze, smiling slightly, and he felt his pulse accelerate. Had she come to this particular Circle K hoping to bump into him? He knew her address, and while it wasn't far, this convenience store was anything *but* convenient to her. In fact, it was well out of her way.

"Do you have plans for dinner?" He picked up his coffee and started toward the front of the store, hoping he sounded casual.

"Charles, would you mind pouring me a cup of coffee too?"

He looked at her, startled. For just a moment her voice had sounded slightly strained. But her smile was wide and relaxed. "The decaf's up a little too high," she explained. She leaned for-ward, closer to him, and lowered her voice. "And I have limited movement in this dress."

The movement she had just made gave him a breath-taking view of the tantalizing fullness of the tops of her breasts. Charles forced his gaze toward the coffeepots. Decaf. She wanted decaf. "Of course," he said, quickly pouring a cup. He put a lid on it as he cleared his throat. "About dinner . . ."

She looked at her watch again. "I've already ordered room service for tonight. I'd love for you to join me."

He picked up both coffees. He wanted to get out of here. He wanted to see Maggie Winthrop in the warm pink light of the lingering sunset. He wanted to offer her his arm and escort her to some four-star restaurant and . . . "Did you say *room* service?"

Charles turned back to her. She took both cups of coffee from him, setting them back on the counter. God, he didn't even think to ask if she wanted cream and sugar.

But cream and sugar wasn't exactly what she wanted. It wasn't even close. She stepped nearer to him, close enough for an embrace, close enough for a kiss, and rested one hand on the front of his jacket, just over his heart. Her other hand went up to the nape of his neck. She gently pulled his head down while rising on tiptoes to meet him and . . .

Her kiss was sheer perfection. Her lips were so soft, her mouth so sweet. He hesitated in surprise for only the briefest of moments before he opened his mouth to her, deepening the kiss. He put his arms around her, pulling her even closer. His hands encountered the cool smoothness of her dress and the perfect softness of her body underneath.

His arousal was instant. He kissed her again, harder this time, pressing her back against the counter. There was no way she could have missed his physical response to her, yet she didn't push him away. On the contrary, she held him even closer, kissing him just as passionately, just as hungrily.

Dear God, he'd died and gone to heaven.

Except when he pulled back to look at her, he couldn't help but see that her eyes were filled with unshed tears. She turned her head, trying her best to blink them away without him noticing.

So he pretended not to notice. "Don't tell me," he said, trying to keep his voice sounding light. It wasn't hard to do because he was breathless. "Someone's following you again."

Maggie gazed up at him. "Actually, someone's following *you*. Agents from a covert government organization called Wizard-9."

Charles laughed. "Wizard-9, huh? Sounds pretty scary."

"Oh, they're very scary." She glanced at her watch again, then picked up the coffee and started toward the front of the store.

Charles followed, taking out his billfold as she set the paper hot cups on the counter near the cash register.

"Anything else?" the clerk asked. He was about seventeen years old and had straggly facial hair that was supposed to pass for a beard. Charles couldn't remember ever being that young.

"No, that's it, thanks."

"Two eighty-nine." The kid glanced up at Charles, and did a double take. "You again? What happened to your last cup? Drop it or something?"

"Excuse me?" Charles asked. Him again? He hadn't been in here in days. And even then, this wasn't the same clerk who had waited on him.

"Yeah," Maggie said. "We had a little accident." She handed the boy three dollars.

"A what?" Charles said. "Wait a minute, I'm paying for this."

"You can pay me back," Maggie told him, taking the change, grabbing the coffee, and heading for the door. "Come on."

When she walked, a long slit up the side of the dress revealed flashes of gracefully shaped legs.

Charles was almost completely distracted. Almost. "But why did you say—"

Maggie turned to face him. "Charles, I've got a suite at the Century Hotel. Will you come and have dinner there with me?"

Charles was confused about quite a number of things, but this was not one of them. "Absolutely."

Charles was silent as they took the elevator up to the seventh floor of the Century Hotel, where her suite was located.

Maggie gazed at the numbers above the door, watching the three light up and then the four. She was well aware that Charles's eyes were on her. She was also well aware that he entertained high hopes of having more than dinner here in her room.

Maggie knew what Chuck wanted her to do. He wanted her to have dinner with Charles. He wanted her to be bright and funny. He wanted her to charm him, to be some kind of super, extra-strength, high-dosage Maggie. He wanted her to try to condense seven years of friendship into one short evening.

And he wanted her to cement the whole thing by spending the night with Charles.

But what was she supposed to do after this whole awful mess was over? What was she supposed to do after she succeeded in convincing Charles to change his entire life, his entire career—assuming one glorious night of sex could actually do that. Was she supposed to spend the rest of her life with him?

She glanced out of the corner of her eye at the man standing next to her. He was a stranger—except he wasn't. Not really. He looked like Chuck. He kissed like Chuck. He even smelled like Chuck—a faint but tangy whiff of some kind of aftershave mixed with fresh-smelling soap, commingling with his own very male, slightly musky, extremely delicious scent.

But what else was Charles missing besides the scar on his left cheekbone?

Chuck had desired her—maybe even loved her, although he hadn't admitted as much—for seven years. Charles had met her two days ago.

She'd fallen in love with Chuck. But every experience Charles had lived, Chuck had too. Was it possible, then, to love Chuck without loving Charles as well?

Maggie shook her head. This was much too complicated.

And then there was Chuck. Did he love her? She'd thought perhaps he did. Last night he'd made love to her so passionately, so emotionally. But maybe he had been simply sating his desire by having sex with someone who looked like the woman he truly cared about—a woman who had died in his arms seven years in the future.

If so, what an incredibly complicated love triangle *that* would be. And if Maggie did what Chuck wanted, she would be involved with Charles, too, making their relationships even more tangled. That couldn't possibly be the solution to *any*thing.

Maggie didn't know *what* the solution was, but the first step seemed kind of obvious.

She had to tell Charles the truth.

And as the elevator doors opened onto the seventh floor and

they headed down the long, elegantly carpeted corridor to the fancy suite that Chuck had used money from Charles's own bank account to pay for, Charles gave Maggie the perfect opportunity to start telling him the truth.

"So," he said. "What's with the suite at the Century Hotel? Are freelance writers making higher salaries these days than I thought?"

Chuck had prepped Maggie. He'd wanted her to tell Charles that she was staying here because she was having the interior of her house painted and the fumes were too strong.

Instead, as she fitted the key into the lock, she turned to look up at Charles. He was smiling—not that tight, grim little half smile that Chuck so grudgingly gave away. Instead, his face was relaxed, his smile wide. It made him breathtakingly handsome. It lit his eyes, defusing some of the hot attraction that still burned there.

But only some of it.

"Actually, I'm staying here because those men—remember, the ones from Wizard-9 who were following you—they're waiting for me at my home, because they want to kill me." Maggie laughed, and it sounded forced and fake. But now she was babbling and she couldn't stop. "It sounds like one of those brainteasers, the one that goes: There's a man and he wants to go home, but he can't because there are two masked men waiting there for him. You know, it sounds really scary, but it turns out the man is a baseball player on third base, home is home plate, and the two masked men are the catcher and the ump."

Maggie pushed the door open and stepped into the room, praying that after that little outburst Charles wouldn't simply turn tail and run. "Except my own personal brainteaser isn't about baseball. Mine *is* very scary."

She turned and looked back at Charles, who was still standing silently in the hallway. "Are you coming in?"

He hesitated. "Are you . . ."

"Crazy?" she finished for him. "No. I'm sorry, I'm a little on edge. Please. Come in, Charles."

"I wasn't asking if you were crazy." Charles stepped into the room. "I was asking...Maggie, are you in some kind of trouble?"

He followed her into the spacious living area of the suite, barely even glancing at the luxurious furnishings, at the gorgeous rose-patterned drapes and matching upholstery. His concern tinged his voice. "Because I have a friend who specializes in getting people out of trouble. I could give him a call and—"

"Boyd Rogers is on leave," Maggie told him, turning to face him.

Chuck had told her about Boyd today as they'd stopped to get his hair cut. Back at that roadhouse, when they'd bought that little illegal gun he wore under his jacket, he'd called Boyd and warned him to make himself invisible. Chuck was afraid Wizard-9 would try to even up their odds by taking Boyd out now, before he became a major player. His old friend had trusted him enough to agree to take a weeklong leave at an unreported destination without a lengthy explanation.

Now Charles *was* staring at her as if she were crazy. Or a mind reader. "How do you know..."

Maggie sat down on the rose-patterned sofa. "Charles, I need to talk to you about your work with time travel."

The change that came over him was extreme. One moment he'd been looking at her with concern in his liquid brown eyes. Then it had changed to wariness with her mention of Boyd. Now...If a look could cause frostbite, Maggie would definitely require hospitalization.

Still, along with the chill, she could also see curiosity in his eyes. She was counting on that scientist's need to know to keep him from simply walking away.

"What are you talking about? Currently at Data Tech I'm working on—"

"It's not something you're doing at Data Tech. Not yet. Right now you're working on your own."

He took several steps toward the door, but then spun around and took several steps back. "I haven't told anyone about my theories. How could you possibly know?"

Maggie smiled. "You're probably not going to believe this—but, then again, if *any*one's going to believe it, it's going to have to be you—"

The chill in the room dropped another thirty degrees as his eyes narrowed. "Are you the one who broke into my house a few days ago?"

She shook her head. "No." She crossed her legs, and the slit in the slim skirt of her dress flipped open. His gaze flashed in that direction. Chuck had certainly been right about the physical-attraction thing. It was strong enough to distract Charles even now, when he should have been at his least distractible. "No, I'm not."

"Then who? Someone has. Is it this Wizard-9 you keep talking about . . . ?"

"No. The agents from Wizard-9 are afraid to get too close to you. It's Chuck they want dead."

"Chuck?"

This was not going to be easy to explain. Maggie stood up. "Do you like this dress?"

With a sudden burst of exasperation, Charles ran his hands back through his hair. His mouth was held in a grim line, his eyes burned with intensity, and with the exception of that missing scar on his left cheekbone, he suddenly looked exactly like Chuck. He even sounded like Chuck as he kept his voice carefully tight and controlled. "Will you please just tell me what the hell—"

"I'm *trying*," she said. "Just answer my question."

"Yes," he said. Some of that control slipped. He clearly wasn't as good at holding everything in as Chuck was. "All right? Yes, I like it very, *very* much—"

"You should. You picked it out for me."

"No, I didn't—*God!* Why am I arguing with you about a dress? You're obviously—"

"Sometime within the next seven years, those time-travel theories you're working on will become legitimate enough for Data Tech to sponsor your research," Maggie raised her voice to inform him. It wasn't long before he closed his mouth and listened.

She continued, more quietly. "And sometime within the next seven years the Wells Project will be born and your theories will become reality. Your theories will work, Charles, but some very bad people from an organization called Wizard-9 will want to get their hands on your time-travel device—you call it a Runabout. They'll use it to go back in time and plant a bomb in the White House that will kill the U.S. President, and then they'll try to kill you too. But you'll escape, and you'll use a prototype to come back in time to try to set things right."

Charles slowly sat down. "My God."

"You'll come back from the future, and one of the things you will do is to pick out this dress for me to wear—a dress that's sure to catch your attention." She sat down across from him. "There are two Dr. Charles Della Croces in Phoenix right this very moment. One of you is thirty-five years old, the other is forty-two. Your forty-two-year-old self—he calls himself Chuck—he's at Data Tech right now, pretending to be you.

"He was in the Circle K with me when you arrived. While I kept you busy he bought a cup of coffee and went out. He took your car over to Data Tech, and the agents from Wizard-9 followed him, thinking he was you.

"You see, Wizard-9 wants to make sure Chuck and I do nothing that will prevent you from developing your time-travel theories. They're following you to make sure we don't get close to you."

Charles was silent, just watching her. Then, as if he couldn't hold it in any longer, he leaned forward, spearing her with the intensity of his gaze. "How does it work?" he asked. "Where have I been going wrong in my equations? Is it the—"

"Whoa." Maggie held up her hand. "I don't know anything about the theories."

"God, I can't believe it actually works!"

He stood up in one swift motion, reaching across the coffee table to pull her to her feet. He grabbed her around the waist and whirled her around the room. "It works, God, it really works!"

Maggie laughed at his totally un-Chuck-like outburst. She'd never seen him act like this before. She hadn't known he was capable of such sheer, unadulterated joy.

But as quickly as he'd started to dance, he stopped. He nearly ran to a small writing desk that sat near the entrance to the room. He opened the drawers, rifling through them until he came up with paper and a pen. He quickly brought them back to the sitting area, and leaning against the coffee table, he began to scribble what looked like equations as he mumbled aloud.

Maggie's strengths didn't lie in mathematics, but she knew one thing. He had to have a mind like a computer to be able to think in terms of the kind of equations he'd just scratched onto that piece of paper.

For the first time she fully realized how incredibly intelligent Charles Della Croce was. For so long she'd thought of Chuck as a kind of a cowboy, a gunslinger, a fighter. But in truth, Chuck *was* Charles, and he was also a brilliant scientist.

She wished, though, that he hadn't forgotten how to smile, to laugh, to break into spontaneous dance.

As she'd seen Chuck do nearly a dozen times, Charles seemed to become aware that he was drumming his fingers impatiently on the tabletop. And just as she'd seen Chuck do, he forced himself to stop.

He was so like Chuck, but even so, she could see the differences. Charles didn't have that hard edge, that suspiciousness, that hard-as-steel toughness that made Chuck seem impenetrable. He still had that same piercing intensity, but he also had a charming touch of youth and innocence—that ability to become genuinely excited.

Both men had the habit of keeping themselves slightly distanced from her by both their body language and a certain detachment in their eyes. She'd broken through Chuck's control a few times, but it had required tremendous patience and hard work.

Charles's control seemed far less anchored in place.

As Maggie watched he threw down the pen and raked his fingers through his hair. "What am I doing? All I have to do is talk to . . . my other self. He can tell me where I'm going wrong. Chuck, right?" He paused. "Why does he call himself Chuck?"

"Because I gave him that nickname," Maggie told him.

He looked at her. Really looked at her. Maggie could practically see the wheels turning in his head. "Are we lovers?" he asked quietly. The chill in his eyes was completely gone. He smiled slightly, almost shyly. "Please say yes."

She nodded. "Yes," she said. "Lovers—and friends."

Charles nodded too. "That's a good combination."

Maggie had to look away. "Chuck doesn't seem to think so."

"Of course he does. I should know because he's me, right? I'm him." He smiled again. "It's funny, when we first met, I had this odd sensation, as if I knew you already—and in a sense I did. Only it was in the future that I knew you, not in the past." He stood up again as if he couldn't sit still another moment. "God, I can't believe it's really going to *work!* Do you know how many years I've been working on these theories?"

Maggie shook her head. "No." Chuck hadn't told her. Chuck hadn't told her much of anything about himself.

"For more than twenty-five years," he said. "I started the basis of these theories back when I was seven years old."

"Why?" she asked, leaning forward slightly. "Why is developing time travel so important to you?" Maybe *Charles* would tell her . . .

But he didn't answer right away. He just looked at her. "It is," he finally said. "It's very important to me. Ever since—" He broke off. "I haven't told you anything about it?"

Maggie shook her head. "Sharing's not exactly one of your strengths."

He changed the subject. "You said I came back in time to 'set things right.'"

She met his gaze. "That's right. Seven years from now your top priority will not be to develop time travel. It'll be to make sure you *don't* develop it. Charles, that's what I'm here to ask you to do. Stop your research. Don't let it go any further."

She'd shocked him. She saw it clearly in his eyes. Chuck never would have let it show. "How can I stop when I'm obviously so close to success?"

"Because if you *don't* stop, hundreds of people will die. Including *you*."

He silently started to pace.

Maggie turned on the couch to face him. "Chuck seemed to think you would do well to go into medical research and—"

"But it's all going to be different now," Charles interrupted her. "Now that I know what's going to happen, I can make sure this Wizard-9 isn't involved in the project."

"There's no way you can do that. They'll kill you and steal the Runabout if they have to."

"So what am I supposed to do? Burn my papers? Erase my computer files? Promise never even to *think* about time travel ever again?"

"Yes," Maggie said. "Please."

He stopped pacing. That wasn't what he'd expected her to

say. He stared down at her. "Are you sure you want me to do that?" he asked. "Just like that, everything will be different. One tiny seemingly inconsequential decision, and my entire life will take an absolutely different path."

"And a lot of people won't die because a bomb *isn't* planted at the White House. And you won't become the target for assassins and terrorists and other crazies who want to get their hands on the Wells Project. And Wizard-9 agents *won't* chase you across the better part of a decade, trying to kill you before you have the chance to change what they've already done."

He stepped toward her, gently touching her cheek with one finger. "And we might never meet. Are you willing to risk that, Maggie?"

"But we *have* met," she countered. "We're here, right now—"

"Are we?" he asked. "I'm here, but are you? Are you from the future? Because if you are, if I make that one little seemingly inconsequential decision, you're going to disappear. You and Chuck will vanish."

Vanish?

"Think about it," he said. "If I don't continue, the Wells Project won't happen. I won't invent the Runabout...."

"I'm not from the future. But... Oh, my God," she whispered. "If you don't invent the Runabout, there'll be no way for Chuck to travel back in time and—" She broke off, staring up at Charles. If Charles didn't invent time travel, Chuck wouldn't have come in the first place. None of the events of the past few days would have happened—including Chuck's appearance in her backyard. Charles was right. If he did what she asked and turned his back on his time-travel research, Chuck would simply disappear. "Will I even remember that he was here? Will I remember him at all?"

There was compassion in his eyes. "I don't know."

Maggie closed her eyes, remembering the way Chuck had kissed her in the dressing room of the tuxedo shop. They were about to leave for the convenience store, to intercept Charles, and Chuck had pulled her into his arms and kissed her so sweetly, so tenderly. She realized now that that had been a kiss good-bye. He'd fully intended never to see her again.

She remembered how Chuck had cried back in the motel when he'd told her how she would die, seven years in the future. She remembered the steely determination in his voice as he swore he wouldn't let it happen that way this time around.

She hadn't realized it, but he was prepared to give up everything for her. Even his own existence.

Right now he was at the Data Tech party, all alone, waiting for himself to cease to be. He knew that if Maggie succeeded, he would disappear. With just—what had Charles called it?—one little seemingly inconsequential decision, the past seven years of Chuck's life, everything he'd done and dreamed and hoped and felt, would be gone.

Maggie stood up. Her legs felt weak, and her voice sounded just as wobbly. "I have to find Chuck." She headed for the door. "Come on, Charles, you've got to help me. We've got to go to Data Tech, and you've got to trade places with Chuck again. I have to talk to him. There's got to be another way."

nine

CHUCK WORKED HIS WAY THROUGH THE crowded Data Tech lobby, heading for the bank of pay phones, careful not to let the Wizard-9 agents get too close.

He'd put some makeup on his scar. From a distance it looked fine. But up close, it wouldn't take long for someone who knew him as well as Ken Goodwin did to figure out that he was the older-model Della Croce.

The way things were going, it was only a matter of time before his real identity was exposed.

He couldn't *believe* the memories that were flooding through him.

Maggie had taken his plan and tossed it right out the window. Instead of trusting that Chuck would know the best way to manipulate his own past self, she had decided to go for the direct approach with Charles. She'd actually gone and told him the truth.

The *truth*.

Chuck cursed himself for a fool. This was his fault. He should have explained to Maggie why telling Charles the truth was a very, very bad idea. He should have told her about that goddamned game of Chinese checkers he didn't play when he was seven. He should have told her that Charles had an extremely powerful and compelling reason to want to continue his time-travel research. Telling him that time travel was possible, and that it was within reach, within less than a decade's worth of work—that wasn't the way to get him to quit.

And now Maggie and Charles were coming here, to Data Tech. He knew even when he dialed the phone that no one would pick up at the suite in the Century Hotel. He knew that if he could remember riding in a taxi alongside of Maggie, then they were already on their way over.

Chuck ran his hand through his hair as he tried to think. Think. He *had* to think. He would continue to be a step behind them if he waited for the memories to kick in. He would remember the door Charles and Maggie came in only *after* they came through it. And when he got there, they'd be gone.

Unless he could remember their conversation. But this time his memories were ghostly and faded, as if everything Maggie and Charles were doing really *did* take place seven years ago. It was hard enough to remember their actions, let alone their words.

No, his best bet would be to second-guess them.

Okay. That shouldn't be too hard. After all, he *was* Charles. What would he do?

He's just been told that his time-travel theories are on the right track. He's jazzed by that, *and* by the fact that he's in the company of an incredibly attractive woman. The potential danger only heightens the excitement he feels. What would he do?

Maggie wouldn't know that Ken Goodwin had augmented his forces, hiring outside help and nearly doubling his number of men. She would have told Charles that there were only four Wizard-9 agents. He'd figure with such limited manpower, Wizard-9 would either watch the back entrances, or keep an eye on the man they thought to be Charles.

And he and Maggie would waltz in through the front door, hoping to be lost in the crowd.

Chuck took the stairs up to the second floor and stood leaning on the railing overlooking the sculpture of a flock of birds in flight. He pretended he was part of a conversation between two vice-presidents and an office manager. He laughed when they laughed, nodded when they nodded, all the while scanning the crowd in the lobby below.

And then he saw them—Maggie in that incredible dress. The sight of her made his heart stop. She had her hand in the crook of Charles's arm as they walked toward the building from the well-lit parking lot. Despite their differences in height, they made a very handsome couple.

Chuck felt a surge of jealousy and anger that he didn't bother to squelch. With a sudden flash of clarity, he could remember what he was thinking, what he was feeling down there as he walked with Maggie on his arm. And he wasn't thinking about Maggie's safety. He wasn't thinking about Maggie hardly at all. He was focusing on his damned theories and equations, on the prospect of meeting his future self and having all of his questions answered. He was an idiot, a fool.

And Maggie . . . Maggie was looking through the glass front of the lobby, searching for him. She found him almost right away, and their gazes locked. Despite the distance and the pane of glass between them, it was as if she had reached out and touched him.

She was angry, she was hurt, she was scared. He could see all that in her eyes. And she loved him. He saw that too.

She wanted to be with him, and God, he wanted the same. But the only way that could ever happen was by talking Charles into giving up his work with time travel. Only then did they even have a chance. He wanted to grab his past self by the neck and shake him until he realized what he had right underneath his nose. Maggie. He had Maggie.

Chuck saw two different cars pull up directly behind Charles and Maggie, and then everything seemed to switch into slow motion.

The doors of both cars opened and several very big men dressed in dark suits burst out. Charles spun around in surprise as they grabbed both him and Maggie and began pulling them toward the open doors of the cars.

As Chuck watched in horror Maggie fought to get away, and one of the dark-suited men grabbed her around the waist. She fought even harder, kicking and scratching and biting. And screaming.

Chuck couldn't hear a thing. The glass windows that separated them kept all outside noise from the lobby.

It was surreal. Inside, the party guests sipped their drinks, talked, and laughed, while just outside an abduction was taking place.

It was as if he were watching a silent movie. He couldn't hear Maggie, but he could read her lips.

She was shouting his name, over and over again.

As Charles and Maggie were shoved none too gently into two separate cars, Chuck couldn't help himself. "*Maggie!*" He sprang over the side of the railing, dropping heavily to the tiled floor of the lobby below.

Someone screamed, several other people dropped their drinks in alarm, and a murmur of voices rose up.

He scrambled to his feet, rushing out toward the parking lot.

But all he saw were taillights as the cars sped away.

Chuck turned back to the lobby doors, well aware that he was the subject of a great deal of attention. In a flash of realization, he knew that he'd given himself away. Sure enough, he could see at least one of the Wizard-9 agents fighting to get to him through the crowd.

Chuck turned and ran.

"It occurs to me that you might be of more use to us dead than alive."

Maggie lifted her chin, giving the man who sat having a late lunch at the poolside table her best version of the evil eye. "My tax dollars pay your salary, don't they? What a terrible waste."

Ken Goodwin just smiled. He had a bland, almost round, friendly face. His wire-rim glasses made him look doubly harmless. Maggie knew he was anything but.

"Dr. Della Croce is very attached to you," he noted in his vowel-flattened New England accent. "And you to him."

Maggie gave nearly all of her attention to a rough spot on her thumbnail. "So?"

Goodwin laughed. "Did he tell you that in his time line, you were married to someone else? He must've yearned for you for years—it's very romantic. Still, he managed to hide his feelings quite well. I'd known him for quite some time, and I didn't suspect a thing."

The afternoon sun was warm on the back of her neck. It felt good after being locked in the chill of the house since last night. Maggie looked up. "What's your point?" she said flatly.

"By killing you, we seem to have sent Dr. Della Croce into a state that I call self-righteous rage. It appears most commonly in war zones, when an entire platoon of soldiers is decimated by a single man. That man is usually defending his farm or his family. Or avenging their deaths. He's got the advantage of knowing the territory and he's driven by this inhuman power, this self-righteous rage."

Ken Goodwin motioned to his men, both of whom carried lengths of rope, and they hoisted Maggie to her feet. They were neither rough nor gentle—they were simply intent upon getting the job done. And that job seemed to be to lash her hands behind her back and tie her feet together.

Maggie pulled away. "Get away from me!"

But her hands were already tied, and strain as she might against the rope, she couldn't get free. Together, the two men had no trouble binding her ankles.

They lifted her up, but Ken Goodwin stopped them with a single gesture. "Not yet," he told them, then turned back to Maggie.

"What we've got to do," he continued, "is push Dr. Della Croce—the one you call Chuck—further over the edge. We've got to make him react rather than act. We've got to lure him here into *our* territory. Then we can take care of him and clean up this nasty little mess he's made."

"Take care of him? You mean, *kill* him."

His smile didn't warm his eyes. "He's already dead. He was listed as one of the missing in the Data Tech lab explosion."

Goodwin looked up toward the house, toward a large picture window on the second floor. "Good, now we can continue," he murmured.

Maggie turned and saw Charles standing in the window, one of the agents holding tightly to his arm. Thank God he was safe. She hadn't seen him since last night, when the Wizard-9 agents had pulled him into one car and her into another. She hadn't even been sure that he was here, at this luxurious ranch well on the outskirts of town.

"I've read Dr. Della Croce's work on double memories," Goodwin told her. "Fascinating concepts. Apparently since Charles here is a younger version of the other Dr. Della Croce, everything he experiences—everything he sees and hears and feels—appear as memories in the older man's mind."

It had worried Maggie that they hadn't blindfolded her as they brought her here, but now she realized that Ken Goodwin *wanted* her and Charles to know where they were—so that Chuck would know too. So that he would come here, to rescue her. So they could catch him and kill him, here on their own territory.

Maggie felt fear slice through her as she gazed up at Charles. She had to talk to him. She had to tell Chuck, through him, not to come.

As she watched through the window Charles turned to the man holding his arm and spoke to him questioningly, gesturing down at her. The man said something back, with a grin.

Goodwin nodded to the men who had tied Maggie up, and they each took hold of one of her arms.

"Hey!" Maggie said as they began dragging her backward. "What are you doing?"

Up at the second-floor picture window, she could see Charles break free from the man who was holding him. He rushed toward the glass as if he were trying to go straight through it. But it stopped him and he pressed his hands against it as he shouted her name, loud enough for her to hear.

And then Maggie felt nothing behind her. Nothing but air as the two men pushed her out and back. With a splash, she went into the swimming pool.

Her hands and feet were tied.

She was in water over her head, and her hands were tied securely behind her back.

Panic engulfed her as completely as the water surrounded her.

She tried to kick her legs, to push herself back to the surface, but the weight of her long dress only dragged her down.

Maggie fought as her lungs burned and her heart pounded. She fought on, knowing that this was a fight that would be very hard to win.

"Get her out of there! Right now! Goddammit, get her *out* of that pool!"

Charles felt the Wizard-9 agent's nose break as he drove the heel of his hand hard into the man's face. It was enough to make the man loosen his elbow lock around Charles's neck. Another hard jab to the man's throat, and he was free. There were no rules. This was street fighting at its harshest, its dirtiest.

And Charles had the advantage. From the way his opponent was pulling his punches, he suspected it was a priority that he be kept alive—and not just alive, but in good health.

He didn't stop yelling at the top of his lungs, screaming his rage like a madman, as he scrambled away from the Wizard-9 agent. He grabbed a chair and swung it with all of his strength across the room at the door as it opened. Two more Wizard-9 agents ducked to avoid being hit. "You bring her up here to me *right now!*"

The room was trashed. And what furniture hadn't been bumped into or knocked over in his fight with the first bruiser, Charles went for now, throwing end tables and lamps—anything that he could pick up—toward the open door. "Now, god-dammit! I want her up here *now!*"

He'd never experienced such a surge of fear as when he'd watched Maggie tossed so casually into the swimming pool, her hands and feet tied. He barely knew her, and most of what he knew about her was based on sheer attraction. Yet the thought of her death made him crazy. He'd never felt this kind of anger before. Or this kind of helplessness.

The agent he'd been fighting lumbered groggily to his feet inside the room, blood streaming from his nose. He turned toward the door, and Charles turned to look, too, brandishing a floor lamp, ready to use it as a weapon against whomever might be trying to come in.

But it was Maggie. Soaking wet and coughing up water, she was pushed into the room, like some sort of sacrificial virgin sent to appease his monstrous anger. Her hands and her feet were still tied, and she fell heavily onto the floor.

Charles's relief was dizzying. Maggie was alive. She wasn't still lying on the bottom of that swimming pool. He dropped the lamp with a clatter and went to her, pulling her up into his arms.

She was shaking and gasping and getting him nearly as wet as she was, but he didn't give a damn. She was alive!

He looked up toward the still-open door and into the eyes of the man who had introduced himself as Ken Goodwin—the head of Wizard-9.

"We weren't really going to harm her," Goodwin said chidingly, looking around at the mess and shaking his head. "We were just trying to get a little message to your future counterpart."

He was lying. Charles knew it. Goodwin was lying. He'd had every intention of letting Maggie drown at the bottom of that swimming pool. It was only because Charles had gone ballistic that they'd pulled her out. Goodwin had been afraid that Charles was going to injure himself in some way, and rather than risk that, he'd let Maggie live.

Charles looked away from Goodwin, afraid the other man would see his sudden realization in his eyes. He had the power. Goodwin and his men from Wizard-9 may have been the captors, but Charles had the ultimate power.

They needed him, and they needed him alive.

Goodwin held up a thickly bound set of papers. It looked like the reports the R&D staff at Data Tech often put together. "I have all the answers to your questions about time travel right here, Dr. Della Croce."

Maggie struggled to sit up. "No! Don't look at it, Charles—"

Goodwin stepped closer. "Why don't we let Miss Winthrop get dried off while Dr. Della Croce and I talk?"

"You *can't* look at it," Maggie continued, her voice as urgent as her eyes. "Charles, please. It's important that you don't ever allow yourself to know how the Wells Project works."

"But, Maggie—"

"Maggie is obviously not a scientist, Doctor," Ken Goodwin interrupted. "She doesn't understand your need to know. Let my men take care of her while you read this report." He motioned two of the agents forward.

Charles would've sold his soul to see inside the covers of that report. But he wouldn't sell Maggie's. He pushed her behind him. "No. She stays here with me or we don't talk at all."

Goodwin sighed.

"Call your men off," Charles said warningly.

"We can do this the easy way or the hard way," Goodwin told him.

Charles didn't hesitate. "The hard way. She stays with me."

Goodwin motioned to the other agents, and they backed off. "All right," he said. "The hard way it is."

ten

MAGGIE'S HANDS AND FEET WERE STILL
tied, and even after Charles set her down on the floor, he held on
to her to keep her from falling over. The door shut, but only after Ken Goodwin tossed the Wells Project report into the closet
after them.

They were locked in an empty walk-in closet. A single bulb
burned overhead as a full set of bolts were thrown on the outside
of the door.

This was Ken Goodwin's hard way. He was pitting Charles
and Maggie against each other by putting them here, in such
close quarters, with nothing but a light and the report that
Charles so desperately wanted to read.

The report that Maggie so desperately *didn't* want him
to read.

In the meantime Goodwin was sitting tight, waiting for
Chuck to show up and attempt to rescue them. Waiting for him
to come into Wizard-9's territory. Waiting to kill him.

"Are you all right?" Charles asked, his eyes dark with concern.

"Charles, you have to help me get a message to Chuck,"
Maggie said as he helped her down into a sitting position on the
carpeted floor. Her dress and hair were still soaking wet, and she

blinked water out of her eyes as she looked up at him. "We have to warn him not to come here."

He looked around the tiny closet. "We have to find a way out of here."

"I was locked in here last night," Maggie told him. "The air-conditioner vent is too small—believe me, I already tried. The only way out is through the door. No, we're in here until they let us out—until you read that report, or until Chuck comes and they kill him. And *that's* why we have to warn him to stay away!"

"Warn him through double memories." Charles bent down and worked to untie the rope that lashed her feet together. His fingers were warm against her chilled skin. He glanced at her. "Can they really be that clear? Clear enough to remember a conversation—a warning?"

"Double memories can be pretty faint. At first it feels like a weird kind of déjà vu. But Chuck said that once you get used to—" Maggie broke off, remembering something else Chuck had said. Something about . . . ? "Charles, kiss me."

He glanced up at her in surprise.

"There was something Chuck told me about double memories and glandular activity. If you kiss me, he'll remember."

Charles hesitated. "Maggie, I don't—"

She pulled her still-bound feet away from him and struggled to her knees. It wasn't easy with the sodden weight of her dress dragging against her legs and with her hands still tied behind her back.

"This *will* work," she insisted. "Kiss me."

He leaned forward, obviously doing this only to humor her. Softly, gently, almost chastely, he brushed his lips against hers.

"Oh please," Maggie scoffed. "I'm not your grandmother. *Kiss* me, Charles. Come *on!* Make it memorable!"

His eyes flared with heat and he pulled her against him so forcefully that nearly all the air was squeezed from her body. And then he kissed her, sweeping his tongue possessively into her mouth, stealing all that was left of her breath.

It was a kiss of pure fire, pure passion. And Maggie kissed him back just as fiercely, just as hungrily, opening herself to him.

He kissed her harder, deeper, inhaling her, consuming her, and her heart pounded wildly as heat surged through her veins.

It was a kiss that *she* would never forget.

"Don't come here, Chuck," she murmured breathlessly, kissing him again and again, praying that her words would stand out in his memory. She had to believe he'd remember. Chuck had remembered their conversation when she'd met Charles at that lunch place in Scottsdale. He'd remembered telling her about carrot cake. He'd remembered *that* kiss. "It's a trap—Goodwin and his men are ready for you. They're hoping you'll make a mistake, that you'll lose your temper and patience. But there's still time. I'm all right. I'm with Charles now and we're safe for the moment. Whatever you do, be careful. Think it through."

She kissed Charles again, telling herself it was only to drive home her words. It wasn't because she wanted to lose herself in the strength of his passion, in the heat of his hunger for her.

Charles was breathing hard as he pulled back to gaze down into her eyes. He cupped her face with the palm of one hand and traced her lips with his thumb. "What is it about you?" he breathed. "What is this power you have over me?"

Maggie lost herself in the midnight depths of his eyes. Eyes so like Chuck's. "Maybe it's destiny," she whispered. "Or maybe it's knowing that in the future we'll be lovers."

He lowered his mouth to hers and kissed her again, so softly this time, so sweetly. Maggie felt herself melt.

"For you, we're lovers right now," he told her. "But I've got to wait seven years. Seven *years*." He gave her a crooked half smile that was so like Chuck's. "Something tells me, as much as I'd like to, it's a little too soon to start the foreplay."

Maggie laughed. When she'd been at the bottom of that swimming pool, she had been so sure she'd never have the chance to laugh ever again.

"Let me get these ropes off of you." He gently pushed her back so that he could untie the rope that bound her feet.

"Charles, thank you."

He glanced up at her as he finally worked the ropes loose. "For letting you communicate with Chuck through me?" He gave her another crooked smile. "It was my pleasure. Literally."

Maggie couldn't keep from wincing as he pulled the rope from her ankles.

Charles looked down and saw that the rough cord had rubbed her skin raw as she'd fought to free herself in the swimming pool. "Oh, God, I'm sorry!" He pulled her feet up and onto his lap. "I wasn't being careful—that must've hurt!"

"I'm okay," she said softly. And she was. She was alive. "You know, I really thought I was going to drown. I thought..." She shook her head.

"You thought Ken Goodwin was going to kill you," he continued her thought, "because he figured that Chuck—that *I*— had traveled through time to try to save you once already. If you're dead, that gives Chuck a powerful reason *not* to terminate the Wells Project before it even starts. In fact, Goodwin's probably banking on the fact that if you're dead, Chuck's going to work to keep the Wells Project alive so that he can have another chance to go back in time and save you."

Maggie shivered. The closet, like the rest of the house, was cold. It was November in the desert, and although the days were warm, the nights could be quite chilly. And the sun wasn't hot enough during the day to heat this big house. "If Goodwin wants me dead, why didn't he just let me drown?"

"Because I wouldn't allow that. We've got to get you out of that wet dress." Charles gently took her feet from his lap and moved around to begin untying her hands.

Maggie turned to look back at him. "That room they brought me to. The furniture in the room you were held in was wrecked. What did you do?"

He glanced into her eyes. "I played what turns out to be our trump card."

She could feel her wrists burn as he tugged gently at the rope and she couldn't keep from drawing in a sharp breath.

"Maggie, I'm sorry. Your wrists are pretty scraped up too. I don't think I can get this rope off without hurting you."

"Just do it. I'll be okay."

He did. It took several long, agonizing seconds, but then the rope finally was off of her. Her fingers were numb and her shoulders ached as she pulled her hands in front of her. "What trump card?" she asked Charles, trying to ignore the tears of pain that were stinging her eyes. She pushed her wet hair out of her face and hiked up her soggy dress as she turned to face him.

"Goodwin needs me alive," Charles told her. "That's how we're going to get out of here. I'm going to hold my own self hostage."

Maggie shook her hands, trying to bring life back into her numb fingers. "How? We don't have enough time for a hunger strike. And I doubt threatening to hold your breath until you turn blue is going to work."

Charles gave her a quick smile. "I haven't quite figured out the how part yet, but I'm working on it." He shrugged out of his fight-tattered jacket and began taking off his tuxedo shirt.

Maggie couldn't help but notice when he glanced down at the Wells Project report still lying on the floor. It was only a matter of time before he reached for it. But right now his priorities were with her. "Come on," he said gently. "Get out of that dress before you catch pneumonia. You can put on my shirt and jacket."

Maggie didn't move, and he turned around so that his back was to her. "I won't look," he added.

Maybe he *should* look. Maybe that would keep him from looking at the Wells Project report instead.

Maggie closed her eyes, still feeling the fire of his kisses. "I can't get the zipper. My fingers..." It wasn't quite true, but he wouldn't know that.

She heard him turn around, felt him touch her gently as he searched for the tiny zipper pull on the back of her dress. The sound of the zipper going down seemed to echo in the silence.

There was no way he could miss the fact that she wasn't wearing a bra. In fact, he probably already knew that from the way the wet fabric of the dress was glued to her like a second skin. Her breasts were clearly outlined, her nipples taut from the cold. Still, the unavoidable intimacy of her completely bare back—bare from the nape of her neck all the way down to the lace of her panties—exposed by the simple pull of a zipper made it obviously clear.

She could hear him swallow, hear his quiet breathing. She could hear her own heart beating in that fraction of a second between her decision and her ability to act.

And then Maggie acted. She pulled the dress off, stepping out of it as it sank in a heavy wet pile on the floor. She didn't know if Charles had turned around to give her privacy, but she had to guess from the way he wrapped his shirt around her that he hadn't.

She turned to face him, pulling the shirt off her shoulders.

He was wearing only his tuxedo pants, and he looked like some kind of exotic male stripper. And she—she was wearing only slightly more than he had been wearing that day, seven years in his future, when she'd first set eyes on him.

Chuck had wanted her to seduce Charles. He seemed to think that Maggie would have no trouble at all, that Charles would be unable to resist her. And from the sudden volcanic flare of heat in Charles's eyes at the sight of her wearing only the white lace of her panties, it seemed as if he was right.

But Charles was not just a man. He was a brilliant man. And the crooked smile he gave her was rueful. "Boy, you *really* don't want me to look at that report, do you?"

Maggie felt herself blush as he reached for the shirt in her hands and held it open for her. Closing her eyes in embarrassment, she slipped her arms into the sleeves. He turned her to face him, and began buttoning the front, as if she were a child.

"Now would probably be a good time for you to tell me exactly why you don't want me to read that report," he continued.

"I'm not sure I can speak and die of embarrassment at the same time," she told him.

He caught her chin with his hand, tipping her head up, and she opened her eyes to find herself looking directly into his eyes.

"I think I'm probably going to spend the rest of my life regretting that I didn't seize the moment and take advantage of you." He smiled crookedly. "God, I don't just think it—I *know* it."

For one brief moment Maggie was certain that he was going to lean forward and kiss her again. But instead of covering her mouth with his, he released her, stepped back, and put some distance between them.

"But you belong to someone else," he continued quietly. "Someone that I'm not—not yet, anyway. And as much as I'd like to let you . . . distract me, it wouldn't be right."

Maggie turned away, picking up the sodden mass of her dress, trying to hide the emotion that surged through her at his soft words. She hung her dress over one of the bars that stretched lengthwise across the small space. "Funny, I was just thinking how like him you are." She turned to face him. "You have to promise me that if . . . something *does* happen to me—"

"I'm not going to let anything happen to you—"

She took a step toward him. "Charles, they have guns and we don't. Think about it. If Chuck doesn't storm the gates, trying to get us out, and if you don't read the Wells Project report, I'm willing to bet that by the time the sun sets, Ken Goodwin will stop trying to persuade you to see things his way—he'll start using force. And the first thing he'll do is take *me* out of the picture—permanently. And Chuck will want to find a way to go back in time again, to save me. Again."

Charles reached for the report, still lying on the floor. "So maybe I should do what Ken Goodwin wants."

Maggie moved faster, putting her foot on it before he could pick it up. "I'm afraid if you read this, there'll be no turning back. I'm afraid once you understand the theories and the equations you used to make the Runabout work, you won't be able to change your entire destiny with just one simple decision. I'm afraid that what you learn will take you past the point of no return."

Charles sat down on the floor, leaning back against the wall and tiredly taking off his black dress shoes. "Maggie, you have no idea how badly I want to look at that report."

She sat down next to him. "Really? Even knowing that in seven years you'll be willing to trade your entire life for a chance to walk away from the information that's in there?"

He was silent.

"If Chuck were here right now," she told him, "he'd be urging you to take all of your theories on time travel and just let them go. He'd tell you that you have the power to end this once and for all. Right here. Right now. All you need to do is make that decision. No, you won't work on time travel anymore. Yes, you'll go back to school, finish up your medical degree, and start working full-time on finding a cure for AIDS. Or cancer. Or *some*thing. Something good. Something that can't be used as a weapon by unscrupulous people."

"If I do that," Charles said quietly, "if I decide right now to do that, you won't ever see Chuck again."

Maggie felt her eyes fill with tears. "I know."

"What if there's some way we can make this work?" Charles

turned to face her, taking her hand and lacing their fingers together. "What if there's something Chuck's overlooked, something he hasn't come up with, some way we can stop Wizard-9
and *still* develop my time-travel theories?" he asked. "Maggie, I
want to talk to him. I want to figure out a way to get us safely out
of here so we can meet him somewhere and try to figure this out."

Maggie looked into the dark brown intensity of his eyes.
Chuck's eyes. "Why is this so important to you?" she whispered.
"Why do you want to develop time travel so badly? What hap-
pened that you want so desperately to go back and do over?"

As she watched, she saw him take an emotional step back,
away from her. His face was instantly more reserved, his eyes almost shuttered. He wasn't going to tell her. Maggie knew he
wasn't, and she got good and mad.

"You're *exactly* like him," she said, pulling her hand away.
"Too damned bottled up to share even the tiniest piece of yourself." She wanted to hit him, so she moved away to avoid the
temptation, scooping up the Data Tech report and hugging it
close to her chest as she sat in the farthest possible corner of the
tiny closet. She glared at him. "Well, guess what, Charlie boy?
I'm probably going to die for you tomorrow, for the *second* time
around. You can at least show me the courtesy of answering my
questions!"

The shuttered look was replaced by shock. "The *second*
time . . . ?"

"I already took a bullet for you," she told him flatly. "Seven
years from now. Only this time around, it's probably going to
happen tomorrow. The least you could do is *talk* to me and tell
me why I'm going to die."

He was struggling to understand. "You knew you'd already
been killed once, and you still stuck around to help Chuck? To
help . . . me?"

Maggie tipped her head back against the wall and closed her

eyes. "Yeah, love's a funny thing, isn't it, Charlie? I'm in love with Chuck." She opened her eyes and looked at him. "And I love you too. You're him, you know. Part of you is Chuck—except for the fact that you don't happen to love me." She laughed, but it came out sounding more like a sob. "How could you love me? You don't know me. But just think, if I had seven years, I could probably make you love me as much as Chuck does. Of course, it would probably take another seven years *more* for you ever to admit it!"

Charles was silent.

"Please," Maggie said. "Give me something. Close your eyes and find that part of you that could maybe love me in seven years. And then tell me why finding a way to travel through time has ruled your life since you were a child."

Charles didn't move. He didn't even blink.

Maggie closed her eyes again. She couldn't bear to look at him as she waited for him to say something, anything. Or nothing at all.

He cleared his throat. "I've . . . I've never told anyone."

He was either going to keep going, or he was going to stop. Maggie sat absolutely still, waiting to see which it was going to be.

Charles cleared his throat again. "When I was seven years old, I . . . um, I realized that life was made up of linear paths. If you took one, you missed the others, and . . . vice versa."

He paused, and she knew he was struggling to simplify, to make his words ones she would understand. "It occurred to me that all along these lines or paths were these . . . moments. Moments in time that either kept a person on track or pushed them onto a totally different path. Sometimes these moments— or decisions, if you will—seem utterly trivial, but the changes they trigger are . . . immense."

He took a deep breath. "From everything you've told me, it

seems as if my decision to continue or to stop trying to make a working theorem for time travel is one of these moments. Quiet. Seemingly insignificant. Yet from everything you told me—the bomb at the White House, Wizard-9's interference, your own death—" His voice broke and he stopped for a moment.

Maggie opened her eyes and looked at him. He was staring down at his stockinged feet, his eyes out of focus, his jaw clenched, mouth grim. He looked up and met her gaze. "It seems the changes this decision will bring are extremely severe— unless we can somehow alter the path again and take us all in an entirely different direction. Unless..." He looked away from her, his eyes narrowing in concentration as he became lost in his thoughts.

"What happened when you were seven, Chuck?" she said softly, gently. Chuck. She'd gone and called him Chuck. The name had slipped out.

Her mistake hadn't gotten past him. She saw his awareness in the flash of his eyes, in the slight twisting of his lips into a half smile.

He didn't want to tell her. He shifted his position. He ran his fingers through his hair. He looked at the walls in the closet, the floor, the ceiling. He chewed on the inside of his cheek. He scratched his ear. He stopped himself more than once from drumming his fingers on the floor.

"Another moment," he finally said through clenched teeth, glancing briefly at her. "It was another one of those goddammed life-altering moments."

Maggie moved so that she was sitting directly across from him. She stretched out her right leg so that her bare foot was resting directly on top of Charles's left foot. The physical contact seemed to ground him, and for a moment he just sat there, eyes closed, absolutely still, as if gaining strength from her touch.

"I was reading a book." His voice was so soft, Maggie

wasn't sure at first that he'd really spoken. "*The Lord of the Rings*. J.R.R. Tolkien. I was three chapters from the end, and I didn't want to put it down."

He paused, and Maggie held her breath as she realized that his eyes were shining with unshed tears.

"My little brother," he said. "Steven. He came into my room. He wanted to play Chinese checkers. But I only had a half hour before my calculus tutor arrived, and I wanted to read, so I told him no. I couldn't play with him. I didn't even look up from my book to talk to him—I just told him to shut the door on his way out, and he did. About twenty minutes later I heard sirens and then Danny MacAllister, the kid from down the street who delivered the newspapers, he pounded on our front door, and God, it was Stevie. The sirens were for Stevie. He was riding his new bike, crossing New Amsterdam Road, and he got hit by a truck. He was killed instantly."

eleven

"OH, CHARLES, NO," MAGGIE BREATHED.

"I don't know what he was doing. He wasn't supposed to ride his bike anywhere but around the cul-de-sac. He must've been mad at me—" He broke off.

"I don't know what he was doing," he said again, softer this time. "I never knew why he did the things he did. He was so emotional. So...illogical. He was five, and he couldn't even read Dr. Seuss yet. He wasn't 'gifted,' but he didn't care—he was just this happy little silly kid. Everyone loved him, especially me. Everything was so easy for him. My father would play catch and laugh with him out in the backyard, and then come inside and shake his head at me for making careless errors in my calculus assignments."

Now that he was finally talking, the words seemed to spill out. "I used to sneak into Stevie's room at night and climb into his top bunk and ask him what he was thinking about, and he would say something like duckies or bunnies, and I would lie there and try to *be* him. I'd make shadows on the walls with my fingers, the way he did, and I'd try to push aside all the numbers and physics equations in my head to make a little room for duckies and bunnies." Charles laughed, a short burst of not very humorous air. "But I never really could."

Maggie's heart was in her throat. She could picture Charles—Chuck—as that terribly intelligent and gifted child, with eyes far too old and sober for his skinny, seven-year-old face and body.

"And just like that, Stevie was gone," he continued. "One game of Chinese checkers. That's all it would have taken to keep our entire family from being destroyed. But I wouldn't play, and my brother died."

His voice broke, and he stopped, turning away from her so that she wouldn't see the sheen of tears in his eyes that threatened to overflow.

"It wasn't your fault," she said, moving closer, wanting to reach for him but afraid of being pushed away. "Didn't your mother and father tell you that?"

"My father left town," he said, his voice curiously flat. He held himself away from her, his shoulders stiff. But try as he might, he couldn't stop the tears that flooded his eyes. One escaped, and he brusquely, almost savagely wiped it away. "I never saw him again. And my mother . . . She lost it. Literally. She went into a hospital and wouldn't get out of bed. She died about four months later. They wouldn't tell me what she died of—I've always assumed she managed to give herself some kind of over-dose of sleeping pills."

"Oh, Charles." Maggie was aghast at the avalanche of tragedies that had begun with his brother's death. "What happened to you? Who took care of *you*?"

"I was sent to live with my mother's elderly uncle in New York."

"That was where the housekeeper made you carrot cake," Maggie realized. "And you ate it even though you hated it."

Somehow it was that image, the image of a little boy choking down something that was meant to be a treat, that pushed

Maggie over the edge. She reached for Charles, wishing that she could hold that little boy in her arms.

He resisted her for only a second, and then he turned and held her just as tightly.

His parents had deserted him at a time when he'd needed them the most. They had selfishly given in to their own pain and grief, leaving no one to hold and comfort their surviving son. Had anyone ever held him? Maggie wondered. Had anyone told him it was all right to cry, that it was necessary to grieve?

He'd been hardly more than a baby himself—only seven years old. He may have been capable of college-level mathematics, but he had been only a *child*.

Maggie could picture him, all alone in his uncle's quiet house, sitting in his room, thinking that if only he could turn back time and tell his brother, yes, he'd play that game of Chinese checkers . . .

"If I could go back in time," she whispered, stroking his hair, his back. "I'd go back to find you. And I would hold you, just like this, and I would tell you that it *wasn't* your fault. I would tell you that it's okay to cry—that you *need* to cry. And I would make sure you knew that someone loved you . . . that *I* love you."

He drew in a ragged breath as his arms tightened around her, as he pulled back to look down at her. His cheeks were wet with tears. "I sure could've used you."

"I would've told you to look at me." Maggie gazed up into his eyes, gently touching the side of his face. "To remember me. And to wait for me to show up in your life again. And I would have told you that the next time you see me, I would be there for you—forever. That no matter the mistakes you think you've made, no matter what you hold yourself responsible for, no matter whether you stay at Data Tech or go back to medical school or get a job washing cars, I'll still love you. I'll always love you. And that, from that moment on, from that moment when we meet again"—her voice trembled slightly—"the only thing that can part us is death."

Charles gazed down at the woman in his arms, knowing without a doubt that her words were not meant only for the little boy he had once been. Her words were aimed just as well at him, and also at the man he would become.

What a powerful thing this love that she had for him was! Without any intricate equations, without any high-tech equipment, without any help from science at all, her love could travel through time and touch the child he had once been, the man he was, and the man he would become. With that love, she could soothe and start to heal wounds that had festered for too long.

And he could look into the warmth and compassion of this woman's beautiful eyes and feel a peacefulness that he hadn't felt in years.

But he felt a yearning too. He wanted her now, not seven years from now. He wanted to pull her chin up and lower his mouth to hers and . . .

As if she somehow was able to read his mind, Maggie brushed her lips across his.

It took everything he had in him not to pull her closer, not to catch her mouth with his and deepen that soft kiss. God, how easy it would be to love her. The depth of her feelings for him was astonishing. He wanted to take that love and keep it all to himself, all *for* himself.

But he knew that everything she said to him was said to Chuck as well. And every kiss she gave him was a kiss Chuck would remember. Charles was merely a transmitter, a medium connecting her to his future self—to the man she really loved.

Still, when she kissed him again, when the sweetness of her lips lingered against his, he couldn't help himself. He gave in to the temptation and kissed her hungrily, greedily, taking what she offered and then some, plundering the softness of her mouth.

And when she tugged him down with her onto the carpeted

closet floor, he could no longer resist. He gave up trying to fight as she pulled her shirt—*his* shirt—over her head, as he filled his hands with her soft breasts, as he touched her silky skin.

She pulled back slightly to smile into his eyes. It was a tremulous smile, barely able to hide the tears that hovered so close to the surface.

But she didn't stop. She unfastened his pants, and he knew if he let her, unless he stopped her, they would make love—right here, right now.

He didn't want to stop her. He couldn't have stopped her if he'd tried. He knew she saw Chuck when she looked into his eyes. He knew she kissed Chuck when she kissed his lips. And when she slipped her panties down her legs, when she helped him pull his own pants down, when she straddled him, surrounding him in one swift, incredible moment with her slick heat, he knew it was Chuck she was loving so completely.

He wished he were wrong. He wished she saw him, really saw *him* as she looked deeply into his eyes, as she moved on top of him.

The sensations he felt were unlike anything he'd ever experienced before, but he knew despite that, it could be even better. It would be a thousand times better if he were the one she truly wanted, if he were the one she really loved.

She moved faster now, each stroke driving him closer and closer to release. Closer and closer to . . .

He caught her hips, trying to still her movement. "Maggie, I'm not wearing a condom. . . ."

Maggie kissed him. "Charlie, there's a really good chance I'm going to die tomorrow. I think that's just cause for irresponsible behavior. Because I don't know if you noticed, but I seem to have lost my handbag, and I'm currently not equipped with any pockets. . . ."

He smiled, sliding his hands down her naked body. "I did happen to notice your lack of pockets." He lifted her off of him, shifting slightly as he reached underneath him, searching for something. "But I have pockets *and* my wallet, and . . ." He tore open the foil packet. "A condom."

"I honestly don't think it matters."

He looked up at her, and his dark eyes were so serious. "I'm not going to let you die." He actually believed his own words.

Maggie couldn't be so certain. All she knew, all she was absolutely positive about was how much she truly loved this man. The line between Charles and Chuck had long since blurred. It had been all but erased as Charles had told her so poignantly about his little brother.

True, she'd damn near had to throttle the story out of him. But he *had* told her. And he'd told her far, far more than Chuck ever would have. Chuck would've finally revealed the cold facts surrounding his family's tragedy. But to talk about his love for the little boy, to express his yearning to live as uncomplicated and carefree a life as Steven had . . . Chuck, with his well-practiced control would never have shared that much of himself.

But Charles had.

She kissed him, loving the way his eyes lit with fire as she pressed herself down on top of him again, as he filled her so completely.

She loved him. Charles, Chuck, the grieving, lonely seven-year-old boy he had once been—she loved them all. Chuck was right all along—he and Charles *were* the same man.

And this moment, this short time they had, locked here together in this tiny closet, might be the only time she had left to share with him.

She didn't care about the fact that at any moment Ken Goodwin or one of the other Wizard-9 agents might unlock the bolts and open the door. She didn't care about anything.

Except for showing this man exactly how he made her feel.

He kissed her, lifting her up and lowering her down so that

she was on her back. She knew just where to touch him, just what he liked, and she saw awareness and a certain vulnerability in his eyes. This may have been his first time with her, but she had been with him before.

She gazed up at him as he set a rhythm that made her blood burn, looking again for that softness in his eyes, praying that for him this was not just a flare-up of lust between two near strangers.

He smiled down at her, an echo of Chuck's tentative, crooked smile. But again, his eyes revealed far more than Chuck's eyes ever would. There *was* more to this for him than sex—she could see it in his eyes.

She pulled his head down and kissed him, claiming his mouth as possessively as he claimed her body. She heard him groan, felt his body tense, and she knew he was as close to his release as she.

She clung to him, holding him tightly, pulling him even closer, wanting to feel as much of him against as much of her as she possibly could, wanting truly to become one.

And then, with an explosion of sensation, with a flare of pleasure so intense, all lines and boundaries between them vanished as they *did* become one. Maggie couldn't tell where she ended and Charles began as they spun together, out of this dimension and into a place where time stood still. There was only the scorching ecstasy of shared release. The sweet joy of complete communion.

Then they sighed—he did. Or maybe she did. Or perhaps they both did. Together, separately, it didn't matter—as slowly they drifted back to earth. Slowly, the sensation of his arms around her, of his weight on top of her, his hair tickling her nose broke through. Slowly, awareness returned. She could feel the carpet beneath her, see spiderwebs up in the corners of the closet ceiling.

Then Charles lifted his head, and she found herself gazing into his eyes. He looked at her searchingly, as if uncertain of her response to what they'd just done.

She smiled at him, running her fingers through the softness of his hair. "I sure am glad I didn't drown today. I really would've hated to miss that."

His face relaxed into a hot, quick smile. "I'm glad too. More than you can imagine." He kissed her hard on the mouth. "You want to get out of here?"

Maggie froze. "You're going to do it? You're going to decide to give up your research?"

He pulled himself off of her, helping her up and handing her his shirt as he quickly found his own pants. He'd turned away, but not before Maggie saw the answer to her questions in his eyes.

No. He wasn't going to quit. Maggie didn't know whether to feel frustrated or relieved.

"You have the power to end this once and for all," she told him as she fumbled with the buttons on the shirt.

"I can't do it," he told her, his voice low. "All my life I've wanted to go back. To save him. I can't just give it up. Not without trying to find another way."

"You don't think Chuck has tried to find another way?"

He glanced at her, his eyes apologetic. "I think that I can't just quit before I have a chance to talk to him. What if together we can come up with a solution that neither of us would have thought of alone?"

"What if you do something to get yourself killed?" she countered.

"Ken Goodwin's not going to risk—"

"Accidents can happen, Charlie. What if they go for me and this time *you* step in the way of the bullet?"

He tried to make light of it. "Then I guess there'll be no Wells Project."

Maggie wasn't amused. "If you're dead, Chuck will be dead too."

Charles was quiet as he slipped his shoes back onto his feet. "Believe me, I'll do my best to make sure both he and I survive," he finally said.

"So how exactly do you plan to get us not only out of this closet but also off this ranch?" Maggie asked. "I'm particularly curious as to how you intend to keep the Wizard-9 agents and their hired guns from shooting great big holes in me as we wave good-bye, driving . . . which car, Charles? We seem to have left ours back in the Data Tech parking lot."

"We'll take one of their cars."

"Wait, don't tell me. You'll hot-wire it, right?"

"No, I'll have them give me the keys. We'll get out of here faster that way." He picked up the rope from the closet floor— the two lengths of rope that had bound her hands and feet. "Here's what we're going to do."

"Are you ready?" Maggie asked. She'd put her dress back on. It was cold and wet and she shivered slightly.

Charles nodded. With his help, she'd managed to tear the bottom few feet of fabric off the dress, shortening it so it didn't go down much past her knees. That would help when it came time to run. "Remember, when they start opening the locks, step back behind me, and stay down."

"But be ready to move fast," she said, repeating his instructions. "And stay close to you at all times. I know." She glanced around the tiny closet, down at the Wells Project report still lying on the rug. She kicked it with her toe. "All this trouble over a bunch of equations."

As Maggie looked back up at Charles, he saw through her bravado. Her eyes were so wide, her face so pale. "Charlie, if this doesn't work—"

"I'm not going to let them hurt you."

"I know that's what you intend—"

"I *promise*."

She kissed him. He could taste her fear. Or maybe it was his own. "I love you."

Charles nodded, forcing a smile. He had no doubt in his mind that Chuck already knew that. "Come on, Maggie, let's get this done."

She took a deep breath. "Okay, I'm ready." Squaring her shoulders, she approached the door. Another deep breath, and then she was pounding on it. Pounding and shouting as if the world were coming to an end. "Help! Somebody help me please! Charles is trying to *hang* himself! He won't let me near him, and I'm afraid he's going to die!"

She kept it up, shouting and banging, pounding and shrieking until there it was, the sound of the bolts on the outside of the door being thrown.

As Charles braced himself Maggie scrambled toward the back of the closet. The door was pulled open, and one of the Wizard-9 agents—the hulking man Charles had had his wrestling match with earlier that day—got a glimpse of him, rope tied around his neck, lashed so that it looked as if he were hanging from the closet pole.

It was true that he had to bend his knees and lift his feet off the ground, which had to look rather ridiculous. And it was also true that the pole wasn't going to hold his weight for more than another few seconds. But a few seconds was all he needed as the Wizard-9 agent rushed forward to rescue him.

Charles released the rope as soon as the hulk was close enough to reach for him, and his sudden unexpected body weight was enough to take the man down. They collapsed together onto the closet floor and Charles had his hands on the man's gun as he kneed him sharply in the groin—all before the other Wizard-9 agents standing in the doorway even realized what was happening.

The hulk was writhing as Charles scrambled to his feet, gun in hand. He could feel Maggie next to him, pressed against his back just as he'd told her. He pointed the gun at the other agents as everything around him seemed to switch into slow motion.

"Hands up!" he shouted, moving forward, pushing them back out of the closet. If they didn't respond to the threat to themselves, he'd point the gun at himself—see how quickly they'd react to the possibility of his ending the Wells Project before it began by way of his own untimely death.

He was banking on the fact that they wouldn't call his bluff.

And then, from the other side of the house, came the unmistakable sound of gunfire. It was the rapid-fire sound of an automatic weapon, and from the way Maggie's hands tightened on his arms, he knew she'd come to the same conclusion he had.

Chuck was here.

But was he on the giving or receiving end of those gunshots?

Before Charles could take so much as a step toward the door, an explosion rocked the foundation of the house. He realized as he looked out the windows that more time had gone by than he'd realized. It was evening. The sky was dark.

He motioned toward the Wizard-9 agents again with his gun. "Drop your weapons."

But before anyone moved, the door to the room was kicked open, and there in the hallway stood . . . himself.

He was dressed all in black. Black jeans, black boots, black turtleneck shirt. His face was camouflaged with smears of grease and dirt, and he was holding the kind of assault weapon Boyd Rogers used in his adventures as a Navy SEAL. He was holding it as if he knew how to use it, and use it well.

Charles stared for a fraction of a second into his own eyes.

Into *Chuck*'s eyes. The man he would become in seven years. The man Maggie loved.

"Get down!" Chuck shouted, and Charles turned to see the two Wizard-9 agents hadn't dropped their weapons when he'd told them to. And still in that same slow motion, he saw them turn and aim their guns at Chuck.

Charles pulled Maggie away, pushing her onto the floor behind a big double bed. He heard the sound of Chuck's gun, heard Maggie scream, and he tried to cover her more completely with his body. There was the sound of shouting voices, more gunshots, then silence.

And then there was the sound of his own voice—Chuck's voice—saying, "You better get moving. The east wing of the house is on fire. It's dry as hell—it's not going to be long before this whole place goes up."

Charles pulled himself to his feet. And found himself gazing down at the earthly remains of three Wizard-9 agents.

He heard Maggie's swift intake of air, and he pulled her away from the sight. "Don't look," he told her, pushing her toward the door.

Chuck was sitting on the floor, leaning against the wall, his gun cradled in his arms, as if the fact that he'd just snuffed out three lives meant nothing to him.

Maggie ran to him, and Charles felt a sharp flare of jealousy that he tried to stifle. She'd been nothing but honest with him. He'd known all along, even while they were making love, that Chuck owned her heart.

But he didn't have to watch as Maggie threw herself into Chuck's arms. He didn't have to watch as she kissed him. Because she didn't. Instead, she knelt beside him on the floor and turned to look up at Charles.

"Charlie, he's been hit!"

Only then did Charles see the smear of blood on the white wall. Chuck's blood. *His* blood.

"I should have remembered the man in the closet," Chuck said through tightly clenched teeth. "But I didn't, and he surprised me."

"But I had his gun—"

"You had *one* of his guns."

"It's his right leg," Maggie told him as he crouched beside her.

Chuck held out his gun to Charles. "Here. Take this and go with Maggie. Quickly."

---

twelve

"WE'RE NOT GOING ANYWHERE WITHOUT you," Maggie said fiercely. She turned to look at Charles. "How bad is it?"

Chuck answered. "It's not bad, but I won't be able to run. I don't think I can even walk."

"I'll carry the gun, you carry him," Maggie said to Charles.

"No, I'll slow you down—"

"So?"

Chuck's eyes blazed. "So I may have taken care of the others and destroyed the Runabout, but Goodwin got away. He could be anywhere. And I know for damn sure that he's going to be aiming his gun at *you*, Maggie. You need to be able to move, and move *fast*."

Chuck had "taken care of" the other Wizard-9 agents. That's what he called shooting them full of bullets and draining the life from them. Maggie kept her back firmly turned to the sight of the three dead men sprawled on the other side of the room. How could he be so matter-of-fact, so emotionless about killing? How many times in the past had he been forced to kill? Or had he always been so callous and thick-skinned?

She risked a glance at Charles. His expression was grimly

identical to Chuck's. Maybe he didn't care. Maybe the thought of those three men never standing up and going home to their wives and children didn't make him sick to his stomach, either.

"Maggie's the only reason I'd risk building another Runabout," Chuck said, his voice harsh. She looked up at him and she could see pain mixed in with the fiery intensity in his eyes. His wound may not have been "bad," but it hurt him badly.

"And Ken Goodwin knows that," he continued. "If you're dead, Mags, I'd keep my theories of time travel alive." He thrust his gun at Charles. "Come on, kid. I'm expendable. I'll be gone anyway when you finally do the right thing and decide to leave Data Tech. So take it and get Maggie the hell out of here."

"You *did* know," Maggie interrupted. "You knew all along that if I could convince Charles to give up his research, you'd just disappear, didn't you? I can't believe you would let yourself vanish without saying good-bye!"

"I did say good-bye," he said quietly.

Her voice caught. "You didn't mention that that good-bye was because you intended to leave me forever."

Chuck's gaze flickered to Charles, who was quietly working to stanch the flow of his blood. "My intention was to never leave you again."

"You mean your intention was for *Charles* to never leave me again." Charles glanced uneasily over at her, and she shook her head. "Don't worry, Charlie, I won't hold you to any promises you made seven years in the future."

Charles straightened up, picking up Chuck's gun and handing it back to him. "Let's go," he said.

Chuck pushed the gun back toward him. "No."

"We're not leaving you here," Charles stated.

"Instead you'd rather risk Maggie's life?" Chuck countered.

Charles glanced back at the dead Wizard-9 agents. "I think we'd be risking Maggie's life if we left you here," he said quietly.

He hefted the weight of Chuck's gun. "Because I don't think I could bring myself to use this the way you can."

"Believe me, you'd use it. If Goodwin pointed his gun at her, you could bring yourself to use it," Chuck told Charles.

"Yeah," Charles agreed. "Maybe I could. But I'd rather not have to find out." He glanced back at the bodies again, the muscles clenching in his jaw. "That's one way I have absolutely no desire to be like you, old man."

"Please, can we go now?" Maggie whispered. "*All* of us?"

Chuck let Charles help him to his feet, swearing sharply, his mouth tight against the pain. He took back the gun, holding it at the ready in one arm while Charles pulled his other arm around his neck. But he also drew his handgun, the small one he'd bought illegally in the roadhouse north of Phoenix, and held it out to Charles.

Charles took it unwillingly, jamming it down into the pocket of his torn tuxedo jacket.

Chuck gritted his teeth. "Let's do it, then."

Both men spoke in unison. "Maggie, get behind me."

Charles proved to be as good as Chuck when it came to taking precautions and evading capture.

He got them into one of the Wizard-9 limousines, and they'd pulled away from the burning ranch house, the flames from the fire cracking and dancing, lighting up the night behind them. They'd hit the gate going fifty, and the big car had plowed right through.

Charles had driven directly down the mountain and into Phoenix, where they quickly left the limo on a side street. The danger and Chuck's injury made borrowing another car a necessity, although Maggie kept careful track of each of the streets from which they purloined yet another vehicle. After this was over, she'd go back and make retribution.

If she were alive.

Charles knew the same trick with switching license plates that Chuck had pulled not so many nights ago. He drove them from one side of Phoenix to the other, making sure they weren't being followed before he shut off the car's headlights and pulled into the driveway of a house that was dark and silent.

"Where are we?" Maggie asked. The neighborhood was up-scale suburban, complete with thick green grass growing on every lawn. In the somewhat cooler darkness of the night, sprinkler systems were going full blast in the yards all around them. She could just imagine the water bills.

"A vice-president from Data Tech is out of town," Charles told her. "He's in Ireland with his family until next week."

"You mean Randy Lowenstein? If it's Randy, we're not safe here. Goodwin will have access to the schedules of all my—your—friends," Chuck said warningly from the backseat. His voice sounded tight. Maggie could only imagine the pain he'd endured during the course of the night.

"This isn't Randy's house. It's Harmon Gregory's, VP of finance. He's not a friend," Charles said quietly. "In fact, I only met him once, when Randy and I delivered something here to his house. I overheard Gregory's secretary talking to mine, heard her mention Ireland." He turned around to look at Chuck over the back of the seat. "Do you still carry a Swiss army knife? Goodwin's men took mine."

Silently, Chuck handed his pocketknife to Charles, who pulled up the parking brake and climbed out of the car.

Maggie turned to look at Chuck.

In the backseat, his face was completely in shadows.

"Are you sure we shouldn't take you to a hospital?"

"I have a bullet in my leg," he said. "They'd have to notify the police."

"How are we going to get the bullet out? What if it gets infected? I don't want you to die." Her voice cracked softly.

He was silent, unmoving. When he finally spoke, his voice was raspy, and he had to stop to clear his throat. "I'm not going to be here long enough to need to get the bullet out."

"But you said you destroyed the Runabout. Can't you just—"

"I did, and although the time pressures are off, that doesn't mean we can just pretend the threat's not still there. We need to convince . . . Charlie . . . to quit his research. I still need your help, Mags."

"Isn't there any other way?"

"No." The word held all of his absolute resolve, but he said it gently.

"How can you be sure? Maybe if you talked to Charles, together you might—"

"Maggie, do you think I haven't tried to find some loophole, some alternative—" He broke off, intentionally taking a deep breath and lowering his voice again. "Here's what we'd need to do. We'd need to hunt down and kill Ken Goodwin. And then we'd need to hunt down and kill his present-day counterpart, because what if, God forbid, he got in touch with himself and tipped himself off as to what you and I did at the Data Tech lab that day. But then, you know, I'd start wondering about the other members of the Wizard-9 organization. Maybe he'd told them. We'd have to kill them, too, wouldn't we?"

"All right," she said.

But he didn't stop. "Or how about Goodwin's wife? Maybe he told her. Should we kill her too? And his children . . . ?"

"Stop." Her voice was only a whisper, but he heard her.

"I'm sorry."

Maggie blinked back tears as she looked out the windshield at Charles. He was working with Chuck's Swiss army knife, doing something to the small key plate on the frame of the garage door.

"I saw your face after I killed those men." Chuck spoke almost inaudibly. "I can do it when I have to, Maggie. But I'm not going to kill everyone that Ken Goodwin might've talked to. I can't do that. Even if you wanted me to, I couldn't. But I know you don't want me to. What I've already done is bad enough for you."

Silence. Outside, Charles made an adjustment with the knife and the automatic garage door slid up.

He quickly began refastening the key panel to the frame.

"Will you help me?"

Maggie closed her eyes for a moment. "Yes."

Chuck touched her then, reaching forward, leaning out of the darkness to squeeze her shoulder. "Thank you."

She turned to face him, catching his hand in hers, keeping him from disappearing once again into the shadows.

"I love ... both of you." She felt tears welling up in her eyes again.

His face looked so tired, his eyes so filled with pain. "There's really only one of us. There *will* be only one of us."

And that one wasn't going to be the man sitting facing her, gazing into her eyes.

He reached forward and caught one of her tears with his finger. "That's a *good* thing. It's going to be a good thing." He touched her cheek, her hair. "Hey," he said, "you don't think I *like* what I've become, do you? Always having to look over my shoulder, always suspicious, ready to kill or be killed ... ? This way I get a second chance, Mags. I can take a do-over. Not many people get that kind of opportunity." His eyes softened as she pressed her cheek into his hand. "It's not like you're never going to see me again. You will. I promise. I'm going to be a little different—no, a whole lot different, probably. *Better* different." He smiled. "But you'll see me again, and I'll kiss you"—he leaned forward and brushed her lips with his—"just like that, and you'll look into my eyes and you'll know it's me. I'll remember everything. Very faintly, but I *will* remember."

Charles opened the door of the car, and the sudden light

seemed blinding. Chuck sat back, letting go of Maggie's hand as Charles climbed behind the steering wheel.

"I'm sorry," Charles said quietly as he shut the door and the car was plunged once more into darkness. "I didn't mean to interrupt."

He quickly pulled the car into the empty garage and shut off the engine. He got out of the car just as quickly, and using one of the buttons near the door to the house, he lowered the automatic garage door.

They were hidden.

At least for now.

Charles was in Data Tech VP Harmon Gregory's living room, sitting in the dark. They didn't dare turn on any lights. Although the houses in this wealthy suburb were quite a distance apart, he didn't want anyone seeing lights on in a house that was supposed to be empty.

He was sitting with his head back and his eyes closed. He was trying to push aside his exhaustion so that he could think, when he heard a radio switched on from somewhere in the back of the house.

He stood up and moved swiftly down the hall toward the bedrooms.

Maggie was in one of those rooms, in the dark, putting plastic trash bags underneath the bed linens to keep the Gregorys' mattress from being stained by Chuck's blood. Chuck was in the bathroom, with the only candle they'd found, trying his best to clean himself up—something he'd insisted upon doing on his own. Charles could hear the water running behind the closed door.

He came face-to-face with Maggie in the hallway as she, too, heard the radio. He tried not to think about the way he'd seen her, sitting in the car, her eyes filled with tears, holding desperately to Chuck's hand as he kissed her. He tried, and failed.

"Is someone here?" she breathed, her eyes wide.

Charles put one finger to his lips and moved forward, trying to see into the room where the radio played. He could make out the shape of the bed and . . .

It was empty.

From the other side of the window shades, he could see the first light of dawn streaking across the morning sky.

"It's a clock radio," he said, crossing the room and raising one of the shades an inch, letting in a little more of the early-morning light. The room was that of a teenage girl, with magazine pictures and posters plastered over the walls. A bright yellow bedspread covered a bed that was littered with a menagerie of tiny stuffed animals.

Maggie was staring down at the radio, a slight frown wrinkling her forehead. "That song . . ."

The melody of the slow pop ballad was hauntingly familiar despite the fact that Charles couldn't remember the last time he'd listened to a Top 40 radio station.

Maggie looked up at him. "We danced to this song at the Data Tech party. Do you remember?"

He did. He remembered it now too. Faintly. Foggily. As if remembering a dream. And it had to be a dream—neither of them had gone to the Data Tech party.

Maggie laughed. "It's a residual memory," she said. "We're remembering things that happened the first time around. Wow, I've never had one this vivid."

That had to be what it was. And she was right. It *was* vivid. Although it was misty, he saw the events played out as if he were remembering a scene from a movie. As if he were *living* a movie. "I saw you from across the lobby," Charles recalled, "and followed you into the dining room. I was determined to find someone who could introduce us—" He broke off, shaking his head in confusion. "But we'd already met, in the restaurant."

"No, we hadn't met before," Maggie told him. "Not the first time. You just came up to me, introduced yourself, and asked me to dance."

"You said yes. I was thrilled." Charles pulled her into his arms and began to dance with her, as if they were there, right now, at the Data Tech party.

"You were very charming," Maggie remembered, tilting her head to look up at him. "I think we talked until midnight. I told you my entire life story—about growing up in Connecticut and coming out to Arizona State U. and ending up in Phoenix—and it wasn't until I got home that I realized you'd told me next to nothing about yourself."

"I wanted to kiss you while we were dancing, but we were surrounded by people we both worked with, so I asked you to have dinner with me the next night instead."

"I agreed to meet you at Tia's."

"A Mexican restaurant near your house?"

"Yeah." Maggie smiled up at him.

"You were late."

"A client called just as I was going out the door."

"When you arrived I remember thinking it was like being hit by a hurricane. You had so much energy. You must've apologized twenty times."

"I was afraid you might've gotten tired of waiting. I was afraid you'd left. I was so glad to see you."

Charles pushed her hair back from her face. They'd long since stopped dancing, but he still held her in his arms. "You called me Chuck."

She nodded, her smile fading. "I know."

"You said I needed a nickname."

"You said you didn't care *what* I called you—"

Charles smiled. "So you started calling me Frank—until I

retracted my statement." He touched her lips gently with his thumb, tracing them. "All I could think about all night long was how badly I wanted to kiss you."

"All *I* could think about was how much I wanted you to tell me about yourself. I'd pretty much decided that if I could get you to open up to me, I'd let you walk me home, and I'd even . . . invite you to stay."

Invite him to . . . His arms tightened around her. "Oh God. Really?"

Maggie shook her head, smiling almost shyly up at him. "I liked you a lot. Right from the start. But I wanted you to *talk* to me. I tried, but you sidestepped all my questions."

"I knew you wanted something more from me," he said quietly, "but I don't—I didn't—feel comfortable talking about myself, about my past."

"I would've settled for you telling me how you felt."

"I felt happy. You made me smile, made me feel so warm. And hot. God, I've never wanted a woman the way I wanted you—the way I still want you. I had this feeling that you were going to walk away from me," Charles whispered. "But I still couldn't give you what you needed."

"You gave me what I needed today." Maggie reached up to touch him. "Was it really that hard to talk to me?"

"No." He closed his eyes, loving the sensation of her fingers in his hair. "Yes."

She laughed, and feeling a burst of that now familiar warmth and heat, he lowered his head to kiss her. But she stopped him.

"You didn't want to talk about your brother's death, but you've never let yourself forget or move forward, away from it," Maggie pointed out. "Even now. You're still tied to what happened when you were a child." Her eyes were so serious as she gazed up at him. "After all this time Stevie's life is still more important to you than your own."

Charles didn't speak. What could he possibly say?

The sound of the bathroom door opening made him step back, away from her. He hadn't liked watching Chuck with Maggie in the car. The least he could do was spare his future self a similar sight.

Maggie moved toward the door. "I better finish fixing the sheets."

"I'll do it," Charles said, turning off the radio. "I'd like a chance to talk to him. Privately. If you don't mind."

"Of course I don't mind."

Chuck appeared in the hallway, holding on to the frame of the door, propelling himself forward by hopping on his good leg. He was unable to keep from watching Maggie as she quietly came down the hall and moved past him.

Charles could read so much in the darkness of the other man's eyes. Did his own feelings and hunger for Maggie show so clearly in his own eyes?

"I'll be in the living room if you need me," Maggie turned back to say.

What did she see when she saw them standing there together like this? Did they look as different as Charles imagined? Did he seem like a mere shadow of his older, more experienced self? Did he pale so utterly in comparison?

Pushing his troublesome thoughts away, Charles helped Chuck into the bedroom. Chuck had already hung the strap of his assault weapon over one of the bedposts, and he checked, making sure it was within reach as Charles helped him into the bed.

"You know, for the past few years," Chuck said, breaking the silence, "ever since the news about the Wells Project was leaked to the public, I haven't gone anywhere without a matched pair of bodyguards. My house—your house—was turned into a fortress. I put in a security system that kept the world out." His voice got softer. "And kept me locked in."

Chuck leaned over, opening the drawers of a small bedside table one at a time, gritting his teeth against the pain in his leg.

"I know what you're trying to do—"

"Let me finish," Chuck interrupted as he pulled a gleaming wooden box from one of the drawers. "I figured old Harmon Gregory might have one of these."

"Have one of what?"

"It's not even locked. And this man has *kids*." Chuck flipped open the box to reveal a shining silver handgun. "It's loaded too. Son of a bitch." He took the gun, then put the box back in the drawer, pushing it closed.

"Over the past few years," he told Charles as he hefted that small but dangerous-looking weapon, "I've had to carry a gun, and I've had to use it. More times than I like to remember. That's your destiny—if you continue to pursue the Wells Project."

He set the gun down on top of the bedside table, well within his reach.

"I just don't see how you can expect me to let the Wells Project go." Charles started to pace. "I don't see how *you* could just let it go. All my life, I've wanted—*we've* wanted—to travel back through time. To fix things that went wrong. To save Stevie. Have you forgotten?"

"Look at me closely, Charlie. I'm your own personal ghost of Christmas future. Look into my eyes, really look, and see what you have to look forward to if you continue on your current path. I've seen a good friend killed. Boyd Rogers."

Charles stopped pacing.

"You didn't know about Boyd, huh, Charlie boy? Well, he died on this path that leads from you to me. And Maggie too. Do you really want to find out what it feels like to have the woman you care more about than anything else in the world die in your arms?"

Charles was silent. He couldn't answer.

"Look at me," Chuck commanded him harshly. "I'm a dead man. I have no future. And it was my obsession to change my past, my refusal to reconcile myself with Stevie's death, that's led me right here. *Right* here."

Charles took a deep breath. "I realize that there are difficulties to overcome," he said, "but surely there's a way to keep Maggie and Boyd safe, to prevent the Wizard-9 agents from using the Runabout to plant that bomb in the White House, *and* still have access to time travel. All we need to do is to think it through—"

"There's not." Chuck leaned his head wearily back against the pillows. "You know, I had plenty of chances to go back and save Stevie, but I didn't. It was one thing to dream about it, but another to actually do it. I realized that I would risk totally changing history."

"By saving the life of one five-year-old boy?"

"Absolutely." Chuck sat up again. "Did you know that the trucker who killed him was driving drunk? Did you know that he went to jail for vehicular manslaughter? If he hadn't been stopped, God only knows who he might've killed either later that afternoon or some other day. He might've killed someone who grew up to play some tiny, stupid, but vitally important part in world history. He might've killed the boy or girl who was destined to grow up to be a mechanic, that due to his or her shoddy work made a car break down before it could get into an accident and kill someone *else*—someone destined to be a U.S. President."

Charles shook his head. "That's ridiculous."

"Is it? One unplayed game of Chinese checkers was all it took to change our life." Chuck shifted uncomfortably on the bed, clearly in pain. "Do you know a man named Albert Ford? Works in accounting?"

Charles was caught off guard by the apparent non sequitur. "I'm sorry, who?"

"Albert Ford. Accounting."

"At . . . Data Tech?"

"Yeah. Blond hair, thinning on top. Average height?"

"I don't really know him. I mean, I think I've seen him around. . . ."

"If you're not careful, Maggie's going to marry him in a few years."

"Albert *Ford*?"

"Yeah."

"And *Maggie*?"

"Yeah."

Charles shot a long hard look at Chuck. "You've got to be kidding."

"Nope. Wait a few years and you'll see. I was invited to the wedding. If you're smart, you won't make the same mistakes I did, and you won't have to live through *that* laughfest. But even if you don't, you *will* have residual memories. They'll be enough to give you nightmares."

Charles started pacing again. "Tell me about residual memories. I've theorized about them, but when I had one—I remembered meeting Maggie at the Data Tech holiday party—it was much clearer than I'd imagined."

"Some are more clear than others. I don't know why."

Charles glanced briefly at Chuck, and the older man's lips twisted into a half smile.

"Yes, I remember rather vividly what you and Maggie did in that closet this afternoon," Chuck said quietly.

Charles closed his eyes. Oh, God. "I'm sorry. I don't know what it is about her, but I couldn't . . . I didn't . . ." He opened his eyes and met Chuck's level gaze. It was almost like looking into a mirror. "She loves *you*," he said. "And as similar as we are, I'm not you."

"Thank God." Chuck's voice rang with heartfelt conviction.

"You don't understand. I have the power to make you

disappear. And by making you disappear, I'll end up taking a different path to the future, a path that virtually guarantees that I'll *never* be you. Not even in seven years. I'm not sure I can handle knowing that I'm not quite the man Maggie loves. I don't think I can handle knowing that she'll always be mourning the loss of a person that I'll never quite become."

"You're so wrong," Chuck argued. "If Maggie loves me, then she loves you, too, because every single bit of you is here, inside of me. The rest of me, the part that's *not* you, is poison. And Maggie knows that, she sees it. There's so much I can't give her."

Charles was silent.

"I've known her for seven years," Chuck continued, "and in only a few days you've given her far more than I ever have. You told her about Steve. You told her how you felt. That's all she ever wanted. It's what I couldn't give her, but you've already gotten past that. She fell in love with me because of the danger, because of the excitement. But with you . . . You've cemented her love for us—for *you*. Don't you see?"

Charles sat down on the edge of the bed, suddenly so tired. When had he last slept? "I have the distinct disadvantage of not having known her for the past seven years," he finally said. "I haven't even known her for seven *days*."

"Double memories," Chuck said again. "You're going to live through everything that I did through double memories. You'll catch up in plenty of time."

Charles smiled. "She's incredible."

"You should tell her you love her."

"But I'm not sure I—You know, it's only been a few days. . . . Assuming that I *love* her seems a little bit premature—"

"Don't forget, I was there too," Chuck reminded him. "In the closet? I remember *exactly* what you were thinking. I remember how you felt. You love her almost as much as I do. In time you'll love her even more."

Charles was silent.

"You have to tell her."

He looked at Chuck sharply, suddenly understanding. "You haven't told her, have you? I can't believe it. After seven years you didn't tell her you love her?"

"Even now, I can't bring myself to say it," Chuck admitted quietly.

"I think you could say it," Charles countered. "I just think you *won't*. I think you figure I'll come off looking like the better man if I say it, but you don't."

Chuck made a sorry attempt at a smile. "We always were too smart for our own good, weren't we, kid?" They sat for a moment in silence. Then Chuck shifted again, in pain. "I know you're going to do the right thing. I just wish you'd do it soon. My leg hurts like a bitch."

"What about Stevie?" Even as Charles said the words he could hear an echo of Maggie's voice. *After all this time Stevie's life is still more important to you than your own*. And he knew what he had to do about Stevie. He had to let him go. Because he *didn't* want to end up like Chuck, burned out and battle-worn, hard and cynical. He didn't want to watch Boyd and Maggie die.

Yet his very attempt to save Maggie would guarantee that he didn't become the man she loved.

"Let him rest in peace," Chuck said quietly. "Spend the rest of your life trying to save the kids who *haven't* died."

Charles stood up. "Do you . . . want me to send her in? To say . . . good-bye?"

Chuck shook his head. "No," he said. "Do it right, Charlie, and you and I will never have to say good-bye to Maggie ever again."

thirteen

MAGGIE SAT ON THE LIVING-ROOM SOFA, watching the sky turn pink and orange through the narrow slit in the picture-window draperies.

She heard the soft rumble of voices fade, heard the bedroom door open and close, heard Charles pause as he came into the room.

"It's Thanksgiving," she said, without even turning to face him. "I just realized. It's Thanksgiving morning."

"Happy Thanksgiving." He sounded anything but happy.

"Charlie, I've been wondering. Chuck said he learned survival skills from his Navy friend. What's his name..."

"Boyd Rogers?"

"Yeah. He said Boyd taught him all kinds of tricks *after* he developed time travel. After his life was first threatened. So how come you know all that stuff too? Like doubling back on our six?"

Charles sat down across from her in one of Harmon Gregory's easy chairs. He looked totally wiped out.

"I'm sorry," she said. "You need to sleep and—"

He cut her off. "No. I want to talk. I'd *like* to talk... if you don't mind."

"Well, I'm right here—dying to listen."

Charles actually managed a smile. "When I was a kid, after I moved to my great-uncle's in New York City—he was a physicist, did I tell you that?"

Maggie shook her head. "No."

"He worked as a professor at NYU. Brilliant man. But strange. He was certainly not prepared to open his home to a seven-year-old. I think he was intending to send me to boarding school. But then he realized that I understood him when he spoke about his work, so he kept me around. In some ways it was an opportunity—I was auditing courses at NYU by the time I was twelve. But in other ways, living in that mausoleum of a house was..."

"Lonely?" Maggie supplied.

Charles nodded. "Very much so." He cleared his throat and shifted uncomfortably in his seat.

He was talking to her. He was actually volunteering information about himself without her having done more than ask a few simple questions. Maggie found herself holding her breath, hoping he would keep talking, wishing there were some way she could make this easier for him.

But only time would ease his discomfort. Only time would make him see that the trust he placed in her was well justified.

She knew the man he'd become if he didn't risk everything and trust her completely. Chuck hadn't taken that risk seven years ago, and this beautiful, precious, newly formed, and so fragile thing that was the seed of their love had been crushed before it could grow. And Chuck had grown colder, harder. Lonelier. And Maggie had ended up married to some fool.

She looked into Charles's eyes, willing him to take the chance and tell her more.

He looked back, and he began to talk. "The house was so silent—I could think for hours on end without interruption. I read all of the books in my uncle's library, and went to the public library for more. My entire life revolved around my research. I knew there was so much I needed to learn if I was going to develop my theories of time travel. I read, I ate, I slept, and—when Jen, my uncle's housekeeper, remembered to send me—I went to school.

"The year I turned ten, I was walking home from school one day, and a gang of high-school kids grabbed me and pulled me into an alley. They had knives and they threatened to use them if I didn't hand over all my money. But I had none. I had nothing of value to anyone but me. I had a picture of Stevie in my wallet, and when they took that, I . . . lost it. I went ballistic and got myself slashed for my trouble. But even that didn't stop me."

Maggie could picture him, ten years old and wire thin, with that burning intensity turning him into a passionate windmill of pounding fists and kicking feet with no regard for his own safety.

"One of the kids pinned me to the ground while the other kids ran off with my wallet—with my picture of my brother. This kid who held me down—Boyd Rogers—was four years older than me, but it was all he could do to hold me there. I don't know, maybe the way I fought won his respect, but he quieted me down by telling me that if I stopped fighting him, he'd go and get my wallet back. He told me we'd trade—he'd give me the wallet if I would tutor him in science and math.

"At first, I couldn't believe it. I thought he was probably making fun of me, but I would have done anything to get that picture back, so I agreed. And when Boyd upheld his part of the bargain, he held me to mine. It turned out he was serious. He wanted a tutor. So I met him at least three times a week after school, in the park. He got a lot of razzing from his friends for hanging out with a ten-year-old from the School of Gifted Geeks, but he didn't give a damn. You see, he had this plan to join the Navy and become a SEAL the way his cousin had done.

And his cousin told him that if he wanted to get into the SEAL units, he had to have a strong background in science and technology. And that's what I helped him with.

"I worked with him for four years—right up until the day he enlisted. And he tutored me during that time too. He taught me how to fight, how to survive on the streets of the meanest city in the world. And he made it impossible for me to shut out the rest of the world. He gave me a life outside of that silent house." He paused. "You know, I've never told any of this to anyone before."

Maggie's heart was in her throat. "I know," she said softly.

"Boyd and I stayed tight, even after he joined the Navy. And when he finally got into the SEALs, back when I was finishing up my doctorate, he started taking me out on survival training missions. He's been like a brother."

He paused again.

"Maggie, I don't want to be responsible for his death."

Maggie looked up to find him studying her face. His eyes were impossibly sad.

"Or yours, either," he added softly. "Especially yours."

She knew what Charles was going to say next, and sure enough, as she looked back toward the window, he said it.

"I'm going to do it." His words seemed to hang in the stillness.

Maggie fixed her gaze firmly on the ever-lightening strip of sky as she nodded. "That's good," she said. "That's what Chuck wants." She straightened her back and forced herself to look at Charles. "It's what *I* want too."

He just gazed at her. He looked so tired, so unhappy, she wanted to reach for him, to comfort him. She wanted him to comfort her.

"He loves you, you know," Charles finally said. "He has for years."

Maggie shook her head. "He's only known me for less than a week. The Maggie he's known for years married some creep from accounting."

"Albert Ford." Charles gave her one of Chuck's crooked half smiles.

"Do you know him?"

"Not well—but enough to advise you not to marry him."

"All right," Maggie said. "I won't."

"Good." He smiled again. "Poor Albert. Little does he realize his entire destiny has just been altered."

"Think of the aggravation—and alimony payments—we've just saved him."

"Of course, it's entirely possible you were earning more than he was. Maybe *you're* the one who's saved from making those alimony payments."

Maggie laughed, and the smile Charles gave her was one of his own—full and warm and filled with pleasure.

But it faded too quickly as they sat for a moment in silence.

"Would you mind—" he started, then stopped.

Maggie didn't say a word. She just waited.

"Would you mind very much if I admitted that I'm . . . scared?"

She shook her head. "No. I would be . . . honored . . . that you shared that with me."

"I keep wondering if this is really the right thing to do. It feels so wrong to give up all those years of research and . . . I can't keep from thinking what if there's something I've missed. What if there's some way . . . ? What if we all just disappeared? Chuck and I could develop the Wells Project on our own."

"With what funding?" Maggie asked quietly. "According to Chuck, even Data Tech had to go to outside sources to get the money necessary to build the Runabout."

"Maybe . . . private investors." Charles was reaching for answers now. "I have some connections—"

"And if you used those connections, Ken Goodwin and Wizard-9 would be able to track you down. And then we'd be right back here, right where we started."

Charles sat for a moment in silence. "It's just . . . It's hard for me to quit."

"It's not quitting. It's foreseeing a dead end and choosing a different path."

"I'm not sure what I'm supposed to do. How I'm supposed to . . ."

"Just decide," she said quietly. "Picture yourself taking another route to the future."

"All right," he said, straightening his shoulders, steeling himself. "I'll submit my resignation to Data Tech first thing tomorrow morning. I'll go back to school, finish up my medical degree. Do you think that's really all it's going to take? A simple decision? Because I've done it. I've decided."

It took all of Maggie's willpower not to glance over her shoulder at the still-dark hallway that led to the bedrooms. Was Chuck already gone? Would it happen just like that? One moment he was there, and the next he was gone?

But then there was a bang as the bedroom door was pushed open.

Maggie turned as Charles jumped to his feet, ready to defend her, if necessary.

But it was Chuck who came into the hallway, hopping out to meet them. The movement jarred his injured leg and made lines of pain stand out around his mouth.

"It's happened." He looked from Maggie to Charles. "I can feel it. I feel . . . different. So why the hell am I still here?" he said, then collapsed onto the floor in a crumpled heap.

Maggie reached him first. "Oh, my God, he's burning up!"

He was. As Charles touched Chuck his skin felt hot and dry.

Feverish. And his wound had bled clear through his bandage. His jeans were saturated too. "He's lost a lot of blood."

"We've got to get him to a hospital!"

"We've got to figure out what I did wrong."

Chuck roused, groaning, swearing softly. "Maggie! Oh, God, they shot her! Gotta get up—"

"No, you don't."

"I'm here, Chuck. I'm all right. You're just having a nightmare." The sound of Maggie's voice seemed to soothe him and he quieted.

Charles took charge. "Grab his feet," he told Maggie. "Help me get him back into bed."

The sheets were stained a bright shade of red. Charles lowered Chuck down on top of them anyway.

Now what?

Chuck was in a great deal of pain, made worse by his feverish state. He drifted, hovering across the line of consciousness, on the edge of some terrible, nightmarish place, and he fought to stay awake.

"Get a towel," Charles ordered Maggie, and as she vanished back into the hallway he glared down at Chuck. "For a registered genius, you are one hell of an idiot. How could you possibly have forgotten the basic rule of first aid? Apply pressure to stop bleeding."

Chuck was pale, nearly gray looking, and his teeth chattered from a sudden chill. "I did. In the car. It stopped."

"Yeah? It looks like it started again."

"I didn't think I'd be around long enough for it to matter."

"Well, I've made my decision. No way am I following *your* path. But you're still here, so it looks like I'm going to have to do more than simply make up my mind to change my future. I don't suppose you have any suggestions?"

Silently, Maggie appeared, holding the towel out for

Charles. He took it, using it to gently apply pressure over the makeshift bandage.

"I'll find some blankets," Maggie murmured, taking one look at the way Chuck was shivering.

"Thanks," Charles said.

She met his eyes briefly before she left the room. Her own gaze was decidedly sober. She knew as well as he did that their situation had just dropped from bad to worse.

Chuck had drifted off again, before offering up any suggestions.

Charles had to answer for him as Maggie brought a pile of blankets into the room and began covering Chuck. "Maybe I have to take action," he suggested, helping her. "Maybe I should call Randy Lowenstein. Tell him right now—today—that I'm leaving Data Tech. I could call John Fairfield at NYU. He always promised that he'd do whatever was necessary to get me into the medical school at the university. He was a friend of my uncle's," he explained to Maggie, "who always wanted me to complete my degree and go into medical research."

He made the phone calls quickly, from the telephone on the bedside table, as he continued to apply pressure to Chuck's still-bleeding leg. He turned slightly away, because he didn't want to see Maggie sit down next to Chuck, on the edge of the bed. But she didn't. Instead, she sat quietly on the floor, away from both of them, leaning back against the wall. She tucked the shortened skirt of her dress in and pulled her knees tightly to her chest, wrapping her arms around them.

He could feel her watching him as he spoke on the phone, and he felt a pang of longing so sharp, he had to clear his throat before he could talk. Chuck loved her enough to die for her. How could he possibly compete with that? After all this was over, what would happen? Would Maggie even want to see him again, or would he remind her too much of Chuck?

And if he asked her, would she come with him to New York? He honestly didn't know. But he wanted her to. He wanted it more than he'd ever wanted anything.

More than he wanted to find a way to travel through time.

He dropped the phone back into the receiver, and Chuck fought to open his eyes. "I'm still here," he whispered.

Randy Lowenstein had expressed regrets about Charles's decision to leave Data Tech, but he'd been supportive and had wished him luck. Dr. John Fairfield, a man whose anatomy classes Charles had audited while still only a child, had been overjoyed that he was intending to complete his medical degree. Fairfield had never understood that Charles had needed to know enough about the human body to make sure that his time-travel device delivered a living, breathing person rather than some compressed bundle of protoplasm to the past. That was Charles's sole purpose for studying medicine. Achieving a medical degree to dangle off the end of his name meant nothing to him. At least not until now.

But despite the sense of forward motion he'd gotten from his phone calls, nothing—apparently—had changed.

"Maybe I need to do more." Charles rubbed his eyes with his free hand, wishing there was time to lie down, to take a nap. He wanted to sit down next to Maggie and pull her into his arms. But he wouldn't do that. Not in front of Chuck. "Maybe I need to erase my hard drive. Maybe I need to delete the files of my research notes."

It would damn near kill him to wipe out nearly three decades' worth of research. But he was going to have to do it—because he didn't want to end up lying on that bed with a bullet in his leg, filled with vividly violent dreams caused by extremely nonresidual memories of Maggie bleeding to death as he held her in his arms.

"Maybe," Maggie said quietly from where she was sitting on the floor, "Chuck hasn't left because Ken Goodwin is still out there somewhere. Maybe this has to do with him. Maybe until we confront him . . ."

Charles turned to look at Chuck. "Confront Goodwin . . . ?"

Chuck didn't answer, held prisoner by his feverish dreams. And then the doorbell rang.

fourteen

CHARLES TURNED TOWARD THE LIVING room and froze, a look of intense concentration on his face, as if he were waiting for something, listening—for what?

Maggie's heart was pounding so loudly, it seemed impossible that he could hear anything over it at all.

"Who do you think it is?" she breathed.

He shook his head very slightly, his eyes still unfocused, still listening.

"Charlie, do you think it's . . . ?" Ken Goodwin. She couldn't bring herself to say the name. It was impossible, anyway. How could he have found them here?

Charles unfroze, glancing first at Chuck, who tossed feverishly on the bed, then turning to meet her gaze. She knew what he was thinking. If it *was* Ken Goodwin, he was virtually on his own. Chuck was out for the count.

"I don't think he'd stop to ring the doorbell," he said. But just the same, he held out his hand for hers, hoisting her to her feet. "Help me move Chuck into the closet. I want you in there with him until I know for sure what's—"

On the other side of the room, a window shattered with a

crash, the curtain billowing as the figure of a man kicked his way through.

Maggie heard herself scream, a scream that ended abruptly as the weight of Charles's body pushed her down onto the floor and knocked all of the air from her lungs. But then Charles was up again, reaching for Chuck, pulling him off the bed and down, nearly on top of them, as the gunman opened fire.

The noise was deafening in the small bedroom. Again, Charles covered her. The mirror on the wall above them shattered, raining shards of glass down on top of them.

But then the shooting stopped.

"I think that's enough," a voice said. "Don't you?"

Charles shifted slightly, and Maggie could see the leader of Wizard-9, Ken Goodwin, standing in the doorway of the room, holding a gun. From his vantage point, he could easily kill them all. He must've come in through the front door.

He nodded a polite greeting, as if he were paying a social call. "Ms. Winthrop. And the Doctors Della Croce. You didn't honestly think I wouldn't be able to find you?" He smiled. "That bullet the elder Dr. Della Croce has in his leg is part of a little pet project I've been working on over at the Wizard-9 labs. It's specifically designed to lose velocity upon impact and remain embedded in the recipient's body, where it acts as a homing device. Clever, don't you think, Ms. Winthrop?"

Charles moved so he was directly in front of Maggie. His face was bleeding. He'd been cut by the flying glass just below his left eye. He wiped the blood away as if it were merely an inconvenience. "You keep that gun aimed away from her."

"Take care of those weapons," Goodwin said to his hired gun, motioning with his head toward Chuck's assault weapon hanging on the bedpost and the handgun on the bedside table.

Charles pulled himself to his feet, carefully keeping Maggie behind him as the gunman followed orders. Chuck still lay on the floor, caught in a feverish nightmare. Charles's own nightmare was far too real.

He could feel Maggie's fingers wrapped tightly around his arm.

"Step away from her, Doctor," Goodwin said almost gently.

"I don't think so." Charles inched his hand down toward the pocket of his jacket. Chuck had been right. If he had to, he would use whatever means possible to protect Maggie.

Maggie's voice was low and urgent. "Charlie, whatever happens, whatever he does, don't continue with the Wells Project. It's not worth it—*I'm* not worth it. I know you don't love me, you couldn't possibly—you don't even really know me and—"

"Move away from her, Della Croce," Goodwin said again as Charles slipped his fingers beneath the edge of his pocket. "You're an extremely intelligent man. No doubt you've figured out what I have to do to guarantee your continued participation in this project."

"Just keep thinking about New York," Maggie told him fiercely. "If you give in and do what he says, he'll use you for as long as he needs you and then he'll kill you anyway. If I'm going to die, at least let my death *mean* something." Her voice shook. "Promise me, Charlie. Let me at least hold on to those pictures of you in New York. I have to believe you'll get there—that you'll be all right."

How could she think that? How could she imagine he'd be all right anywhere without her? But then Charles knew. He'd never told her he loved her. And he did. He loved her.

"Put this one up on the bed." Goodwin nudged Chuck with his foot as he spoke to his gunman. "And rouse him. I want him to be awake."

This was it. Charles knew this was his chance. As the gunman slipped his own weapon over his shoulder and bent down to lift Chuck onto the bed, Charles dropped his hand into his jacket pocket, praying the handgun Chuck had given him hours before was pointing in the right direction.

It was.

He aimed it at Goodwin and fired, right through his pocket, like some kind of dime-novel gangster.

It all happened so fast. The look of shock on Goodwin's face. The bloom of bright red on the white of his shirt. Maggie's hands pushing him away, pushing him down. The sound of Goodwin's gun as he squeezed off one final shot before his knees crumpled and he sank lifelessly to the ground.

And just like that, Goodwin vanished.

The gunman staggered back with a cry of alarm as Charles scrambled to his knees, pulling his gun free from his pocket. As he aimed the handgun at the man he saw from the corner of his eye that Chuck, too, had disappeared.

"I have no desire to kill you too," he told the gunman. "Just slowly put down your weapons."

The man's hands were shaking as he obeyed.

"The girl's been hit," he said.

The words didn't make any sense to Charles. At least not at first. The girl's been . . . ?

But then he turned and saw the blood.

Maggie.

Charles dropped his gun, fear and anguish hitting him like a battering ram to the chest. Goodwin's final bullet had hit Maggie.

"Call 9-1-1," he shouted as he reached for her, searching for her pulse, praying she was still alive. But the gunman was already gone, out of the room, the front door slamming behind him.

The bullet had gone in her lower back, just below the ribs, as she'd pushed him down and thrown herself across him. Once again, she'd taken the shot that was meant to kill him.

He reached for the phone himself, dialing the emergency number as he worked desperately to stop her bleeding.

"Don't die," he told her. "Goddammit, I'm not going to let you die!"

"Dr. Della Croce?"

Charles looked up warily as the police detective came into the small cinder-block room.

He'd been questioned for hours, first at the hospital, and then here, in this interrogation room at the police station. He'd told his story over and over again to all shapes and sizes of detectives. To the precinct captain. To a psychiatrist who was clearly trying to evaluate his sanity.

He knew it sounded crazy. Time travel. Who would possibly believe it?

The worst of it was, they seemed to think he was the one who had shot Maggie.

Maggie's surgery had taken an interminable amount of time. She'd come through it alive, but when he'd been taken from the hospital she still wasn't out of danger. She was placed under guard in the intensive-care unit.

Charles wanted to be there, sitting next to her, holding her hand, telling her to hang on, to fight to stay alive.

Telling her that he loved her.

Instead, he'd been taken here. And while he hadn't quite been put in a jail cell, the door to this little room had been securely locked each time he'd been left alone.

He'd tried to focus his thoughts on Maggie, tried to reach out to her across all the city blocks that separated them.

Her love for him had defied the boundaries of time. Surely his could touch her across such a short physical distance. . . .

"How is she?" he asked the detective, praying that the news was good.

"She's corroborated your story," the man told him.

Charles's heart leaped and he stood up. "She's conscious?"

"Yeah. Not that we believe her any more than we believe you, but at least we seem to have removed you from our list of suspects. Ms. Winthrop insists you didn't shoot her. Although I think it's the fact that the ballistics lab verified that the bullet the doctors took out of her didn't come from your gun that's working the most in your favor."

"I want to see her."

"Well, she's asking for you, too," the detective told him. "So let's go."

The drive to the hospital took forever, as did the elevator up to the intensive-care unit, but finally Charles was there.

Maggie was asleep. She looked so tiny in that bed, hooked up to every monitor imaginable. An IV tube was attached to a bag that sent a slow but steady drip of a powerful painkiller into her arm. Charles took her chart from the foot of her bed.

"You can't read that," the nurse admonished him.

He gave her a long, level look. "Yes," he said. "I can."

She was silent as he opened Maggie's chart and quickly read the doctor's notes, saw from where the bullet had been removed, saw that it hadn't come near her spine, saw that none of the damage it had done would be permanent.

Her injuries were serious, but she would live.

If she wanted to.

The nurse watched him warily as he replaced the chart.

"I'm going to sit with her," he told the woman.

"Visitors aren't supposed to stay long," she told him. "There's no chair."

"Then I'll stand." Charles reached out gently and touched Maggie's hair, touched her hand. "Hey, Maggie," he said quietly, unable to keep his eyes from filling with tears. "I'm here." His voice broke and he couldn't go on. All he could do was hold her hand, hope that she felt the pressure of his fingers against hers. He didn't care what anyone said, he wasn't leaving her side again. He needed her to hang on. He needed her to come back to him. He wanted her to open her eyes and look at him while he told her that he loved her.

The nurse stood and watched him for several long minutes before she silently left the room.

She came back with a chair.

Charles couldn't remember the last time he'd slept. But every time he felt himself start to drift off, he forced himself to sit up straighter and have another cup of coffee.

He was determined to keep talking to Maggie. He was sure that somewhere, even if only in the back of her subconscious mind, she could hear him.

And he wanted to make sure he was there and awake when she opened her eyes again.

At first the nurses tried to talk him into taking a nap. But after a while they gave up and brought him a fresh cup of coffee every time they came in to check on Maggie.

The only problem with coffee was that after drinking about three cups, he was forced to leave Maggie's side for a minute or two.

And naturally, he was in the bathroom when she woke up.

"She's asking for you," one of the nurses told him as he walked out of the men's room.

Charles ran down the hall, praying that he'd get to her before she slipped back into a painkiller-induced sleep.

He burst through the door. "Maggie!"

Her eyes were closed, but she spoke. "Chuck."

Chuck. She wanted Chuck.

Charles felt sick. He felt his heart drop down into his stomach. She wanted Chuck, but Chuck was gone. Forever.

He felt a surge of emotions. Grief for her loss. The pain and despair of his own dashed hopes and expectations. Fear that if she knew the truth, if she knew Chuck was gone, she'd give up her fight to stay alive.

Charles reached for her hand, uncertain how to tell her.

As his fingers touched hers her eyes opened.

He could see both her pain and the medication she was being given to numb it in her eyes. She was barely able to focus, and she blinked up at him, trying to clear her foggy vision.

"Chuck," she said again.

The cut on his cheek. No doubt she saw it and in her grogginess she mistook him for his future self. He started to shake his head, to tell her no, but she reached for him, pulling him closer, clearly wanting to tell him something of great importance.

"Chuck, it's . . . okay," she breathed. "You can go now. I'm going to be all right."

She tried to squeeze his hand, but her grip was impossibly weak. Charles couldn't speak. He didn't know what to say.

"I love you," she whispered. "I'll always love you, and remember you. But I have to . . . be honest."

She fell into a silence that lasted so long, Charles pulled back slightly, thinking she was once again asleep. But her eyes were still open. They were filled with tears.

"I know why you wanted me and Charlie . . . to be together. You were right. . . ."

"I don't understand. . . ."

"You knew if I could love you, if I could love the man you've become, despite all you've done and all you wouldn't tell me . . . then I would love Charlie even more." Her eyes closed and the last of her words were spoken on a sigh. "And I do."

Charles sent a silent prayer of thanks to Chuck, wherever he was. It didn't matter that he wasn't going to take Chuck's dark and dangerous path. It didn't matter that he was never going to become Chuck.

He was already something better than Chuck.

He was Charlie.

And Maggie loved him, just the way he was.

Maggie's throat was sore. Her mouth and tongue were dry and tasted like the floor of a barn.

Her eyelids were heavy and glued shut. It took close to forever to pry them open, but when she did, she was rewarded by the sight of Charles, fast asleep in a chair next to her bed.

From the looks of the hospital room, from the number of empty coffee cups scattered around the room, he appeared to have moved in.

How long had she been here?

Judging from the growth of stubble on Charles's chin, it had been quite a few days.

She tried to moisten her lips to speak, but when she opened her mouth, she made barely more than a dry-sounding rattle.

Nevertheless, Charles sat up, instantly alert.

"Hey," he said, his lips curving up into one of his truly fabulous smiles.

He poured some water from a pitcher into a waiting cup, and held it out for her, positioning the straw so that it reached her lips.

The water was almost as refreshing as his smile, and she sighed deeply with contentment—then realized that deep sighs, in fact, deep breaths of any kind, were no longer in her repertoire.

"Hurts, huh?" Charles's eyes were dark with concern as she stifled a groan.

"Yeah," she managed to rasp.

"You're going to be okay." He took her hand. "You woke up just in time to watch them move you out of the ICU."

The cut on his cheek was starting to heal. "You're going to have a scar," Maggie whispered, "right where Chuck did."

Charles nodded. "Probably."

"Funny," she said.

"He's gone, you know."

Maggie looked into Charles's eyes. "Not all of him. Not the best part of him."

He gave another of those slow, wonderful smiles. "We've been driving the police crazy, you and I."

She laughed, and discovered that laughing was something else she shouldn't do a great deal of for a while.

"I told them the truth," he continued after she'd recovered slightly, "but they haven't exactly taken the time-travel part of the story and embraced it. They remain stumped by the blood on the sheets. They've done DNA testing, and it's obviously my blood, but they know that amount couldn't possibly have come from the cut on my cheek. . . . I told them about Chuck being shot, but every time I mention him, they send another shrink in to evaluate me.

"And the bullet they took out of you—it's unlike anything they've ever seen before. But whenever I tell them it came from a gun that was made seven years in the future, they get really tense."

Maggie bit her lip. "Don't make me laugh!"

"Enough of the neighbors saw Goodwin's hired gun running out of the house. I think the police suspect we were being held hostage by him, and that the trauma created this odd delusion we share about time travelers."

"I don't care what they think," Maggie told him. "I'm just glad that it's over."

Charles nodded. His eyes were soft as he touched her hair, as his thumb stroked her cheek.

"So," she said a bit breathlessly, "you're off to New York."

Something shifted in his eyes. "I am."

Silence. Maggie broke it by clearing her throat. "So," she said again. "I guess I'm wondering if you're going to ask me to come along, or if you're going to let me slip away. What's it gonna be, Charlie? Are you going to spend the next seven years pining away for me the way you did the first time around?"

Her words didn't get the smile she expected. In fact, he took them dead seriously, not as the rather lame joke she'd intended.

"I think," he said slowly, "I'm the only man in the world who can learn from mistakes that I haven't even made yet." He paused, and Maggie nearly drowned in the midnight darkness of his eyes. "Maggie, please do me the honor of becoming my wife and come to New York with me."

Maggie laughed, then grimaced in pain. Of all the things she'd suspected he'd say, *that* wasn't one of them. Marry her. He wanted to *marry* her. Was it possible . . . ?

Maggie searched his eyes and found what she was looking for. *Yes.* He loved her. It wasn't like Chuck's love—fueled by years of disappointment and frustration and pain. Instead it was new and fresh, like her own love for him, accompanied by wonder and delight and that ever-burning heat of desire. Her eyes filled with tears. "Oh, Charlie—"

He leaned over and kissed her gently.

"I love you, Maggie," he told her, almost as an afterthought. "You have no idea how much."

Maggie smiled. "Yes, I do. And yes, I'll marry you."

She knew that he loved her just from looking into his eyes. But she sure did like to hear the words.

epilogue

HE STOOD IN THE BEDROOM, DIZZY, WON-dering what he was doing there. He'd come upstairs to get something and then . . .

The room seemed somehow different to him. The carpeting softer, the colors more subdued, the floral-patterned bedspread unfamiliar. And the view out the window . . .

It wasn't the desert. Instead of the flat arid landscape, he found himself looking out at snow-covered hills. New England, he remembered suddenly. This wasn't Arizona. It was Massachusetts.

It was Thanksgiving in Massachusetts. It was their third Thanksgiving in this house in this little town that he and Maggie loved so much.

Maggie . . .

He turned as he heard her push open the door, as she came into the bedroom. *Their* bedroom.

She was wearing a dark blue velvet dress that swept all the way to the ground and almost entirely concealed her softly swelling abdomen. Their second baby. She was pregnant with their second child. She wore her hair down around her shoulders, and as she gazed at him she looked so beautiful, his breath caught in his throat.

His wife. Of nearly seven years now.

"Are you okay?" she asked softly.

He nodded, unable to speak. He couldn't remember the last time he'd been this happy. Yet, at the same time, he *could* remember. He could remember every single day of the past seven years, waking up with Maggie in his bed. He remembered the joy of shared mornings and the quiet intimacy of late nights spent talking and making love.

He remembered the afternoon nearly three years earlier when he'd helped his wife give birth to their daughter, Annie. He remembered holding their precious baby in his arms, of rocking her to sleep. He remembered the chubby toddler Annie had become, the way she raced to greet him every day when he came home from work. He remembered it all. It was so good, so sweet. It was the life he'd always dreamed of having.

He could tell from the way Maggie was standing, from the look in her eyes, that she knew. She stepped forward unhesitatingly, into his embrace, and he held her tightly, so much so that he was afraid he might hurt her. But she held him just as close.

"Hello, Chuck," she whispered.

"Mags." It was all he could manage to say before he kissed her.

It was funny. The pain in his leg. The fever from the bullet wound. Gone. All gone. All of the anger and resentment and bitterness he'd carried with him for so long was gone. Just like that. Gone. He'd thought he'd simply be gone as well, but he'd been wrong....

He wasn't gone. He was back in his own time. But it was a different time. A better time.

And he was Chuck, but ... he wasn't. He felt so different. So happy. So at peace and so content with his life.

He'd thought that wanting Maggie so desperately for seven years, that loving her from a distance, had made his love so powerful, so sharp and strong.

But he realized now that the love he felt in those rapidly fading memories was nothing compared with the incredible love that had grown from having and holding her for the past seven years.

He didn't want to be Chuck. And he wasn't. Not anymore. Not ever again.

She pulled back to gaze into his eyes, and it was as if she could read his mind. She gave him one of her wonderful, gorgeous smiles. "You're Charlie now."

He managed to smile, too, despite the tears in his eyes. "I am. Thank God." And he was. The memories he had of the past seven years of his life with Maggie were so much stronger, so much more real than the ghostly echo of that other life he'd had.

Maggie stood on her toes to kiss him again, and Charlie felt himself sigh.

He was Charlie Della Croce, and he was home.

about the author

Since her explosion onto the publishing scene more than ten years ago, SUZANNE BROCKMANN has written over forty books, and is now widely recognized as one of the leading voices in romantic suspense. Her work has earned her repeated appearances on the *USA Today* and *New York Times* bestseller lists, as well as numerous awards, including Romance Writers of America's #1 Favorite Book of the Year—three years running, in 2000, 2001, and 2002—two RITA awards, and many *Romantic Times* Reviewer's Choice Awards. Suzanne lives west of Boston with her husband, Dell author Ed Gaffney. Visit her Web site at www.SuzanneBrockmann.com.